MARVEL

A NOVEL OF THE MARVEL UNIVERSE

BLACK PANTHER

PANTHER'S RAGE

A NOVEL OF THE MARVEL UNIVERSE

BLACK PANTHER

PANTHER'S RAGE

SHEREE RENÉE THOMAS

Titan BOOKS

MARVEL

BLACK PANTHER: PANTHER'S RAGE
Print edition ISBN: 9781803360669
E-book edition ISBN: 9781803361093

Published by Titan Books
A division of Titan Publishing Group Ltd
144 Southwark Street, London SE1 0UP
www.titanbooks.com

First hardback edition: August 2022
10 9 8 7 6 5 4 3 2 1

FOR MARVEL PUBLISHING
Jeff Youngquist, VP, Production and Special Projects
Sarah Singer, Associate Editor, Special Projects
Sven Larsen, VP, Licensed Publishing
David Gabriel, SVP of Sales & Marketing, Publishing
C.B. Cebulski, Editor in Chief

This is a work of fiction. Names, characters, places, and incidents either are the product of the author's imagination or are used fictitiously, and any resemblance to actual persons, living or dead, business establishments, events, or locales is entirely coincidental. The publisher does not have any control over and does not assume any responsibility for author or third-party websites or their content.

A CIP catalogue record for this title is available from the British Library.

Printed and bound in Great Britain by CPI Group (UK) Ltd, Croydon, CR0 4YY.

To Mr. Chadwick Boseman

Greatness Never Dies

CHAPTER ONE

HARLEM SHADOWS

NIGHT BECAME her. When he watched Monica, the blue tinge of club lights shimmered across her velvety skin. He knew that she had become as much a part of him as the molecules of night. In a few months, to T'Challa's surprise, she had become his necessary thing: the air he breathed.

He inhaled the intoxicating scent that was her own, a mixture of jasmine and gardenia, fragrant and sweet as the royal gardens in Birnin Zana. T'Challa sat in an art deco den crammed with small rectangular tables. Flickering candlelight reflected in glittering mirrors. On stage, Monica emerged from the darkness into the soft, warm crescent of light, her full lips a plum blossom above the silver microphone.

"She's beautiful," N'Jadaka said, raising the glass of amber cognac. "I can see why you're so smitten."

"Careful, friend," T'Challa said with a playful growl. He unbuttoned his navy-blue blazer, revealing a yellow embroidered tunic. "Instead of watching *my* lady, when are you going to get a real woman of your own?"

N'Jadaka laughed. "Brother, please. I meet a real woman every night."

T'Challa chuckled, shook his head. It felt good to be at peace for a change, in the presence of a friend's warm banter and the talented woman he loved. They were in Minton's, where Monica Lynne was the headliner, performing in what he hoped would be her final show in the United States before he whisked her away to finally see his home in Wakanda. It was a question he'd pondered many nights as he paced his Striver's Row apartment, staring out of the brownstone's bay windows onto the tree-lined streets below.

How to make a new life when his old one had become unrecognizable.

Located in Harlem between 7th and St. Nicholas, Minton's was tucked away on the first floor of the Cecil Hotel. The historic night club had seen the birth of bebop, the evolution of jazz. A steady stream of greats made the club their musical dueling ground, from Thelonious Monk and Coleman Hawkins to Dizzy Gillespie and Miles Davis. Music hung in the air. Huge black-and-white portraits of legends like Billie Holiday, Sara Vaughan, and Ella Fitzgerald adorned the brightly painted walls behind patrons who dined on low country gumbo and sipped ruby-colored drinks in fine, fluted glasses.

In the breath before the band emerged and the first notes hit the air, T'Challa leaned into the silence, anticipating the voice he had come to love so much. Monica Lynne, a songstress and dear friend. Their troubled hearts had crossed paths in a most unusual manner, one that had bonded them in unanticipated ways.

"You're always so wound up, Mr. Heavy Is the Crown," N'Jadaka said, a sly smile on his broad face.

"That's *King* Heavy to you, N'Jadaka," T'Challa said, cutting his words with laughter. "And you could never wear this crown."

"I heard that, King," N'Jadaka said without missing a beat. "Let me get you another drink. Loosen you up, Your Majesty. I thought tonight was supposed to be a celebration for you and your future queen." Waving at a passing waiter, N'Jadaka wore an antique red coral bead necklace, his tight black tee strained across his broad chest and six-foot-six frame. He sat back from the table and stretched his long legs. Few outdressed the staff at Minton's, but somehow T'Challa and N'Jadaka managed the incredible feat. The front of the house was all black vests and bow ties, tailored suits and stylish pocket squares. Dapper Dans and Harlem's most stunning starlets dotted the crowded room. "Another yak, straight up, and get my friend whatever he's drinking. You *are* drinking?" N'Jadaka said with a smirk.

T'Challa smiled, his eyes narrowed. "If all goes well, we'll raise a glass of Wakanda's finest."

Brassy horns punctuated the night as glasses clinked, and soft voices whispered in the candlelight.

"*East of the sun and west of the moon...*" the woman with a heart-shaped face and deep brown eyes sang, her hair a sparkling dark crown atop her head. The musicians gently toyed with the tune, playing with the rhythm. They tied and untied knots of harmony and sound, weaving around Monica's clear voice as she conjured echoes of the Ella Fitzgerald rendition of the song while still making it her own.

She shimmered in her emerald dress, the soft lights iridescent against the only mural in the club that had survived the long rush of years. The famous jazz singers huddled in a faded bedroom and the lone, sleeping woman in the bright red dress captured on the back wall, just over Monica's shoulder. A hush came over the room, the music enchanting, a lethal combination of a classic reinvented with mastery and skill. Old cares and worries were whisked away in the wake of Monica's healing voice. She sang, staring out into the crowd, her eyes locking onto T'Challa's. The dream of a faraway, forever kind of love was just the dream that T'Challa had in mind.

"And your ring?" N'Jadaka asked, breaking the spell.

"I have something special waiting," T'Challa said. "Wakanda's own, from the Great Mound."

N'Jadaka's jaw stiffened, his face a passing shadow. T'Challa saw the old pain in his new friend. Their paths had first crossed at Avengers Mansion. After the epic battle against Klaw, avenging his father's murder, T'Challa had thought he would feel peace. But peace abandoned him. Instead, anger burned in his heart, consumed his waking thoughts. Rage and grief coursed through his spirit like twin poisons. T'Challa fled his homeland, seeking an outlet for his rage. He hoped to find the peace that had eluded him since his father's murder. He knew vengeance was a dangerous drug: one that could taint the judgment of even the most level-headed leader. After being away from home so long, T'Challa had been heartened to meet a fellow Wakandan, especially one unjustly exiled as a child.

T'Challa was only a boy himself at the time of Klaw's invasion. N'Baza, his father's most trusted confidante, trusted no one. Man, woman, enby, child: all those suspected of collaborating with Ulysses Klaw were identified as traitors to the realm and swiftly expelled from Wakanda's borders.

"I know it is a source of pain for you, my friend," T'Challa said. "But remember, we have vowed to make new memories."

N'Jadaka was silent—his eyes unreadable, seemingly devoid of emotion. That was one bond they shared. Each man wore a mask of his own. Grief and loss were as much their common ground as their homeland.

"A time for new vows…" N'Jadaka said.

"And perhaps a time for a new leaf," T'Challa replied with a slow grin. "You seem to have caught someone's eye."

N'Jadaka scanned the room to rest his eyes upon an elegant woman seated at the bar.

"Whoa, that's what I'm talking about," N'Jadaka said, all teeth and raised eyebrows. "Some of the most beautiful people in the world, right here in Harlem."

Dressed in a black and gold form-fitting leopard print dress with a short black bolero jacket, a matching silk scarf around her neck, she smiled at them.

N'Jadaka leaned forward, working his signature charm. He

pointed at himself but, to his surprise, the woman shook her head.

No. He frowned for a second, then she pointed her gold stiletto nails at T'Challa, who was chuckling at his side.

Yes, the woman nodded, cat eyes narrowing.

"Damn," T'Challa whispered between clenched teeth. "What are you doing?" he asked as Monica sang to the crowd, watching the scene. Her improvisational style was influenced by Betty Carter, Shirley Horn, and Nina Simone. As she sang, she evoked sighs and appreciative claps from her listeners.

"Heavy is the crown!" N'Jadaka said, laughing.

"Finally," T'Challa said, relieved as a sharp-dressed waiter arrived with their drinks. "Please refresh hers, on me." T'Challa pointed at the smiling woman. "With my apologies. Tell her my heart is already taken, but I am deeply flattered."

N'Jadaka sipped his cognac, watching T'Challa closely. "What's that under your drink?" he asked.

T'Challa frowned. Resting beneath a cloth napkin was an odd envelope. The last time the Panther King had received one of them, it was not good news.

Voices in his head seemed to come from a distant place, calling, tempting him with old promises, threatening to reopen ancient wounds. The stained, brown leather folio was a shadowy enigma with no hint of sun, no hint of the mysteries that were to be revealed. Someone—not any postman from this land—had secretly delivered the missive, a letter with no postmark or return address. T'Challa needed neither—the Seal of Wakanda was stamped into the thick, heavy envelope.

Strange news delivered from his homeland whose name was precious currency, its language unspoken. Who was the waiter and where had they gone? T'Challa reached for the folio, his eyes steely.

"What is it?" N'Jadaka asked. His finger traced the rim of his glass.

T'Challa didn't answer. The air was thick with the scent of spices and perfume. He ran his thumb across the seal and unwound the leather tie. For a society that prided itself on its advanced technology, Wakanda favored old-world traditions. Discretion was one of them.

T'Challa opened the folio and slid a heavy, handmade sheet of paper out. He grasped the letter by one of its deckle edges and read silently.

Your Highness,
Please forgive this intrusion. An urgent matter requires your presence and guidance.
Wakanda has lost its regent, N'Baza. Please return home as quickly as you can.
Your kingdom is in grave need of the Black Panther.
Your loyal servant,
Communications Specialist Taku

N'Baza. Gone. Such earth-shattering news should not have been confined to the limits of mere paper. T'Challa felt the crash of mountains crumbling in his chest. The weight of the knowledge left him speechless.

The exiled one sat quietly at his side, as if he could sense the waves of grief rolling off the Panther King's spirit.

"T'Challa," N'Jadaka said, his voice raised with worry. "Is something wrong?"

"I'm beginning to wonder if things will ever be right."

Uncharacteristically, N'Jadaka did not have a ready reply.

T'Challa slipped Taku's letter back into its leather case. "I'm sorry, friend, but I must return home at once."

The room erupted into ecstatic applause. Monica thanked her band and the guests, and graciously stepped off the stage. A cone of light followed her, the happy faces of her audience beaming all around. She shook hands and bent every now and then to peck a cheek. T'Challa slipped the envelope in his jacket and watched Monica as she wound her way through the crowd towards him, the long emerald dress trailing behind her like a great peacock's cobalt and green-golden feathers.

It wasn't her beauty. It was her kind spirit and her voice—that remarkable voice—that had drawn T'Challa to her. Despite the dangers they had seen, the traumas they had experienced, something about each other rang out like a bell, musical notes in the air. Together T'Challa hoped they might create a new song of solace, camaraderie, a home.

He and his younger sister Shuri had suffered such great loss. The only family they had now was each other. If Monica agreed, he hoped to add her to their circle.

"Hi N'Jadaka," she said, glancing at him.

He nodded. "You were magical, as always."

"Thank you." She leaned in and kissed T'Challa on his cheek, whispering, "Hey handsome."

"Monica," he said, his voice offering just the hint of a deep purr. "Stunning as always. Love what you did with Ella's classic performance."

"A special song," she said. "You'd think it was written for me and you."

"Funny that you should say that."

She smiled and stroked his arm. "Glad you enjoyed the show. This new band is working out well. But it looks like the real performance was happening at the bar."

N'Jadaka burst into a fit of laughter.

"Girl, you are something else," T'Challa said. "What are you drinking?"

"The same thing you sent your friend," Monica said and winked.

"Really?" T'Challa chuckled. "I sent her apologies, but you, Ms. Monica Lynne, can have my whole heart."

"Well in that case," she said, her smile broadening, "I'll take your heart and a glass of pinot." She slid into the chair next to T'Challa's, watched him closely, then squeezed his hand gently. "What's wrong, T?"

For a moment, T'Challa didn't answer. She had a way of knowing things sometimes; things felt rather than said. Monica sensed his moods as easily as she navigated complex vocal arrangements.

"Maybe we can discuss it later?" she asked gently, glancing only briefly at N'Jadaka, who quietly sipped his drink.

"No, my friend can hear this as well," T'Challa said with a heavy sigh. "Tonight, I received notice. I must return home…"

"Oh," Monica said, crestfallen.

"To bury N'Baza," T'Challa finished.

"No!" Monica gasped and she shook her head in disbelief.

"You know that man has been like a father to me. I'm sorry, but this is not how I thought our evening would end."

"I'm so sorry," Monica said, then added. "He was your regent, right?"

T'Challa nodded.

"I see."

"When do you plan to leave?" N'Jadaka asked, signaling for the check.

"Immediately," T'Challa replied, watching Monica. "I should be in Wakanda within a few hours."

"Of course," N'Jadaka said. "I hate to see you go, friend, but I understand—you have to take care of your people."

Monica was silent, then spoke, her voice soft and comforting. "I know this is a lot, and I know you're a king, but are you going to be alright, baby?"

T'Challa looked contemplative, his thoughts careening. He could hear Monica's steady heartbeat above the night club's conversations, the clink of glasses, and soft jazz music playing from the house speakers. He needed her steadiness. When he returned home, the nation would lean on him, but T'Challa knew he needed someone to lean on too.

"Monica, come with me." It wasn't how he had planned to ask her to visit his homeland, and it wasn't the best of circumstances. But it came from his heart, and it felt right.

She stared at him. He could see her mentally working through the practicalities. Finally, Monica spoke. "I think I can take some time off, let these freshmen stretch their legs. But no matter, T, you shouldn't have to do this alone. You know I'm there for you if you need me."

"I need you," he said. And it was true.

"My condolences," N'Jadaka said. "Check in with me when you can."

"Check in?" T'Challa said. "Why don't you close up shop for a while? Your antiquities are already collecting dust. It's about time you come home."

Shock and what looked like a glimmer of hope flitted across N'Jadaka's face.

Moments went by.

"Well damn," T'Challa said, glancing at Monica and then back to N'Jadaka. "That's the first time I've ever seen you speechless."

N'Jadaka ran his hand through his locs, his eyes misty. "Never thought I'd get a chance to see Wakanda again. Thank you."

"You're welcome, my friend. It's going to be some homecoming," T'Challa said, squeezing Monica's hand. She stared at him again, then stroked his cheek.

"Indeed," N'Jadaka said and signed the check.

CHAPTER TWO

WAKANDAN BLUES

BIRDSONG AND a deep humming filled the air as the royal motorcade wound its way through the Golden City. The surprisingly sparse crowd released cheers and ululations, punctuated by wailing and lamentations. The disparate rhythms and wondrous sights filled Monica with a sense of foreboding. T'Challa sat stonily by her side, while N'Jadaka stared out his window.

A native New Yorker, born in Bed-Stuy, raised in Harlem, she had never seen skyscrapers such as these. Coppery metal towers rose all around her as if they were golden rays born from the sun. Huge sculptures of historic Wakandans loomed in the distance. Other kinetic public art spun in the wind, as if propelled by sound, runes and magical spells culled from the centuries, carved into them in ancient Wakandan script.

The crowd's collective voices sounded alternately celebratory and dirge-like. The rhythm and cadence reminded her of the blues. Sorrowful with the soft, tearful sadness of old Spirituals, but like the poet Langston Hughes once said, "hardened with laughter."

Monica was still adjusting to having ridden in a Quinjet.

The hybrid-winged aircraft reminded her of a giant wasp. It had whisked them away in the cover of darkness, along with T'Challa's armed Wakandan guards. She slept fitfully most of the night; at some points, not at all. Now she stared, wide-eyed, at the evidence of riches as they rolled past. Far more than she had ever seen.

Monica knew that T'Challa was a king, not the kind in a deck of cards with ring curls and a big Joe Namath fur coat, or the romanticized ones people spoke of wistfully from Black history's past. To be a king was one thing, but to be the Panther King was apparently another. Such opulence and obvious affluence, stability and an unbroken history was breathtaking to see. To think that this was T'Challa's natural world and she was now in it—that was something she would have to reflect upon and get used to.

Born to a young single mother, she and her sister had never had much; from what she gathered from N'Jadaka, he never had either. To be dropped into such a world was as thrilling as it was unsettling. *But it isn't about me now,* Monica thought. *It's about T.* He needed her in the way she had once needed him. Almost losing your life had a way of putting things in perspective. She couldn't imagine the kind of pain his little sister must be going through, to have lost her parents—one murdered, one missing—and now her most trusted guardian. At least Monica still had her mother when her father died, even if that sometimes felt like it wasn't enough. There were serious political implications as well, but Monica didn't have the energy to fully consider the first one. If Regent N'Baza was no longer there, then clearly T'Challa would need to be. It was that irrefutable fact that made her heart sink.

Now the sound of flutes and pipes joined the cacophony as an organ grinder dressed in ceremonial robes and a mime performed together. Children laughed, their bright, moon-like faces full of glee. Red-and-gold striped banners emblazoned with the Black Panther symbol waved in the sky. More traditional red-black-and-green flags dotted the crowd. Suddenly a sharp whistle pierced the air. A loud explosion followed. Monica screamed.

The crowd cheered. *Fireworks.*

An astonishing display of colorful smoke, as vivid as any rainbow, painted the sky like holograms. T'Challa chuckled as Monica recovered, her hand on her throat. She steadied her breathing. After another dazzling display, she squealed in delight, joining the crowd's wonderment. A muscular Black Panther with a gold collar, stunning as any mural, pounced—then disappeared in a cloud of sparkling smoke.

Three robed musicians danced along the road, playing giant many-stringed koras. The gourds were the largest Monica had ever seen: certainly larger than any instruments in her collection. She had played a blues club, Ground Zero, in Clarksdale once—after her Beale Street tour in Memphis and the sets at Wild Bill's and the Green Lounge. There were rumors that a farm in Mississippi grew a similar special species, but these instruments were extraordinary. Monica gazed at the beautiful koras, nodding her head to the tranquil music that gave voice to the song of the wind. Monica unrolled her window to hear them better. A Dora Milaje, one of the royal armed guards, twitched and narrowed her eyes, but T'Challa motioned for her to be still.

"Can you hear that?" Monica asked, unaware that the Black Panther, the ghost of the forest, had enhanced senses that allowed him to hear and distinguish sounds from great distances.

Like now, T'Challa could hear Monica's heart race with excitement. Being attuned to her in this way made T'Challa a most attentive lover. He drew her closer to him, pulling her into his great arms, inhaling the intoxicating scent from her hair and gorgeous skin.

"You're shining," he said. "I love to see you happy. It is my only wish for you."

Without thinking, Monica kissed him, her hand on his firm jaw. The guards discreetly looked away.

"This is how you welcome a king," Monica said. "T'Challa, they missed you."

A twinge of guilt and pleasure coursed through the Panther King. Seeing his people united in their grief moved him—gathered together to celebrate his return and the passing of the great leader N'Baza.

Water fountains shaped like black panthers in a range of poses gushed from elaborate vibranium and marble bases. The natural marble was in hues she'd never seen. A flock of birds too exotic to be peacocks, fluttered overhead. Iridescent feather plumes sparkled and glimmered in the bright sky, a constellation of stars in broad daylight.

Monica caught glimpses of all the varied fashions of Wakanda. Like the Golden City itself, the wardrobes were a stylish mixture of the old and new. Mohawks and elaborate braids, nose and ear jewelry, wrists full of bright, shining gold sailed past her. Her eyes devoured all that she could see, heart and mind full, imagination set afire by the sheer volume of artistry.

"T, you actually live here?" she said, wonderment in her voice. "This is breathtaking."

"Yes, I forget sometimes. I've been here since the day I was born," T'Challa said.

"I don't think I'll ever forget this."

Riding through Birnin Zana's golden streets, Monica felt as if she'd been whisked into *The Wizard of Oz*. But this was no Emerald City fronted by a hurley gurley hustle man. She knew from experience that T'Challa was the real deal. He'd saved her once, from a national hate group singling out Black activists, and her life had never been the same.

Monica stopped counting the number of men and women immortalized in the city's public art spaces. Here, even a child, a small girl, was celebrated in stone. One could tell that the Wakandan kingdom stretched across the ages. The evidence of the centuries remained in the faded volcanic rock that some of the older buildings were made of, in the shining vibranium-reinforced buildings of the newer structures, and in the carved sculptures and graffiti murals that adorned many walls. Even the playgrounds reflected the empire's noble culture. Children joyfully splashed in a pint-sized replica of Warrior Falls. Others posed before façades of signature buildings from the Golden City adorned with Wakandan symbols. Two little boys called out as they climbed atop a miniature Wangari tree, its trunk wide enough to hold three slides. Monica watched them as they slid and tumbled into a fit of laughter at the bottom.

No one would ever grow up not knowing who they are, Monica thought. The world around them reflected a different story, more affirming than the one Monica and her older sister Angela had known. In Wakanda, the children grew up never questioning their greatness. The evidence of that love and possibility, of their people's tremendous contributions, their stability and success surrounded them.

A priceless legacy not easily stolen or erased.

If Monica didn't know T'Challa, she would think him crazy to have left Wakanda. She saw no unhoused citizens, no garbage, none of the refuse that comes with despair, intentional neglect, and inequity. The children and the elders looked well cared for, and no mentally challenged citizens were left alone to struggle without aid, wandering aimlessly in public or private spaces like they did in the US. Who would ever leave such a place?

"Killmonger!" A shout erupted from the crowd. A mime on impossibly tall stilts wearing a wooden mask that obscured their features hovered in the air. They were dressed in purple and gold raffia-fringed mud cloth. The crowd moved back as the figure danced and spun on one leg, the other raised toward the sky.

"Ooh, look!" Monica cried. "Can we stop here?"

T'Challa whispered a command in Wakandan. The limo eased to a crawl, the motorcade slowing down all around them. *Killmonger?* Wakandans did not celebrate war or death. Disturbed by the outcry, he turned to Monica, but her excitement dispelled his concerns.

Monica clapped her hands as the car windows sank into the door panels, her laughter joining the crowds as the masked dancer performed zany tricks. They gyrated to music that reminded Monica of popular Afrobeats, each move a precise and more elaborate version of the newest dances. The people clapped in time as the dancer sang a little song, whispering at first. *"Killll, kill, killll, monnnnn, ger! Killll, kill, killll, monnnnn, ger!"* Puzzled, the crowd joined them.

"Is that Wakandan?" Monica asked.

"No. I've never heard that chant before," T'Challa said, watching the performer. The Dora Milaje seemed unsettled.

Monica stared at the dancing harlequin, and T'Challa shook his head. "The clowns and puppets are the favorites of children, Monica."

"This dancer is giving me life, but why are they chanting like that?"

The car slowed to a stop, then N'Jadaka spoke. "I think this is where I get off."

Puzzled, Monica frowned at him. Even for the cosmopolitan, consummate contrarian, this move didn't make sense.

"I know you will have your hands full, honoring N'Baza in the way he deserves," N'Jadaka said. "But I feel my place is with my people. Home is not just a place, a palace or a shanty. It is a feeling." He waved at the lively crowd gathered along the Golden City streets, his hand on his heart. "T'Challa, welcome home, but I have not felt my home for many long years."

He grabbed the weekend bag he'd hastily packed overnight—a considerably smaller load than Monica's, which trailed behind them in another vehicle.

"I want to find the grounds where my parents were laid to rest— if they in fact rest," N'Jadaka said. "The hand of Klaw razed me." He paused, his eyes still, dark waters lost in thought. Then the storm passed. "I need to trace those roots back to the village where I was born," he said, his voice somewhere between hopeful and mournful. "I trust you will understand, T'Challa."

T'Challa bent his head, as if listening to a sound far off. "I do."

"Then I thank you for bringing me this far." N'Jadaka hoisted the bag on his shoulder. "I wouldn't be here without you."

"No need to thank me, N'Jadaka. Take care of yourself and I will see you again. I hope sooner rather than later."

"Yes, you will."

N'Jadaka closed the limousine door behind him, his signature red coral bead necklace bounced on his throat as he quickly disappeared into the chanting crowd.

Monica watched the top of his head, the dark locs wrapped in a high bun, until it was no longer discernible. The silence in the car made her wonder if she had misjudged T'Challa's mercurial friend. His moods had always made Monica uneasy, the quicksilver shifts from charming to something indescribable—not quite melancholy, not quite malice, something in between. But T'Challa trusted him, so Monica kept her peace.

For a moment, the couple sat in silence. Monica contemplating what the future might hold. T'Challa contemplating Wakanda's dark past. As N'Jadaka had just reminded the Panther King, his friend and his family weren't the only casualties of Klaw's murderous obsession or of Regent N'Baza's firm reign. Returning N'Jadaka home could never make up for the years he had lost outside Wakanda's walls of protection, but it might offer a way to heal.

A convoy of painted bicycles rode past, streaming tassels on the handlebars and wheels. They spun in a circle, weaving in and out, with giant marionettes hoisted atop them. Fully functioning, connected by wire, each cyclist could turn the head of the creatures with a flick of their wrist. There was a giant serpent, beautifully painted in black, orange, and gold. It writhed and spun its head. A pink tongue flickered out to the delight of the squealing children. A green dragon shook its wings, and a pale skeleton did a Bojangles jig, rattling its many bones.

"*Killll, kill, killll, monnnnn, ger!*" the crowd chanted. "*Killll, kill, killll, monnnnn, ger!*"

T'Challa wrinkled his brow at the crowd's fervor. A question formed in his mind. Then, without warning, the purple-robed masked dancer did a series of back-to-back somersaults, vaulting into the air. The crowd roared, pointing with delight, their mouths open *O*s.

"Death to the panther demon!" the dancer cried.

The crowd gasped in shock, mirroring Monica's own confusion. Before she could speak, the dancer darted towards them, stilts stabbing the earth. The masked dancer leaned back as if doing a limbo, then forward, so close Monica saw the chisel marks on the unfinished wood.

"Killmonger," he whispered. "Killmonger!"

The dancer spat in Monica's face. The shock made her scream out in horror.

T'Challa snapped.

Suddenly the limo was full of Wakandan cries and curses. Car doors were flung open; the passenger window shot up; the Dora Milaje guards and T'Challa leaped out.

One second, T'Challa was dressed in his formal, light-colored, embroidered travel clothes; the next, his entire body and face were enveloped by an extraordinary black suit, so dark and smooth it looked as if black water, the night itself, had risen up and swallowed him whole.

Sharp anti-metal claws emerged from his fingertips like silver lightning.

The Black Panther released a guttural growl. The sound was so menacing that, if you heard it in the jungle or on a street, you would think you had already been eaten.

The masked dancer ran off, ditching their stilts, disappearing into the crowd. But Monica suspected they wouldn't be gone long. She had seen the Black Panther in action. He'd taken on a nation of violators. When he moved, the whole world seemed to tremble beneath his feet. A mere clown buckjumping on stilts or running on flat feet didn't stand a chance against the Panther King.

A Dora Milaje guard handed Monica a beautiful handkerchief, sympathy in the guard's eyes. She fought off tears as the limo sped off.

"Ms. Lynne, we are sorry for this. Whoever that was, that jambazi, meant no disrespect to *you*," they said, their voice full of the beautiful lilting accent Monica had come to love. Everything sounded better in Wakanda. Even lies. "We should arrive at the palace in a few moments. Our physicians are some of the best in the world."

"Physician?" Confusion made Monica's question a whisper.

"Your Highness requested that we take you to his personal doctor, to ensure your health. Forgive me, but to say more might displease him," said the guard.

"Thank you," Monica replied. "No apology needed. I get that he thinks I may have been poisoned."

"Forgive my lapse in etiquette, Ms. Lynne. I am Adebisi, Captain of the Dora Milaje." The guard offered Monica a steely handshake. "I will escort you to the royal palace. No more harm will come to you. I promise." A slight growl filled the guard's voice.

The Dora Milaje guard did not speak again. Her eyes now flat, displaying the blank neutrality that Monica had come to recognize sometimes in her own love. "Better safe than sorry," she said. Something her late mom, a former healthcare aide, often said. They all sat together in silence, the urban fixtures of the Golden City now giving way to a more idyllic and rural setting.

Fields of tan and lavender-colored crops dotted the landscape. A few giant purple horned rhinos grazed in the field. The limo sped up a twisting hill. Monica's ears kept popping. Then, a sound like a rocket's explosion filled the air, followed by gunshots.

"What was that?" Monica asked, fear gripping her heart. T'Challa was out there, back in downtown Birnin Zana.

"Fear not. Our king is The One Who Puts the Knife Where It Belongs."

The guards faced forward and not another word was spoken, in Wakandan or English.

The motorcade sped down the Path of Kings, a winding road flanked by various larger-than-life monuments to the royal line that began with Bashenga and continued to T'Challa's late father, T'Chaka. The air had the scent of cinnamon and other spices that Monica didn't recognize, an aroma that T'Challa said came from Wakanda's special trees. The tree bark and the bright yellow-orange-and-crimson flowers were sometimes used as a cooking ingredient or for healing.

Feeling a bit carsick, Monica was surprised and relieved when the motorcade finally stopped before a tall, wide gate covered in Wakandan symbols and a panther motif. More armed guards flanked the perimeter. Clad in red and gold, the Dora Milaje, all women, silently held traditional spears and dangerous-looking high-tech weapons Monica didn't recognize.

An oral command opened the gate to reveal a palace so stunning, even the lore of fairy tales did not do it justice. The palace grounds were flawless. A ribbon of luscious green blossoms were arranged in patterns that evoked the Wakandan script. Monica gasped audibly, shaking her head.

She stood in silence, wavering between marvel and worry. Her line of thought was broken when she saw the surprise and distaste on the face of the man who now stood before her.

Adebisi whispered in Wakandan to the man who was obviously a military leader of some sort. *Could this be...*

"W'Kabi," the man said, his voice a deep bass. "I am the Chief of Security and the General of the Taifa Ngao." He saw Monica's blank face and continued. "I am the Shield of the Nation. It is my honor to meet you, Ms. Monica Lynne of the United States."

Monica smiled, no teeth. She knew a hater when she saw one. This W'Kabi was with it, straight buggin'.

"Nice to meet you, Mr. W'Kabi, Mtemi ya Taifa Ngao," Monica said, mindful of respect and decorum. This was the man T'Challa trusted with his life. After hearing her speak his true title in Wakandan, he spoke to her with slightly less antipathy.

"I am sorry your journey was not more comfortable," W'Kabi said. "We will have your things sent to the King's personal rooms. In the meanwhile, would you please go with Daktari Mganga to our newly-expanded research hospital? She will see that all is well with you."

Dr. Mganga peered at Monica, her face pleasant but her eyes questioning. Monica nodded at her.

"It is our honor to welcome you, Ms. Lynne. I am Mganga, protégé of the Great Mendinao. Our king must hold you in the highest regard," the elder said.

"How do you know that?" Monica asked, weariness from the journey beginning to take hold.

"Because you are here."

DORA MILAJE guards followed their king as he raced through the parting crowd. Echoes of the Killmonger chant played through his memory as he leaped atop the statue of Azzuri the Wise, the creator of Wakanda's global spy network. Azzuri, T'Challa's grandfather, was the Black Panther who defeated Captain America in hand-to-hand combat during the Second World War.

"Your Highness, over there!" yelled a man, huddled near a bush with his wife and child. They were in one of the city's public parks. He pointed at a circle of interlocking apple guava and Wangari trees.

"Bad Panter, Bad Panter!" the toddler cried, ecstatic. He had one little tooth in his mouth.

T'Challa dove for the copse of trees. He could hear the masked jambazi's desperate gasps for air as he crashed through the town square. But the people's cries would have revealed the culprit's whereabouts even without T'Challa using his enhanced hearing. He was slowing down, fear overtaking him.

Rage filled the Black Panther's heart as he stared at the assailant. The masked one trembled before him; panthers petrify their prey before pouncing. T'Challa wanted to tear this person apart, for disrespecting Monica, for disrespecting him. He dove onto the jambazi, knocking them down. The wood mask flew into the air to reveal a wild-eyed man. A skull painted in sickly yellow neon. Two hundred solid pounds of fury bore down on the defiler.

The Black Panther snarled. "Who are you? What is a Killmonger?"

Delirious, the man wept and laughed. "Your replacement," he said.

Underneath the hysterical man's laughter, T'Challa heard the soft ticking of a timer. *An IED*!

T'Challa rose and opened the laughing man's purple robe.

The timer read one second, then zero…

"Killmonger!" the man cried, his last words.

A silent explosion ripped the man apart and threw the Panther King across the clearing. He landed with a crash against a Wangari tree. The bomber's blood mixed with the fruit of apple guavas. The Black Panther's vibranium suit had absorbed most of the bomb's force and all the sound, protecting him. Now the Black Panther released the force of the explosion into the air. The boom shook all the fruit from the remaining centuries-old trees.

T'Challa stood up, only to face a volley from three R24 assault rifles. It was the cyclists from earlier, the roving marionettes. The rider of the dragon bike screamed at the Panther King.

"False King, you follow no true god! Bast is a demonic spirit, and you are a puppet of the outworlders."

T'Challa spun and rolled, deflecting the cloud of bullets with his suit and gaining ground on the murderous traitors. He snatched one rifle from the serpent biker, tossing him into the top of a tree, and pummeled the dragon into unconsciousness. All that remained was the skeleton.

"We are beyond death," the skeleton rider shouted as he flung his weapon to the ground. He beat his chest, his face emblazoned with the same sickly gold paint that now glowed in the twilight. "Killmonger has shown us K'Liluna, the true god of Wakanda. We are the Death Regiments. No longer will colonizers rule Africa. No longer will Wakanda tolerate weak kings, scraping and bowing to foreign powers. Down with the Hidden Kingdom!" the Skeleton cried. "The future has been revealed!"

"Nice speech," the Black Panther said, then punched him in the throat.

"YOUR HIGHNESS, I must speak with you with much urgency."

T'Challa walked past his chief of security, nodding. "Yes."

Blood and other unspeakable matter clung to his suit. Only his face was revealed, his eyes dark and broiling with fury.

"Where is Monica?"

W'Kabi looked baffled.

"Taifa Ngao, I will ask you once more. Where is Monica?" T'Challa roared.

W'Kabi lowered his eyes. "Ms. Monica Lynne is unharmed according to Daktari, Your Highness."

T'Challa was relieved that she was physically well, but he wouldn't say she was unharmed. He had brought her to Wakanda at the worst time. He had some explaining to do.

"She has not yet dined," W'Kabi began. The Panther King bristled. "It was offered, but Ms. Lynne preferred to wait for you. She is resting in your chambers."

"Have Shuri meet us for dinner in one hour."

"Your Highness, she is training—playing," W'Kabi said, correcting himself, "with the Sacred Eighteen."

"With Okoye and Nakia again?"

W'Kabi nodded.

"Ms. Lynne…" W'Kabi began, pursing his lips despite himself.

"My guest here," the Panther King said. He saw the question before it was formed. "Indefinitely."

"Of course, Your Majesty. Captain Adebisi has already taken it upon herself to guard Ms. Lynne." He turned to leave.

T'Challa had known W'Kabi all his life. He read the disapproval in the man's posture.

"W'Kabi," he said, "I know it is urgent. I have just survived an IED explosion by an apparent suicide bomber. We will speak on that, on this Killmonger—whoever he may be—on Regent N'Baza's ceremonies, and on whatever else I need to know. But tonight, I must make amends to someone very important to me. This was not my plan."

W'Kabi looked thoughtful. "I understand, T'Challa. Is it your plan to…?"

"Make her my queen? It is."

The Chief of Security—who had trained T'Challa himself, who had advised the late Regent when the Orphan King was too young to rule—looked surprised, then scandalized.

"Do you mean, Your Highness, it is your intention to make an outworlder our queen?"

The muscles in T'Challa's face quivered. The last time W'Kabi had seen the usually even-tempered leader this furious was when he went to face Ulysses Klaw.

"A jambazi spat in my future queen's face—in my presence. I am covered in his blood now. I will not tolerate your disrespect. *You*, and *all of my subjects* in the Golden City and beyond, will treat Monica Lynne with the respect she deserves."

The Shield of Wakanda made the "Wakanda Forever" signal and left his king pacing the room like a restless panther, furious.

T'CHALLA QUICKLY showered in one of his private rooms. He skipped his oversized Zebrano hardwood soaking tub, large enough for two, though he sorely needed a hot bath after the day's battles. He knew this old fear, the old worry. At night, before he met Monica, before he avenged his father and killed Klaw, he dreamed of the shore, of strange storms blowing through his palace. Of the water rising from volcanic rock, not the River of Grace and Wisdom, the Red Sea or Indian Ocean, but a new ocean formed from his pain and fiery tears. The water rose like lava from an erupting volcano, and there was nothing he could do about it.

They want to break your spirit, but Bast has chosen you.

He could hear his father's voice. A warning not to let anger rule him, the way it ruled so much of the modern world. T'Challa kept a binder of obituaries, of his people and of others, so when the fiery rage—the desire to destroy and take life rather than uplift and affirm life—threatened to overtake him, he would know who had died while he lived, in what he once thought was his prison of privilege and luxury. When T'Chaka died, T'Challa added his obituary, kept it for history. But the secret book of names, of the dead, did not help him then. Rage had won out. If he wasn't careful, it could win again.

When he came out of his rainforest shower, he folded over, as if the breath had been pulled out of him. He stilled himself, meditating on the pain in each tender part of his body. He had taken blows, but an explosion always rocked him. T'Challa dressed to face Monica, his toughest battle yet. He was still sore, but he wouldn't show it. He walked in the great, high-ceilinged bedroom, back straight, eyes radiating warmth. But he didn't have to pretend how much he enjoyed seeing Monica.

"T'Challa," she said. Her voice soothed some of his pain.

"Monica."

She wept in his arms. He held her until her tears stopped flowing. Another broken dam he felt powerless against.

"I'm sorry I brought you here. If I had known, there is no way I would have carried you into such danger. With my regent dead and me being away for a year, Wakanda is clearly unstable—far more unstable than I expected."

"All of this in a year?" Monica asked.

"I was selfish, fleeing my own demons. Now, to my own people I am seen as a demon."

"Not all," Monica said. "It was clear that so many truly love you."

"With war, sometimes it only takes a little. Cunning is greater than strength."

"And your wisdom is your strength, T'Challa," Monica said.

"Then I must be strong enough to part from you. Monica, I must send you home to safety. There are too many unknown variables here."

"And you know what's not one of them?" Monica replied. "Me. You always take care of everyone else. Who will be there for you? I don't want to go, T. I want to stay here with you, killer clowns or not."

He laughed. "That's my brave sunbird, voice of a million years."

"Sunbird?" she said. "I think I like that."

"Good, let's get you some dinner. Don't want you starving for me, too. I likes'em thick."

Monica laughed all the way to the impressive dining room.

The table was seated for three, but six diners were present.

Shuri stood smiling at them, mischievousness in her eyes. "You're late," she said. "You asked me to come to dinner, which I did, but you were not here when I came. A princess like myself should not be dining alone." She tossed her beautiful braided hair, regal and glittering with jewels.

T'Challa shook his head. "Monica, you've met Captain Adebisi."

The Dora Milaje leader stood behind Shuri, a tall, grim figure. She offered her king a nod and crossed her arms over her chest—a gesture old as the line of Bashenga. *Wakanda forever!*

"So, Okoye and Nakia?" T'Challa asked.

The two girls, one tall and slim, the other short with little round cheeks, looked on nervously.

"I invited them. Looks like you brought a guest. What is this now, *Coming to Wakanda*? Where's Arsenio?"

Nakia laughed loudly, then covered her mouth. Okoye elbowed her friend, shaking her head *no*.

T'Challa sighed. "Monica, meet my little sister, Shuri. Shuri, meet…"

Shuri cut her brother off. "Hi Ms. Monica, pleased to meet you. But *you*," Shuri said, pointing at T'Challa. "So, you leave me alone for a year, to fight crime with Captain America, Iron Man, and the Mighty Thor," she said, sarcastically. Nakia was trying but failing not to giggle beside her, while Okoye kept her composure as usual. "Having all sorts of fun! And when the party's over, *now* you want to come for me?"

T'Challa glanced at Monica who smiled, amused. "Oh, I like your sister," she whispered.

"Then you can have her," T'Challa said, pulling out Monica's chair.

CHAPTER THREE

A RAGE IN WAKANDA

WITH MONICA asleep in the palace bedchambers, T'Challa breathed in the early morning air, sitting astride his father's old motorcycle. The sun had not yet risen, and he needed to clear his head from the long journey back home and decide how he would handle N'Baza's sudden death. After his experience in Bustani Msitu, home of the linked Wangari trees, T'Challa began to suspect that his regent's death was not from natural causes. Today W'Kabi would have questions. T'Challa had a few of his own. For now, he needed to think in a place that brought him peace and clear vision.

He rode until the golden palace was far behind him, until the roads narrowed and all that remained were the paths of the ancients, the first Wakandans. Here in the hills where the goddess Bast first graced Bashenga, the city looked foreign, as if it had risen from the ground fully formed. But T'Challa knew the blood and sweat baked into every brick, the tears of hope that shone on the shimmering glass-and-vibranium girded walls.

He left the bike his father had loved so well leaning against a flat-topped acacia tree. He wove his way around the abandoned obelisks and carved sculptures of panthers reclining in trees or peering from behind tall green grasses. T'Challa climbed atop the hill and filled his lungs with the scent of gazania daisies, wild dagga, and jasmine. From a hill covered in soft grass overlooking the Golden City, he watched the morning sun lean through the blinding blue sky. Wet morning dew cooled the soles of T'Challa's feet, relaxed his mind for morning meditation. He loved to see his city like this, when the sun's golden rays cast a glow over the heart and soul of Wakanda. No longer sore, he thanked the Panther God Bast for saving his life once again, and for the opportunity to watch the sun rise over his kingdom, the land of his birth.

He stared out at beautiful Birnin Zana, the Golden City with its rising towers and hanging gardens, and thought of his father. He wished Wakanda's slain king could see what the city had become. T'Challa took a sweet breath knowing that his father would be proud of their progress, of the empire that was now a technological marvel. But yesterday's confrontation with an unknown enemy from within Wakanda's borders would have his father fuming in Djalia, the ancestral plane.

As always, T'Challa hoped that the once-great king would be proud of the man that he was struggling to become.

"We are living your dream, father," T'Challa said as the golden light spread across the waking city. "I promise I will not let this threat destroy your vision or the kingdom we have built." The Panther King turned from the golden haze of sun and metal towards the dense countryside that reached out to beautiful Lake Nyanza.

He decided to visit Griot G'Sere, who lived near Warrior Falls. He wished to discuss plans for N'Baza's homegoing ceremony. He wanted more answers before he met with his security chief.

Standing on the rolling hills, T'Challa's heart was heavy, his mind filled with scenes from his youth. Regent N'Baza, the stern elder full of magic and mystery, carried himself like the long line of healers and shamans that formed his bloodline. With his ceremonial headdress and somber robes—he refused modern dress—the elder had been like a father to T'Challa, and was the only one he trusted to rule the kingdom in his absence. After all, the regent served as the surrogate king of the Wakandan empire, protecting his little sister Shuri and their people. N'Baza's loss was a heavy blow, but the elder had lived many long years of glory and great service. No matter how he died, he would be missed.

His grief a cloud around his shoulders, T'Challa rode in silence until the acrid scent of burning wood filled his nostrils. His enhanced senses picked up singed flesh and something else. Fear.

In the distance he spied a ribbon of black smoke rising, then noticed several more—from opposite sides of the village. Alarm rippled through him. Eyes dilated, his enhanced vision searched for the source of the fires. No factories or machinery operated in that direction. There, among the verdant hills and giant baobab trees, were only the villages where the griots kept Wakandan history alive through vibrant song and poetry. It was said that when an elder dies, a library burns, but in Wakanda the elderly griots were not just libraries; they were the memory of the people, connected to the oldest lineages in the land. Smoke clouds like those meant more than accident or death: they meant destruction.

Within seconds of his mental command, the Black Panther suit materialized to envelop his body, a dark shroud made of shifting layers of vibranium nanotech. The Panther King's armor was flesh and spirit, nanobots and neurology. G'Sere had once called it mojotech, scoffing that it was high culture rootwork, magic indecipherable from science.

T'Challa ran until the grass gave way to dense brush interspersed with giant baobab and acacia trees that swept the sky like huge brown and green fans. Taking to the treetops, he leapt from branch to branch, his body agile, fast, sure. He raced across fat leaves that spread beneath him. Vibrant colors swept above and under, all around the Black Panther.

The scents of burning leaves and blood irritated his nostrils. He heard tortured screams intermingled with derisive laughter.

When T'Challa swung into the opening, he found two soldiers standing on opposite sides of a cage that had been hoisted and suspended in midair. A series of ropes extended to the baobab branches above. Staring intently, one held a spear, the other an assault rifle. Their crudeness, the inhumanity of the trap turned his stomach. It reminded T'Challa of everything that his father fought against. Years of injustice boiling around Wakanda's serene borders.

Another whiff, and T'Challa caught the scent of old G'Sere, one of the most respected and wisest of all the griots in Wakanda. T'Challa listened to the wind as the old griot moaned and cried to Bast for mercy.

Clearly Bast had heard him, because the Black Panther was there.

A closer look revealed old man G'Sere curled like a newborn behind rusty bars and a steel floor wet with blood. Open wounds covered the elder's chest, leaking red all over the white, ceremonial robes festooned around his arms and legs in ragged strips.

The cage itself reminded T'Challa of the stories that his father had told him when he was only a young cub. Stories of an ancient history that had preceded both of their lives. Tales of a terrible industry of blood and suffering, tears and lamentations lost in an unforgiving sea. Like a merciless wind, hateful foreign lands filled T'Chaka's cautionary tales of tyranny and suffering bodies shining slick with sweat. Black skin covered in welts, beautiful, good people, whose flesh reflected the great darkness that held the stars. Only cruel hearts would force others into bondage.

T'Challa cursed under his breath, but the next sight nearly ripped his own heart out of his chest. Instead of strangers, he saw the once good-natured souls, Tayete and Kazibe—young men his father had trained himself. The treachery hurt the Panther King's spirit. Once, those faces had helped T'Challa and W'Kabi bring solace and comfort to desperate souls who had lost so much during Klaw's invasion. Now the Black Panther saw those same faces twisted and contorted with hatred. The lack of respect for the elder's ways was one thing, but the cruelty was quite another. The faces that he saw in front of him were just as grotesque as the twisted figures from Dante's *Inferno*. T'Challa had been called a demon, but this was truly unholy.

Filled with malicious rage, the pair prodded the old man with their spears. Over and over, Tayete and Kazibe thrust their spears into the cage.

"Tell us what we want to know, G'Sere. There is still time for you to live," Tayete said, grunting as he nudged the old man's arm.

Kazibe grinned and nodded in approval. Then his grin turned into confusion, fear, suspicion. "Do you hear that? Over there." Kazibe pointed toward the rustling trees standing behind Tayete. They looked as if they had been swept by a great wind.

"Kazibe, you are much too craven. A bird caws, a cub purrs and you're ready to jump out of your skin. Look at yourself. Stop being such a coward."

"That's not a…." Kazibe's eyes went wide with fear.

Before Kazibe could catch his breath, before the word *cub* could tumble from his lips, the Black Panther snatched Tayete, swung him in a circle, and threw the treacherous turncoat into a tree.

"Kazibe! I have known you since you were a boy. Your father served our fallen king bravely. My own father trained you both as if you were his sons." T'Challa glanced at the cage. The sight of G'Sere stretched in his own blood brought back faces that the Black Panther had tried, to no avail, to bury in his subconscious. The face of his father, struggling with all of his might to live. Staring into T'Challa's eyes, hoping for one more second. The face of Klaw, laughing with triumph.

Kazibe hung his head in shame, but Tayete rose and puffed out his chest, a defiant young cock. "Like a son but not a son," he said. "We want to be more than errand boys, delivering grain and tissue," he said but his wavering voice defied him.

They had seen the Black Panther in action but never against his own.

With one foot the Black Panther kicked the spear from Kazibe's hand. He smashed his other foot against Kazibe's jaw. The blow was met with a loud crunching sound, and Kazibe's fearful eyes rolled in his head. T'Challa watched Kazibe's knees give in as the deserter toppled to the ground. He wanted to strangle the soldier, but he first turned to the cage to release Griot G'Sere. He heard a familiar clicking and pulsing sound—a vibranium-powered assault rifle.

"Not so tough now, are you?" Tayete grinned. The rifle throbbed in his grasp. Light poured from the front and the sides of the bulky weapon, accentuating the hatred in Tayete's eyes. "You've been gone a long time, *T'Challa*. Everything is different now."

The Panther King barely had time to register the insult of being called by his first name by a soldier without any rank. The wretch who had betrayed him, his people, and brought pain to one of T'Challa's most loyal aides. The violation could not stand.

T'Challa could have allowed his vibranium armor to absorb the blast from Tayete's assault weapon. Instead, the Black Panther dodged the sizzling beam, and sliced the gun into pieces with his black claws before picking Tayete up by the neck.

"You haven't tasted Wakandan air in many moons." Tayete kicked and struggled against the Black Panther's grip, like a small child. "Don't worry. You won't taste it for long. Wakanda has a new king and a new god now."

"Anyone who wants my throne can challenge me any time, at Warrior Falls, but this is the coward's way."

T'Challa hurled Tayete into Kazibe just as the other soldier was standing up. Kazibe broke Tayete's fall. The thought of someone who had betrayed his father challenging the throne filled him with ember-hot anger. He started toward Tayete and Kazibe, tangled together on the floor, but stopped mid-step when he heard G'Sere moan.

"Mtoto, leave them," the elder whispered. "Their blood is not worth staining your soul."

Beat by slow beat, T'Challa heard the life draining away from the elder who had shared secrets and stories with him as a boy. The Orphan King would go to hear them more than he would openly admit. Hearing a story read aloud can bring comfort to a hurting heart. To hear his old mentor leaving the realm of the living in such a poor state saddened T'Challa deeply. G'Sere deserved better.

A shaking, blood-stained hand reached through the bars of the cage. G'Sere's wrinkled face stretched with pain, the time remaining to him unknown. His arm trembled as he collapsed. T'Challa leapt onto the cage and gripped the bars, prying them apart with his claws. He pulled open a gap wide enough to remove the elder.

Behind him, dazed and confused, Tayete and Kazibe had recovered and scrambled up, scuttling away. The Black Panther heard their mincing steps and Tayete's faint mad laughter drifting in the wind.

"Mtoto, My King, you have returned," G'Sere said, his voice strained.

T'Challa kneeled beside G'Sere and took the griot in his arms. The old man smiled with bright shining eyes, his voice weak.

"They said you would never return, but I knew they were wrong," G'Sere said, his breathing labored. "I told them you would never abandon Wakanda." G'Sere squeezed T'Challa's wrist with a soft trembling grip, weakening by the second. "They tried to make me denounce you. So many others have already sided with him."

"This Killmonger, who is he?" T'Challa asked.

"He is misplaced vengeance returned. Follower of K'Liluna the Betrayer. She feeds off rage and vengeance. Please, My King, be careful." G'Sere struggled to breathe. "Rage may help you cut a swath through your enemies but be careful it does not turn back and consume you. Stay on your father's path. The Betrayer has hooked her claws into Killmonger's spirit and granted him extraordinary power, but remember, T'Challa, none is greater than the avatar of Bast. Find harmony in the chaos." With those mysterious words, G'Sere grew silent. After a moment, his head lolled. He was gone.

T'Challa stroked G'Sere's soft gray hair, grief filling the space where the elder had once been. "Do not worry, my friend. The people who did this to you will face justice."

He turned to the bright, merciless sky. Tears burned his eyes. "I promise. On my father's life, on my very own, on the land of my ancestors. I promise in the presence of Bast herself. The men who did this to you, and whoever commands them, will pay for your blood with their very own, G'Sere."

T'Challa held the elder and rose, barely feeling the slight man's weight. Then it hit him: He had only just returned to Wakanda, but it would be the second day T'Challa returned home with someone else's blood on his claws.

The Black Panther carried G'Sere's body back to the small settlement of low-level quarters and flats that bordered the edge of the Great Mound. The trek felt long and arduous, not physically but spiritually. The Black Panther walked the entire way, head down, staring at what remained of the one who had filled others with so much life and song. He would miss G'Sere's solemn face and playful spirit. One who lived with so much fire and knowledge, magic and whimsy.

As T'Challa walked, one of G'Sere's songs played itself in the Panther King's mind.

Away in the mountain (away, away)
Bast gave us a king (oju iwaju wa fun wa)
Bast gave us a king (the future is for us)

T'Challa felt eyes watching him through peepholes, parted curtains and cracked doors. The villagers stared from rooftops, peered from behind parked vehicles glimmering in the Wakandan sun. When they saw their king carrying one of their own, they joined his weary march. One by one, the people of Wakanda emerged from their homes and their hiding places. Soon the street was filled with onlookers. When they saw G'Sere's lifeless body, furious wailing rose like a terrible storm. Grief swept over the streets like a great fire, their sadness a dark cloud eclipsing the village.

Before long, T'Challa reached the humble home G'Sere shared with his wife, Noxolo, their three children, and other extended family members. T'Challa remembered the way well. With his dead mentor in his arms, T'Challa had never felt more distant from his homeland.

He saw the unspoken accusation in the eyes of his people. As king, the absent king, he was more responsible for the elder's death than the killers. He felt the unforgiving glares, as if they sensed something foreign and unfamiliar in the Black Panther's demeanor. *And now he has returned with an outworlder?* No one said the words aloud, but the Panther King felt them all the same.

He kneeled, placing the body on the ground, ashamed. He didn't even have a wrap to cover the griot. He didn't wish the family to see G'Sere in this way. T'Challa silently ordered the Black Panther suit to retract from his torso, removed his shirt, and covered the elder. He left his mask on to hide his shame. A murmur rippled through the crowd that gathered as G'Sere's family rushed from their home.

When they saw the lifeless body, battered and bloody, the stains spreading through T'Challa's garment, they howled with grief and indignation. In less than twenty-four hours, the ululations that had greeted the Panther King's return had turned into lamentations. In Wakanda the elders were as sacred and revered as the Wangari trees. To abuse one in this manner was a sacrilege.

G'Sere's wife, Noxolo, looked anything but peaceful. She fell atop her husband and covered his bruised face with kisses and tears.

Then she looked up at the bare-chested Panther King, loathing and hatred burning in her eyes. Her grief made her tongue reckless.

"My husband believed in you when no one else would. He trusted you to protect Wakanda and protect all of us. Where did his trust, his blind faith get him? You let the vipers in. Usurpers did this to my husband—and you did, too. Yet you dare call yourself King of Wakanda?"

"Mother!" One of G'Sere's sons cried. Horrified and devastated, he grabbed his mother to lead her away. She fought her son more fiercely than she had tongue-lashed the Panther King. Her other children had to drag the poor woman away. "I fed you from my own table!" she whispered, weeping. "Wakanda needs her king, Mtoto! G'Sere had faith in you."

Only one member of the crowd remained. A child not more than ten years old. He stared at T'Challa with tears rising in his eyes. The expression was familiar. He stared with all the desperation of a son who had witnessed his father slain before his eyes. With all the rage of a panther driven to wrath.

Blood spilled in my kingdom because of my absence. T'Challa raised his head to the blazing sun overhead. Listening for direction. He had come to this ancient place seeking peace but all he had found was death. And the ghost of Klaw laughing and mocking him. The sound of hatred.

You let him die.

CHAPTER FOUR

FIRE IN THE VALLEY

T'CHALLA CHOSE to walk back to the palace, alone with his thoughts. He left his father's motorcycle by the tree. It would need to be retrieved later—or not. Sentimental trinkets and nostalgia were the least of his worries now. Griot G'Sere had helped him, just not in the way he planned. A curious pattern was emerging, one that was proving more concerning each passing hour.

From its hills, rumored by the late G'Sere to hold the remains of giants and creatures from the empire's past, Wakanda had never looked so beautiful to T'Challa. He loved this ancient land of his birth, its varied people with traditions that went back thousands of years, its mystic mountains that held old spirits and rivers that whispered back to you, its legends and lore. But the empire was anything but tranquil. The realization that something sinister was afoot—and had been for some time—left the Panther King deeply unsettled.

As T'Challa walked, the midday sun bore down on his bare neck and back. Sweat pooled across his muscular shoulders. The walk felt like a necessary penance, each step tamping his anger and sadness.

The hard-packed, brick-red soil of the dust roads turned into stone-cobbled and then paved streets. As the afternoon bore down, the paved streets turned into a system of golden highways that led straight to Birnin Zana, the Golden City, seat of the empire's government.

He tried to see it through Monica's eyes. The palace façade was shaped like an enormous black feline, built in loving and unending dedication to the Panther God Bast. It was devastating to learn that two of his father's young soldiers had lost their faith in the wake of the nation's struggles—and that some Wakandans had grown so hopeless that self-immolation seemed like a reasonable option. All those miserable revelations made each step heavier than the last.

T'Challa wondered what K'Liluna the Betrayer, the god G'Sere mentioned, had promised this Killmonger and his minions. Bast spoke rarely to the people anymore, instead ruling through her chosen avatars, promising them refuge and respite in a world that offered neither. T'Challa's royal family was of that special lineage, born of those who, over time, had always had the goddess's ear. The deity watched over the people of Wakanda like a giant matriarch guarding her faithful children, ready to pounce and devour any threat that neared them.

As T'Challa walked shirtless and bare-chested through the streets of his city, he wondered if anyone would recognize him in his current sorry state. He was too tired to feel shame. He wore no royal clothing or Wakandan regalia. Still, throngs of people drove by, waving and blowing car horns, screaming blessings, grateful for the return of their king. Wakandan citizens leaned out of their windows and opened doors. It was a very different reception to the one he had received in the village. The loud, tumultuous din echoed through the streets. All the fervor and the fanfare did nothing to lift T'Challa's dejected spirit.

A small retinue of black jeeps pulled up. Sleek aircars hovered just above the ground, all hurrying toward T'Challa. Leading the pack were two huge vehicles: massive, armored steampunk elephants, with a single lone figure riding atop one of the mechanical beasts. The sight brought some light and levity to T'Challa's heart, a sense of wonder. The tight-lipped man steering the metal-plated pachyderm could only be Chief W'Kabi. T'Challa knew the conversation they must have would be a hard one, but it would be honest. Given all that he had seen, he would have to set some of the royal conventions aside to speak with W'Kabi frankly, as old friends, as they once did.

Wakanda's top military officer wryly waved at T'Challa from atop his mechanical beast. It was outfitted with the thick, intricately woven blankets of the famed weavers of Birnin Okowe. The elephant mech raised its massive trunk and golden tusks. Its trumpeting rumbled and rolled through the air. Even from his elevated, woven seat atop the elephant, W'Kabi's grim features shone just as sourly and as reliably as they always had. Their tense conversation regarding Monica had not been forgotten but seeing W'Kabi's bemused look brought a much-needed smile to T'Challa's face.

"Morning, Your Highness. Ms. Lynne said you were gone when she woke, and Taku said he could not reach you. So, what happened?" he asked, glancing at the shirtless king. "You decided to go to Birnin Man?"

T'Challa chuckled. "No, I'm trying to keep up with you, Hannibal."

The two burst into laughter. W'Kabi threw the Panther King a flask of cold water and a shirt. "This should slake your thirst, Fabio."

T'Challa choked back laughter. The cool interior of his vibranium-technologically-enhanced mask had been a life saver on the long walk back to the city, but he welcomed the refreshing drink nonetheless. "Aw," he said, retracting his mask and taking a gulp from the flask. "Water is life."

"That it is."

W'Kabi climbed on top of the mechanical elephant's head, leaped into the air and completed two somersaults before he landed in a crouch in front of T'Challa. The monsoon wind from the distant sea brought the scents of ripe fruit, blossoms, and rain.

"Getting a little rusty," T'Challa said, a weary grin on his face. "My grandmother could flip faster than that. Hell, Shuri can."

"Never, My King," W'Kabi said as he stood to his feet. "I have brought you transport."

"I noticed," T'Challa said, glancing warily at the other elephant mech.

"All joking aside, My King, we must hurry back to the palace. There is much to discuss. There have been *developments* since your *absence*."

T'Challa did not like the emphasis that W'Kabi placed on his words. Still, he shook W'Kabi's hand and grabbed the shoulders of the general in an affectionate gesture. T'Challa remembered W'Kabi's early days as a foot soldier and ranger in Wakanda's army. In those days, W'Kabi had been just as ridiculous as Tayete and Kazibe. *But W'Kabi's mood had been so much better in those early days,* T'Challa mused to himself. So had his own. War had a way of lingering with you. No matter which side you are on, an ending doesn't mean it ends.

"General W'Kabi, you are right. It has been too long since I've spent any time with the most treasured and qualified member of our Wakandan army."

"Flattery gets you everywhere," W'Kabi said as he climbed back on the machine. "Hop on."

T'Challa nodded in appreciation, stroking the massive side of his elephant. He admired the stained-glass-like mosaic that formed its skin. It looked wrinkly but felt smooth to his touch. "I needed that time, but my people needed me more. I realize that now."

W'Kabi looked relieved as the Black Panther vaulted onto the mechanical elephant's back.

"Your people have longed for your return as well, My King. But you are here now. The turmoil you found at the edge of the city is only the beginning of the problems that plague Wakanda."

T'Challa glanced at the company of soldiers and high-tech vehicles, idling behind their general with the poise of a bed of coiled cobras waiting to strike.

"Where is Taku?" T'Challa asked as his mech began to slowly lumber towards the palace. He wouldn't want to get on the wrong side of that beast, he mused, then turned his thoughts back to the matter at hand. He should have used his communications specialist to search for this Killmonger group straightaway; instead T'Challa had thought he could avoid the inevitable, if only for a little while, by darting out to the outer villages and spending some catch-up time with his old mentor. The excursion to the Griot Village turned out to be a blessing and a curse. T'Challa had left with information but had lost an old friend and the trust of people he cared for.

"Taku is back at the palace, waiting to brief you. We have emergency transmissions coming in from all over the kingdom. Taku insisted on translating these communiqués personally." W'Kabi's voice grew serious. "We do not know who we can trust anymore."

For a moment, the Shield of Wakanda looked as if he was thinking of something to say, or as if he was thinking of the right way to say what he was thinking. His thoughts swirled behind his grave features. The man looked as if he had never been a child. T'Challa waited while the general sorted his thoughts.

"Your Highness, this is a very difficult time to have an outworlder—a foreigner—in our midst."

"Careful. She is not foreign to me."

"I know, My King. We are doing our best to accommodate your guest, but she may be safer in the US, away from these internal difficulties."

T'Challa shook his head as the general dipped up and down, riding his elephant. T'Challa knew Monica well, and she had made herself clear. A return to Harlem, so soon? She wouldn't hear of it. "Monica has witnessed difficulties on a scale that might surprise you. There were many demons haunting her across the shores. A moving target was on her back. That is how we met. And that's part of why I asked her to come here. There are things that have bonded us together. I do not intend to break that bond."

W'Kabi nodded, not quite agreement but acceptance. "Well, let's get out of here. The people have seen more than enough of your Chocolate Thunder show." He laughed and pushed a button near the great elephant's giant ear. It raised its head and released a thunderous trumpet, then galloped off.

The Black Panther tapped his elephant and it rumbled, great ears flapping. Five tons of power propelled him across the golden road, racing through the air. He laughed. W'Kabi had brought him the Ferrari of elephants. It sped into the golden afternoon sun, leaving the convoy of royal guards behind.

THE PANTHER King and the Shield of the Nation rode back to the royal palace, where they joined Taku in an underground war room. The trio stood before a bright monitor that covered an entire wall.

"Display map," T'Challa commanded as he turned on his Kimoyo beads. The Wakandan AI-enhanced communications system projected a map of the empire across the flat screen. Around the southern edges of the empire, near Azania and Niganda, icons of bursting flames marked the border attacks and conflict areas. Chief W'Kabi stood on one side of the Black Panther; communications specialist Taku stood on the other.

"Why didn't you tell us you would be leaving the palace grounds this morning, My King?" Taku asked. In his worry, he did not hide his irritation. "You left without alerting anyone—not even your guest. And this is the same thing you did a year ago. Before you assigned Regent N'Baza, no one knew your intentions."

T'Challa let his spirited communications specialist do what he did best—speak.

"No one could find you, until we learned of your exploits with the Avengers *through the news*. Even then, when we reached out to you, you never replied to our correspondence. Shuri, your own sister, said you barely responded to her holos. My King, what happened over the past year? The silence is unlike you."

T'Challa felt the sting of words, his chest filled with embarrassment and despair. *What happened?* He wanted to shout. *My father happened. Mother happened. N'Baza, G'Sere.* The names in his secret book went on and on. But this time, the obituaries

T'Challa collected to remind him of the costs of his choices were the result of his long absence. No one would openly blame him in *The Daily Panther* or other papers, but nevertheless the Panther King felt the sting of these last two deaths.

He thought about his father. Saw once again the pain distorting T'Chaka's face in his final moments. In his mind, he heard the magnified droning of the sonic weapon that killed the Great Isolationist. He hadn't always agreed with his father, but it pained him to see T'Chaka wracked by guilt, questioning his legacy and some of his most significant choices, at the end.

The question in T'Chaka's eyes was the question T'Challa asked himself—*am I a just king? Or have I done my people a grave disservice?* T'Challa wanted to change that legacy of isolation and neutrality to build a bridge connecting Wakanda to the global world. But there were risks: internal and external. He thought about the constant challenges and the betrayals, even from his closest confidantes.

"And this Monica—the foreigner that you have brought into our most guarded levels of security," continued Taku. W'Kabi stepped closer to Taku, attempting to warn him of the mistake he'd already made the previous day, but T'Challa spoke, his voice low and lethal.

"Taku, enough. You have one more time to call my future queen a foreigner."

Shock spread across Taku's face. *Queen? Of Wakanda?* "I mean no disrespect, Your Highness," he stammered. "But the Dora Milaje have been uneasy. They are not in the loop, have not been informed of your movements, and they are struggling to serve you as they pledged. You know well their only mission is to maintain your safety."

T'Challa knew it was important for his two closest aides to express themselves freely at this crucial time, but he still wanted to choke the messengers. Just a little. Instead, he said, "I have spoken with the Dora Milaje."

Taku looked as if he expected more, but T'Challa had turned his attention back to the map projection. Two more flaming icons emerged. One appeared in the east, near Lake Nyanza and the other spread toward the west, near the Great Mound bordering Canaan.

Unbidden, his thoughts drifted to Monica's lovely voice. *"Together in the stars,"* she sang. *"We'll dance to love's sweet harmony…"*

Find harmony in the chaos. Those were Griot G'Sere's last words. The first time T'Challa heard Monica sing, she was in a cramped basement lounge nestled in Brooklyn. Her voice had moved the Black Panther to tears. Now the thought of her singing to him, telling him to be strong and faithful, girded T'Challa; dared him to dream more boldly for himself and his people. In this time of tectonic shifts of culture and alliances, he could not afford to fail. The future of the Wakandan empire could be at stake.

"W'Kabi," the Panther King said, taking a deep breath. "You spoke of dissatisfaction in the ranks. Disapproval over my decisions. I can tell from your actions and from your demeanor that you blame me for these attacks and murders. But I want to know how you have let an insurgency build right under your nose. These attacks are highly calculated and well planned. I don't have to tell you that they must have taken months of careful strategizing to be successful."

"Months, perhaps years, My King." W'Kabi's grim voice and stare remained steady. "The rumors came long before the attacks. First, you abandoned your kingdom when we, your people, needed you the most. News of your adventures with the Fantastic Four and the Avengers gave the impression that you had turned your back on Wakanda and betrayed us for Westerners. Some even said, after all these years refusing to help our neighboring countrymen—right across our borders—in the name of King T'Chaka's careful isolationism, you chose to assist the same nations that enslaved our countrymen, ravaged their lands, and now exploit every natural resource they possess."

T'Challa held his tongue and listened, then he spoke calmly.

"My sojourn was necessary for the advancement of Wakanda. My actions are for the greater good of my people. Even when I move in secrecy, know that I am always putting Wakanda first. During my missions with Tony Stark and Reed Richards, I gathered vital intelligence and formed key alliances that will prove very useful to Wakanda's future." The Black Panther paused.

"Wakanda forever," he added. "It's never a question."

Taku bristled. "If it was vital, Your Highness, it might have proven useful here. Perhaps we could schedule a debriefing—"

"*I* determine what is vital and useful, and when I wish to divulge it." T'Challa chose his next words carefully, mindful that all responsibility ultimately fell upon his shoulders as the Panther King. "W'Kabi, Taku, trust me as you long have. There is a method to my madness—"

W'Kabi scoffed. "Shakespeare, eh? 'Do not stand in a place of danger, trusting miracles.' Azzuri the Wise."

"So now you quote my own grandfather back at me?" T'Challa asked.

He gazed at the map hologram and rubbed his chin. These attacks could have been in the works long before he left Wakanda to join the Avengers. Shuri's face, her braids bouncing on her shoulders, came to mind. She had grown so much over the past year, more confident and sociable under the tutelage of the Dora Milaje. When their father died, the child had become a mere shadow of herself. The thought of anyone harming his sister made T'Challa sick. She was his only remaining close family.

He forced himself to remain present, to think of how high this treacherous talk had risen. He wondered just how dangerously close Wakanda was to a civil war. And to think that these rebels were not lone wolves, but many people in pockets throughout the kingdom who had become dissatisfied with the Orphan King's brief reign! It was a thought that troubled and shamed him. Was it the whole hand or just a finger? Either way, the empire could not risk losing even that.

He thought of Monica again. He decided that he would triple security around his sister and his American love. African American, as she called it. T'Challa knew the moniker spoke to their origins and the cultural connections they had managed to maintain, despite centuries of deep erasure. But even knowing that history, the term always made him pause. The thought of explaining that concept to Monica, let alone his own people, put him on edge, reminding him that blending Monica into Wakandan culture might require education, listening, and delicacy on all sides.

"W'Kabi, organize a search team. We are going to investigate these attacks. Maybe we can find some clues as to who or what group is responsible."

"Not a group. A man, My King," Taku said. "His name is Erik Killmonger."

"Yes, I keep hearing about this Killmonger, but who is he?" T'Challa asked.

"We don't yet know his identity, but he is said to be a charismatic leader hell-bent on war and usurping the Wakandan throne."

"Then why doesn't he challenge me at Warrior Falls like a real leader would?"

"Because he is said not to want any royal lineage in Wakanda's government at all." Taku spoke with a low voice. "His name is insignificant. It is unconnected to any blood or family in Wakanda that we can trace. Nevertheless, it is a name whispered throughout the country. His followers grow by the day. I tried for months to send you communiqués on Erik Killmonger, but when I did not receive a reply, I gave up."

"Taku, these whispers," the Black Panther said, irritated, "explain them to me."

"My King, the whispers began while you were in New York." Taku stared uncomfortably at the ground and shook his head. The ebony, red, gold, and rainforest-green marble mosaics formed a kaleidoscopic pattern that his eyes traced. Above them, the history of Wakanda and its relationship to the goddess Bast played out on the ceiling, in the same colorful, tessellated marble and stone motif.

"I understand. You needed time alone," Taku continued. "But things were happening on the outskirts, mostly. A couple of soldiers got into a brawl at a nightclub. One of them pulled a gun; the other screamed 'Erik Killmonger!' as if a proclamation. The man with the gun was so shaken, he left without firing a single shot. The next night someone set fire to the club—and chained the doors shut.

No one survived. We sent the messages, marked urgent, but you never replied. For a year."

Outwardly impenetrable, inside T'Challa bowed his head in shame, conflicted by the memory of unanswered messages piled inside his Kimoyo. His thoughts careened, a mosaic of the passionate love and danger that had consumed him the past year. One moment he was listening to Taku's extensive grievances; the next he was back at the Great Mound, deep within the dark cave, facing the man he swore he would kill. T'Challa had finally avenged his father, but the horror of Klaw, his body disintegrating, transforming into pure sound *right before his eyes*, was a nightmare that haunted him each night.

Vengeance didn't feel as good as he had thought it would.

His memory shifted to his New York loft in Harlem, Monica singing in his ear, her fingertips brushing his chest. The scent of her perfume all around him. He didn't recognize it at first, but over time it became clear. Monica's voice had a way of relieving T'Challa's pain, easing his spirit.

I had to leave to return to myself.

T'Challa struggled with that truth. He wanted to confide in his two friends, but pride wouldn't allow the Black Panther to reveal weakness. Especially to his soldiers. So, he kept the real reason of why he left Wakanda and stayed away for a year to himself. He let the whole nation believe a lie, because the lie was easier than confronting the truth.

A rising din of voices caught his attention, but the sound was thirty feet away. At first, the Black Panther thought the voices were bickering, but when he listened closer with focused intention, he heard comradery, which only confused him more. Then he heard the voice, and suddenly he understood the fervor very well indeed.

"Monica," T'Challa said. A smile stretched across his face despite himself. His two closest aides were unaccustomed to seeing this side of their king. *The Black Panther in love?*

Monica Lynne stepped into the room surrounded by a retinue of Dora Milaje. Red coats, cowrie shells, leather cuffs, battle spears, and all. But there was something else. T'Challa was shocked, as he had never seen his personal guards so at ease in someone's presence other than themselves. Formality and stealth were their trademark strengths. The new generation, which his little sister Shuri was intent on joining, still needed work. That the guards, even Captain Adebisi, treated Monica with such care, made him appreciate them even more. It was as if they had a silent agreement to try to ease the awkwardness of Monica being away from home, surrounded by strangers, dropped into a whole new, increasingly *dangerous* world—something, he realized, they would all be quite familiar with.

In the old days, it was said that the Dora Milaje were treated as the Panther King's brides. One or two would be offered from each of Wakanda's eighteen tribes and trained from a young age to become the world's fiercest warriors, to serve as the personal royal guards of the Black King. Back then, the Adored Ones were trained in martial and other deadly arts as they were today, but also served as wives for the king. T'Challa's grandfather, Azzuri the Wise, had done away with that particular tradition, though the royal family long believed it was T'Challa's *grandmother's* idea.

Somehow, Monica had managed to win over Wakanda's fiercest warriors. The Panther King smiled. *She must've sung to them,* T'Challa thought. *Of course she did.*

"T," Monica said, as she ran toward T'Challa. She wrapped her arms around his neck and planted a huge kiss on his cheek, right beside the corner of his mouth.

"T?" mouthed one of the women warriors. The formation tittered, then resumed their trademark stance.

Wide-eyed, Taku only stared, the communicator rendered speechless, but W'Kabi was scandalized. The Dora Milaje stood, watching to see how events might unfold. By reflex, T'Challa's hand went to Monica's waist, but he had enough self-control to pull himself from her embrace and stand beside her. He was the Black Panther in this moment, not "T".

"We went to the Golden Fields, T'Challa," Monica said, correcting herself. "Beautiful. My grandmother would love your gardens. Perhaps one day, we can watch the sun set over the Wangari trees and the grassland. But for now," she said, turning to smile at the guards who towered over her, "I've been invited to visit Mrs. Chandra. I'll see you later, perhaps?" she asked, seemingly unaware of W'Kabi's disbelief.

"My wife," he said, "has invited you to our home?" He managed to sound more at ease with the idea than he looked.

Even T'Challa was amused by this development. More of a homebody, Chandra was a private sort, not often seen entertaining. This surprised no one, as the Shield of Wakanda wasn't the most jovial of husbands.

"Adebisi told me about these special flowers that grow out near the River of Grace and Wisdom." T'Challa nodded approval at Adebisi, the Dora Milaje leader, whose hair was braided in a new style that was distinctly more Uptown than Wakandan.

"She said that it is tradition to cook with the blossoms, to add the river's gifts to your meals. Who couldn't use more grace and wisdom now?" Monica said. She hoped to impress T'Challa with her knowledge of Wakandan culture.

She squeezed T'Challa's hand and waved goodbye to his trusted aides. "Bye, Taku. W'Kabi," she said, her eyes mischievous. "I'll see you around." She turned to T'Challa and paused. A sly grin curled across her face. "One more thing, T."

"Uh oh," T'Challa said, raising his eyebrow.

"Captain Adebisi agreed to train me so I can defend myself—if you don't mind me working out your Adored Ones?"

"Adebisi's tough. Don't say I didn't warn you," T'Challa said, admiring Monica's assertiveness.

"I'll show her some basic panther stances. Nothing major, Your Highness." Adebisi stood beside Shuri. "It would be my honor to train your companion."

"It looks like the decision has been made." The Panther King could not hide the smile raising his cheeks.

"Good. It's settled then. If you don't mind, we'll start right now." Monica turned to the holoscreen lit with burning red icons. "You have your hands full anyway. I'll catch you later, Your Majesty." She smiled and winked.

The Dora Milaje marched out, flanking Monica Lynne on both sides.

For a moment the three sat in silence.

"Now that was interesting," offered Taku.

"Guess who's coming to dinner?" T'Challa said, laughing. W'Kabi did not look amused.

"My King, we were discussing grave matters concerning your empire." He frowned and shot a frustrated glance at Taku, who stopped smiling immediately. W'Kabi pointed at the map projection with its flaming icons. "Is it wise to expose an outworlder to these matters?"

T'Challa felt a flicker of anger rising in the back of his throat like a serpent. The Panther King made a note to himself to speak to W'Kabi later, alone. There was much they needed to say to one another, but this was not that time. Aloud, he asked his most pressing question.

"Could this Killmonger be a son of Klaw or some other enemy?"

The list of villains in the world was long. T'Challa was sure he had gathered more than a few new enemies fighting alongside the Avengers and the Fantastic Four.

Taku admitted it could be a possibility, but as far as they knew, Ulysses Klaw had left no descendants. "But the people he recruits, his Death Regiments, are said to have extraordinary powers. What specifically, we are unsure."

T'Challa's eyes flickered, the anger triggered by the memory of the traitors' attack. "I haven't yet seen any evidence of that," he said, "unless extraordinary audacity is one of them. Two of them attempted to torch Griot G'Sere's village. And they staged an attack on the day of my arrival." He shook his head. "A crew of clowns on bicycles with puppets, R24s, and psychedelic skull paint…"

W'Kabi and Taku exchanged glances. "Clowns? You didn't mention—" the Chief of Security said, confusion on his face.

"You had to have been there."

They studied the map with its burning icons, blooming across the kingdom like some airborne disease. Another pair of conflict flames dotted the map, this time near the River Tribes, small historic villages outside the Golden City. The memory of G'Sere dying rose in T'Challa's mind. The elder had shown his love and loyalty, even in his last breath. Too much had been taken. Killmonger had to be stopped.

T'Challa felt the old rage returning. Over the past year, knocking out villains and beating bad guys to a pulp with the Avengers and the Fantastic Four had been an outlet to control the rage that still burned through him after his father's assassination. T'Challa knew the time for talk was over. Villains only responded to action.

"W'Kabi, gather the forces. Taku, alert the medical and human dignity staff. We are going to stamp out every flame of this rebellion, and when we are through, we will track down this Killmonger and end him."

UNDER THE beautiful soft shades of the waning sun and the coming twilight, the silvery rays of the day star and the full moon played against the velvety green foliage of locus trees. For the Panther King, the sound was not as idyllic as the scenery.

The air was hot and humid, thick with smoke as the sleek motorboat sped down the river. T'Challa leaned into the air, W'Kabi and Taku at his side. For miles he had been hearing the low frequency sound he could only describe as severe pain. The royal guards were packed in multiple boats behind them. Burned wood and charred flesh filled the Black Panther's nose and stung his eyes, even beneath the mask. Screams and moans surrounded them, deafening in their despair. But at this distance, only he could hear it. When the Panther King peered through the smoke, his enhanced eyes caught flashes of the wounded staggering amongst the charred ruins. They looked like the walking dead.

He flinched when he saw a lifeless arm lying on the ground, the brown limb jutting from the shadows. The historic boathouses, famous for their bright colors and clever names, had lined the banks of these ancient rivers for centuries. Now they and their owners lay in a burning, smoking heap, with few survivors.

Amidst the destruction, a shrill scream pierced the twilight.

"Killmonger! Killmonger!" The maddening voice screamed until it turned into a fit of sobbing.

Interspersed throughout the madness, the screaming, and the tears, stood the Black Panther, watching his people fling themselves into the waters, fire and despair overtaking them.

Behind the Black Panther's boat, a small detachment of Dora Milaje rode on large futuristic barges, designed to carry cargo. Hopefully it would be survivors this time. The fleet of barges was powered by the absorption of vibratory energy by vibranium molecules, a property Wakandan scientists discovered some time ago. The scientific principles of vibranium conversion had advanced greatly since those times. T'Challa's own research into the material's relationship with sound waves had been one of his greatest moments before he defeated Ulysses Klaw. It was scientific discovery and collaboration, a shared desire to improve and expand knowledge, that had helped transform Wakanda from a series of warrior clans to a nation of technological progress. But now that growth was threatened by a mysterious enemy who sowed the seeds of discord.

Leaving a few guards to watch the boats, the others sped ahead to begin the rescue. T'Challa, W'Kabi, and Taku disembarked and walked along the riverbanks. The remains of the elaborately carved fishing boats were dashed against the shore. One—shaped like a giant seahorse with a carved trunk, scales, and wings—was turned on its side. They had walked a few meters when they realized they were not weaving around driftwood and river refuse but were stepping over parts that once belonged to people. The realization left a sick taste in their throats.

Taku offered a prayer. He poured libations in the name of the defenseless dead and Bast. T'Challa surveyed the carnage, horrified at the level of destruction that had rained down on these humble people. Located south-east of the River of Grace and Wisdom, Birnin Okan Odo, River's Heart, was known for its colorful bamboo and coconut thatched houseboats, as well as its annual festival dedicated to the goddess Bast and its river elders. Its green, lush forest and fertile soil made it the home of the empire's most skilled fishermen and water whisperers.

It was said the tribe in this village could call the water up by will. Fishermen sang songs and whispered to waves, summoning the river's most fat and desirable specimens. Seafood from their waters made its way to dinner tables and plates throughout the kingdom.

The few that remained—those who had not fled or were not cut down in the fiery wrath of the Death Regiments—wandered around, wailing, lost. There would be no festival this year. And now the songs of water were prayers to Bast and the river to deliver them from Killmonger's Death Regiments and fire.

"We give praise to the universe, praise to Mother Earth, praise to all nature, and its beings," Taku said, W'Kabi and the Panther King joining him.

"We give praise to our guiding spirits, praise to our ancestors, praise to the newly dead. May Bast look over you and have mercy on you, and may your name be a blessing to all who knew you."

To T'Challa, it looked as if the culprits had come in the cover of night. A series of stealthy attacks around the perimeter of Wakanda, designed to destabilize the empire by erasing its borders and terrorizing its people.

"These heartless rebels travel like phantoms," W'Kabi said, pain and anger in his voice. "We only see the ruin after the carnage has been completed. We don't know how many there are or who they are because there are so few survivors." The disgust in the general's voice and the sadness on his face needed no explanation.

"No one wages war with ghosts," T'Challa said.

In the old days, T'Chaka would have consulted the visions of the ancestors. T'Challa preferred a more substantial solution. Something that could be backed up with quantifiable data—or a fist and a boot.

"You left Wakanda, Your Majesty," W'Kabi spoke, softly at first. He was staring at the great plumes of smoke rising from the ruins of the village. The one and two-story thatched houseboats were all ablaze. A thick, oily scent filled the air, turning their stomachs. "Though I didn't care for Taku's tone, he told you the truth," he said. "Your people *needed* their king. They called for you, but you did not answer. I am sure you had your reasons; and yes, you defeated Klaw before you left, avenging the nation, but the minds of your people were scarred by the horrors that his men inflicted before we were able to stop them. We have been here before, My King," W'Kabi said, surveying the senseless destruction all around them.

Taku discreetly walked away, in search of a survivor he might comfort and, if possible, gently interview. A handful of Dora Milaje followed him, while another handful remained with the general and the king. Others guided the injured to the barges, where supplies and refreshments were stored. But there were so few, the rescue mission threatened to turn to a mass interment.

With a mental command, the Panther King removed his vibranium armor. He wanted W'Kabi to see him as T'Challa, to speak his heart, as it was clear much weighed on it.

It was time.

"Your military, your Dora Milaje, your family protected your kingdom in your absence. But the people, like those who suffer here, wanted a *leader*. Visible, recognizable, connected to the nation. Despite our greatest efforts, that was the one thing we could not offer them. The vision and guidance of Bast's avatar, the Panther King."

T'Challa walked with his friend, listening and filtering out the scent of fear and terror that permeated the air.

"These poor peoples' destruction is as much the work of our hands as it is this fiend's. The choices we have made left space for true evil to emerge. That's where this Erik Killmonger came in. In the leadership vacuum that was created."

W'Kabi's attempt to soften the verbal blows at the end touched T'Challa.

"The vacuum 'that was created' versus the vacuum *I created*?" he asked. "Don't pull your punches now, W'Kabi. It is beneath you, friend."

"It is as a friend that I speak to you now, and not as your general," W'Kabi said. "Something happened to you out there, across the Great Water. Though you have returned and look the same, you are changed. And it is not simply because you have fallen in love, My King. There is something else. And that is the problem. The people need to know that you are the same leader, the king that took the throne honorably at Warrior Falls. That they are your priority."

T'Challa and W'Kabi weaved their way around large mossy river stones as they talked. The royal guard fanned out around them. T'Challa kicked over one, revealing an ochre-stained petroglyph. In Wakanda, no matter the region, the evidence of the ages was all around them.

"N'Baza was respected as regent, but he was not king," W'Kabi said. "We deeply revered him, as his homegoing ceremonies will demonstrate, but he did not fight for the title at Warrior Falls. He was unable to consult with the Goddess because he was not chosen to be her avatar. Killmonger became a symbol of the people and their suffering, and you, My King, became a symbol of the elite who claim to have their best interests at heart. An elitist who travels the globe with outworlders while the people in his nation struggle to put the pieces of their war-torn country back together."

"W'Kabi, you go too far." Taku emerged from a grove of trees, what was left of Birnin Okan Odo's sacred shrines. His hand rested at the hilt of a bejeweled dagger strapped at his hip.

W'Kabi glanced at the blade, at the intense fury building in Taku, and laughed derisively, amused. "Communicator, you need to stick to your devices and leave the weapons to me. You can say your peace, but I cannot? Calm yourself. You do not wish to parry with me."

"Enough. Let W'Kabi finish, Taku." The Panther King raised his hand, gestured for Taku the Communicator to stand down and unhand the hilt of his dagger.

"It was Erik Killmonger who answered the people when you grew silent," W'Kabi continued. "Whoever he is, he gave them something to believe in. When a people lose hope, they lose their future. Despair replaces joy, and fear strangles faith. You cannot build what you cannot conceive. That's why so many have turned against the throne. Even some amongst our own ranks."

They reached the outskirts of the village, but T'Challa felt the heat and heard the cries before he saw their faces. He ran to the edge of the blue water. A couple with a round-faced child huddled in a small skiff tied to what was left of the dock. The family and much of the town was surrounded by fire. Behind them a burning boathouse collapsed on itself. The woman stared blankly into the air. Her baby wailed in her arms.

"Bast, *buk chiuta,* please save us from the Killmonger," the woman prayed in the language of the rivers, her voice ragged, hoarse. She stared up at the shifting sky, as if awaiting an answer. The wind picked up from the river's face, sending a wave of the most unimaginable stench. *Suffering.* The circle of fire rose, choking the air with smoke and unbearable heat. The father screamed, "Save us!"

T'Challa dove into the water.

By the time he hit the surface, his Black Panther armor had already spread from the nanotech in his necklace and Kimoyo bracelets, covering his head and body in a sheath of inky purple-and-black shining vibranium. Taku called after him, then shot a dagger-like glance at W'Kabi. Even beneath the waves, T'Challa could hear Taku scolding W'Kabi as T'Challa swam toward the flames.

"Is that the action of a man who ignores his people, W'Kabi? Go ahead and follow your king, Shield. Swim through the fire yourself," Taku said coldly.

The Black Panther sliced his way through the currents that would have sucked an ordinary man to the bottom. When he reached the boat, an explosion rocked the burning house behind them and sent the remainder of the structure tumbling to the ground. For a second, the Black Panther lost himself in the flames, in the memory of the sieges that Klaw had led against his father and then the kingdom of Wakanda itself. T'Challa had done so much to rid himself of the fury and the rage from that experience. It was a fact he had been taught all his life, like everyone in the empire, that Wakanda could never be taken. Klaw had made that a question.

At the root of all anger is fear. This Killmonger with his Death Regiments had renewed the fiery rage and anger that battling Klaw had ignited inside the Black Panther.

As he swam, pulling each of the screaming river family from the flames, he felt it building at the base of his skull, rage just inside the bone hollow of his temples. It surged through his arms and throbbed in his chest and hands. His own fire threatened to unite with the flames.

Safely ashore, the woman stared at the embers of her home and wept. Then she covered her eyes and lay her head against her man's heaving chest. She cradled their baby with both arms, thanking Bast and the river spirits for sending the Panther King to rescue them. The man embraced his family and stared at the burning houseboat, thoughtful.

"Ever since we were young newlyweds, my wife and I dreamed of owning our own home right in the heart of Wakanda where you lived, Your Highness. We are just humble people, both from this river village, but we dreamed that our son might someday live a life of importance in the Golden City. Death Regiments did this. Look at our home," the weary man said. Flecks of soot and debris covered his smoke-stained skin. "Look what they did to my brother." He pointed at a dark lump sitting in the shadows at the back of the skiff.

The Black Panther turned to a sight so chilling, it made him shudder. He wondered if the poor man had even known Killmonger's name before he died.

"Most of the families were allowed to leave this place as Killmonger's men sacked and torched our homes, but my brother was an avid supporter of you, My King—even in your absence. Killmonger's forces made an example of him—" the man looked around at the wreckage that was his home, "—and of us."

"I will restore your home, your village. Replace destruction with justice," T'Challa replied. "I cannot return your brother to you, but trust I will stop this Erik Killmonger. And he will pay for your pain with his own."

The woman turned to T'Challa, not quite satisfied but sated. "Killmonger is a menace. I saw him break every bone in a man's body, just to hear the bones snap. Our neighbor. Then he attacked our brother, who attempted to resist him." She shook her head, eyes filled with heavy tears. "It was like he was cleaning one of the fishes from this very river. The entire time he was murdering our brother, Killmonger was calling for you, My King. He told everyone how spineless and pampered you were. Said Wakanda needed a strong leader. Someone who could protect us. Someone who will not abandon us or give our resources away to the world."

She stared at the Panther King, watching his eyes. "But who would protect us from *him*?"

The woman held the baby before T'Challa. Tufts of wet, curly black hair rose around his tiny face. The child stared back at him, owl-like and silent.

"You are all he has, My King. He cannot survive, none of us can, if Killmonger is our future." She handed the baby to her husband, then grabbed T'Challa's arms, as if drawing strength. She whispered prayers of blessing and protection, ancient rites of the people who spoke with rivers. Holding him as tightly as she had held her own child.

"Please save us, My King. If you do not stop Killmonger, he will destroy all of Wakanda."

W'Kabi and Taku joined them, standing quietly behind the Black Panther. T'Challa wrapped his arms around the grieving mother, her wise words strengthening him, his presence giving her hope amid great loss.

Taku and a few royal guards guided the family away to join the others on the medic barges. They would be given new homes and shelter in the Golden City while Wakanda helped to rebuild their river village. For now, W'Kabi stared at T'Challa, his eyes glinting with grief and thinly veiled fear.

"I never thought I would see this day," he said. "Erik Killmonger has turned Wakanda against itself."

T'Challa flinched at hearing his own thoughts spoken aloud.

"Wakanda can never be taken," the Black Panther said, "unless she is taken from within."

"How can we fight when the enemies are our families?" W'Kabi asked. He spoke now, not as the leader of the Taifa Ngao, but as a husband, a father, and a man with many kin and friends throughout the kingdom. "All this blood and fire..."

The Black Panther surveyed the ecological and infrastructural damage. The people of Birnin Okan Odo would be recovering from the psychological costs for many years. "We must find this Killmonger and stamp out him and the Death Regiments."

"But we must be careful, Your Majesty," W'Kabi said, "that we do not become the fist that blackens our own eye. There have been increasing whispers and rumors of an Erik Killmonger for months. He was more of a shadow, a myth among back alleys and the outer villages. But the blatant attacks did not begin until you and Ms. Monica Lynne arrived, Your Highness."

Something was needling the Panther King, a murky mystery that plagued him like a worrisome thought not yet formed.

T'Challa listened to his Chief of Security with one ear and pricked the other ear toward the fires and the ruined river village. T'Challa heard a woman's laughter from deep within the flames. A taunting voice, unfamiliar but menacing.

Taku placed his hand against the communication bug planted in his ear. He frowned and raised his head wearily.

"My King, a mass column is marching near the pool of Warrior Falls. The company is being led by a large man walking beside a..." Taku frowned, listening. "A two-tone leopard?" He asked, incredulous. "Wait, what are you saying?" He listened and exhaled. "I'm told it is a very large leopard, a rare one. Yellow with black spots in some areas, black with yellow spots in others. Whatever it is, it is no joke."

"A leopard?" T'Challa replied. "Pound for pound, they are the strongest of the world's big cats. Somebody has a point to prove."

"The armed guards have already been deployed," Taku said. "But they have been ineffective in stopping the advancing forces. They say this man that leads them, the one who walks beside the black-gold leopard, is Erik Killmonger."

At the mention of Killmonger, the Black Panther's anti-metal claws sprung from his fingertips. His jaw hardened.

"He's shouting his own name like a rallying cry, Your Highness, as he fights his way through our forces."

"Well, he won't be fighting for long," W'Kabi said. He clicked on his Kimoyo beads, sending instructions to Wakanda's army.

"He has pronounced himself to be the choice of Wakanda's people," Taku continued, his brow wrinkling, forming a deep worried groove as he listened. He paused. "And he is calling for you to meet him in open combat, Your Majesty." Taku's face reminded T'Challa of a popular meme, red Dixie cup and all.

"I will meet this Killmonger in open combat—alone," he said, silencing Taku and W'Kabi's objections. "Deploy the Dora Milaje to assist the Shield of Wakanda with the Death Regiments at the bottom of the Falls, but Killmonger is mine."

The Black Panther looked at the desolation that now filled Birnin Okan Odo.

"Yes, Your Highness, but I'm afraid most of the Shield of Wakanda has already joined the combat—to no avail."

The Black Panther's astonishment was visible even through his mask.

"We are fighting fellow Wakandans," W'Kabi said to the Panther King. "Iron strikes iron. It will be a long battle. It may be a stalemate for now, but the night is young," the Shield said.

"Complete the extraction and rescue," the Black Panther said. "Send the Wakanda Interior to finish putting out these fires. Let the survivors know that their King is rebuilding and replanting."

The triumvirate roles of statesman, national symbol, and spiritual leader was a balance T'Challa's father had navigated expertly. The

Panther King found some roles easier than others, but balancing them all at once still took great effort.

Taku and W'Kabi watched their king. The fury emanating from him made the air crackle, electric and hot.

"To Warrior Falls," the Black Panther said. "Wakanda Forever." Taku, W'Kabi, and the Black Panther folded their arms across their chests, the ancient symbol for Wakandan resilience. With firelight and smoke set against the smoldering bamboo trees and vines, the Black Panther's fearsome claws shone in the moonlight.

CHAPTER FIVE

HEAVY IS THE CROWN

T'CHALLA LEAPT through the trees and vaulted over the rocky escarpments that led to Warrior Falls. Fury mixed with nostalgia and painful memories, filling his guts, churning inside his chest. As a child, his father had brought him to the beautiful, mystic place many times. T'Chaka taught T'Challa his first combat lessons there, testing his agility and skill with the spear and dagger. Those were wonderful things for a father to teach his son; the Dora Milaje were teaching little Shuri those hard-won lessons as well. But the most important lessons that T'Challa cherished were the conversations he and his father had sitting on the rocks. Near the waterfall's edge they spoke of many things as they watched the sun set over Wakanda.

T'Challa raced to confront an enemy greater than any Wakanda had yet faced. Even Ulysses Klaw had not wrought such destruction. No one ever had the power to turn the Wakandans *against themselves*. Not until now.

The Black Panther crouched low with his belly to the ground and crept over the top of a river-smooth rock. When he peeked over the edge of the cliff atop Warrior Falls, he saw the two fools, Tayete and Kazibe. The good souls turned traitors, murderers who had tortured and killed Griot G'Sere, leaving him a lifeless lump in T'Challa's arms. The pair were guarding the main path that led to the top of Warrior Falls. *The enemy must not be so wise if they trust these fools to protect them.*

"Kazibe, did you see the way I handled the panther demon?" Tayete asked, as pompous as ever. "Did you see him run from me like a zomo rabbit in the presence of a hungry lion?" Tayete raised a rusted machete that glinted in the rising moonlight as if the long shaft of metal were slicing through flesh and bone. "When we destroy the royal palace, I will deal with the Black Panther myself," he boasted, scrawny chest puffed up like a rooster. "I will hand him to Killmonger in bits and pieces."

Kazibe saw T'Challa first.

The Black Panther stood on a jutting ledge that hung just above and behind the heads of the turncoats. The Panther King stared at the round-bellied traitor. Small flashes of deep purple light glimmered across his vibranium armor. Kazibe stepped backwards, mouth hanging open in shock, and bumped into Tayete, but Tayete was too distracted. Too wrapped up in his daydream.

"Tayete," Kazibe whimpered.

"When the time comes, I will make the panther demon beg for mercy," Tayete continued. He ran his fingertip along the edge of the machete. "Then I will make T'Challa beg me to kill him." Tayete laughed into the wind. His voice filled with malice. "What makes a royal better than me?"

"You know what they say about wishes?" Kazibe stammered.

"What are you babbling about, Kazibe?" Tayete said.

Kazibe pointed and backed away.

The Black Panther leapt off the cliff and kicked Kazibe in the face. T'Challa ducked Tayete's machete and swept the man off his treacherous feet. By the time Tayete hit the ground, knocking the wind out of his chest, T'Challa had disarmed him and pushed the tip of the traitor's own blade against his scrawny throat.

T'Challa felt the rage coursing through his body, racing through his arm. It would be so easy to kill him, to squash him like the annoying insect that he was. He squeezed the machete handle until the wood wrapped in oily rags and dirty string cracked and crumbled in his hand. It would be so easy to slit the traitor's throat, to leave his head on a pike like the warrior clans of the past. But this was not the path his father had taught him. T'Challa threw the machete over the cliff.

"You killed a man who served Wakanda his entire life. A loyal, generous man who touched countless souls with his wisdom." T'Challa squeezed Tayete's neck with his gloved hands, pressed his black claws into the skin until the traitor squirmed and wept.

He would draw no blood but would extend the terror. Griot G'Sere might not approve, but the wretch before T'Challa had earned at least that.

T'Challa's heightened senses, honed and crafted since he was a boy, alerted him only moments before a wide crescent-moon blade swung at his head. The dark metal warbling past his jaw pushed the Black Panther into action. There was only one metal that throbbed and pulsed with harnessed kinetic energy like that: *vibranium*.

Too many thoughts flashed in T'Challa's mind, careening all at once. First, he wondered how the shadow had gotten so close before triggering his panther senses. At the same time, T'Challa's mind reeled at the thought of someone with the audacity to swing a vibranium weapon at *him*.

The man that swung the curved blade stood nearly seven feet tall. His entire body was composed of raw muscle. Honed and chiseled. He had long locs that flowed in the wind behind his swift movements. The man wore a red coral bead necklace, brass bracelets, and a leather belt adorned with skulls and runes.

"N'Jadaka?" T'Challa asked, confusion and shock in his voice.

"Surprise!" N'Jadaka said. Satisfaction on his face. "Wussup, bruh? I was wondering how long it was going to take you to figure it out. I guess the answer was never." He laughed. "An Oxford Man, huh?"

T'Challa recognized the face immediately, but he couldn't reconcile the psychotic killer with the man he thought he knew. A whirlwind of rallies, philosophical discussions in his classroom, viewings at the antique store he claimed he owned, and nightclub scenes full of laughter and cheer rolled through the Black Panther's mind like an old movie.

"Your family has bled Wakanda for years, T'Challa," N'Jadaka said. "It's time to turn the power over to the people. Power. You studied that in America, didn't you?"

"You would know better than me," T'Challa shot back. "You spent your life in the US, remember? What do you even know of Wakanda?"

Killmonger bristled. For a moment he seemed lost in time, lost in some distant, painful memory, *deep in the mines, red dust on his feet and hands.*

Behind the muscle-bound man, on a stone ledge that stretched just above Erik Killmonger's head, three giant leopards radiated malevolent hunger. They paced back and forth, saliva dripping from their fangs as they stared down at the Black Panther. Two were yellow with the trademark black rosettes, but the third, almost twice their size, was most unusual. Parts of it were golden yellow with the traditional black spots, but other parts were as black as the Black Panther himself, only with golden yellow rosettes that glowed like great eyes. It watched T'Challa closely, snarling with a ground-shaking growl.

"What's the matter?" N'Jadaka said. "Cat got your tongue?"

The three leopards threw back their heads, their roars raucous, raspy coughs, as if laughing.

"Who are you really?" T'Challa asked the man who had pretended to be his friend.

The largest leopard shrieked, then emitted the rapid hoarse cough again, a signal to the others. The two golden leopards jumped down from their ledge, landing next to Killmonger. They stood on either side of him as Killmonger petted them.

"Erik Killmonger," the man said, stroking one of the leopards on its golden head. It purred like the tamest of cats. "N'Jadaka is a name I'd prefer to forget."

"No one will remember your name when I am through. From this moment on, N'Jadaka, you are dead."

The Black Panther crouched as he circled Killmonger, his attention focused on the leopards. He knew Killmonger intended to release them at some point. When was the question. He'd been outnumbered before, but not atop one of the highest waterfalls in Wakanda. He needed to position himself as far away from the waterfall's edge as he could, without ceding Killmonger the advantage. He knew he could not allow himself to be surrounded—or taken to the hard, cold ground.

Killmonger made a signal and the leopards retreated. He lunged at the Black Panther, simultaneously blocking a black boot aimed at his temple. Killmonger laughed when the Black Panther spun around, circling him, and aiming another kick at his chest. The blow landed, a rib crusher, but Killmonger *did not fall.*

Damn.

"N'Jadaka was weak but useful," Killmonger said. "There's a whole lot of pain wrapped up in the name N'Jadaka, a history I'd rather forget, but it served its purpose." Killmonger sliced T'Challa's arm with the vibranium blade. He just missed an artery, the brachial. The Black Panther's suit maintained its integrity—barely.

"And what purpose was that, you fiend?" The leopards screeched and growled behind Killmonger, pacing back and forth, eager to leap into the fray.

"It helped me get to you. A few times I thought the jig was up, the ruse would fall apart, but—"

Killmonger's head swung back, jaw assaulted by a bone-crushing blow from the Black Panther, but to T'Challa's surprise, Killmonger looked unshaken, as if he'd only been tapped.

"Killmonger endures the pain, true indeed," the cunning brute said. "But Killmonger dishes out pain, too. Get this work!"

He threw a jab that narrowly landed on the Black Panther's jaw, but even the glancing blow left a solid impression on the Panther

King. *Killmonger got hands*, T'Challa thought, gritting his teeth. Time to rethink his strategy. The two foes fought fiercely, testing each other as they alternated blows in rapid succession.

"So, N'Jadaka, professor and part-time antiques dealer, you are the psychopath they whisper about?" T'Challa said huffing, nearly out of breath but incredulous. They circled each other, staggered between heart-stopping blows, then stepped back to regain their ground. "You are the fiend who has turned half of Wakanda against itself?"

The Black Panther vaulted off his hands and flew into Killmonger with a flurry of feet and punches and acrobatics. The assault threw the brute off-balance, surprised him, but not long enough for T'Challa to take him to the ground.

"If you wanted my throne, you could have asked. Challenged me like a true brave Wakandan. Not slunk in the background like the coward you are," T'Challa said. "Warrior Falls was always available to you, but you ravaged the countryside like a crazed berserker. What honor lies in that? You killed G'Sere," T'Challa growled. The memory of the griot's bruised, sunken face and the cruel wounds that drained him of his life made T'Challa want to return the favor.

But Killmonger parried each of T'Challa's blows with ease, smiling even. It was the same self-satisfied grin that T'Challa had seen numerous times over the past year. Now, looking at him, T'Challa realized he should have known who he was the minute Taku reported that the murderous rebel had been seen *crying out his own name* as a rallying cry. Only a narcissistic, deeply insecure and unstable person would do that—and be serious about it. Thinking back on their interactions, T'Challa knew N'Jadaka had led his psychotic pep rally with a straight face. He cringed inside realizing how much access he'd granted the man, even trusting him in his Harlem home and in Monica's presence—a mistake he would never make again.

The pair fought their way to the edge of the jutting rock where the thunderous waterfalls rushed past and filled the air with an all-encompassing song. Killmonger's vibranium scimitar slashed

T'Challa's thigh, but the attack left Killmonger's defenses open, and the Black Panther smashed his elbow against Killmonger's rock-like jaw.

Killmonger stumbled backwards a couple of paces and fell in the water. Blood painted the foam red. T'Challa wrapped both hands around the brute's massive throat. With bloody rage filling his mouth and his eyes, he pummeled Killmonger's face with blow after lethal blow. An image of G'Sere singing the history of Wakanda flashed through T'Challa's mind. The song included the story of T'Challa's own birth. The Orphan King, the Panther King, saw N'Jadaka's evil smiling face. And then he heard that wry laughter mocking him, and he could not tell whether the laughter was real or memory.

The two smaller leopards paced the jutting ledge leapt toward T'Challa. Golden fur gleaming, the black anti-metal in their claws shining like star-lit obsidian. Purple flames glowed in the beast's eyes like precious jewels. These were no ordinary leopards, and their big mate shrieked and called to them from the upper ledge.

The twin leopards knocked T'Challa off Killmonger, but the Black Panther tumbled and recovered to wrestle the fierce beasts through the water. He did his best to avoid the leopards' deadly fangs and claws without hurting the animals, but his confidence in dispatching them without taking their lives grew dim.

Erik Killmonger stood coldly watching the Black Panther battle, while the larger leopard's cries grew shriller and more furious. Killmonger wiped the blood from his mouth. He laughed at the Panther and the leopards tussling, clawing, and roaring their way over the stones and the crashing river water.

"I told you when we first met, T'Challa, 'I'm going to change the world for the better.' To do that, I've got to start right here in Wakanda."

One of the leopards sank its teeth into T'Challa's forearm as the other beast crushed the Black Panther's shoulder between powerful jaws. Light poured from their mouth and eyes. T'Challa realized the leopard's teeth and claws had been capped and crowned, enhanced with anti-metal implants. Recognizing the material, instantly, he wondered how the rare mineral had fallen into N'Jadaka's possession. With quick cat reflexes, he managed to catch the beast's mouth as it lunged for his throat.

The other leopard paced the ledge, shaking its massive black-and-gold head at T'Challa and growled. In its laughter, T'Challa heard the echo of a mysterious voice that had plagued and mocked him since his return. The creature laughing...

What was it? The leopards roared; each had its cavernous vibranium-laced mouth wrapped around the Black Panther's forearms. Both giant cats were crushing down with all their strength, pressing T'Challa to the merciless ground.

"You killed innocents, your own people, burned their villages. Set ancient legacies ablaze. Do you hate Wakanda that much?" T'Challa asked, tossing one of the leopards against the craggy rocks.

Killmonger hung back, his breathing finally at a normal rate, his body recovering from the Black Panther's relentless blows.

"It is not Wakanda I hate. It is the worthless sycophants who lead and bleed it. None of you have the vision to see what Wakanda can truly be. Because people are clothed and well-fed, you think you have done your duty. You sit in your royal palace, but you know nothing of true suffering. The whole world cries with people who could be free with the power Wakanda has, but you wield it only to profit from your precious extraterrestrial mineral. It's not even something you earned yourselves. A freak of nature sent the meteor hurtling to your patch of land from the sky. An accident of fate. You are still the directionless warrior clans which you have mythologized so much. Shiny skyscrapers and hovering aircraft are easy, but can you revolutionize and free a world?"

T'Challa stomped on the other leopard then lifted it up by its tail. The uber-leopard whined and screeched from the ledge, but wordlessly Killmonger held it off.

"Nice speech," T'Challa said. "Did you practice that for ACT-SO? Was that your Easter speech? I give you high marks for self-righteousness and imagination, with your revisionist history, but your lack of ethics disqualifies you to continue in the next round. You have no moral ground to stand upon," T'Challa said. "No one wants your blood-soaked vision of the future, one that can't discern true enemies from friends. Evil from innocence. You tortured and killed my people, our people. You murdered one of my oldest friends just to lure me to this waterfall so you can run your mouth. Stop your madness while you can, N'Jadaka. You are trying to take what can never be yours. You hold no honor, no moral rights over me or anyone in the kingdom. You are just a frightened, lost feral soul—no more in control or self-aware of your traumas than this poor leopard I hold in my hand."

Gripping its tail tighter, T'Challa spun the golden beast in a wide circle, then swung it like a bolo and slammed it into Killmonger's chest, tossing the man and the cat against the great mountain that held Warrior Falls.

T'Challa had climbed Warrior Falls with the intent of killing Killmonger, but something in the man's speech made him hold back. Griot G'Sere had cautioned the Black Panther not to allow his rage to consume him.

Stay on your father's path, the griot had said before he died.

T'Challa tapped his Kimoyo beads, speaking quickly while the golden leopard remained stunned. "Gather the Council. I'm bringing Killmonger in," he told Taku. He turned to Killmonger, who lay slumped against the cliff wall, dazed and surprised. "The trap you set for me is the trap you laid for yourself, N'Jadaka." Disgust shaped the Panther King's words. "You were a set-up, a charlatan from the first moment we met in New York. And to think I trusted you with your sob story and called you *friend*."

He walked toward Killmonger but sensed motion behind him, turned just in time to see the remaining twin leopard and the black-gold leopard leaping at him. He clothes-lined the smaller leopard, which fell back with a whimper, choking. The black-gold leopard howled, diving at him. T'Challa ducked its giant paws and spun around before leaping into the air. He unleashed a flurry of blows, repeatedly punching it in its great temple and mouth. The black-gold leopard screeched and howled, slinking back, swiping with its great claws, giving T'Challa just enough time to edge away.

Still disoriented, Killmonger struggled to get up, blood dripping down his face and neck as he watched his injured leopards stumble on their great paws like wounded cubs.

"That's going to be a nasty headache," T'Challa said, the anger still broiling inside him. Clouds of mist and the scent of overripe fruit and blossoms drifted all around them. The Black Panther glanced over his shoulder. He didn't want his back to the five-hundred-foot drop, but the black-gold leopard had recovered and was inching forward, eyes blazing. Wary now, the beast's fearsome fangs dripped blood.

The golden leopard pounced at him with a shrill screech.

The Black Panther stepped aside. He could hear the leopard's screams as it plunged over the cliff.

The black-gold leopard wailed, enraged; it slashed at the Black Panther, knocking him to the ground. The remaining gold leopard snarled and joined the larger cat.

T'Challa strained on the ground with labored breath, trying to channel his panther strength into his arms, to keep the two remaining leopards from crushing him.

Visibly weakened but standing, Killmonger shuffled over to where the leopards lay atop T'Challa, trying to tear through the vibranium suit. "That's enough, Preyy," he said to the massive black-gold beast.

Killmonger made a clicking sound and the golden leopard eased up, but the massive one continued trying to rip the Black Panther's head off.

"Now, Preyy!" the brute barked, as if speaking to a fellow soldier instead of three hundred pounds of rippling, pissed-off leopard muscle. He stamped his boots in the wet dirt; the black-gold leopard reluctantly removed its great jaws from the Black Panther's throat, but it kept T'Challa pinned down.

T'Challa stared up at Killmonger, the rage returned; embers flickered in his eye.

"All those innocent people," he said. "Their villages destroyed. And for what? You could have tried to murder me in New York. Why bring all this destruction here?" he asked.

"I did what I had to do." Killmonger stared down coldly at T'Challa with unmasked hatred turning his eyes into stone. "Defeating you in America would have been meaningless. The Wakandan people need to see you fall in the place where the Panther Kings rise. No, T'Challa, Wakanda has had enough puppet kings and naked emperors. It's time for the people to rule Wakanda. It's time for you, your weak god, and your pathetic lineage to die."

The Black Panther strained against the crushing weight of the great leopard, his breath slow and ragged.

Killmonger sneered, the red bead necklace like blood on his throat. "I thought you would have put up more of a fight, Panther King. I guess your reputation is as false as the so-called royal blood you claim flows through your veins. Should have known." Erik Killmonger released a shrill cry, a rolling jackal-like high note that thundered from the back of his throat.

The two leopards pounced, clamped their vise-like jaws down on T'Challa's limbs. The vibranium suit was the only thing saving him from the force of their fangs. T'Challa begged Bast for forgiveness for what he would do next. Then he rose and jammed his fists inside the golden leopard's mouth, his anti-metal claws partially extended. The startled yelps disturbed T'Challa, but he couldn't allow the fight for Wakanda to end this way. His people needed him.

The Black Panther withdrew his claws and smashed the wailing leopards' heads together like cymbals. He threw the smaller of the beasts into the sharp rocks protruding from the stone overhang. The yelp let him know the mark hit its target. He could not fight them both off again. He had to finish them.

T'Challa tried to support himself but stumbled. The extent of his injuries, bruised ribs joining his cuts, and the weight of his conscience had drained most of his strength. He stumbled and fell into the flowing water, near the ledge. Weary, he closed his eyes, while the great black-gold leopard wailed in grief, the repeated screams echoing through the Falls with the deepest pain. A flock of jewel-toned birds scattered in the darkening sky.

Erik Killmonger straddled T'Challa's chest, kneecaps pressing the bruised ribs. He pummeled the Black Panther's face with blows until lights and shadows were all that was left. No pain or physicality. T'Challa's mind had drifted past the threshold. Pure meditation now, as he had been trained. Another memory of time spent in Warrior Falls with his father.

There was no reason why Killmonger should still be able to stand. T'Challa stared at him and saw something red and dark swirl inside Killmonger's eyes. The Black Panther wondered how this Erik Killmonger could challenge the power of the sacred Heart-Shaped Herb.

Killmonger took the vibranium dagger from his belt and held it underneath T'Challa's chin. The vibranium blade crackled and surged with an energy that seemed foreign to T'Challa. The physicist in the panther pondered the possible alloys used to forge Killmonger's weapons. *N'Jadaka*, the Black Panther thought, as he clenched his jaw.

"You, your father, your father's father: all of you have bled Wakanda—sold us to our enemies. You're no better than those who sold others for trinkets, Venetian glass, rum, sugar, tobacco, umbrellas, and cotton. I wear this necklace as a reminder of the blood spilled."

T'Challa sputtered at the dissonance. "You razed an entire river village! Centuries of history up in smoke, let alone the hundreds of lives lost in your madness."

"A necessary sacrifice for a greater vision," Killmonger said. "One you would never understand. That's why you gots to go, T'Challa. Your line ends here. *Black Panther No More.*" Erik Killmonger lifted the glowing vibranium blade into the misty air and brought it down with all his might—plunging the knife into T'Challa's chest. *Iron strikes iron*, W'Kabi had said. Vibranium met vibranium. T'Challa's panther suit began to glitch and dematerialize.

Killmonger smiled, satisfied, as he stood over T'Challa. Then he grabbed the Panther King's throat with both hands and lifted him into the air. Erik Killmonger held T'Challa over the rushing waterfall that foamed and crashed over jagged rocks growing out of the river hundreds of feet below.

"We don't need a new king. We need a new Wakanda," Killmonger said, his voice full of grim anticipation.

T'Challa struggled in Killmonger's arms. His injuries were extensive, but there was something else behind them. Something draining his energy. He stared up at the sky and imagined he saw his father, little Shuri, and then, Monica's face. "What kind of future will your kingdom have, N'Jadaka, built on death and suffering?"

Erik Killmonger cracked a knowing smile that parted the corner of his mouth. He squeezed T'Challa's neck.

"The future no longer concerns you. Your reign ends now. Heavy is the crown."

Killmonger tossed the Black Panther over the cliff. The Panther King heard the thunderous sound of the falls and felt the harsh wind against his face, then the brutal ice-cold spray of water.

CHAPTER SIX

WOMEN OF WAKANDA

"MONICA, WHAT is it the elders say? 'When elephants fight, it is the grass who suffers.'" Chandra turned to her, sprinkling fragrant spices and fresh blossoms into a beautifully painted ceramic bowl. "There are people here who will fight and fight until there is no grass left."

She pushed the steaming bowl over to Monica, who graciously dipped her spoon. Chandra's grave eyes had a distant expression, as if they carried pockets of memory, burdens like stones she carried from place to place. "How is it?" she asked after Monica had taken two spoonfuls.

"Good," Monica said.

Light poured in through the loft apartment's curtainless windows, filling the kitchen with a honey-gold warmth. A pair of giggling voices drew Monica's attention, and she noticed two small faces peeking around a corner that connected Chandra's kitchen to a modestly decorated dining room.

"Our boys," Chandra said, shaking her head.

"May we play outside, Mother?" the taller boy asked.

Chandra nodded, smiling sadly as they bounded away. She turned to Monica. "Like you, love has bound me to Wakanda." She looked as if her marriage to W'Kabi had seen better days. "Leave this place while you can."

Monica was startled. This was not the tea she thought she was coming to enjoy.

"The mountains speak of war."

"The mountains speak?" Monica asked, bewildered.

"Some of our people believe the mountains are alive."

"As in sentient?"

"Yes, like you and me. Alive and thinking. My tribe believes that the mountains speak to each other, the way scientists believe the trees speak through their roots and leaves," Chandra said. "In Wakanda, even far up north where I was born, the mountains have plenty of opinions, and I agree with them. They speak of war. I fear that Wakanda will witness grave suffering, and not from an outside enemy but from the enemy within."

"Well, the reception wasn't exactly what I was hoping for," Monica said, politely. "There was a moment on the drive, that first day, that made me want to turn around and fly home again. If people could fly, I would have been gone."

Chandra chuckled. "I heard it was less than satisfactory. W'Kabi was very disturbed…" She paused, too gracious to finish the sentence.

Because of my presence, Monica thought. She knew it wasn't just because of the terrorists. The Shield of Wakanda looked less than thrilled with the Panther King's guest.

"Everything happened so fast," Monica continued. "I could barely form the thoughts before the motorcade took off and we were gone. Like something out of a comic book," she said. *Like old times again,* she thought, remembering how she and T'Challa first met.

"Surely you knew danger would accompany a man with such responsibilities as our king," Chandra said. Monica's jaw tightened just slightly. She had prepared herself to be grilled. She had expected to be hazed at some point, just not so soon, and not by W'Kabi's beautiful and regal wife. The mother of two, she carried herself with an efficiency and serenity that Monica admired.

"Let me put it this way. T'Challa and I have had some adventures, so I knew danger was a possibility. But it's because of him that I still have my life."

"Oh, our king faced many dangers while he was away." Chandra peered at Monica, the afternoon light streaming through the cozy orange-and-indigo tiled kitchen. "You have healed wounds in his spirit, and he in yours," Chandra said, a knowing look on her smooth face. "You are a lovely couple. Looking at you, I understand why he stayed away for so long," the woman said, her compliment startling Monica. "I remember the days when W'Kabi courted me," she said, her voice wistful. "When love was clear in his eyes and not just empty words that came from the hole in his face." Monica could hear the grief in Chandra's voice when she said her husband's name.

Chandra sprinkled tushen, the healing herbs she'd gathered from her garden, and fresh fruits from the great Wangari trees into the traditional soup of her village and stirred. She was from a remote hamlet in the mountains, up north past Birnin T'Chaka, way up near the borders of the Jabari-Lands.

The sound of her wooden spoon created a drum-like rhythm that naturally made Monica wish to sing to it. Trying to ease the mood, Monica started off slow at first, her voice low and soft.

Surprised by her guest's spontaneous singing, the deep lines in Chandra's face began to relax. Her expressive eyes, with their long, dark lashes, brightened up above her sculpted cheekbones. She joined Monica, tapping the soup spoon in time as they sang, their voices echoing off the sloping walls of the high ceilings. Small items and woven baskets of Chandra's nomadic mountainous people were scattered throughout the space.

Chandra added lyrics in her mother tongue, songs that goat and cow herders still sang.

I come from the land
where the belly of the earth

is atop this old world, atop this old world
I come from the land, where the tall grasses rise and fall
Atop this old world, atop this old world

Adebisi and startled members of the Adored Ones walked in to find the two women, arms linked, singing and jumping in time. The Adored Ones watched in silence until their captain, Adebisi, began to tap her traditional spear in time with the two dancers. The others clapped a syncopated rhythm that added to the complicated beat.

Moved by the shared experience, Monica sang from her heart. She did not know the meaning of Chandra's lyrics, but the spirit of the hauntingly beautiful song inspired her. Just as her notes seemed to carry them all to the sky, Shuri and her two older, taller shadows burst into the kitchen, three more Adored Ones right on their heels.

"Princess Shuri!" Adebisi said, sharply. "You are entering an elder's home. This is not the royal palace."

"I am sorry, Captain Adebisi," the little girl said, visibly chastised. "We were told Ms. Monica was singing, and we wanted to hear her."

"Wouldn't want to miss this show," Nakia said slyly.

"May we stay, please?" Okoye pleaded.

"Join us," Monica said. The three Dora Milaje-in-training yelped with happiness. "But first, breath lessons. All singing begins from deep within, with the first breath."

As the group engaged in vocal warm-up exercises and games, they filled Chandra's kitchen with joyful sounds. Monica listened as the edges fell from Chandra's voice, revealing a softer tone.

As if sensing the sudden dip, the sadness in Chandra's register, Monica turned to face W'Kabi's wife and began to sing a song of hope and strength directly to her.

Shuri, Okoye, and Nakia joined Monica. Linked hand-in-hand, they sang a song that had no lyrics. Scatting is what Monica called it. Wordless but full of meaning, the song lifted their spirits and spoke of the better days they all hoped for themselves and the Wakandan kingdom.

"You have a gift, Monica Lynne," Chandra said when they finished.

"Thank you—" Monica began, blushing, but Chandra cut her off.

"No, I do not mean for entertainment, though I know that is part of the work that you do. I mean for healing. Not every soul has this gift, and even those who do, don't always express the inclination. Some healers remain dormant, their gifts lost to this world, but you must not waste yours. The voice Bast—" she corrected herself. "That the Great One has given you is a gift of rare healing, one that the men we both love need dearly, and indeed the Wakandan people need now more than ever."

"Chandra, you touch me with these kind, kind words. My mother, Jessica, was a healer," Monica said, thinking of the natural herbs Chandra had introduced. "As a health aide she helped ease the pain of many others. Hard, exhausting and necessary work. I know she was a blessing to many who were fortunate enough to find themselves in her care. In the end, my sister Angela and I could only work and pray to help ease her own pain. She carried us alone after our father, Lloyd, passed, and the burden was heavy sometimes, the road hard. I don't think we appreciated it then as much as we do now. She always wanted me to live my dream," Monica said.

"And what dream was that?" Chandra asked gently.

Monica had a faraway look in her eyes, as if she was trying to focus on something that remained ever out of reach. "I was going to say that I was living my dream, but I have changed, and I no longer know what it is. I guess I would say, I want my voice to do its work in this world. I think, whatever that is, I would be happy with that."

"Then find the path of intention. You must consciously tap the part of your voice, that gift, that creates healing. It is there. I felt it when you sang to me. I know the others did, too." The women warriors and the younger ones in training nodded solemnly. Shuri looked at Monica with a new glint in her eye.

"A wise elder once said that a healer's power, whether through rootwork, mojotech, story or song, comes from courage, not ability," Chandra said. Shuri and her friends listened intently. The Dora Milaje listened as well. "You must be self-aware and have the wisdom to know when and how to wield the healing gift the universe has granted you. Thank you, Monica," Chandra said, her eyes wet, almost shining.

"For what? Your generosity today has been incredible."

"For reminding me of *my* voice," Chandra said, "and the gift the mountains gave me so long ago."

o———o

PAST THE royal courtyards and beyond the Igi Iya gardens, where the Mother Tree grew tall, Monica Lynne danced and sang on the banks of the River of Grace and Wisdom.

It was the following morning. After the serious conversation with Chandra that blossomed into song, Monica had welcomed the chance to loosen up and spend some special time with T'Challa's only little sister and her two closest friends. Young Shuri, Nakia, and Okoye crooned the vocal arrangements they learned from their new music teacher and big sister from New York.

"Listen."

Monica raised her hand, as if conjuring the high notes from thin air. Magic it was, and little Shuri and her mates attempted to reach as high as the songbird—the name Mrs. Chandra had given her—high enough to reach over Warrior Falls or crack a glass in Asgard.

Okoye clapped her hands, her beautiful moonlike eyes shining with delight, while Shuri and Nakia danced the Gwara Gwara.

"*Don't bother to compare!*" the children warbled. Monica sang along, and Captain Adebisi and the Dora Milaje harmonized with them, to the shock of even Nakia.

"Adebisi, I did not know you had such a beautiful voice," Shuri said.

"It is as fearsome as her fighting," Nakia said, giggling. Okoye discreetly stepped aside, well out of reach of the expected playful jab.

Adebisi laughed, her braided hair in a high bun. "I have plenty of talents, unknown to the likes of you," she said with a smile. "You three have gotten away from your studies long enough. It is time for your training to resume."

The bright smiles were replaced with frowns.

"Since Ms. Monica has taught us something today, perhaps it is time for us to teach her something, too," Shuri said. Nakia cheered up at the suggestion.

"The women of Wakanda are wise and wily, Ms. Monica Lynne," Nakia said. "We are wickedly awesome warriors, too." She flipped through the air, arching her back, landing first on her hands and then on her feet. Delighted, Monica cheered and smiled until the little warrior-in-training performed another cartwheel; then, spinning, she kicked Monica's feet from under her legs. The songbird, T'Challa's sunbird, tumbled down.

"Nakia!" Adebisi cried. "You will run thirty laps for your insolence." But the captain needed not worry that Nakia might go unpunished. Shuri and Okoye chased Nakia down and began demonstrating why the Adored Ones, even the younger ones in training, were the fiercest warriors in the land.

The three friends sparred, seriously at first, and then playfully exchanging jabs, straight punches, and palm strikes, running freely under the beautiful Wakandan sun.

"If I had learned that as a little girl, my life would have been different. What a world you have here in Wakanda," Monica said wistfully to Adebisi.

"Wakandans live in the same world, we just try to live it differently. At least we did until…" Adebisi stopped herself, the warrior remembering that she was still a captain. "The world is a dangerous place. It grows more serious by the minute. But you are safe with us, Ms. Monica. You are the honored guest of the king, and we have pledged to protect him and all those he loves with our lives." She looked pointedly at Monica, as if she was privy to a big secret.

"I thank you," Monica said. "Let us pray it does not come to that."

"Well, to that end, let us introduce you to a few of our signature moves. You came here to learn, right?" Adebisi shouted, "Shuri, Nakia, Okoye, come."

The girls ran up to the women, almost out of breath.

"Today's training will conclude with one of you teaching Ms. Monica the three elements of the Panther's Attack."

"Allow me, Ms. Monica. It is not easy," Princess Shuri said gravely, her eyes round and serious. "In time, you will get the hang of it. But it hurts like crazy the first few times."

"Yes," Okoye said. "Nakia, do you remember when Shuri first tried it with you?"

"It was nothing. She got the best of me, beginner's luck," the child said, and they all laughed.

"Then let us begin," Shuri said, arms outstretched.

An hour later, the sun had rolled across the sky, and Monica was thoroughly exhausted.

"Hold up, girls. I'm bone-tired," Monica said, gasping for air. She held up one finger, wrapped her other hand around her stomach. "Give me a minute to catch my breath."

The cool breeze from the River of Grace and Wisdom was a welcome reprieve from the day's exercises.

"You need to cool off, Ms. America!" Nakia ran behind Monica, and laughed, pushing her into the river.

"Sistren!" Okoye and Adebisi said in union, voices stern and forceful. The little warrior started toward her mischievous partner.

Nakia, the youngest of the Dora Milaje, squealed with glee and leapt into the water, fleeing Okoye's wrath. Shuri followed, flipping, twirling midair, laughing until she made an acrobatic splash in the river. The current was calm and languid. The refreshing waters were a welcome end to a long and enjoyable day.

From the riverbank, Okoye chuckled and folded her arms, quietly practicing the notes Monica had taught them. Then a dark blotch caught her eye. It floated down the river, a shadowy but vaguely familiar silhouette, completely out of place.

She squinted, craning her neck to see. From a distance the figure could have been a piece of driftwood or a crocodile, though they were rarely seen in this part of the winding river. Okoye ran a few paces up the riverbank to get a closer look at the floating mass, Adebisi not far behind her. To the child's horror, a closer look revealed a floating body, its arms and legs spread out as if it were an effigy. The face was turned down into the water. Whoever it was could not have survived that.

Then Okoye noticed the panther suit visibly glitching, materializing then dematerializing back and forth, over and over again. Anger and horror shaped her face as she cried out and jumped into the water.

Laughing and splashing water at Nakia and Shuri, Monica turned her head, shielding her face with her forearm. As soon as she saw the shape, she knew.

"T'Challa?" she said, his name barely a whisper. She screamed for Adebisi and stomped clumsily in the water. She stared at the glitching panther suit and hesitated for a moment before she wrapped her arms around T'Challa and cried.

Monica's screaming cut through Shuri and Nakia's water war. When Shuri saw her brother's floating body, her laughter turned into terror.

"T'Challa!" Shuri called out. She rushed to the Panther King's free arm, but Adebisi and the Adored Ones had all leapt into the river and surrounded him.

Nakia wrapped her arms around T'Challa's chest and cried, "Beloved, my beloved!" The child buried her face in T'Challa's chest. Okoye and Shuri were too stricken to tease their friend about her crush on the Wakandan king. When Monica tried to gently pull Nakia back, the young Dora Milaje smacked her hand away.

"This is all your fault!" Nakia hissed at Monica. "We should have been protecting our king instead of running around with his Ms. America."

"Calm yourself," Okoye said, gripping Nakia's shoulder. "It was our Beloved who put Monica in our charge."

"You are released," Adebisi said hoarsely, cutting through the girls' chatter. "Tell no one of what you have seen today."

T'Challa was covered in gashes all over his arms and legs. His chest was full of dark reddish-purple bruises, his thighs criss-crossed with cuts. A huge opening in the failing panther suit revealed a devastating wound.

Adebisi whispered to her soldiers in Hausa.

"It's okay," Monica said quietly. "I know it's vibranium. It's the only thing that could have possibly done all of this."

"What happened, T?" she whispered as the women warriors pulled their fallen king from the river's waters and carried him along the twisting banks. Monica tried to wrap her arms around him, but she settled for rubbing the back of his head. She stroked his cheeks as she cried, the women walking briskly.

"Please, Ms. Monica," Adebisi said firmly. "We will update you and Princess Shuri of his condition as soon as we can. For now, we must go."

The women carried the Panther King high, sprinting along the riverbank.

"It's the wrong direction," Monica said, growing alarmed. "The new research hospital is the other way! Dr. Mganga showed me when I arrived."

"No, Ms. Monica," Adebisi said as they carried the Black Panther away. She pointed at the great, mist-topped mountain in the distance as the Royal Talon Fighter hovered into view. *The mountains speak,* Chandra had said. *They speak of war.*

"Doctors cannot save him. Only the Heart-Shaped Herb can."

CHAPTER SEVEN

A SSSERIOUS SITUATION

NORTH OF Warrior Falls, hidden near the abandoned mines of Mena Ngai, the Great Mound where Klaw died, his body transformed into pure sound, a great din and fire climbed the night. It called K'Liluna from timeless beginnings wrought in ancient flame, the Leopard God of redemption, whom some called vengeance.

For her avatar, Killmonger, the time had come.

Further south, between Warrior Falls and Birnin Bashenga, hidden in plain sight, the Death Regiments had built a training outpost over a burned village. Here, Killmonger conditioned the bodies and minds of his faithful soldiers. They learned three basic objectives: assassinate the royal family, destroy the Golden City, and install Erik Killmonger, N'Jadaka the Great, as the new president of the Democratic Republic of Wakanda.

A crowd of trainees sat on wooden benches around a pit that dropped fifteen feet into the soft, pliant earth. A plank the width of a diving board stretched over the deep hole. At the bottom, a nest of snakes hissed and snapped. Garden snakes no bigger than shoestrings, rattlers and sidewinders, cobras and pythons large enough to swallow an adult and still have room for seconds.

Horatio Walters had chosen the name Venomm after he pledged his loyalty to Erik Killmonger. He didn't care that the name had already been taken. He would be the greatest Venomm that ever was. Now, he stood with his dusty boots spread on the middle of the plank. His eyes bulged, mouth split in a mad grin. He stared at the serpents slithering below. A writhing ball of motion, the snakes rustled and hissed, swaying at the crazed figure balanced above. His sleeveless field jacket revealed two scaly arms, round and hard with muscle. Something had chewed his face to the bone: scant tendons and strips of dry tissue remained. His bright blue eyes reflected the night crossing the translucent horizon.

He raised the giant magenta-and-black rock python, a symbolic offering to K'Liluna. The snake stretched its wide mouth underneath the stars, tail wrapped around Venomm's arms and thigh.

A pale, scaly hand caressed the snake's head, brushing its chin with its fingertips. Venomm smiled and cooed to his pets. Outside the pit, the trainees stared and whispered. Nearby, Erik Killmonger stood between Tayete and Kazibe. The two fools turned traitors.

"You have done well," Killmonger said, his attention focused on the man with the scaly arms and the burned face. "Thanks to comrade Venomm, Wakanda stands on the cusp of its greatest era. Our march on Warrior Falls was nothing. Wait until we take the Golden City."

Killmonger glanced over his shoulder and found the braggart Tayete's face ashen at the sight of the snakes, his eyes stretched wide with fear. The image of a craven Tayete made Killmonger smile. For a second, just a second, he remembered the day he mastered his own fear. He stared as if he did not recognize Tayete.

"Do you like what you see?" Killmonger patted the traitor's shoulder. "Only a handful of people have seen this place and lived. Thank me later."

"How does he control that thing?" Kazibe whispered.

"Control?" Killmonger laughed ruefully. "Through love, as with anything. Venomm has loved snakes since he was a child. For some reason, they love him back. Serpents are his closest friends."

Killmonger led Tayete and Kazibe to the edge of the pit.

The two fools peered cautiously at the nest of vipers, watching Venomm and his python finish their dance. Venomm left the plank covered in sweat. He raised his hand and let the rock python twist around his arm until the serpent's head nested in his palm. He raised the python's head and rubbed its cheek against his own.

"Gentlemen," Venomm said and nodded. The skin from his face had been burned away decades before. The tissues left were smooth and shiny, lacerated strips that swept his face, criss-crossed his jaws and forehead. His nose had burned away completely, leaving a black nub shaped like a spade or an upside-down black heart. The flesh around his eyes sank into puffy, red rings, sad and resigned. The world had been unkind, but with his serpents he was strong.

The magenta-and-black python raised its great head when K'Liluna's avatar grabbed Venomm's shoulders. Safely behind Killmonger, Kazibe observed the man with the burned face and the giant python with curiosity, while Tayete stared with wide, fearful eyes.

"Are your friends enjoying Wakanda, Horatio?" Killmonger asked.

"Call me Venomm. Horatio's dead. Nobody cared about him anyway." Venomm spoke with a hard Southern drawl that stretched his words.

"Venomm it is, with two *M*s." Killmonger laughed, but anger refused to leave his eyes. He faked an uppercut, patted Venomm's shoulder, while the python reared and hissed.

Tayete and Kazibe stared. Frozen, their eyes betrayed fear. Then, just as fleeting, the darkness left Killmonger's face, the light returned to his eyes and his mouth slanted into that sly, charming smile that had won over so many of Wakanda's citizens and torn the once united and cohesive nation asunder.

"You're right," Killmonger said. "So, *Venomm,* I hope you and your friends have gotten some exercise. I promised you a place where you could perform your rituals." Killmonger wrapped his muscle-bound arm around Venomm's shoulder, guiding charmer and companion past Kazibe and Tayete. The fools stumbled backward as the python snapped and hissed.

"I promised you an entire kingdom," Killmonger continued. "One that would revere you and praise you as one of its most precious saviors. Our time has come. T'Challa is a memory. All those years waiting to face him: it was almost a disappointment. I overestimated Wakanda's beloved king." Killmonger laughed. "Next, we crush the Dora Milaje and the Taifa Ngao." A huge smile spread across his face.

"You said, verbatim, that my friends could feed on T'Challa's remains," Venomm said, the rock python's face suspended next to his own. "We had a new trick planned and everything. Watch Jolene the Great Python swallow a black panther alive—whole. I wanted you to watch my friend digest T'Challa, while he screamed until he couldn't scream no more." Venomm winked at Tayete and Kazibe. "Sounds like fun, don't it?"

Tayete's face went pale. His hands shook at his sides, and the muscles in his neck and arms constricted with fear. Kazibe stared, his gaze steady and curious, even when the python hissed and brought its face within inches of his own. The snake spread its jaws, revealed a set of long, glistening fangs plated with lustrous vibranium. The glowing, purple scales that covered the serpent's body matched its metallic-tipped fangs and winked in the sun like so many precious jewels.

"The rock python is native to this region of Wakanda, and I've seen more snakes than I care to remember around my village," Kazibe said. "But never one with vibranium enhancements." Kazibe looked as if he wished to ask a question but lost his nerve. He returned to his silent study of the black-and-magenta serpent.

Venomm chuckled. He touched the side of the snake's head and turned its attention away from Kazibe until the snake's green, glowing gaze came into direct contact with his own blue, blazing eyes. He patted the top of the snake's head, as the serpent closed its eyes and nuzzled its brow inside his palm.

"You got a weird cast of characters, Killmonger," Venomm said, stroking Jolene. "But I like weird. Makes me feel like I can be myself."

"Don't worry, Venomm. The whole world and all of the ancestors will witness our triumph and your greatest performance yet." Killmonger spoke with his massive back turned to his soldiers. "Without their precious king, the Black Panther's old regime will fall when we begin our grand finale. We will strike Wakanda in the heart. For now, Venomm, I need you in the mines at the Great Mound. Making sure the comrades down there stay on task."

The snake charmer nodded, as the python coiled around his neck and rested its chin atop his head. Venomm walked away, carrying the serpent coiled on his back and around his arms, towards the flats that comprised the outskirts of Killmonger's settlement. Killmonger, Tayete, and Kazibe watched as the man and his pet disappeared into the thick, black Wakandan night.

"T'Challa was a puppet for the superhumans across the Atlantic." Tayete's voice rose as he spoke. "Yet one of them commands us. His skin is covered with scales like the reptiles he loves. His face has been burned off. What does he know of Wakanda, her people? One of us…"

Before Tayete finished his thought, Killmonger planted his fist into the soldier's solar plexus. The traitor's eyes bulged, and his cheeks puffed with the air rushing from his lungs. Tayete fell to his knees and Killmonger spun to roundhouse-kick him in the face. What little strength Tayete had vanished, and the fool-turned-traitor collapsed as if the entirety of his body, all his bones, had been reduced to gelatin.

Blood shed from wars a thousand-fold danced in Killmonger's eyes. Tayete crawled backward. Kazibe's face had gone as pale as Venomm's, as if he had felt every blow. He stood there trembling, helpless, more terrified of Killmonger than Venomm's snakes.

"You do not ask, soldier. You act upon my command." Killmonger wagged his finger in the cowering man's face. "Never question me. I am not T'Challa. You should have left your questions in that cursed palace." He smiled and placed his fists against his hips. "But it's all right, Tayete. I like you. Therefore, I am going to teach you. And I am going to give you this one bit of advice." Killmonger crouched in front of Tayete. "Never let Venomm hear you talk about his face. His snakes are always hungry."

○———————○

BACK AT the royal palace after only a few days of rest among the shamans of Mount Kanda, T'Challa felt less pain, if not fully replenished.

"So, it's true. The Panther King lives!" Shuri said, interrupting his thoughts. Relief covered her face as she darted into T'Challa's lab. She walked by several prototypes of the panther suit. "New suit, who are you?" she asked, eyeing them. "You've been busy, big brother. I heard you broke out like a fugitive."

T'Challa laughed. "It takes more than a few healers to hold me down," he said, hugging her. She held on as if she would never let him go. "Worried, were you?"

She punched him playfully. "Me, worry? I thought I'd have to suit up and take Killmonger out myself. But when I saw you floating down the river—" Eyes shining, she clasped his hand.

"I know I've been gone a long time, Princess, but I don't intend to leave you again. You're stuck with me," T'Challa said.

"But your Adored Ones whisper of war," she said, her face serious. "I don't want to lose you, too. Let me fight."

The desperation in her voice, something he was unaccustomed to hearing in his brave little sister, pierced him. She was a warrior at heart, a panther through and through. So much was at stake. Embracing her now, he knew he held Wakanda's future in his hands.

"We can fight in many ways, Shuri." T'Challa considered the youngest Bashenga squeezing his midsection. "I appreciate the kindness you've shown Monica and the training."

"That's nothing special. The self-defense was her idea." Shuri pulled away. "You know she loves you, T'Challa. You better not hurt her."

"I care for Monica deeply, Shuri. In fact, I'm hurt that you would even suggest..."

"Be careful. You may not *intend* to hurt her, but your throne will make stuff complicated. Look at your track record."

Shuri and T'Challa walked through the halls of the royal palace until the pair were standing outside the Tranquility Temple. Inside was a lavishly decorated chamber filled with life-size statues and scented torches all dedicated to Bast, the Panther God.

"How are your injuries healing?" Shuri asked.

"I'm fine, little sister." The Heart-Shaped Herb had repaired the Panther King's broken bones, the torn muscles in his back, and the knife wound in his chest, but he was still sore.

"You're not indestructible, T'Challa, and that's okay," Shuri said.

Amazed at her maturity, he realized Shuri had grown up even lonelier than him.

"Remember. As things stand you are an heir to the throne of Bashenga, but what if you had to fight for it?" The Black Panther folded his arms and watched his sister squirm around for a comeback. A sharp pain knifed T'Challa's back, reminding him of his body crashing through the water underneath Warrior Falls. He looked forward to relaxing in his favorite lounge chair.

"I told you. I'm ready." Shuri rushed to her brother's side.

"Not yet," T'Challa said, forcing himself to keep his back straight. "But the day may come when Bast requires you to serve on the battlefield. The Panther God herself will call on you. Until then, be patient and prepare."

"I've been preparing forever."

"Forever is good. Between you and your friends, I see limitless potential."

WITH THE Heart-Shaped Herb working to heal his injuries,

T'Challa sat in his favorite parlor, the Chambers of Tranquility, surrounded by the Dora Milaje, his councilors, and Monica, who watched him furtively. Although he was not yet one hundred percent healed, he was out of mortal danger. The Panther King had fled the shamans like a fugitive, despite their protestations. Even Dr. Mganga could not persuade him to rest longer.

The memory of N'Jadaka's betrayal fueled him, kept him restless, eager to seek revenge. He knew he needed to rein in his emotions. His panther spirit fed on the darkness permeating the room. Placed throughout the chamber, golden candelabras turned darkness into a theater of flickering shadows and worried faces.

Black curtains embroidered with golden thread draped the walls. A thick rug covered the center of the marble floor. Engraved bowls filled with incense, spiced flower petals, and fragrant oils filled the room with the scents of lavender, mint, and cedar.

In one corner, where the shadows were darkest, a claw of black panthers stretched their lazy bodies. They yawned and licked their ebony paws with round faces and emerald eyes as alluring as any model posing on the cover of a fashion magazine.

W'Kabi stood next to T'Challa, as grim as ever. In one hand the general held a spear topped with a silver-black blade that surged with the energy of harnessed vibration. The weapon's shaft—forged from tempered, gray steel—bore a series of engraved glyphs and sigils that recorded the ancient, blood-soaked history of the Taifa Ngao.

Communicator Taku held a small tablet in the palm of his hand, which emitted a hazy hologram inches above the screen. An array of colors coalesced to depict a small, sunlit village. A closer look revealed the burning boathouses that had led T'Challa to Warrior Falls and Erik Killmonger.

N'Jadaka. The name of the confidant-turned-nemesis triggered a lightning bolt of pain that jolted up T'Challa's back and throbbed around his temples. The Panther King's thoughts raced back to New York, back to N'Jadaka's deceitful smile—charming enough to disarm Doctor Doom. The treachery broke T'Challa's heart and filled his spirit with the conflicting forces of vengeance and deep regret.

Near the edge of the black carpet, where the shadows from the candlelight flickered across marble, Zatama, trusted advisor and member of the Tribunal Council, quietly conversed with one of the royal servers, Tanzika. Even in the dim light, shadows shifting through the room, T'Challa noticed the almost imperceptible revulsion that wrinkled the corners of Zatama's eyes and raised the edges of his mouth into a slight sneer.

Tanzika listened intently, her delicate hands gripping the handles of a metal cart decorated with a pristine gold-and-black cloth that fell just above the wheels. The top tray was covered with empty plates and gilded cutlery, spotted and smeared with the remains of the day's lunch.

The Panther King noticed the glint in Zatama's eye, his close proximity to Tanzika—body language that revealed more intimacy than the pair realized.

Beside T'Challa, Monica stretched across the lounge chair. He sensed her discomfort. She had experienced a lifetime of hurt and violence rolled up into one unforgettable week. The Panther King knew it would have been best to send her back to New York, but T'Challa needed her. Now. First and foremost, he loved her. Floating in the waters beneath Warrior Falls, his only sadness had risen from the possibility of never seeing her again.

Monica offered T'Challa a smile that warmed his heart, filled him with a surprising sense of hope and resilience. He focused all his reserve, all his trained poise to keep himself from kissing her right there in front of his entire court.

Steps away, Adebisi stood with her spear planted into the thick, plush carpet, staring silently straight ahead. She saw but did not see, heard but did not hear. The face of an Adored One was discretion and vigilance. She had witnessed the horrors of war and killing in Wakanda once before, but that was from an external enemy. Never from people she'd call her own.

At this stage in the game, the Dora Milaje and Monica were the only people in the room—in Wakanda—whom the Panther King trusted completely. Killmonger's treachery had struck Wakanda at its core, turned half the country against itself. The thought of civil war sent a sharp pain through T'Challa's forehead. He wanted to go back to sleep with Monica in his arms. A part of him regretted his return, even though his people needed their king more than ever. For a sliver of a moment, T'Challa thought about letting Wakanda have Killmonger if that was what his nation and her people truly wanted.

He imagined N'Jadaka turning Wakanda into a dictatorship, a military state, the kind of place that had once sparked intense debate between the two Wakandans back in Harlem. T'Challa would never let that happen, not as long as he lived and breathed and walked the earth. T'Challa wondered if there was any of N'Jadaka left anymore. What would it take to break through the pain and anger coursing through Killmonger's veins, to discover the true essence of the boy N'Jadaka once was before he was captured and sold to Ulysses Klaw?

Theirs was a shared pain. They possessed a common enemy, or so he had thought. But they had been diametrically opposed—and now they would always be.

"All my time in America, I dreamed of the day I could return." The Panther King stared at a sculpture of a black acacia with limbs that branched under a vaulted ceiling obscured by jet and candlelight. Perched on one of the lower branches, carved from a block of obsidian, Bast in her panther form stared down at her avatar.

"My return was supposed to be a celebration," T'Challa said. "But I have brought death and destruction to Wakanda." *N'Jadaka.* Just thinking the name crushed T'Challa's heart.

"You came back for a reason," Monica said, squeezing T'Challa's hand. "I'm here for a reason, too."

Monica smiled and leaned towards him. She sang and stroked his face. His jaw stiffened, then relaxed under her gentle touch. A tune to heal his soul and his body.

Sweet healing, let me love your pain away
Follow my voice, with you I'll always stay

Divine fire, impenetrable darkness, coalesced in her eyes. Remnants of the Heart-Shaped Herb warmed in his veins, and the panther spirit that stirred within him finally rested. Monica's voice worked with the sacred elixir, repairing the tissue in his chest and abdomen. T'Challa closed his eyes and shook his head.

"Did I do something wrong?" Monica smiled up at him.

"Do you ever stop being amazing?" T'Challa asked. Loving her changed everything. Almost enough to take away the pain that T'Challa felt. Almost.

But even in the comfort of darkness and the healing voice of a beautiful woman, the faces of the fallen, the victims of N'Jadaka—Erik Killmonger—swam through his mind. He saw G'Sere singing Wakanda's history, the griot's face alight with joy and song; the faces of the slain; the burning boathouses. He would never forget Birnin Okan Odo's wailing survivors screaming amid the flames and the corpses. There weren't enough pages in his book of secret names to contain all the souls that were lost.

T'Challa remembered the mother who held her baby with one arm and embraced her grief-stricken husband with the other; saw G'Sere's weeping wife and their children mourning over the griot's lifeless body. Finally, T'Challa saw the light disappear from G'Sere's eyes and the slack expression of death that turned his face into something empty and cold.

"N'Jadaka will pay," T'Challa said, returning his attention to the statue of Bast that watched from the black tree limb above.

"Your Majesty, has violence become our only way?" Zatama asked, bowing before the Panther King.

"Watch your tongue, Zatama," W'Kabi said. The Dora Milaje bristled around him. He stood to his full height, gripped the ceremonial spear with both hands, commanding all his grim darkness. "T'Challa is Bast's avatar, and he is still your king."

Still your king? T'Challa thought, noting how the situation made him second-guess every word.

"Let Zatama speak freely," he said.

"This Killmonger is the sower of discord, the willing agent of violence and destruction." Zatama stared anxiously at the ground. "Your Majesty, you are the son of the Great Isolationist, of the line of Bashenga. Bast chose you as her sacred avatar. The people who have drifted will return to you, if—" Zatama's voice faltered.

"Speak," T'Challa said, dulling the edge in his voice. "You have my ear."

"If they know their king is here to stay, here for Wakandans. Some believe—"

"I know what *some* believe, and they are wrong. I have sacrificed everything for my people."

Zatama let the king's words linger in the air before choosing his own carefully.

"The Panther God favors strength and cunning, but not war and death. This is civil conflict. Perhaps a more diplomatic approach is what is needed. We are filling our cities with our own blood. How long before Killmonger makes it to Birnin Zana?"

"Your Majesty," Taku said, interrupting. "The Kimoyo has detected Death Regiment soldiers moving around Warrior Falls. They appear to be coming out of the water." He offered the tablet to T'Challa.

Light rose from T'Challa's palms, casting an image of water that crashed from hundreds of feet above, a pool of violent froth and the mouth of the great source that fed all the other rivers in Wakanda. Crossing the riverhead, across a wall of verdant plant life, a column of warriors marched toward the waterfall. They were bare-chested except for plates of armor that covered their hearts. They wore neon sigils and runes tattooed on their arms, and painted skulls covered their ghastly faces. Broken bones adorned the Death Regiment's uniforms, their eyes devoid of emotion, as empty as the dark void that separated T'Challa from the ancestors watching over him from Djalia.

Monica's soft hand touched T'Challa's arm. The light from the hologram accentuated the fear and the shock that furrowed her brow. She squeezed T'Challa's bicep and leaned against his side.

"Does it have to be you, T? Can't you send your Shields or your Dora Milaje?" Her eyes filled with tears. "You haven't fully healed yet," she said, peering at him. "You're not invincible, you know."

"I am Wakanda's greatest living warrior," the Panther King said. "It is my responsibility to protect my people. Monica," he said more gently, "I have already neglected my duties once. I will not abandon my people again. Not ever, even if that means placing myself in mortal danger."

T'Challa squeezed her hand, then stood to face his court. The room grew silent as the group gathered, waiting on their king's commands.

"W'Kabi, prepare a company of your best men. In fact, double security around the Great Mound and Warrior Falls."

"Yes, My King. At once," W'Kabi said, cutting his eyes at Zatama, who looked crestfallen. A mischievous smile curled the side of the Shield's mouth.

T'Challa tapped an icon at the bottom of the Kimoyo tablet. This gesture switched the camera to a panoramic view. What T'Challa saw sent his mind into a spiral of pain and memory. He turned to Monica.

"Do you see this? Here, at the base of the Great Mound?" He pointed at the holo. "Someone has detonated a huge cache of explosives. My father died here, protecting Wakanda's most valuable resource. This is also the place where I avenged his death." The pain in T'Challa's voice surprised him. Seeing enemies at the Great Mound again hurt as deeply as it did on that fateful day.

"I have spent years running from these memories, yet they always draw me back to the same place, the same destiny. An enemy far more dangerous than Ulysses Klaw has turned half of my own people against me. I must face this threat now or lose everything I have ever loved."

CRASHING WATER filled T'Challa with a sense of dread. He remembered falling, the raging white water biting his skin, shredding his damaged suit like razors, the spray filling his nostrils. He came so close to death that day; he saw his father's smile, his father's glowing eyes—*a divine ambassador sent to welcome another Panther King to Djalia.*

The hot lightning, the burning shafts of pain aching in T'Challa's back and arms, reminded him of N'Jadaka's betrayal. A black arrow of disciplined muscle and silent rage, he made his way back to the sacred ground where he had fought for his life, for everything he loved and lost it all.

The Black Panther slipped over a dark branch high enough in the trees to conceal him from the soldiers walking below. Even from the treetops, T'Challa smelled N'Jadaka's scent clinging to the traitors, the two fools—Tayete and Kazibe. The Panther King remembered the survivors limping and coughing through the flames and the smoke, the victims sprawled throughout the carnage.

"Now that the panther demon is finished, we can have anything we want." Tayete laughed and spread his arms. "Wakanda is ours for the taking."

"Why are you always so loud?" Kazibe asked. He raised his index finger to shush Tayete.

"What does it matter? The panther demon is finished. He should be glad that he died at the hands of Killmonger." Tayete crouched and clawed as if he was grabbing someone. "I would have tortured T'Challa until he begged me to kill him. Then I would have paraded his head through the Golden City."

T'Challa flew like a bullet and kicked Kazibe in the back. The traitor's eyes bulged, and his arms and legs flew behind him. Kazibe's knees went out and the traitor fell like there was no ground beneath his feet. Tayete looked as if he wanted to scream or rip his hair out. Instead, he grabbed the automatic rifle slung across his shoulder and fired a burst that ripped through the trees and vegetation, sending lush, green blades flying through the air and broken branches falling to the ground. Evading the gunfire, T'Challa allowed the smoke and the debris to obscure his presence. Perched in a treetop, he watched Tayete lower the assault rifle that surged with a purple light T'Challa would have recognized anywhere.

But how? the Black Panther thought. How had Killmonger gotten his hands on so much vibranium and anti-metal? The weapons, the plated claws and teeth on Killmonger's leopards, none of it made sense—unless N'Jadaka's treachery had found its way into the Panther King's inner circle. The thought turned his stomach as he dove toward Tayete. T'Challa raked his claws across the assault rifle, slicing it to pieces, gashing Tayete's arms. The fool cried out and fell to the ground.

"Stay away, if you know what's good for you," the traitor said, scooting backwards on his hands and knees.

"I know exactly what's good for me." T'Challa could not hide the mirth in his voice. He grabbed Tayete's collar with both hands, pulled the traitor up until the pair faced each other, their noses only inches apart.

"You're supposed to be dead. You—you must really be a demon," Tayete said. Trembling in T'Challa's grip, his legs went slack, and a dark, wet spot spread across the front of his pants. He gripped the Panther King's hands, struggling to free himself. "You had better unhand me, now, p-panther demon. Killmonger's Death Regiments are right behind us. Surrender now, and I will make sure they show you mercy."

T'Challa laughed. "You stink, Tayete, with fear. Did you soil yourself?" He sniffed the air. "We must clean you up, make you presentable. How about a nice warm bath?" T'Challa hurled the protesting fool into the raging water.

The Black Panther turned to Kazibe, who took one fearful look at the approaching king before jumping from the grassy ledge to join his friend in the foamy pool below.

T'Challa watched as the two fools disappeared in the froth and the gray-blue haze of the rushing river. Somewhere downstream, the two would pull themselves onto dry land. They would dry themselves off and return to their mischief, but T'Challa would never kill them—not unless his own life hung in the balance. Tayete and Kazibe were pitiful and wretched, but they were still Wakandan.

Who would leave those fools to guard anything? T'Challa shook his head.

He heard footsteps marching in the distance. Hundreds ascending the main steps to Warrior Falls. They would pass soon. The Black Panther vaulted up into the treetops, hid in the shadows and waited for the company to march below. He wanted to see the men who had turned against him and taken up with N'Jadaka.

Kill, Kill, Killmonger!

The Black Panther pressed his claws into the tree bark as his mind returned to the masked rebel that had spat in Monica's face.

The stench of Killmonger's Death Regiments brought the Panther King back to the present. Killmonger's signature scents, blood and death, rose with the climbing breeze. He imagined the stench reaching the heights of Djalia, all the way to the Panther God's throne. Caught in the wind, the trees and the grass whispered. A rabbit shot across the worn path that stretched below. A flock of thrushes sped over the trees. The Panther King watched the Death Regiments rise from the jungle dressed in camouflage, green denim, and dungarees adorned with human bones. *The Death Regiments.* T'Challa remembered the fear in Tayete's eyes when he mentioned Killmonger's merciless band of mercenaries and rebel assassins.

The Death Regiments passed under T'Challa, marching in single file across the base of the shallow river. Unaffected by the hammering downpour, they disappeared into the plummeting waterfall one by one. Not one soldier looked back. If they noticed Tayete and Kazibe's disappearance, they did not show it.

The Black Panther waited until the last soldier vanished, then slipped down the tree and followed the column into the crashing water.

Warrior Falls dropped a thousand wet fists, sharp blades that chopped and battered the flesh beneath his vibranium suit. The pounding, slicing water sparked his bruises, the memory of his fight with N'Jadaka, and the five-hundred-foot plummet from the top of the waterfall.

He thought of Monica's hands, soft on the outside yet as strong as the precious metal hidden beneath the Great Mound. T'Challa imagined those wonderful hands massaging the muscles in his back and neck. He let the memory of her sweet voice carry him through the all-encompassing roar of the water.

T'Challa emerged from the falls and found himself in a huge open space, dark and silent, inside the abandoned vibranium mines that he had closed after the murder of his father and the defeat of Ulysses Klaw. The Black Panther stood amongst digging machinery, tools, and railways long abandoned and derelict. To his surprise, he found none of the Death Regiments that had disappeared inside the waterfall. They'd left no trace of their passing, not a bone or a single footprint. The Black Panther sniffed the air, but the stink of blood and death that had risen from the path outside had all but vanished. Even the air felt still and undisturbed.

Flickering lights and machinery grinding in the distant dark told the Black Panther that the mines were not abandoned after all. He heard the drone of electromagnetic rail cars rambling back and forth through the darkness under the Great Mound. He smelled the vibranium wafting up from the depths of the mine, a frightening and disturbing scent. He stared into the depths and watched a magnetic train speed away into the cavernous womb of the mountain's interior.

This mine should be closed, T'Challa thought. His next reactions filled his mind with an escalation of horror and rage that he could hardly contain.

He stepped forward, intent on finding the thieves who were stealing Wakanda's most precious resource. The Black Panther walked with his head held high in the darkness and his fists balled at his sides. Still, all the greed, the lies, the troubles attached to the Wakandan crown had worn T'Challa's spirit to a crumpled shadow.

Lashing through the night, the whip wrapped around the Black Panther's neck. First, he thought of N'Jadaka, but something was wrong. The smell was different. The scent of blood and suffering that Killmonger left on everything he touched permeated the air. Still, the smell was not nearly as strong as its source.

A storm of thoughts rushed the Black Panther, but there was no time to think. Instead, he leapt from the cliff, allowing the whip to squeeze his neck. T'Challa grabbed the lash and tensed the muscles in his arms and shoulders, using the taut whip and the strength of its wielder to act as a tether.

"Looky here, I've caught a big ole rat dressed up like a cat!" Venomm cheered as he stepped from the shadows. His face twisted into a pale, grotesque sneer. The scales on the skin of his arms shone bright even in the darkness of the abandoned mine.

The Black Panther allowed his body weight to give him the momentum he needed to swing underneath the jutting cliffside. T'Challa leaped through the air, swung underneath the rock, and came up soaring over the disfigured villain. Black claws raked across the scaly whip but failed to cut the braided metal.

Impervious to vibranium, he thought as he spun free of the whip and kicked Venomm in the chest.

The blow sent the scaly villain flying backward, but before the Black Panther could charge for another strike, Venomm's rock python shot from the darkness overhead and wrapped itself around the Panther King's body. His arms pinned to his sides, T'Challa struggled in the snake's grip as it opened its mouth to reveal fangs covered in the lustrous black metal that bore the conductive properties of vibranium but the resistance of some stronger metal.

Maybe it's an alloy of vibranium and titanium—perhaps even adamantium, T'Challa thought.

"You're supposed to be dead, Ta'Charlie. Killmonger said he killed you himself." Venomm stood and balled his open hand into a fist. When he did this, the magenta-and-black rock python squeezed the Black Panther inside its massive coils. Shock filled him. The creature had been augmented by vibranium.

T'Challa felt the bruises from his fight with Killmonger sing to the darkness under Warrior Falls. Without warning or reason, that final night in Harlem reeled in his mind as the serpent squeezed him. He saw N'Jadaka smiling, raising a glass to Wakanda. T'Challa remembered the music. Monica singing like he was the only soul in the packed room. The best night of his life had been a lie.

"Don't matter no-way," Venomm said, chuckling. "You'll be dead by the time he sees you."

The python squeezed T'Challa's upper body, opened its mouth around his head. T'Challa stared at vibranium-tipped fangs.

"Killmonger's building a new world," Venomm continued. "A place where people like me are loved and respected, even feared. There's no way in hell you're gonna ruin that."

T'Challa asked Bast for forgiveness, then commanded his panther suit to blast the rock python with a shockwave that left the snake writhing in a painful rope of black and magenta scales curled around his feet.

Screaming some indecipherable war cry, Venomm lunged at T'Challa, but the Black Panther found the rock python's attack more impressive. He ducked the flurry of swinging fists and punched Venomm in his rib cage. T'Challa felt the bones break under his fist. Venomm's wry smile surprised the Black Panther as a pair of king cobras shot from behind a shadowy rock pile, wrapped around his ankles, and pulled him over the cliff. Just before he fell into incalculable darkness, the Black Panther grabbed a sharp horn of stone jutting from the cliffside.

"Why is Killmonger doing this? All the killings and burning? I thought he wanted to build a new Wakanda," T'Challa said. One clawed hand slipped from the rock and left him swinging desperately over miles of bottomless darkness.

"That's the funny thing," Venomm said, as he ground his bootheel into T'Challa's fingers. "Killmonger says we have to destroy Wakanda, rebuild it from the ground up."

"Is that so?" T'Challa asked. He yanked his hand from underneath Venomm's boot for a black, breathless second. Suspended in midair, he grabbed Venomm's ankle.

The Black Panther knew the shock would force Venomm to plant his foot into the ground, creating a nice counterweight for T'Challa to brace himself against. He swung his foot up and kicked

Venomm in the jaw with a vibranium-coated bootheel. With his jaw broken and legs turning to jelly, the scaly soldier almost fell off the cliff himself, but T'Challa grabbed his collar. The Black Panther hefted Venomm in the air with one hand, taking a moment to watch him kick his feet over the dark chasm.

"Your Killmonger is not what he appears to be," T'Challa said. He loosened his grip on Venomm's neck for one second, allowing him to panic over the thought of plummeting through oblivion.

"It's too late, anyway," Venomm laughed. "Your people have already chosen Killmonger. Even now he's preparing his assault on the Golden City, and everyone who opposes him will die. Then the meek shall inherit the Earth." Venomm squealed and kicked his feet, as he hugged T'Challa's forearm for precious life.

The Panther King slammed the snake charmer into the rocky plateau standing behind them. Gripping Venomm's collar, T'Challa pressed one knee into Venomm's chest.

"Killmonger will pay for all his crimes. Trust me," T'Challa said. He bent forward, so his face would be closer to Venomm's. The Panther King stared into his opponent's pale blue eyes. "Everyone who works for Killmonger—everyone who assists him, all his sympathizers—will share his punishment in full."

CHAPTER EIGHT

MALICE BY MOONLIGHT

THE NIGHT after the Black Panther defeated Venomm in the mines underneath the Great Mound, he took Monica to the Igi Iya gardens behind the royal palace. Even in the open air, with countless stars and the cherry moon gleaming overhead, he felt closed in. His fight with Venomm replayed in his mind.

Killmonger says we have to destroy Wakanda and rebuild it. The same man who had raised his glass and drank to T'Challa's health wanted to end everything the Panther King loved.

The red moon showered the Golden City with a flourish of pink brilliance. The stars filled the dark with precious gems, limitless worlds crafted from pure light. A host of clouds raced overhead. *Like rush hour traffic in Harlem.* T'Challa thought about the times when his life was simpler.

The Panther King took Monica's hand and led her to the edge of the garden where golden torches shot purple and red flames into the night. Beyond the flambeau, a steep one-hundred-foot drop overlooked a shallow tributary fed with runoff from Warrior Falls and the River of Grace and Wisdom. The Golden City sprawled across the countryside, a wide cloak fashioned from gilded thread.

The garden perfumed the air with wild freesia, treasure flowers, and bush lilies. The breeze that carried the sweet scents felt cool against T'Challa's face, and Monica's hand felt warm inside his own.

T'Challa wrapped his arm around Monica's waist, and she lay her cheek against his heart. He took a deep breath, inhaling the scent of her hair, her skin: perfume and powder scented with tiaré and coconut oil, the faint spice of her sweat. He pondered his lost friendship and the man he had called brother, but N'Jadaka was gone, replaced by a murderous psychopath who called himself Erik Killmonger.

"I called N'Jadaka *brother*." T'Challa's voice deepened with anger and sadness. "I'm supposed to be a king with the instincts of a panther. None of my enemies have ever gotten that close. I welcomed him into my home."

"You're a king, not a god," Monica said. "Even the best of us make mistakes in judgment." She stroked his cheek. "To err is human. That's why I love you—because even with all your gifts, you're still a kind, loving man."

"But I am the avatar of Bast, and I rule by her grace. I can only imagine her displeasure."

Monica raised her eyebrow. "I traveled all the way across the Atlantic Ocean for a fugazi?" She laughed and pushed T'Challa's chest. "Stop looking sad, T. I'm joking with you."

The Panther King tried to smile. He'd been trained to mask his emotions his entire life, but Monica always saw through his stoicism. He could never hide his feelings from her. Instead, he kissed her, and she returned the loving gesture. They held each other, there in the fragrant garden, caught between the red moon and the Golden City. T'Challa squeezed Monica's waist while she nuzzled her nose against his Adam's apple.

"I am sorry for bringing you into all of this," he said. "You left the United States for me."

"And walked right into a war zone," Monica said, her voice dry with sarcasm. "I could have stayed in New York for that."

Shadows darted through the garden just beyond Monica's shoulder. He had never seen a shadow ripple like black liquid. Sensing the heat rising from the shadows, T'Challa grabbed Monica just as the dark bodies armed with black blades leapt from the stirring bushes. T'Challa instinctively summoned his armor, felt it wrap around his body. One assailant sliced at T'Challa's throat and met a bone-crushing fist, full force. The Black Panther felt the jawbone shatter beneath his knuckles. He kicked another dark figure reaching for Monica, who shrieked in shock at his side. The shadow assassins circled the Black Panther and Monica Lynne. Scouts from the Death Regiments. Skulls decorated their shoulders, chests, and faces. Belts fashioned from bones glowed around their waists in the pink moonlight.

"Stay close," T'Challa said to Monica, who braced herself. He thought of N'Jadaka grinning down at him, as the Black Panther plummeted through a battery of relentless water. He remembered the fiend's smile on that last, fateful night in Harlem, feigning friendship. A shadow morphed into the shape of T'Challa's friend-turned-nemesis. The Black Panther jumped and spun in midair, kicking the shadow's face with a black boot.

"T'Challa!" Monica screamed, barely ducking a blade.

More shadow assassins leapt from the darkness, armed with blades of all sizes, greatswords and spears, machetes and daggers. They crept in grim silence around T'Challa and Monica, circling the pair.

"I want you to deliver a message," T'Challa said to the shadows. "Your leader will never win. Wakanda will prevail, and as for you—"

T'Challa leapt through the advancing night. He cut throats and broke bones until only one assassin remained. Monica cringed as T'Challa rammed his fist into a shadow man's face.

The Black Panther meant to spare this one to send N'Jadaka a message, but when he grabbed the assassin, he saw Klaw laughing instead. T'Chaka's death shone fresh in the hateful eyes of Wakanda's deadly nemesis. Rage filled his chest, and before T'Challa could strike, the face became that of N'Jadaka, who now lay prostrate beneath him.

For a moment, T'Challa saw the warmth in the smile that was once his friend's. Laughing, the visage then morphed into Erik Killmonger and promised that the nation T'Challa had loved his entire life would fall forever. Everyone that T'Challa loved would bow to Killmonger—or die just like Griot G'Sere.

Infuriated, T'Challa unleashed a flurry of deadly blows at the laughing face. He punched and punched, even as bones cracked beneath his fists. Blood covered the Black Panther's forearms, splashed his chest and mask. Somewhere beside him, he could hear Monica's cries for him to stop, but her voice sounded distant, as if he were in a dream. T'Challa remembered the screaming that had followed Klaw's attacks on the Great Mound and the burning villages sacked by Killmonger. All he could see now was his own red-blooded fury.

Another shadow emerged from the garden, a short figure with a long walking stick. As soon as the hand touched T'Challa's shoulder, he forgot about the helpless bloodied form that had now returned to its origin—a faceless shadow that bubbled as it sank into the ground. T'Challa reached for the shadow beside him, and the darkness dissipated, yielded to a brown hand wrinkled around aged knuckles.

Scattered around the garden, shadowy forms sank back into manicured grass and paths of neatly arranged polished cobblestones. Monica cried out, "Control yourself!" When T'Challa looked up, he found a set of curious brown eyes and a comforting smile that reminded him of G'Sere's expression as his soul seeped from his body.

Wakanda's legendary chief physician and shaman, Mendinao, stood before him. The elder wore a blue headwrap, a blue undershirt under a maroon tunic, and a heavy indigo jacket despite the temperate breeze that blew through the garden. A short, sturdy man, Mendinao stood at eye level with T'Challa as the Black Panther was kneeling, straddling an imaginary enemy that had sunk into the earth. As Mendinao squeezed T'Challa's shoulders, gold and jeweled bracelets crowding the shaman's wrist clinked with a song all their own.

"Easy, Panther King. The first part of your trial is complete," Mendinao said. Monica exhaled, relieved, beside him. The physician had been Wakanda's most talented healer since T'Chaka was a boy. "The Heart-Shaped Herb has been prepared. I am told you did not complete your treatment at Mount Kanda." T'Challa did not answer but hung his head in shame. "Before replenishing your sacred powers in full, I must warn you of another effect of our sacred herb. It has the ability to magnify your inner impulses. Balance is key." Mendinao squeezed T'Challa's shoulder.

"Then I have failed Wakanda, Mendinao," T'Challa said. He grabbed Mendinao's forearm. The Panther King's voice shook with uncertainty and regret.

"You are Wakanda's champion, My King. You are the greatest of all the avatars." Mendinao cupped his long, soft fingers around T'Challa's face. Kindness flickered in the shaman's eyes.

T'Challa imagined his father, his king, smiling. The son stared into the night. "I'm sorry." The words lingered in the air until T'Challa leaned forward, resting against Mendinao's chest.

"I failed you, father. I let you die," T'Challa said.

Monica, her own eyes wet and shiny, reached for T'Challa, but Mendinao's gaze stopped her mid-gesture. He shook his head and patted the Panther King's back.

"Do not let the ghosts of the past haunt your future, My King," Mendinao said. "Your past is merely an abstraction, no more real than the shadows you fought this evening." The healer stepped backwards and stared into T'Challa's eyes. "You are the future, Your Highness. Do not let your rage drive you."

Mendinao's voice became soft, and the light in his eyes surrendered to shadows. "The Heart-Shaped Herb enhances all of your strengths, both physical *and spiritual*," the great healer said with emphasis. "If your mind is filled with rage, the Heart-Shaped Herb will magnify that emotion. Rage is a low frequency. It is beneath you, T'Challa. Self-control and discipline are key. You are Wakanda's only hope against our greatest threat."

The healer extended his hand; spindly fingers wrapped around the bottom of a cup filled with a smoking liquid brewed from the Heart-Shaped Herb. T'Challa smelled the pungent, earthy scent deep in his soul. The fragrance recalled the memories of every other time that he had drunk the elixir, precious drops that allowed him to protect the people and the way of life he loved with all his existence.

T'Challa accepted the steaming goblet. As the steam rose into the air, he stared up at the confident eyes and respectful smile of the shaman. Behind Mendinao, yellow shafts hovered above the Golden City. Past the heart-red moon in the cold dark beyond the world, T'Challa saw his father and mother. He saw G'Sere singing the stories of their ancestors, and he saw Bast perched on a black branch, watching all the world.

INSIDE THE dark, sleepy palace, Zatama, the most respected member of Wakanda's Tribunal Council, woke to a blade pressing on his throat. The sharp edge broke the skin, sent a red tear sliding down his neck. A hard foot pressed on Zatama's chest. His waking eyes focused on a dark figure with muscular legs, round hips, and high cheekbones. The woman wore a huge afro and skull-shaped earrings that dangled from her earlobes. The alabaster bones and skulls that denoted Killmonger's Death Regiments decorated her belt and hung from the flag end of the spear that pinned Zatama to the bed.

"Would you like to keep breathing?" The woman spoke in a hushed voice, without whispering.

Frozen beneath the spear tip, Zatama did not move. Instead, he stared, clenching his jaw as the woman stood over him. It was dark in the room, and shadows obscured her face.

"Wise decision. Living is good," the woman said, her husky voice extending every syllable that seeped from her malevolent smile. "Life will be even better once the Black Panther is dead."

"Who are you?" Zatama dared to ask. His muscles stiffened in his back and limbs.

"Malice," the woman hissed. Somehow her voice filled the room. "Allow me to pose my own question. Think carefully before you answer—your life hangs in the balance. You captured my comrade, the one who calls himself Venomm. Where is he?"

Anger rippled across Zatama's face. He shook his head and waved his arms, but Malice raised a finger to her lips and made a shushing sound.

"Quiet," Malice said. "Don't worry. I'm a professional. You will live if I so choose. First, slowly and calmly, you will tell me exactly how to find Venomm. Then, you will show me."

Zatama cursed silently. Then, underneath the shadows and the madly smiling skulls, he began to whisper. His eyes went round and black as he told Malice everything he knew about the underground holding cells where Venomm had been taken. Malice watched Zatama intently. She stared into his eyes, as if her gaze could detect any hint of deception.

"Now you will lead the way," Malice continued. "Don't worry about anyone disturbing us. The guards in this part of the palace have been neutralized." She smiled.

The pair left the bedroom, creeping through the dark as Zatama trudged ahead, weeping. Malice had collapsed her spear and stored the weapon in a sheath strapped to the small of her back.

"Don't worry about the cameras, Councilor Zatama. No one will know you betrayed T'Challa unless we want them to," Malice hissed.

Zatama led Malice through the first checkpoint, and Zatama flinched at the sight of the men standing in front of him. Before he could speak out and warn the soldiers, Malice had killed them both, silently and efficiently. She smiled as the guards fell to the ground. Malice raised a single finger, adorned with a skull ring that shone despite the failing light.

Evading the cameras with ease, Malice worked her way through the dark corridors. She eliminated four more sentries on her way to the holding cells. Malice and Zatama entered a long hallway lined with tiny, empty rooms on both sides. Around the corner, a soft

light flourished.

Voices drifted from the corner. Both spoke in even tones that fit well with the somber hall. One voice, deep and rich, embodied the nobility of Wakanda. At the sound of this voice, Malice's hand tightened around the hilt of her dagger.

The other voice was ragged and spoke in long drawls. It carried a slight hiss at the edge of every word. A subtle, deep sound that came as naturally as breathing to its host. Venomm.

"I gotta admit," Venomm said inside the prison cell, shifting on his cot. "You don't react to my face like most people." The snake charmer sounded exhausted.

"Wakanda is not like any other place in the world," Taku said, his voice amiable, disarming.

"It's not?" Venomm said, skeptical. "Looks like the same piss-hole prison to me!"

Wakanda's chief of communication chuckled. "Well, it's true you're not getting the royal treatment, but you earned that. I know what people see when they look at you, but what do you see when you look in the mirror?"

Venomm narrowed his eyes, considered his jailer, Taku. His eyes seemed to fill with fire and poison, and in that moment, Taku thought Venomm bore a strong resemblance to the striking black-and-magenta snake they had wrestled away from him. When they caught them, the serpent was wrapped around Venomm's chest and torso as if she grew there. His closest companion, the loyal snake gave quite a fight, clearly used to executing Venomm's every command.

Venomm stared at his reflection in the plexiglass. "I see a man who ain't never had a friend. Not one," Venomm replied.

Taku tilted his head, leaned toward the plexiglass that separated the two of them. "Correction. You've never had any *human* friends."

At this, Venomm's eyes went from hard accusation to a cruel mixture of defiance and life-long grief.

"You miss your snake," Taku said gently.

Venomm slammed his fists into the plexiglass. "Where's Jolene? If you hurt her, I swear I'll kill you."

Taku smiled. "Don't worry, your friend is alive. In fact, she's doing quite well. Would you like to see her?"

Venomm looked skeptical, but hope glimmered in his pale blue eyes.

"I told you the truth, Venomm," Taku said. "Your snake—Jolene—is fine." Taku produced a flat disc, a crystal plate no bigger than his palm. Multicolored light swirled in the plate and coalesced into a three-dimensional picture.

Venomm pressed his face into the plexiglass. For a moment it looked as if he might crash through the clear, synthetic confines. Instead, he raised a fist and pressed his flat scaly palm against the clear surface. His eyes were wild, a mixture of desperation and joy. The emanating light depicted a sunny, lush jungle scene, and Venomm watched his rock python, Jolene, slither around a huge Wangari tree limb, its massive body weighing the branches down.

"You see? Your friend is getting the royal treatment." Taku smiled. The light from the hologram threw shadows against Taku's sympathetic face.

Venomm looked relieved, the scars on his cheeks and forehead relaxing. "Ever since I was a kid," Venomm mused, "I always loved snakes. Snakes get a bad rap. Know what I mean? In Sunday school, the snake took all the blame for Adam and Eve's foolishness. I always knew there had to be more to the story. Poor snake, blamed for man's sins."

Venomm spoke in a far-off voice, as if he was in a distant place, long ago.

"I loved snakes so much because I knew what it was like to be an outcast. People don't treat different right. Folks been hating me my whole life. Even before my accident, nobody ever loved me. Nobody but my snakes." Venomm laughed at himself. "Back then I didn't think my life could get any worse. Boy, was I wrong."

He stroked his chin thoughtfully.

"All of the kids in my neighborhood made fun of me. I was the weird snake boy who walked around with reptiles in my pockets. Girls thought I was creepy. Even my teachers disliked me. At school the principal was always going through my pockets, trying to see if I brought any snakes. Tried to tell them; the snakes were my only friends, the only things that ever loved me. Of course, snakes are bitey sometimes. Nobody's perfect. But snakes aren't like humans. They only bite when they feel threatened. The kids at my school, my teachers—heck, even my own family—used to hurt me all the time, and none of them ever had a reason. Bullies. Back in those days, I was a nice boy. I remember. Don't let nobody tell you Venomm always been like this. Back then, I never hurt no one. Even when they deserved it. Looking back, that was my biggest mistake."

Malice leaned forward, her ears piqued, hearing Venomm's voice. She moved silently through the darkness, one hand covering Zatama's mouth, while the other pressed her knife to his throat.

"There's nothing wrong with a gentle spirit," Taku said, comforting, empathetic even. "People ridicule me for being soft, sometimes. I know how it is."

"I didn't understand back then. The world ain't no place for the weak. Whatever it takes, you got to be strong. That's why I look like this. Because I was weak."

"You can't blame yourself for the actions of others," Taku said. "And it's not about how you look. It's who you are and who you choose to be. Accidents happen, Horatio. People survive."

Venomm guffawed incredulously. "Don't give me that mumbo-jumbo mind trip, Taco! *It's all about the inside,* eh? Heh! I was a handsome boy before my accident," Venomm said. "I ain't know it but I was." He spoke in a dreamy haze. "But I was too different, and that's why they hated me."

Just beyond the cone of light cast from inside the prison cell, Malice pinned her captive against the wall, squeezed her hand around Zatama's angry mouth. She pressed the knife to the councilor's back, right below his kidney, until the tip broke the skin. The councilor groaned and swiped at the air.

"When Bruce Morgan asked me to be his lab partner, I was surprised," Venomm said. "I remember being so happy. It was my sophomore year, and he was the first kid to talk to me in high school—like a real person. The coolest kid wanted to be *my* lab partner. I thought the world had finally accepted me, that my life was gonna change. I ironed my best shirt that morning, even left my snakes at home." He paused, covered his head with both hands. His jaw clenched. "Who throws acid in a kid's face?"

For a moment, silence filled the space between the two men.

"Do we need to stop now, Horatio?" Taku said, concern softening his words.

"I'm alright," the charmer replied, pain in his voice. "I can keep going. I remember the screams were mostly my own, but I heard laughter, too. Later, Bruce said he didn't know what he had in that glass, or how it got there. But I heard him laughing. I still hear him sometimes in my sleep.

"Rolling around on the floor, screaming in the middle of chemistry class, my face on fire, that was the worst day of my life. Nobody even looked at me after that. I left school, and Bruce Morgan got two weeks' suspension. He got a vacation while the rest of my life was ruined. Don't that crack you up? After Bruce Morgan I couldn't go anywhere, not even to the corner store. After my pops left, my mom cried every night. She couldn't stand to look at me. Spoke to me like I was already dead. I know she blamed me, but it wasn't my fault. That's when I started going into the woods."

"Venomm," Malice hissed under her breath. "Fool. Make your enemy reveal *himself*—like Erik taught you."

"I got my first bite playing by the river." Venomm chuckled. "I didn't see the water moccasin until it was too late. After it got me, I fell out crying and hollering. Of course, nobody came. I thought I was gonna to die right there. But nothing happened. I waited for the poison to kill me. But it was the opposite. Instead of dying, I got stronger. That snake's venom gave me power. That's how I picked my name, you know.

"By the time I met Killmonger, I had become a fine connoisseur of serpents. He was a good mentor, not like those busters I used to know, and he put me on to some new things. But I'd been studying snakes on my own for years. Taking night classes here and there.

Even if he hadn't shown up in the parking lot after class when those thugs tried to hurt me, those Bruce Morgans would have died that night. My babies would have made sure of it. Erik's a good guy. You just don't understand him, that's all. He gave me the confidence to finally get my revenge on Bruce Morgan. Get it out my spirit. He's got some demons of his own. But yeah, Jolene ate good that night."

Venomm smiled at Taku and winked mischievously as Malice raised her spear high above Taku's shoulder.

THE MOON had passed without notice until it sat in the north, where it hung red and bulbous, a sleepless eye, watching over Wakanda.

"How can so much beauty contain so much death?" Monica asked. She stared at the Golden City glowing before her. She thought things would be different in Wakanda. She had only met two Wakandans back in the United States. The first had seemed pompous, elitist. But somehow, she had fallen in love with this man, and she had fallen more deeply than she could have ever imagined. She had traveled across an entire ocean with this man, who was born a king, and stepped into the middle of the Terrordome.

"Everyone hates me here. You know that, don't you?" Monica folded her arms.

"No one hates you," T'Challa said gently. "Wakanda has remained insular for thousands of years. Most of my people have never spoken with someone born outside its borders." T'Challa wrapped his arms around Monica's waist and pulled her closer.

"Hating me is, like, the only thing your people seem to agree on."

"What about Shuri and Chandra? Even the Dora Milaje have grown fond of you. I have never seen Adebisi be that kind to anyone."

"T'Challa, they spat in my face the first day." Monica tilted her head and stared at him as if she was speaking to a child.

"That was not my people, Monica. Those were my enemies. The real Wakanda loves you. The people who love me love you. There are some who need a little more time."

"Like W'Kabi," Monica said.

"W'Kabi is a bit old-fashioned, even by Wakandan standards."

"Your chief of security is a mess. I get an earful every time I talk to Chandra."

T'Challa chuckled and held Monica's hand as they followed a gilded walkway back to the rear of the royal palace. Precious gems and lustrous stones glimmered beneath their feet.

Inside, T'Challa and Monica found darkness and unsettling silence. A giant panther statue dedicated to Bast towered above, staring at T'Challa with silver-black eyes and sharp teeth. He sensed the danger before he saw the shadows.

When the black figures stepped from behind the statue, T'Challa jumped in front of Monica and blocked a dark spearhead that swung at his face. Any other time, T'Challa would have moved at a blinding speed, removing Monica from the spear's path and disarming the assailant, but the Heart-Shaped Herb was still working through his system, and he was not as quick as normal. Or so he thought when the spear tip slashed through his arm, displacing the nanoids in the Black Panther's armor.

"Monica," T'Challa said as he grumbled in pain.

"I know the drill," Monica said and stepped back.

"T'Challa," Malice's husky voice rang through the dark. "I was hoping to meet the great panther demon. Killmonger will never know that his old friend was alive and well."

"What made you think I wouldn't be?" the Panther King said, claws extended. "Tell N'Jadaka that I look forward to our next encounter."

"This will be the end for you, panther demon." Malice stepped from the shadows, using Zatama as a human shield.

Venomm emerged from the shadows behind Malice with a wounded Taku as his hostage. He had taken Taku's service pistol, and now held the gun under Taku's chin.

"I told you, Ta'Charlie. It's too late," Venomm said. "You're no match for Malice, and Wakanda has already chosen another leader."

"Malice?" T'Challa laughed. "I used to believe that N'Jadaka was my brother," T'Challa said. He stood in front of Monica with his arms spread and his fists balled. Even in the dark, the Panther King's armor glowed at the edges. "He lied to me. He could have lied to you as well."

"Oh, you won't be laughing for long, black cat!" Malice said, spinning her skull-faced spear. Venomm chuckled and hissed behind her, burrowing the pistol's barrel deeper into Taku's chin.

T'Challa watched them carefully in the dark. If he had taken all the Heart-Shaped Herb, he would be able to see Malice and Venomm as clearly in the darkness as in a fully lit room. Still, even without the full power of the Heart-Shaped Herb, T'Challa saw well enough. He sensed them as well, which was even better. Still holding Zatama hostage, Malice ran at T'Challa, while Venomm put the gun barrel to Taku's temple.

"Killmonger saved us," Malice said. "Your precious Wakanda didn't lift a finger." She tossed Zatama like a sack of yams, then raised her hand and brandished the skull-adorned spear above her head. "He gave us power." Twirling her black-bladed weapon, she leapt at T'Challa, swinging the spear at his face. He dodged the slash and blocked Malice's boot right before it kicked him in the mouth.

Monica called T'Challa's name as he drove Malice backwards with his own flurry of punches and kicks, flying knees and elbows. Malice blocked all T'Challa's advances, then swung the spear's skull end at T'Challa's head. Metal and wind sang above his head. The skulls spat fire, along with a vaporous cloud that sizzled as it dissipated inches from his face.

"Killmonger has corrupted half of Wakanda," T'Challa said. "In turn, something vile and unspeakable has corrupted him." The Black Panther pounced forward and pivoted on his hand to kick with both feet.

Malice parried T'Challa's feet with her spear, but the Panther King punched her with his other hand. He followed with a crushing blow, a fist in her stomach. Malice doubled over; her eyes went wide as the air rushed from her lungs. A string of blood flew from her mouth. The Black Panther landed on the balls of his feet, waiting to land the final blow.

"How did you disrupt our security?" T'Challa grabbed Malice's throat and raised the Death Regiment soldier so her feet were kicking in the air. "*How?*" T'Challa roared.

Malice grunted and wrapped her legs around the Black Panther's neck. As she twisted, he felt the muscles tighten and squeeze. Before he could react to the blur wrapping around his back, Malice landed behind the Panther King and drove her vibranium spearhead through his panther suit, driving through his flesh.

T'Challa heard raised voices outside the royal palace. An explosion sent chunks of wall and broken statue flying across the room. The blast buried Venomm and Taku in piles of rubble. W'Kabi, the Shield of Wakanda, stepped through a huge gaping hole in the wall, his iron and vibranium spear slung over his shoulder. Venomm crawled around the rubble until he found Taku's service pistol. The snake charmer fell on his back, aimed the gun at W'Kabi.

"I told them to kill you." The Security Chief pointed his spear at Venomm. The silver-black blade pulsed with gleaming streaks of purple.

Wide-eyed and trembling, Venomm fired the gun at the mass of muscle charging him like a jet-black rhino—but missed. Taku jumped out of the way and Venomm threw the gun just before W'Kabi hacked the firearm in half, with purple and black flames trailing the vibranium spearhead. The snake charmer fell on his back. W'Kabi pressed a shiny, black boot into his chest, watching him squirm and struggle until W'Kabi wedged the spear tip against the worn nub that used to be a nose.

"Those burning villages, the death of our griot, G'Sere, the assault on Warrior Falls—that was your work, outworlder." W'Kabi pulled at Venomm's nostril with the tip of the spearhead.

"No, W'Kabi! He is our prisoner." Taku grabbed W'Kabi's arm, restraining him and whispered in the Security Chief's ear. "He has information that we need."

"Forget his information," W'Kabi answered with a growl. "The penalty for attacking Wakanda is death."

Malice planted her heels and spun her spear above her head. Blood ran down the side of her mouth, but her eyes glowed with the same red fire that pulsed and flickered inside the skulls at the base of her spear. Malice drew her arm back and hurled the flaming weapon at the Black Panther.

T'Challa caught the spear just before the blade pierced his mask. He grimaced as the edges broke through his vibranium gloves, digging through his palm and the undersides of his fingers.

"Only fools and elders believe in kings and gods they can't see." Malice grunted as she drove the spear through T'Challa's grip.

The blood from his lacerated hands ran down his arms. Malice was one of the strongest opponents he had ever faced. T'Challa held onto the spearhead with one hand, grabbed the shaft of the spear with the other.

"I have questions for you, Malice," T'Challa said. "The vibranium in your spear, where did it come from?"

"You speak as if Killmonger has stolen something," she said, her voice full of contempt. "He is the true avatar. Everything in Wakanda belongs to him, including your miserable life." Malice gritted her teeth and struggled to push her spear through T'Challa's hands.

"You are out of options," T'Challa said. "You must return to N'Jadaka and report your failure. Tell him the Black Panther lives!"

Malice stared into the Black Panther's eyes for another moment before releasing her weapon and running toward a nearby window. The Black Panther hurled the spear past Malice and shattered the glass, allowing Malice to leap out into the night.

CHAPTER NINE

BROKEN SPEARS, BROKEN TRUST

A WEEK after Malice's assault on the royal palace, Kantu crouched in the brown grass and stared at the charging rhinoceros. Concealed by the deep golden brush, he had placed himself directly in the charging rhino's path. Nine years old, still a boy, he gripped a dagger he found while playing along a riverbank. With the weapon in his hand, Kantu felt like a warrior.

He watched as the men of his village circled the stampeding rhino. Two of the villagers held a metallic net spread between them like a huge blanket. Swinging poison-tipped spears, others poked and taunted the charging beast, but most ran from the creature.

The rhino had jet-black eyes that glowed red around the edges. It stomped and swung its huge twin horns, silver and shiny. Kantu had never seen a rhino with silver horns, and he had never seen one this close to his village. Mostly the rhinos hung around Lake Nyanza, playing in the water and grazing in the nearby grasslands.

Kantu had never before seen a rhinoceros attack without being provoked. This one was found running wild at the edge of his parents' farmland, destroying crops and chasing the farmers out of the fields.

To no avail they had tried appeasing the rhino with yams and stalks of grain. Now Kantu gripped his black knife, hoping the beast would run near and give him the opportunity to slow it down by wounding its belly. The adults could handle the animal from there.

Kantu felt the breath rising and falling in his small chest, the sweat gathering on his forehead, around his back and skinny arms. The rhinoceros was almost upon him. The boy gripped the blade and prepared for the beast's charge.

The rhino's skin, even on its underside, rose in thick plates that looked impenetrable. Gripping the black knife like some touchstone that would tether him to reality, Kantu trembled and stared up with wide determined eyes, caught in the charging rhino's shadow.

At first Kantu thought a missile had struck the rhinoceros, but the projectile formed into black arms and legs, the unmistakable mask of His Majesty, King T'Challa. Awestruck, Kantu watched King T'Challa and the rhinoceros tumble and crash into an acacia tree, destroying a metal shed. Pressed between the rhinoceros and the remains of the shed, T'Challa shook his head and lumbered to his feet.

The rhinoceros galloped around the clearing of battered trees and boxes and charged the Panther King, its black eyes filled with unbridled rage. The king stood his ground, welcomed the rhinoceros with open arms. Just before the rhinoceros hit him, the Black Panther grabbed its horn and swung onto the rhino's back. With the Panther King atop its muscular shoulders, the rhinoceros bucked and twisted. The beast rolled across the ground to free itself without success. It ran into Wangari trees, slammed itself into an outcrop of stones. The rhinoceros and T'Challa thundered across a small stream. Throughout the ruckus the Black Panther held on. He whispered in the beast's ear and patted its side as it ran in ragged circles.

"Calm down, my friend," the Panther King said. "You are safe here. Remember, the lands you destroy belong to good people, those who require the bounty of Wakanda and the gifts of Bast to survive. Just like you."

Purple and silver light pulsed through the Black Panther's suit. The vibranium fabric absorbed the kinetic power created by the stampeding beast, the crashing sheds, the falling trees, the villagers scrambling for safety. T'Challa held onto the rhino as the suit turned the vibrations into an energy field, a brilliant film that throbbed and hummed, as it expanded around the rhino. He leapt from the rhino's back and watched the beast pace inside the energy bubble, examining its new confines for some means of escape. The rhino rammed the bubble, but the impact sent the beast flying backward. Stunned, the animal finally lay on its side, its belly rising and falling with each heavy breath.

The Black Panther heard Monica call. He turned and spotted her walking toward him, from the wheat-brown farmland and tilled fields that stretched toward a row of quaint and colorful ranch-style homes. A child half her height held her hand by the fingers, pulled her toward the Panther King and the captured rhino.

"You can't leave him trapped like that, T," Monica said as she stood beside T'Challa. Clearly their short excursion to see Alkama Fields, Wakanda's fertile farmlands, was going to be more dramatic than the couple planned. "What are you going to do with it?"

"This animal is under some form of mind control," T'Challa said, pointing at the rhino. "That red light shining in its eyes: something is driving this poor creature mad. This is N'Jadaka's work, but I can fix it. I must."

The rhino stumbled to its feet, rammed the energy bubble and fell again, this time to sleep. T'Challa wondered if his own downfall had finally come. Would he stumble and collapse, destroying his father's legacy?

Where are you, N'Jadaka? T'Challa wondered how Killmonger had managed to avoid detection in the month since their fight atop Warrior Falls while weaponizing everything in Wakanda, turning the country's greatest resources against the throne.

In fact, it seemed N'Jadaka had come very close to replicating vibranium. T'Challa's lab tests on the weapons taken from Malice and the augmented scales that armored Venomm's python revealed a substance that evoked much of the induction properties of vibranium, while proving to be just as strong. *If not stronger,* T'Challa worried.

He suspected N'Jadaka had discovered a method for synthesizing the Heart-Shaped Herb as well, which might explain the host of superhumans assembled under his command—Venomm, Malice, and the Death Regiments who had attacked Monica, Griot G'Sere, and Birnin Okan Odo. N'Jadaka must have ingested the concoction before their fight at Warrior Falls, making him more arrogant than ever. The samples of N'Jadaka's DNA that T'Challa had gathered from his own wounds only bolstered his suspicions. He had observed the synthesized substance through his own microscope in his labs, watched it glow and swim across a pristine glass slide.

The Black Panther entered the sonic bubble and patted the snoring rhino. Loud rumbles flew from the beast's nostrils, lifting its side in long steady rhythms.

"All it needs is a baby bottle and a blanket," Monica said and laughed, holding on to Kantu. She hummed to him, as he wrapped his arms around her and rested his cheek against her hip.

"You know that's a vibranium dagger," T'Challa said to Kantu, pointing at the black-and-silver-tinged blade. He pondered its origin. No one would willingly leave such a weapon, even if they dropped it.

"Kantu," a woman called from behind them, her voice harsh, authoritative.

T'Challa and Monica turned to see a yellow-robed woman running toward them. Even from a distance, the woman's hostility shone through her eyes, her pursed mouth, the rigidness in her outstretched arms and rod-like back. A short man with brown skin and a bald head strolled behind the woman. T'Challa saw excitement and relief beaming from a smile that consumed the man's entire face, the smile of a man preparing to meet his king.

"Kantu, get over here, now," the woman commanded, adjusting her yellow matching gele.

Monica released the boy, extended her hand to shake the woman's. Her handshake refused, Monica used her open palms to cover her heart.

"You must be this brave young man's mother," Monica said politely.

"And father!" the bald man said, interrupting. "Thank you, My King! Thank you for saving my son and our humble farm." He clasped his hands and bent down to kneel.

"Thank Bast, M'Jumbak," the Panther King said. "Fortunately, her avatar happened to be nearby." He surveyed the damage caused by the charging rhinoceros. Felled trees and metal sidings from broken shelters were strewn across the farmland.

"Your Majesty, you—you know my name?" M'Jumbak's eyes grew as wide and dreamy as his awestruck voice. His wife shook her head, smiling beside him.

"Everyone knows the greatest farmer in Alkama Fields." T'Challa patted the man's back and laughed. "The greatest farmer in the world and his gorgeous wife, Karota, whose beauty and cleverness are unrivaled throughout all of Wakanda. For you have made this fertile land bountiful indeed."

The Panther King bowed.

Karota accepted the compliment with a reserved smile. "Thank you, My King," she said. "Thank you for saving my boy. I don't know what we would have done if you weren't here to help us."

"I would have taken the rhino by myself," Kantu said. "I would have knocked it out and given it to the king to show my loyalty." The boy growled at Monica's side and made gestures like a Birnin Zana wrestler. "One day, I am going to join the Taifa Ngao and protect Wakanda from the bad guys trying to destroy our land, like Killmonger. Maybe one day I will be the Shield."

Killmonger's name turned M'Jumbak's gaze into downcast fear and shame. Karota side-eyed Monica, wrapped her arms around her son, and dragged the protesting child toward a small farmhouse rising in the distance, past rows and rows of golden corn and wheat.

"I am sorry, My King. Kids have such wild imaginations." Now M'Jumbak smiled nervously as he scooted away from his King, taking Karota's lead.

T'Challa watched the husband and wife carry their child back to their farmhouse, their fields, and their good life together. The thought made him pull Monica to his side. He wondered if his Harlem city girl would ever embrace the other side of the ocean, even in a golden city, even with the king who adored her.

"Did you see the way she looked at me? She's not feeling me. Just like everybody else in this country." Monica sighed and rested her cheek against T'Challa's chest.

"My people are wary of outsiders, I will admit, especially out here near the borders—but our sovereignty has been tested many times." T'Challa rubbed Monica's hair, smooth against her head, with the back of his hand. He stared at the couple disappearing into the distance and the quaint farmhouse—shining bright orange against the blue horizon.

Back in her yard, Karota now spoke loudly and brazenly, unaware of the Black Panther's enhanced hearing.

"Did you see our king cavorting with that—that *outworlder*?" Karota growled.

"You will not disrespect our king, woman. He saved our farm and our lives." M'Jumbak spoke in hushed tones, his breath heavy with the walk back to their farmhouse. "Besides, he remembered our names, Karota. The king knows who we are."

"What do you expect? He's the king," Karota responded with a dismissive tone. "He is privy to information concerning all of Wakanda's citizens. And it is true, we have done well," she said with a satisfied smile. "He probably researched our names while he was riding that rhino."

"As soon as I am old enough, I am going to pledge my service to the Shield of Wakanda!" Kantu's voice bubbled with youthful energy.

"And with that outworlder on hand, he wonders why half the kingdom has lost its mind. It's a shame. King T'Chaka must be turning in his grave."

T'Challa had known Karota and M'Jumbak since he was a child. His father kept track of the most efficient agriculturalists in the kingdom, and he always spoke highly of them. "Farmers are Wakanda's future. Even the greatest cooking pot cannot produce food," King T'Chaka would say.

Karota kept their family together, long respected for running the farm's logistics. M'Jumbak supervised the fields and drove the harvests to the open markets in Birnin Zana. Smiling M'Jumbak: his reputation as a salesman had traveled far and wide throughout the kingdom.

T'Challa pulled Monica closer, wrapped her in his arms. He promised himself that he would make a suitable home for his queen in Wakanda. All they needed was a little time.

I am the king. He caught himself before he spoke aloud, holding Monica close.

"Is there any place in the world that's safe?" she asked, her voice filled with foreboding.

T'Challa stared at the rows of maize and wheat, yams and cassava. His mind took him back to Harlem. He heard Monica singing, saw N'Jadaka smiling. The night the Panther King had escorted his greatest enemy into his own backyard. The deaths, the burning and the bloodshed were borne from T'Challa's decisions. He closed his eyes and took in Monica's scent—as much as his lungs would allow.

The ride back to Birnin Zana was quiet. T'Challa thought it would be an uncomfortable ride, but Monica snuggled next to him.

"It's your queen-to-be," she sang comically before the two fell over each other laughing.

Wakanda raced by the window, a series of orange fields, brown savannahs, and rising hills, all yielding to a gilded city, a shiny pot of burnished illumination. Daylight filled the window with a warmth that had always comforted T'Challa. He turned to Monica and found his love dressed like an angel in cascading sun rays.

T'Challa and Monica were soon rushed into the vast retinue of civil servants, soldiers, and Dora Milaje. Monica hated the way T'Challa's Taifa Ngao guards always looked around her and never directly at her, unlike the Dora Milaje. None of them spoke to Monica outside of the formalities they owed T'Challa.

Over the past month, however, Monica had grown accustomed to T'Challa's *concomitants*. The word had irritated her when T'Challa had first used it in reference to the young, powerful women who guarded him night and day.

Why don't you just say companions? Monica had asked. *Because they are not my companions,* T'Challa had said. *You are.* It wasn't long before she understood. T'Challa was telling the truth. What they experienced in Harlem was real. Their love was real.

Inside the palace, T'Challa took Monica to a huge sitting room filled with embroidered couches and soft carpet that fluffed five inches high. Everyone from dignitaries, councilors, and the Dora Milaje milled about the parlor. Spread throughout were huge columns decorated with sculpted panthers. T'Challa and Monica sat on a black couch gilded with glittering thread, bejeweled with polished vibranium.

"Our throne, my queen." T'Challa bowed and showed Monica to the black and gold sofa.

"I'm no queen," Monica said, her lips curved into a bow. "I'm more interested in working for the people than ruling them." She gave T'Challa a sly smile. "Let me sit in your lap."

T'Challa blushed, but he did not resist. When she kissed him, the Panther King forgot about his pained spirit.

Monica leaned against T'Challa, her fingers tracing his jaw. "I told you," she said. "Look around. Everybody in this room is wondering why you're with me. All of these beautiful, more-than-worthy elegant women of Wakanda, and you chose a soul singer. Might as well give them a show."

"People stare at you everywhere you go," T'Challa said. "It was just like this back in New York. There's something special about you, Monica."

"This is different, T." Monica playfully punched the Panther King's chest. From the corner of her eye, she saw two of the Dora Milaje move toward the couch, gliding on silent feet until T'Challa made a hand gesture that stopped them and sent the gorgeous pair of killer bodyguards back to their positions standing against the wall.

"See what I mean?" Monica asked. "I'm the poster girl for everything Wakanda hates. You need your people behind you, one hundred percent. All of them. Having me around is weakening your relationship with your country and your kin. I don't want to be responsible for your downfall, T'Challa—or theirs." Her voice went deep and serious.

Before he could respond, an elegantly dressed woman balancing a huge plate loaded with food and drink atop her head entered the parlor—Tanzika, who served the royal family. She kneeled without spilling a drop and presented the spread to her King as a retinue of attendants swept in. One by one, they removed the dishes from the plate atop the woman's head and set the meal on a low-standing table that flanked the black couch.

Tanzika stood, bowed her head, never taking her eyes off the king. She stared at him the way someone might stare at the sun. Unable to look straight on, for all its brilliance; unable to turn away, for all its glory.

"Your Majesty, for dinner this evening we have grilled scallops in white wine, asparagus, plantains seasoned with garlic and pepper, and roast lamb with mint and ginger. I hope you and your..." she paused, "...*guest* enjoy your meal." Tanzika gave a stiff smile that did not meet her eyes. She handed the couple two pieces of heavy flatware wrapped in linen and raffia.

"It would serve you well to remember that Monica Lynne should be treated like any member of the royal family."

"Yes, My King." Tanzika bowed and returned to the commotion floating around the sitting room.

The Panther King focused his enhanced hearing on Tanzika's voice and followed it through the royal palace. He focused on her footsteps first, and the light scratches her feet made, brushing against the white carpet as Tanzika made her way through the crowd. He paid close attention to the rhythm of footsteps. *Swoosh, swoosh. Swoosh, swoosh.* His ear followed until her footsteps clicked against polished marble. T'Challa noted the tapping until it stopped. Then he waited for Tanzika to fill the silence.

"Zatama, why are you standing here by yourself?" Tanzika asked. "Everyone's back in the parlor having fun."

T'Challa clenched his jaw, listened carefully. Monica complimented the food, but T'Challa only half-heard her speak. He furrowed his brow, concentrating his attention on Tanzika and Zatama.

"He actually has her sitting on the throne with him," Tanzika complained. "I can't believe it: an outworlder gallivanting around the royal palace like she owns it. How can we come together as a nation when our king flouts the customs that have kept this country independent and great, truly great for years beyond reckoning?"

"You're like everyone else, Tanzika," Zatama answered. "The only thing you care about is reality television and music videos. For people like you, all of this is a game. But I see the path that Wakanda is taking. If we wage war within our borders, how can we call ourselves a civilized nation?"

"What are we supposed to do? Hand the country over to Killmonger?" Tanzika asked.

"We have become a nation of violence and ignorance, no better than those who claim democracy one day and persecute their people the next. I do not want that for Wakanda, but no one listens to me."

Disappointed in what he overheard, T'Challa stopped listening there. Tanzika and Zatama's conversation worried the Panther King. He did not hear any treachery in their voices, but who was to say that wouldn't change? How long would it be before his followers used his mistakes against him?

Like N'Jadaka, T'Challa said to himself.

OUTSIDE OF Birnin Zana, brilliant yellow light gave way to shadow. Most recently the shadows had given way to fire and suffering. Mere miles from the Great Mound and Warrior Falls, Wakanda's dark region separated the automated wonder of the Golden City from the stretches of brown and green savannah that led to the heart of Alkama Fields. In this darkness lay the abandoned ruins of Birnin Kasuwa and the great Necropolis of Wakanda.

The farmers in Alkama Fields were all familiar with the ruins of the city Ulysses Klaw had invaded. A place of heartache and destruction, Birnin Kasuwa was abandoned after the war, save for a lone memorial near the ruins left to mark its memory. The road to the old commercial center stood outside Wakanda's ancient burial grounds. Some elders believed the city should never have been built there, so close to the burial grounds of the nation's dead. The farmers hated driving through the Necropolis, but the trek around the wasteland and the great cemetery cost an entire day of travel.

M'Jumbak had heard stories of the old ruins and the Necropolis his entire life, but the horror of the old tales was nothing compared to the real world. Not for M'Jumbak. As a boy, he used to laugh at the frightened children and the superstitious elders afraid to venture through the Necropolis at night. In his youth M'Jumbak and his friends would play raiders in the burial grounds, and as the companions got older, they would venture into the Necropolis to hang out and drink homemade wine.

M'Jumbak stared at the cemetery. Half of his mind went back to his childhood. The other half shook him away from his reveries, with the thought of Karota and the curry goat and grilled fish waiting for him on the kitchen table. He gripped his shirt pocket. The sale at the market in Birnin Zana had been profitable that day. M'Jumbak parked the hovercraft and the empty trailer that had carried his harvest to the markets. He thanked Bast for sending her avatar and saving his crops, as he slammed the truck door and stood before the City of the Dead, where generations of Wakandans were buried, including their kings. M'Jumbak entered the burial site and leaned against a tall headstone that had been planted in the ground for at least a millennium, maybe two.

He pulled a brown bag from his pocket, produced a short, stout bottle, and held it up to the moonlight. M'Jumbak admired the green glass on the bottle and the way it caught the failing beams cascading over the cemetery. He chuckled and unscrewed the top. Only a few extra minutes, but that's all he needed for a couple of quick swigs. Then he would get back on the road and head to the house. Karota was waiting, probably calling, but the reception in the Necropolis was terrible. The thought made M'Jumbak giggle with mischievous glee.

"To you, my dear king." M'Jumbak raised the bottle. "Thank you for blessing us with your presence. I don't care what they say. I knew that you would never leave us." M'Jumbak took a long guzzle and winced with the heat of the liquid burning his mouth and his belly. He raised the bottle once again. "To your woman, Monica. I'm glad that you have found love. Who cares *where* you found it?" M'Jumbak's head wobbled as he professed his allegiance. His elbow slipped from the headstone, and he almost fell, but he caught himself.

The noises made M'Jumbak believe that his stomach was growling. He hadn't eaten all day, since before he left the farm and headed for the markets in the Golden City. Also, he knew that Karota had prepared his favorite meal. She always cooked after they argued, and they argued a lot. He knew that they would eat first, put Kantu to bed, then the real making up would begin. This thought also made him smile.

But the second noise was much louder. It sounded like gears grinding, like some half-metal beast waking from a century-long slumber. He heard stones and dirt shifting. He could have sworn the ground beneath his feet was breaking apart. M'Jumbak looked at the bottle and flung it to the side. Now the darkness grew closer, inched forward, closed a slow circle around him. The noises clarified, took the shape of hurtful moaning, half-human and evil.

The dirt crumbled under M'Jumbak's feet. Broken rock and soil, hissing through the cracks, accentuated the moans and the angry growls that grew louder. The noises came from the cracking earth separating beneath him. Staring at the breaking ground, he saw the first fingers scratch through the surface. M'Jumbak stumbled backward. Terror spread across his face as a skeletal hand burst through the ground. The wiry fingers wiggled and curled in the night air.

To M'Jumbak's horror, a skeletal arm broke through the dirt, then two arms and a skull, beaming like the moon. Red flames lit the eye sockets and the open jawbone. Bony hands pulled at the dirt as the skull screamed its way above ground. M'Jumbak took another step and slipped on the spilled bottle. He fell on his back and elbows, watched the cadaver free itself from the grave. Blood-red fire burned where the cadaver's heart would have thumped, had the skeleton been dressed in flesh. The jawbone stretched and cracked. The monster scowled as it crawled out of the hole.

"Kantu!" M'Jumbak whimpered. "Karota!" Tears ran down his cheeks. He pictured his wife on the porch of their farmhouse, waiting. One hand on the green post that they had shared for twenty-five years. In his mind, he watched her stare at the fields and the distant darkness that should have produced her husband hours ago.

Another hand broke the ground and grabbed M'Jumbak's wrist. The farmer yelped and snatched his arm away. Before that cadaver could climb from the ground, three more monsters composed of bones and shadows started their climb to the Earth's surface.

She'll think I got sidetracked, drinking or gambling. She won't wait up. She'll put Kantu to bed, and my boy will cry himself to sleep, believing his father does not love him.

The thought coupled with the sight of the ghouls falling on top of him drove M'Jumbak to madness. Something broke in his mind, and he took the only chance he saw for escape. He fled through his screams, followed his ravings until they led him deep inside himself. He felt the first cadaver bite his face, but hardly felt the second bite around his throat. As the enchanted skeletons pinned the farmer to the ground, all the sensation in his arms and legs escaped. While the skeletons bit his flesh, the farmer screamed until he couldn't hear himself, until his voice turned to blood song.

○————○

BACK IN the royal palace, T'Challa clapped as a troupe of young griots entertained the royal court with ancient poems and love songs dedicated to Bast. In the song, a faithful king pledged his love to the Panther God, praised Bast's beauty, and promised to spend a lifetime—a thousand lifetimes if necessary—to win Bast's love.

"This song is considered taboo to some of my people," T'Challa said. He rubbed his finger against Monica's chin and stared into her eyes. He felt the entire room watching.

"Taboo or sacrilegious?" Monica raised her eyebrow. "I guess it depends on perspective, you know. Your people are very protective of your culture. I understand." She paused for a deep breath.

Monica sat up, wiped a lonely tear with her finger. When T'Challa reached for her, she shook her head and said no, pursed her lips and stared at the griot.

"I'm all right," she said. "There's something in this music. I've never heard anything like it in my life."

"Most of these songs have been written and rewritten over thousands of years." T'Challa turned to the griots playing and singing. "They change the words and add their own parts, but somehow the crux of the song has stood the test of time. A warrior dedicating his life to his Goddess."

The entrance at the far end of the parlor slid open. Rifle strapped to his shoulder, Councilor Zatama stormed into the parlor. Dark, glowing eyes followed the royal councilor as he strode toward T'Challa. Hands rushed to sheathed blades, but the poised Dora Milaje waited for their king's signal. Zatama stood before T'Challa and Monica. The councilor's face was screwed into a bitter scowl. When he pulled the rifle from his shoulder, every blade in the room pointed toward him. T'Challa raised an open palm, a gesture for the Dora Milaje to sheath their weapons.

"This weapon was designed here in Birnin Zana," Zatama said. The councilor flung the rifle to the carpet. Anger rose from his heaving chest to his furrowed brow. "Somehow Killmonger has accessed our weapons supply." Hesitating, he raised his head to meet the gaze of his king. "Treachery has wormed its way into Bashenga's house. W'Kabi wants to hang Venomm and Malice right now. We must find an alternative to your civil war. All this bloodshed and infighting. We have disgraced Wakanda before the Panther God. We must change our course or risk losing everything."

"That rifle... is it Wakandan design or a replica?" the Panther King asked, though he already knew the answer. He paid close attention to Zatama's every word, Zatama's every move.

"It looks just like..." Councilor Zatama stared at the rifle lying at his feet. His voice quaked and his stammering revealed his confusion.

"I did not ask you to tell me what the weapon looks like." T'Challa's voice was stoic, but his expression was grim as stone.

Zatama looked at his king for a moment, then bent to pick up the weapon. He turned the rifle over in the light, rubbed his finger along the metal housing.

"I—I don't know, Your Majesty," Zatama said. Head lowered, his chest sank in shame. "I will take it to the lab for further testing."

The Panther King nodded, but his Kimoyo beads lit his wrist and buzzed, each bead a different color, before he could offer Zatama any encouragement. He tapped one of the beads, brought up a hologram that lit his palm, the illumination spilling between his fingers. A picture of Taku, solemn and grave, stared at T'Challa from the hologram.

"My lord, a farmer from Alkama Fields is here, urgently seeking your counsel."

M'Jumbak, T'Challa thought. *Why has he come to the royal palace in the middle of the night?* The idea filled the Panther King with apprehension. Worry that he could not show in either his voice or his face.

"Good, Taku. Bring him to me right away." T'Challa turned to Monica. She sighed and stroked the back of his head.

"Looks like your job is never complete," she said. The worry on her face made T'Challa take her hand.

"This farmer is not a he, my lord," Taku said.

M'Jumbak's wife Karota ran into the parlor, escorted by Taku and a group of stone-faced Taifa Ngao.

"My Lord, My Lord," Karota cried out and flung herself at her king's feet, her eyes filled with tears.

Monica looked taken aback. Tears filled her eyes, and she stretched her hand toward the woman who had only hours before shown the Harlem native so much hatred and xenophobia. Taku reached for Karota, but T'Challa shook his head. The communications chief nodded and returned to his place behind the sobbing farmer.

"It's M'Jumbak. He left for the market not long after you saved our farm—even though you said you would reimburse us for our damages. You had already done so much. He said he wanted to do his part. He took a shipment of crops to the markets here in the Golden City, but he never returned. No matter where he goes or what he's doing, he always returns in time for dinner, and he always puts our son to bed." Karota held her forehead as the words rushed from her mouth.

T'Challa knelt beside Karota, held her hands, helped the farmer's wife to her feet. She fell against him and cried.

"He went to the burial ground to drink. I know it," Karota said. "He always goes there. He kept going even after the war and all this Killmonger nonsense started. I told him it wasn't safe, not anymore, but he wouldn't listen."

"Should we send a search party, Your Majesty?" Councilor Zatama said. He bowed his head, slung the rifle over his shoulder.

"No, Zatama, I will go," T'Challa said. "I am Wakanda's protector. M'Jumbak is one of its greatest and most loyal subjects." He patted the woman's back. "I will find your husband, Karota. Until then, go home to your son and rest." The Black Panther turned to Monica.

"I will return soon. Until then, the Dora Milaje will attend to your safety," T'Challa said. He managed a weak smile and took her into his arms.

"Be careful, T," she said, staring up into his eyes. She hugged T'Challa's neck, shuddered against his body.

OUTSIDE, THE cold pressing his face and arms, the Black Panther left the Golden City on a black motorcycle, racing against the nightfall, racing against the rage burning his heart. The high rises and the luxury cars of the Golden City flashing beside him filled T'Challa with a sense of accomplishment and purpose. When he reached the stretches of dilapidated buildings and ruined streets that bordered the Necropolis, T'Challa slowed the sleek, black motorcycle to a purring crawl.

Before the foreign invasions that sent T'Chaka to the ancestral plane, Birnin Kasuwa had served as one of Wakanda's main hubs, a distribution center that stored, refined, and shipped goods and precious materials throughout the countryside.

That was before Ulysses Klaw. The "modern colonial," they had called him. Klaw had paid special attention to Birnin Kasuwa, hoping to cut out Wakanda's heart just as the villain had cut off Wakanda's head when he murdered its king. Many of Klaw's victims had lived in or near the district and the Necropolis. A monument was placed in their memory, a living wall shaped like a chain link, or two great serpents facing each other. The victims had been captured and forced to work in the mines surrounding the Great Mound—forced to steal Wakanda's precious vibranium for the empire's enemy. Others were used as human shields in Klaw's short-lived assault on Wakanda. Fewer still were the Wakandans who aided Klaw willingly.

After T'Challa's first victory against Ulysses Klaw, his uncle, N'Baza, had ruled with a heavy hand. All Klaw's collaborators were either exiled or executed, depending on their crimes and level of allegiance to the invader. The memory of that era left a visible mark of grief on the land.

The stretch of abandoned black buildings, this wasteland between Birnin Zana and the Necropolis, now looked nothing like the vibrant center it had once been, flourishing with commerce all those years ago. The land had seen the worst of the Purifying. Many of the exiled—and even some of the executed—had been innocent, forced by rifle barrel to work for Klaw in the mines.

N'Jadaka had been one of the latter. Now the land was home to many ghosts.

The bleak nightscape, the ruined buildings near the Necropolis, reminded T'Challa of how rotten and twisted N'Jadaka's heart had become. The wind whistled between the dilapidated warehouses, and T'Challa could have sworn it carried a distant scream. Perhaps a child or a denizen suffering on some distant shore.

He rode slowly through the ghost town until he found M'Jumbak's pickup truck parked in front of the old cemetery, walking past a fountain that looked decades deep in disuse.

T'Challa stood before a pair of huge pylons that flanked the open gate. One was carved into the shape of a woman's body, a panther's face, robed and hooded. The panther woman offered a basket. *Filled with the waters of Djalia,* T'Challa thought. The other column was carved into a panther-man with a bare chest, armed with a raised hammer. *Building the road to the ancestral plane,* he mused again. He followed a set of footprints that started near the abandoned truck and led him into the burial ground, where only names forgotten by the world rested.

Moving slowly, the Black Panther padded into the cemetery. The deeper he went, the more he regretted coming to the Necropolis alone. Something about the burial ground unnerved him. The ground felt hollow and restless, shifting and sliding under his feet. He stared at the leaning headstones and rocks growing from the barren earth and sparse weeds. Before long, he spotted a lumpy shadow sprawled between a circle of tombstones. T'Challa stood over the pile of twisted limbs, clenched his jaw at the sight of the lifeless eyes that stared back, piercing the Panther King's soul.

T'Challa remembered the light shining in M'Jumbak's smile. The farmer's handshake had been firm, but his entire body had trembled when he greeted T'Challa. M'Jumbak had watched his King with unabashed pride, even as his wife muttered in his ear and his eager son tugged on his tunic.

T'Challa kept that light, those smiling eyes in his heart as he crouched beside M'Jumbak's mangled body. The ground shifted and broke apart. Hands and faces punched and butted their way out of the dirt and into the open air. Skulls shorn of skin, reduced to strips of rotten flesh, screamed and hissed at the Black Panther. He brandished his silver-black claws and found himself surrounded by rotting cadavers. Stretching their mouths and arms, the skeletal ghouls moaned and lumbered toward T'Challa.

He grabbed M'Jumbak, hoisting the fallen farmer over his shoulder. He remembered Karota's tearful, red eyes and her pleading. The Panther King had promised to return M'Jumbak home to his family. He would not leave this man, who had been filled with so much warmth and life, with these decayed agents of death.

When T'Challa pulled at M'Jumbak's tunic, the broken bones piled inside shifted, rearranging themselves. A crooked hand grabbed T'Challa's wrist, the grip even stronger than it had been earlier that day. The bones in M'Jumbak's neck popped and cracked as the head twisted to face his back. The eyes were filled with black fire, burning the farmer's face from the inside and distorting his smile into an evil grin. The undead farmer opened his mouth with a rattling growl, his jawbone ripping apart.

T'Challa recoiled from M'Jumbak instinctively. Repulsed, bewildered, tossed into utter despair, he watched M'Jumbak rise, bones snapping in and out of their sockets, growling at his feet. Animated cadavers rose from the broken earth. Long, fleshless fingers, hard as gravestones, locked around the Black Panther's arms and legs. Wakanda's king struggled as skeletal hands wrapped around his throat, squeezing the indestructible metal girding his windpipe.

One skeletal ghoul—taller and bulkier than the rest but fleshless all the same—stood over the struggling Panther King. Bones wrapped in darkness shaped into muscle, fire burning in the cadaver's chest and eyes. The misshapen union of shadow and bone looked down at T'Challa as if the specter was the king, and T'Challa was nothing more than a vagrant, a helpless insect struggling for one last moment in the world of the living.

"The Panther King comes to the Necropolis seeking the Death

Regiments. Well, T'Challa, here we are. Are we everything you expected?" The cadaver raised its bony palm wrapped in shadows and flame. The flames in the cadaver's eyes, its jagged voice, and the incessant moaning of its undead companions filled the night. A foul mist spread through the graveyard, enveloping T'Challa in fetid air, filled with sickness and hopelessness.

The cadaver rested its fleshless knuckles against bone-round hips covered in dark haze. It raised its head to the starless night and laughed with all the madness and maleficence of a bloodthirsty, deranged despot. The monster raised a hand engulfed in flames. Streams of fire spread up the cadaver's forearms. The undead horde tightened their grips on T'Challa's limbs, their own hands tattered with ribbons of rotting flesh.

"The Necropolis belongs to me. I am Baron Macabre, and this is my dominion." Composed of waxy flesh, exposed bones, and shadows, the cadaver wore shredded crimson rags around his bony skull and scrawny waist. He held his burning hands over the struggling Panther King.

As the flames grew, T'Challa felt his skin burning inside his armor—like bare flesh set to an open blaze. The panther suit was designed to withstand many things, but not psychic attacks. He clenched his teeth and groaned, refused to scream, refused submission to the agents of death, agents of N'Jadaka.

"Ah, yes, you feel it! The Black Panther feels pain. There is pain in death, so much pain." Baron Macabre leaned towards T'Challa. "Where is your Panther God now? I feel your life force leaving your essence in her silence." Baron Macabre laughed, balled his fist. The flames shot from his eyes, surged around his forearms. The fire spread from the Baron's hands, consuming the Black Panther's body.

This time T'Challa did scream and writhe, struggling against the vise-like grips of the cadavers. With the last vestiges of his sanity fleeing quickly through the flames and the searing agony, T'Challa watched the disjointed body of M'Jumbak crawl on broken limbs that moved like spider legs, until it sat next to the Baron, nuzzling its cheek against the Baron's legs.

More hands and moaning faces jutted from the ground, wrapping themselves around T'Challa's chest and torso. T'Challa felt himself being pulled into the ground, but it was too hard to concentrate beyond the burning sensation that ate its way through his entire body, through the sound of his own screams. Through the flashing delirium, the fever-pitched visions sped before his eyes like an endless reel of microfiche. T'Chaka smiling and dying. Klaw laughing and dying. G'Sere singing Wakanda's history and dying. The countless, faceless villagers cheering for their king and burning and dying.

As the air filled with char and ash, the zombies began to sink, and he knew that he was sinking into the ground with them, being dragged into the world beneath the shadows. T'Challa did not fight. The ground beneath him felt cool. A part of him even welcomed the shadows. There were no enemies in the darkness underneath. No responsibilities. There was only darkness, and after that, nothing.

Only rest. Only peace.

IN THE palace, Zatama sat in his bedroom at a desk covered with books and a rainbow assortment of Kimoyo beads. He rubbed his forehead for a moment, took a sip from a large glass of wine, then typed on the Kimoyo tablet resting atop his cluttered desk:

The entire kingdom is losing its mind. No one knows who to trust. Who is loyal to Wakanda? Who is keeping the faith of our beloved Bast? Who has lost their faith and joined Wakanda's greatest enemy? Who among us is in league with the bloodthirsty Killmonger?

I have known W'Kabi most of my life, since the days when he was merely a low-ranking foot soldier in the Taifa Ngao, since my first days as a young councilor on the Court Tribunal. He was always a formidable fighter, but over the years he has sacrificed his humanity.

Now, W'Kabi's mind has been so corrupted by war, fighting and all the senseless killing that has taken place over the last few months, he can no longer discern reality from fantasy. He has become a dangerous man. He is a threat to T'Challa and the entirety of Wakanda. The other night, W'Kabi would have killed Venomm (Horatio) had I not intervened. For a moment, I thought W'Kabi wanted to kill me.

Even worse, our king, our beloved leader who has always been the voice of reason, is losing his sense of balance. Ever since he was a child, tragically forced into the never-ending drama of political intrigue by the murder of his father, our king has always kept a level head. He has always controlled his emotions. As a highly trained scientist, he has always allowed logic to lead him and guide his decision-making. But lately the king has changed. It's as if all the violence and the pressure of ruling has begun to erode his brilliant mind. I knew that something was wrong the minute he stepped off that Quinjet with the foreigner walking beside him, their arms affectionately interlocked. Love can also be a form of madness, a force that throws you off balance. I saw the madness of passion in his eyes, and I see it every time he looks at her. A king needs a queen, I will be the first to admit this, but a king should never lose himself to anything. Not even a woman. He should always protect himself, even from his own heart. Even from the love of his own queen.

I hope that something changes soon, if not, I fear…

Someone knocked on the door, breaking Zatama's concentration. The soft rapping roused him from his troubled writings and his musings, which were even more unsettling. *Why didn't they use the holo buzzer or Kimoyo beads to announce their presence?*

"Who's there?" Zatama asked. He stood in the dim lamplight. The councilor tried his Kimoyo beads, but his tablet powered down to a gray, opaque sheet. Every reset failed to connect, and all he heard was static. Something was blocking the signal.

Who would be so impolite as to come unannounced, knocking at my door?

The first name that crossed his mind was W'Kabi. Zatama sighed. The two old colleagues had unfinished business and much to discuss. For some reason, the automatic latch and slide function failed. *Everything is broken. Broken spears, broken trust,* Zatama mused to himself in exasperation.

He muttered a curse as he headed for the door, his robes swishing as he walked, then he paused. He would have to open it manually. As impatient as the general was, Zatama should have heard W'Kabi's grumbling by now. But oddly, there was only silence in the hall.

Zatama turned back, pulled a vibranium dagger from an engraved leather sheath, mounted on the wall above the iroko wood desk. "I'm ready for you this time, Malice."

He stepped into the living room, as the door opened and hissed, the sound of a whisper, a blade's edge raking stubbled skin.

"Why did you come back?" Zatama said. His voice trembled as he raised the dagger above his head.

But the opened door revealed an empty threshold. Zatama frowned and lowered the dagger. Long ago he had chosen a path of peace. Blades and bullets were not his weapons of choice. Words and reason guided him, and he hoped, compassion. Cautiously, he poked his head into the corridor.

To his surprise, a woman obscured in speed and darkness leapt through the open doorway and tackled the councilor, forcing him back into the palace apartment. She cupped her hand over his mouth, as his eyes widened in shock and recognition, cutting his throat with a silver blade that winked through the dim light.

Blood gushing from his throat, Zatama struggled, gurgling through the hand clamped over his mouth, desperately clawing the carpet, seeking the dagger he dropped when he hit the floor. The killer whispered into Zatama's ear.

"Sorry, friend, but times are changing," she said. "Wakanda is on the verge of a new day. I wish you could live to see it, but we must all make sacrifices for a better nation, a better tomorrow. Killmonger will build the greatest empire in the history of the world. Let that thought comfort you as you journey on to Djalia."

A single tear rolled down Councilor Zatama's face at the sound of the killer's voice. With the final dregs of life spreading across his robe, a dark red river, he raised his hand and raked his nails across

the killer's face.

Eyes glassy and lifeless, there lay Zatama. Blood pooled around his head, a crimson halo.

HAD THE Black Panther not been so consumed by the hands dragging him down into the earth and the searing pain through his suit, he might have felt Zatama's presence leave the physical plane. He might have felt the councilor's life-force ripple out from the Wakandan royal palace and start the fathomless journey to the distant realm of the ancestors.

But T'Challa found himself occupied by his present circumstances—mind, body, and spirit. The more he fought, the more hands he found jutting from the soft soil, pulling at his body, pulling him down, down, down into the soft burial ground. Unseen flames engulfed his body, cooking his internal organs from the inside out.

The burning is all in your mind, the Black Panther thought. *If it was real, my suit would be burning, melting against my skin. If the pain is imaginary, I can control it.*

The task was much easier said than done. Still, T'Challa took a deep breath. He did his best to surrender to the pain and accept the sensation. That was the first step. The second step was to relax his body, allow the cold decaying hands to wrap around him, allow the dirt to cover him. He stared up at the creature who had once been a farmer, who had greeted the Panther King with a handshake and a smile warmer than the noonday sun spreading across the veldt. Now what was left of the poor farmer's body was cold, even though black flames poured from his mouth. Cold flames imbued with the power of death, the power to burn the soul without marking the flesh.

But T'Challa knew the warmth, the healing power of other suns—of love and life itself. The third step was to embrace a power strong enough to conquer death, the force of his own mind and memory.

T'Challa raised his head and met Baron Macabre's gaze. Swift as a shadow, the Black Panther reached out. From somewhere deep within, he found the strength to pull free of the hands and the gnawing mouths dragging him down. With the invisible death flames smoldering inside him, he grabbed the Baron's skeletal wrist, pulling the undead assailant down into the makeshift grave.

Razor-sharp lightning bolts coursed through T'Challa's veins at the Baron's touch. Still, the Panther King pulled until the Baron's face was only a thumbnail's length from his own. The putrid stench of death filled T'Challa's nose and lungs, but he held onto his captive.

"What's the matter?" T'Challa asked as Baron Macabre struggled.

The Black Panther felt the death flames growing inside him, but he resisted the fiery pain, focusing on the memory of Wakanda's golden sun. The psychological pain grew so intense, he wondered if he might sustain physical damage. If so, the sacred Heart-Shaped Herb would heal him. *First, I must make it out of this grave alive*, he thought with no little sense of irony.

Baron Macabre wrestled against T'Challa's grip, his face contorted in desperation. The cadaver sent a bolt of pain so powerful that T'Challa temporarily lost all sense of his surroundings, bringing him to the edge of a dark void where sanity had no authority. Still, he refused to release the Baron. Instead, he flipped the Baron over, breaking the grips of the rotting hands that tugged at his limbs.

In one motion, one moment as still as the cold, bleak night, the Baron was underneath him. Now with his hands wrapped around the Baron's throat, T'Challa began to squeeze.

The malevolent energy that had seared his bones seemed to invigorate the Panther King. He felt the darkness coursing through his chest, flowing into his arms and hands as he sank his claws into the Baron's neck. The bones cracked.

The Baron gasped, surprising T'Challa. *So, the dead breathe*, he thought. With searing pain wrapped around his bones, T'Challa squeezed even harder. He felt the black flames swelling in his entire body, and he knew the fire burning inside was his own rage. That's when T'Challa heard his father's voice speaking gently inside of his mind.

150   *Acknowledge the rage, my son, but never let it consume you.*

T'Challa loosened his grip on the Baron's neck. The cadavers fell on top of him, but now with his own fire blasting through his veins, T'Challa was more than a match for the Baron's undead minions. He fought them off easily, ripping the arm off one cadaver swinging at his head, kicking another so hard that his foot went straight through the cadaver's chest and kicked another zombie in the face.

With the strength of his ancestors and the Heart-Shaped Herb energizing him, the Panther King leapt from the clutches of the moaning zombies and vaulted into the trees overhead.

"Incinerate him! Don't let him escape. Burn his soul to the bone," the Baron commanded.

"Nothing you do can stop the inevitable," T'Challa said. "Your leader will fall, and you with him." Derision filled the Black Panther's voice as he leaped, scrambling across the canopy of trees, making his way toward the graveyard exit. There, Killmonger's Death Regiments were assembled between the pylons, blocking the gateway that separated the world of the living from the kingdom of the dead.

Armed with stolen Wakandan assault rifles—powered by stolen vibranium—the two fools, Tayete and Kazibe, stood with wide, fearful eyes staring into the dark hazy burial site.

"Fancy seeing you two here," T'Challa called out as he flew from the darkness between the Death Regiment's gunfire. With one foot, light and nearly weightless, T'Challa used Tayete's helmet as a stepping-stone to land, catch his balance, and leap away into the night, while the Death Regiments fired their rifles at the escaping target.

Flipping through the air, T'Challa landed on his motorcycle and sped off, a barrage of bullets thundering in his wake. Spurred on by the images of the dead eating away at his consciousness, he made good time on his return to the royal palace. The image of M'Jumbak spitting hellfire from his eyes and mouth tormented T'Challa the most. The Panther King promised himself that he would return to the Necropolis and retrieve M'Jumbak. He would return the farmer's body to his family: Karota and their son, Kantu.

T'Challa remembered Baron Macabre's breath, pungent with the odors of death and evil. He wondered if the zombies were really dead, if he could return the creatures to the world of the living. Maybe there was some way he could return M'Jumbak to his family and restore the peace and sanctity that the farmer had known before Killmonger's violent assaults on Wakanda's outer villages. Anything that would spare him from having to deliver the heartbreaking news.

But T'Challa chased those notions from his mind. He did not wish to instill false hope in himself, and he refused to mislead Karota and Kantu if he could help it. Difficult days lay ahead, for M'Jumbak's family and his own.

He rode past the silent gilded monuments of the Golden City, weaving between the skyscrapers, darting through back streets until he had prepared his words for Karota. When he arrived, he parked his bike in the courtyard behind the royal palace. The scent of wet grass wafted from the river's bank, and T'Challa breathed deeply, taking in the cool, night air.

He needed to see Monica right then. Even though the stench of death clung to his armor, and his muscles still ached from the burning black flames, he needed to see Monica. He needed to hold her, and he needed to be held. He needed to hear her voice and stare into her eyes. He needed her song. More than anything, he needed to curl up next to the light that waxed behind her eyes and her smile. T'Challa wanted something to pull him from the netherworld's border and back into the world of the living. He needed something to remind him that he was alive. That he was a man. That he was worthy to be loved.

T'Challa entered the palace through one of the high windows near the hallway that led to the bedchambers he shared with Monica. He perched on a windowsill while the automatic locks disarmed, and the window opened itself. Even the royal palace had been designed to yield in the presence of its king. T'Challa dipped inside the window and hopped to the floor, thirty feet below. The first thing he noticed was the abnormal amount of foot traffic crisscrossing the hallway. Taifa Ngao officers ran past him.

T'Challa grabbed one of the officers, a wide-eyed foot soldier who immediately kneeled before him.

"What's going on? Why all this commotion?" T'Challa asked.

That's when he heard Monica's voice—distressed. Before the young soldier could answer, T'Challa had released him and started his own race down the hall. His armor dematerialized, revealing a black coat and pants trimmed in heavy embroidery around the sleeves and pants cuffs. The voices grew louder as he approached. The Panther King heard the deep bass of W'Kabi and Adebisi's authoritative bark. The three of them—W'Kabi, Adebisi, and Monica—were arguing.

"Let me go," Monica said. "I don't know what you're talking about."

"You don't know?" W'Kabi asked. "The proof is right here."

"There must be some mistake. Ms. Lynne would never do something like this." Adebisi's familiar gruff echoed through the corridor.

T'Challa turned the corner and found a group of soldiers crowding his door. Taku stared at the ground, eyes lowered in shame. The Panther King saw his Shield, jaws clenched, nostrils flared. It was the look that W'Kabi wore when he wanted to fight. Over the years, T'Challa had seen that face more times than he could count. Adebisi stood before W'Kabi and appeared to be blocking his path. Finally, T'Challa saw Monica. Hands pinned behind her back, she struggled in W'Kabi's grip.

This time, T'Challa could not contain his rage. Rushing past Adebisi, he grabbed W'Kabi's throat, pressed his old friend, his top-ranking general, against the wall, claws extended. T'Challa heard the gasps and felt the shocked eyes staring at him. They bore holes in his back. He heard Monica yelp, a barely audible noise, and shoved past those eyes too ashamed to face him.

"I warned you, W'Kabi," T'Challa said through clenched teeth. "You have mistreated Monica since she arrived, but now let me tell you. For your own safety, this better be the last time I have to say this. Monica is more than my guest. Monica is a part of me, just like my arm, my leg, or my heart."

"T'Challa," Monica called out behind him.

The relief in her voice evident, T'Challa knew that she was crying, even though his back was turned to her. The sadness and the pain in her voice triggered him, but he needed to remain calm. No matter what, he was the king. T'Challa took a deep breath and loosened his fingers from W'Kabi's throat. T'Challa saw rage and fire in W'Kabi's dark eyes as he rubbed the thick welts rising on his neck. The Panther King imagined W'Kabi would have killed him on the spot if he could.

Good, T'Challa thought, furious at all the intrigue and deception that he had encountered since his return. *If you are my enemy, W'Kabi, let it be known.*

"My King, remember your crown," Taku said, his voice filled with worry. He stood next to T'Challa.

"Yes, remember your people, My King," said W'Kabi.

Fury, hot as the Baron's diabolical touch, seared through T'Challa.

W'Kabi stood with his chest out. "A grave misjustice has happened and it is your doing, Your Majesty. You were the one who brought this foreigner into our midst. You allowed her to desecrate our beloved land, our traditions."

T'Challa felt the eyes of his subjects, felt their confusion and revulsion.

"And now you have allowed the unspeakable. This outworlder has spilled blood right here in the royal palace!" W'Kabi was yelling now. Somehow, he had found the courage to raise his voice even higher, step even closer to the Panther King.

"Spilled blood?" T'Challa asked, bristling. The words in connection with Monica's name were ludicrous to him, as was the manner in which W'Kabi spoke to him. It was as if T'Challa had escaped the Baron's clutches only to return to an upside-down world. He could still feel the cold dead hands that had tried to drag him into the sour ground. The cold flames that had burned the Black Panther without leaving any marks on his skin. Not a scar.

But right now, W'Kabi's words hurt more than any of the

undead's flames.

"This foreigner—excuse me, your *guest*—has spilled blood in Wakanda," W'Kabi hissed. He looked at Taku and held out his hand.

Taku handed W'Kabi a dagger, a short blade with intricate runes carved into the hilt. W'Kabi held the blade in the air and allowed the light to run the course of the metal surface. The blade shone, and dried blood coated its surface.

"This must be a mistake," Adebisi said, turning to T'Challa. "Your Majesty, you know Ms. Lynne better than any of us. She would not harm anyone in this palace, not even W'Kabi." She growled when she spoke the Taifa Ngao's name.

"This blade took the life of Zatama. The blood on this blade comes from Zatama's heart," W'Kabi said. "First we lifted the foreigner's fingerprints from the blade. Then we reviewed the footage from the surveillance cameras around Zatama's room, and I saw her with my own eyes. I saw her cover Zatama's mouth and plunge the blade into his chest."

T'Challa felt his world crumble before his eyes, beneath his feet, felt himself sinking down, down, down into a dark, cold place. He could have sworn that the cold, undead hands were pulling him back into oblivion once more, into a hell of his own fashion.

This can't be. No, no, no.

T'Challa turned to Monica. She closed her eyes and lowered her head, as tears streamed down both their cheeks. For the first time since T'Challa had known Monica, she was speechless. In his mind he saw a man smiling, genuine happiness filling his eyes. T'Challa heard the man laughing. T'Challa felt himself falling from the edge of Warrior Falls. The man's name kept repeating in his mind.

N'Jadaka.

T'Challa clenched his teeth. N'Jadaka had taken so much, so quickly. He made a silent promise. N'Jadaka or Killmonger, whatever he called himself, would pay. And he would pay this debt in full.

CHAPTER TEN

WAKING THE DEAD

T'CHALLA STROLLED the gardens behind the royal palace. The path that he walked, paved in lustrous cobblestones, led him to the River of Grace and Wisdom where Monica had found him floating, half-dead, defeated by a man whom he had once called friend and brother. A man he once loved just as much as any family member— as much as his own sister or the memory of a mother that had died bringing him into this troubled world or a king who had died protecting his family and his kingdom.

A cool breeze swept into the garden and took T'Challa's mind back through the open door of memory. Two nights before on the eve of Councilor Zatama's murder, he had stood with Monica beside this very river, held her in his arms, hoping for that moment to never end. T'Challa stared at the blue haze of the morning and sighed. For a moment, he could have sworn that he had caught her scent perfuming the wind. His love had flown with him halfway across the world. She had left her homeland to help him reacquaint himself with his, and now she was a prisoner. T'Challa had promised to protect her and failed.

Lost in reverie, he walked along the bank of the river, unaware of the creature floating beneath the water just behind his heels.

By the time T'Challa saw the fifteen-foot crocodile's explosive launch out of the water, the time for escape had passed. Even with his enhanced reflexes, T'Challa barely had time to catch the jaws of the crocodile before they wrapped around his head. His armor did not have time to materialize fully, so the crocodile's sharp teeth cut his hands.

T'Challa noticed the black eyes filled with the same coldness he had found in the Necropolis burial grounds, as the amphibian had snatched the Panther King into the water. The crocodile spun T'Challa around and around, above and below the surface of the river.

Somehow the Black Panther managed to pull his fragmented thoughts into coherency. His panther suit materialized, but he felt warm blood soaking the inside of his vibranium armor. The crocodile whipped its head back and forth, tossing him like a rag doll.

He wrapped his legs around the crocodile's waist. The strength of the beast surprised T'Challa. He might as well have been wrestling with the Juggernaut or the Hulk.

No, nothing is like the Hulk.

The crocodile shook its teeth loose from the Black Panther's grip, wrapped its mouth around T'Challa's head.

Enraged, the Black Panther gripped the croc's razor-like fangs, more enhancements courtesy of N'Jadaka, and pried its great mouth open until he heard its jaws crack. Grief filled the Panther King's heart as blood gushed, turning the water into pink haze—not unlike the beautiful dawn that T'Challa had witnessed only moments before. Now the Black Panther swung the crocodile around, hurling the beast out of the water and launching it into the open air.

T'Challa swam for the surface and allowed himself to float on top of the water. Exhausted, he did not resist the hands that grabbed under his armpits and pulled him back to the bank of the river.

Back on dry land, the Black Panther crawled as far as he could and fell in the soft grass. Allowing his mask to dematerialize, he swallowed a huge gulp of air. The shock of cool air in his lungs made T'Challa gag and cough, coupled with the realization that the entire country, the land that he loved, had turned against him. It wasn't just disgruntled farmers or small cohorts of overly ambitious soldiers.

It was the land itself caving under his feet, the trees, the birds, the wind. The Great Mound. Vibranium. The Heart-Shaped Herb itself.

He imagined Bast staring down and wallowed in shame. He covered his face with black gloved hands, wet and slick with saliva and blood.

Mercy, Great Mother! What have I done to make you disfavor me so? What have I done to make you forsake me?

A shadow stood over T'Challa, blocking the unforgiving sunlight. The shadow offered a hand to pull the king out of the damp grass sticking to his backside.

"My King," Taku said. "It is all right. Let it go. Let it all go."

T'Challa blinked, focused on the brown face and the sympathetic smile framed in ethereal shafts. He thanked Bast for the wet goop that masked his tears. He grabbed the hand reaching down, pulled himself up, and stared at the river that looked so peaceful, now. The crocodile lay on the opposite shore, panting, its belly turned upward.

Taku sat next to his king in the soft mud, staring at the placid, dying crocodile.

"What are we going to do with it?" Taku asked. His voice, exhausted, depleted. "Throw it back into the river? Leave it for vultures?"

"We need samples for testing. I suspect the source of its augmentation, but I must be sure."

"You think it's the work of Killmonger?" Taku asked. Disbelief and shock furrowed his brow.

"I know it's Killmonger." T'Challa almost said "N'Jadaka" but caught himself. "The stampeding rhinoceros I found in the farmlands, the animated corpses in the Necropolis, the giant leopard that attacked me at Warrior Falls. They're all connected to Killmonger, but there's another power at work as well, and I hate variables."

"Something more dangerous than Killmonger?" Taku said, astonished.

"Doubt all you like, Taku," T'Challa said. He stared at the crocodile, still spilling the dregs of its lifeforce.

"I interviewed Monica last night," Taku said, staring at the sky. "I understand why you love this woman so deeply. That's why I came looking for you. She needs you, T'Challa, and you haven't seen her once since her arrest."

"Careful, Taku. W'Kabi might label you an outworld sympathizer."

"W'Kabi loves to grandstand, but do not mistake his love. He would give his life for you at a moment's notice." Taku took a deep breath and stared his King in the eye. "Please forgive me, Your Majesty, but I must ask. Why haven't you been to see Monica?"

"I need to clear her name, find Zatama's killer, and time is not a luxury I can waste, Taku. I must exonerate Monica before she appears before the Tribunal." T'Challa studied the sky reflected in the river. "I have failed nearly every person I have ever loved, starting with my own father. I will not fail Monica."

"You are not a failure, My King. You are Wakanda's most beloved savior. You are the greatest of all Bast's gifts," Taku said. "Monica needs you. She needs your physical presence. She is alone and far away from home."

The walk back to the royal palace was slow and arduous. T'Challa carried the crocodile like a shawl draped around his shoulders, its tail dragging along the ground behind him. He needed the weight on his back and his legs to take his mind off the weight burdening his spirit. He walked beside Taku. Unnatural silence spread between the two men, a deep chasm filled with flames and suffering bodies flailing in the murk.

T'Challa left the crocodile in the palace laboratories and headed toward the quarters where Monica had been confined under house arrest. He did not stop to bathe. He did not change clothes. He had not been to his bedchambers since Monica's arrest: the traces of her lingering in the room only deepened his sadness.

He took the elevator down, made his way through the series of corridors that led to the chambers where Monica was being held. Paintings of kings past, from Bashenga the First to T'Chaka the Great Isolationist, lined the hallways. The portraits all stared at T'Challa with flat, black eyes that somehow managed to express disapproval.

He found Monica's chambers heavily guarded, even more so than usual. W'Kabi's doing. The thought brought some ease to T'Challa's heart—even though he was sure that reassurance was not the effect that W'Kabi had desired.

She is safe.

The soldiers moved from T'Challa's path quickly enough. Still, he detected their disdain. No one spoke or even sighed. He noticed their rigidity. The pain in their eyes could not be hidden so easily. T'Challa nodded and strode through the parted sentries, his jaw clenched, chin held high. He met the unsure eyes with a strong gaze of his own.

Inside the chambers, T'Challa found Monica stretched across a lavishly ornamented chaise longue with a hand-carved frame engraved with ancient Wakandan script. At the sight of her, T'Challa's stomach tightened, and the blood pounded inside his chest. She wore a long silk dress that clung to her curves and draped over her feet. A pair of headphones covered her ears, blasting some phantom music. She hummed, scribbling notes in a composition notebook.

Ever the songwriter, T'Challa thought with a wry smile. The bittersweet thought reminded the Panther King of Griot G'Sere. He had wanted them to meet so badly. If anyone in Wakanda could have related to Monica, it would have been G'Sere. The old griot could have made Monica's transition into Wakandan society much easier. Now the couple were pretty much alone. The sight of his love confined in this gilded prison was too much to bear.

Just as T'Challa had gathered the courage to interrupt Monica's songwriting, she raised her head. She looked startled at first, before a wide smile spread across her face. She flung the headphone to the carpet and leapt into T'Challa's arms.

"T, what took you so long?" She wrapped her arms around his neck. "It feels like I've been waiting forever for you to get me out of here."

T'Challa's gut knotted with regret as he contemplated his next words. What would he say? How could he tell Monica the truth without upsetting her? He refused to lie or mince his words. He owed Monica more than that. He respected her too much. Besides, she would have seen right through the lie anyway. She always did.

"You didn't come here to free me, did you?" Monica asked. Her back stiffened in his arms. She backed away, her eyes desperate.

"That's the first time I've seen you write since you got here," T'Challa said. He didn't know what else to say. Monica's voice had brought him back from the edge many times. He could not imagine his life without her. Her music had saved him. Her singing voice always felt like a cat purring, lowering blood pressure and stress hormones, resetting tendons and broken bones. The healing endorphins released in his mind brought peace to his spirit. Some called it the healing frequency, from 174 to 285 Hertz. Whether she knew it or not, Monica's voice had remarkable range and a unique effect.

"Stay on topic, T'Challa," she said. "W'Kabi, your *Shield of the Nation,* has accused me of murder. Look at me—they put me in prison," Monica cried, raising her arms. "I came here to support you because I love you. How in the world did I end up in jail?"

"No harm can come to you, while I live."

"While you live?"

"I didn't mean it like that," T'Challa said. "I just meant that this is a formality. I will take care of everything. Don't worry, Monica. I must find Zatama's true attacker. Proving your innocence is our best option. N'Jadaka has sown the seeds of discord in my house. I must expose the source of this corruption.

"So, I'm a pawn in some messed-up Machiavellian drama?" She bit her lip and shook her head, turned her back to T'Challa. "While you're proving my innocence, make sure you get me a plane ticket.

I want out as soon as possible. I love you, T'Challa. I promise I do, but I didn't sign up for all this."

Oh no, T'Challa thought. *She's gone full Color Purple.* She'd be calling him Harpo before the night was through. He had to do something fast.

"Monica, the security recordings show you knocking on the door, you cutting Zatama's throat. The murder weapon has your fingerprints. Whoever did this means to destroy you, me, and this entire kingdom. I must locate the killer, and time is not our friend."

"Why would you bring me here if so many of your people hate *outworlders* so much?"

"Much of Wakanda is hostile toward outworlders. We have a long history of defending ourselves against foreign occupation, but that is not the complete story of us. I have seen the way my Dora Milaje, and my own sister, interact with you. They love you, Monica, and so do I."

"If everybody loves me so much, why am I being held against my will for a crime I did not commit? Riddle me that, Panther King!"

"N'Jadaka is trying to poison my country. He has managed to turn Wakandan against Wakandan. Something that has never happened before. No one knows who to trust. My question is, how did it go so far?"

They both were silent. They knew, at least in part, the answer to that. T'Challa had been missing in action, with Monica, who was now imprisoned. There was no question in her mind why she was there, even if it wasn't true.

He fell onto the chaise longue and covered his head with his hands.

Monica stood before him and wrapped her arms around his shoulders, allowing the Panther King to rest his cheek against her stomach.

T'Challa sang, recalling the lyrics of Luther Vandross's "If Only for One Night," her favorite song. Monica moved back, shocked.

"T!" she squealed. "You're singing? That's not fair. You know I love Luther."

He sang on, warbling as best he could. No match for the master crooner, but his heart was in the right place. He held Monica until her eyes closed and the night was full of stars. Then the Black Panther laid her across the chaise longue and slipped out into the darkness.

Visiting Monica should have silenced the ghosts haunting his memory, but the time with his love left T'Challa with more questions and a deeper sense of urgency. He needed to free Monica before it was too late. The Tribunal Council would meet in one day. They would decide Monica's fate based on presented evidence. If T'Challa could not offer evidence clearing her of the accusations, the council would deliver a guilty verdict and sentence Monica to death.

T'Challa sat on his throne, resting his jaw in his palm, brooding. Since the farm uprisings and the trouble stirring in Wakanda's breadbasket, W'Kabi's Taifa Ngao had scoured the country searching for Killmonger and his base of operations. He had found nothing. They had searched Warrior Falls, the Great Mound, every major city, even the farming villages—and found no traces of Killmonger or his Death Regiments. T'Challa had heard similar news from the soldiers he'd sent to investigate the Necropolis.

These were the thoughts plaguing T'Challa when Tanzika brought his evening meal. He noticed the smoking venison and yams and shook his head. *Don't the cooks know any other recipes?* T'Challa shook his head and reached for a piece of succulent meat. He plucked the crispy flesh from a set of skewers simmering in brown gravy.

"Have you taken Monica her dinner?" he asked.

Before Tanzika could answer, W'Kabi marched into the room. Behind him Karota followed, her head lowered, and her fingers folded in front of her heart.

Flanking W'Kabi and covering his rear were Taifa Ngao armed with energy swords and spears, clad in vibranium-laced armor. The soldiers stared at T'Challa with blank expressions, stone grim, which barely masked the disdain that many of them held for their king.

"T'Challa," W'Kabi called. He pointed at the Panther King, who now sat attentively on the black and gold throne that had been carved into the likeness of the Panther God. W'Kabi's eyes were red with fury and spittle flew from his mouth as he approached the base of the throne. "What are you going to do with the outworlder? You allowed her to distract you and keep you away from your duties. Now she has spilled Wakandan blood inside the royal palace. Zatama dedicated a lifetime of faithful service to the House of Bashenga. How many more of us must sacrifice ourselves for a king who has turned his back on his nation?"

The parlor fell silent. Tension and anxiety filled the room. Even the soldiers flanking W'Kabi looked nervous. Tanzika looked as if she were about to drop the empty serving dish that she had only moments before handled with all the grace of an interpretive dancer.

T'Challa took a moment to quell his own anger before he responded. T'Chaka had never had to deal with such open insolence. Still, there were Wakandans who had pledged their allegiance and their service to the deceased Panther King's nemesis Ulysses Klaw. Considering that thought, T'Challa welcomed W'Kabi's open insubordination. *Open is always better, T'Challa.*

T'Challa raised himself to his feet and stood in front of his throne. He watched the fearful soldiers shrink behind W'Kabi. This was not a good sign. Fear rendered its host malleable, a puppet ready for manipulation. T'Challa would counsel W'Kabi on this later. Wakandan soldiers had to be fearless. Even in the face of certain death.

"You speak as if I do not wear the burden of every death. As if I do not hear the screams of every tortured soul. Yes, last night, blood was spilled in our royal palace. And I promise you the true killer will pay with their own blood. I promise you that every death, every suffering Wakandan, will be avenged by my hand." T'Challa's voice began to rise. He thought of the king's decorum that he had worn like impenetrable armor for most of his life. He decided to shed that armor to bare himself; an open book for all those brave enough to read its portentous pages.

"Last night, outside the protective walls of the Golden City, I saw the dead rise from their graves," the Panther King continued. "I fought against doomed souls who had already left this earthly plane but had failed to make the blessed flight back to Djalia. I felt the cold, burning hands of death squeezing my throat."

In a flash of black muscle, the Panther King leaped from his throne. Before the soldiers could gasp, much less react, T'Challa was among their ranks. T'Challa did not touch the general, but he stood so close that he could smell the sweat forming in W'Kabi's pores. T'Challa also smelled alcohol and mouthwash, which disturbed him. Another subject he would broach with his Shield in private.

"Last night those cold, burning hands tried to pull me down into the grave with them. It would have been easier to surrender to the dark void, to lay down in the grave with those doomed souls, but I refused."

"My King, I, I did not mean…" W'Kabi spoke with his eyes lowered and a new sense of temperament calming his voice.

"I am Wakanda's king. I am her sole protector. Her last line of defense, as they say in the West." He took another deep breath to calm himself, but the stench of liquor almost unhinged the avatar.

"You want to know why I left, but you never asked me. You only assumed. You want to know so badly. You have your top officers here with you. Go ahead, ask me. Ask me why I disappeared from the land that I love. The land that my people spent thousands of years building and cultivating, protecting from foreign invasion."

"My lord, I, I…" Deflated by shame, W'Kabi shrank from the Panther King.

"The memories of my father's death. Holding him in my arms, watching him struggle for those final precious breaths. The vengeful blood on my hands, in my eyes, drove me to the edge of insanity. After I killed Klaw, I thought the thirst would be quenched, but it intensified. I wanted more. I could have killed a thousand men with my bare hands, and it would not have been enough. I was in no state to rule. But I was chosen. I had to deal with the demons haunting my memories, so I could be the king that Wakanda needed, a king that Bast would favor."

"Your Majesty," Taku stepped forward. "Remember your guest. Karota has come seeking news of her husband."

Karota stared at T'Challa with wide, expectant eyes, filled with hope and hopelessness. He remembered M'Jumbak, how the farmer crawled on his belly, spat black flames. T'Challa opened his mouth but found that he could not produce any words to comfort the farmer's wife. Karota ran past Tanzika and W'Kabi and wrapped her arms around T'Challa's midsection. She buried her face in her king's chest and wept loudly, calling her husband's name.

T'Challa embraced the woman. He patted the back of her head and stared at the soldiers and the courtiers. All their faces betrayed bright fear, confusion, and sadness. But because he was their king, he detected something else—disappointment.

"I will avenge your husband." T'Challa spoke to the widow weeping in his arms, the soldiers and the courtiers, the faithful and the treacherous alike. Most of all, he hoped that N'Jadaka was listening. *Yes, my friend, I am going to find you, and you are going to pay.*

After Karota left the parlor, T'Challa took to his study and prepared for his return to the Necropolis. He searched his Kimoyo and the books in his library, but found no histories that explained the zombies he had fought the previous night. T'Challa quit the research and prayed to Bast for an hour, promising to vanquish N'Jadaka and every other Wakandan who followed K'Liluna. He spent another hour lifting weights and two more sparring with Shuri.

Later that night, T'Challa returned to the Necropolis. This time he went by foot. The Black Panther needed to run. The night called through the wind, the buzzing electric cars whizzing through the Golden City, and the nocturnal creatures that scurried through the veldt outside of Wakanda's capital. He welcomed the burning in his legs as he leapt across the gilded buildings in the city proper and the trees along the roadside, finally reaching the forests that separated Birnin Zana from the abandoned ruins that led to the Necropolis and the burial grounds that bordered the Alkama Fields.

T'Challa felt the same foreboding, the same sense of unease that he had felt the night before. A small part of the Black Panther regretted leaving his Dora Milaje and W'Kabi's Taifa Ngao back at the palace, but he thought better in solitude. Also, he preferred having the Dora Milaje near Monica, and W'Kabi was just as faithful to Wakanda as he had ever been. W'Kabi would make sure that Monica stood before the Tribunal Council. That was the law of Wakanda, and W'Kabi would uphold Wakandan law to the end.

T'Challa moved slowly, cautiously through the old cemetery. The smells of things both dead and undead filled his nostrils and knotted his stomach. Something scurried in a patch of bushes and stones on T'Challa's periphery. M'Jumbak emerged from the shadows, spraying black flames from his eyes and his mouth. Horrified by the farmer's terrible fate, T'Challa leapt into the air and met the undead creature with a flying side kick. His foot landed in the center of M'Jumbak's chest, knocking the creature back into an outcropping of crooked tombstones.

The creature that had once shook T'Challa's hand and smiled with all the glory of a fresh Wakandan morning righted itself almost instantly, flipping from its back to its belly in one motion. Its limbs positioned like spider's legs, the creature scurried back and forth, hissing and spitting.

"M'Jumbak, can you hear me? The ruler of Wakanda, the avatar of Bast, your king, calls you. Come forward. It is time for you to return to your family, time for you to rest."

The creature's eyes widened with dismay, a brief moment of recognition. It hissed and spat, then turned toward the night, releasing a bloodcurdling scream that erupted from some place deep within. T'Challa swore that the pitiful sound could have ripped the creature in two, it was so anguished.

A keening began, a wailing dirge song that shook the earth beneath T'Challa's feet. Unlike the night before, the undead moved much more quickly. They sprang from the ground tossing dirt in all directions. They crept from behind black trees and crooked tombstones. Before T'Challa could register the onslaught, the undead Wakandans surrounded him.

This time there seemed to be even more reanimated cadavers; the moaning and the wailing sounds were much louder. The groaning burrowed inside the Black Panther's skull; he wanted to cover his ears. Instead, he crouched and bared his black claws. He did not move from his stance, and he kept his eyes on the creature that had once been M'Jumbak.

"You have come to greet me again," T'Challa said. The rage burned in his voice. "Where is the Baron?"

The cadavers answered with moaning and croaking. They collapsed their circle around T'Challa, but this time he was ready. He leapt into the air and spread his legs, kicking two of his assailants in their faces. He brought his elbow down on the neck of another. T'Challa kneed another monster in the stomach. He remembered the shadows that had tested him in the palace garden. He remembered Mendinao's advice. *But what does the old man know of war?*

T'Challa hurled a wailing cadaver into a tree. He kept his eye on M'Jumbak as he fought his way through the undead. The creature perched on top of a wide gray tombstone. It reared on broken legs and spat black flames in the air.

"You should not have returned, T'Challa," the cadavers said in unison. Regrouping, they circled the Black Panther. "Be patient. I will bring you the fight you seek if you give me the chance." The undead creatures spoke with the same sarcasm, the same bass, the same throaty drawls.

"Macabre," T'Challa growled. He grabbed the first cadaver in reach. "Where are you? You can't hide forever," the Panther King yelled.

"I am not hiding." The cadavers all spoke in the Baron's voice. Even the undead farmer spoke with the rest of his horde. Black flames rolled from his mouth and eyes.

"Enter the grave to seek death," the corpses said, mischief and delight cracking their voices. "You've come to the right place, T'Challa. Now, down you go. But first you face *my* beloveds." The cadavers rushed the avatar. Their laughter rang through the Necropolis.

Hands burst through the ground and grabbed T'Challa's ankles. They pulled and tugged as more monsters threw their weight upon him, burying him inside a fresh grave that opened up under his feet.

He struggled against their supernatural strength, replenished by the sound of Macabre's voice.

T'Challa fought as the clawing hands, the pressing bodies, drove him into the earth under his feet. M'Jumbak's disjointed shell, host to some phantom power harnessed by N'Jadaka, sat on its crooked gray tombstone and watched the Black Panther, his face approximating confusion and regret, until the Panther King was completely submerged.

T'Challa fought the zombies while falling through black space punctuated by jutting rock and black pipes protruding from the shaft's side. The panther suit calculated a fifty-foot drop before the bottom smacked him senseless. The impact sent the zombies flying in all directions. T'Challa staggered to his feet. The vibranium in the panther suit had absorbed most of the impact, but his head spun, and his stomach felt like he'd left it back in the burial grounds. Doubled over, he grabbed his knees, and caught his breath.

All around, bodies were strewn and broken. They bled black-crimson on a marble floor designed like a chessboard. Black and white squares stretched in two directions down a long hallway.

So, the dead can bleed, T'Challa thought. He stood over lifeless glass eyes staring at him through a broken mask, a thin hull that resembled bone and scant, putrid flesh. The black fire, the moaning, extinguished. Back in the Necropolis, the hands strewn across the marble had felt so cold around his arms and his throat.

"Keep going, you won't be able to turn back," Macabre blared. "What about Shuri, your Dora Milaje, poor Monica? How is she going to make it?"

The arrogance, the condescension, the violent mirth brought the Black Panther to the edge.

He stood in the dark and stared down both ends of the tunnel. One end tumbled into utter darkness that could only take the Panther King deeper into the earth. Down the other, distant lights emanated and swirled—an underground Aurora Borealis.

"Which way did I go, T'Challa?" Macabre's voice rang through the dark. His tainted spirit corrupted the earth itself.

The darkness was the Black Panther's friend, the gift of Bast. But T'Challa was not looking for a friend. He was hunting his enemies. Enemies who befriended and betrayed him. Enemies who spilled blood under his own roof.

T'Challa bared his claws, stalking through the dark tunnel toward the light. He moved with the deadly grace of his namesake. As he made his way, the lights became stronger and brighter. Even with the lenses in his mask, T'Challa had trouble seeing. He felt the Heart-Shaped Herb grow warm in his veins as his eyes adjusted to the assaulting light. After a while, the tunnel yielded to a room filled with light. Mirrors covered every wall, rendering misshapen images of the Black Panther.

Macabre's derisive voice filled the Panther King's skull and threatened to burst his head open from the inside.

"I told you to turn around, T'Challa. Now it's too late," the Baron said. "Don't worry, my comrade and I are here to greet you. We will most assuredly give you the death that you seek. Allow me to introduce another member of the Death Regiments, King Cadaver."

T'Challa fell to his knees as Macabre's voice burrowed between his ears. He gripped the sides of his head and did his best to keep his balance. T'Challa's own ill-shaped, mirror images mocked him as they spun and spun in concert with the flashing lights and the laughter that hammered inside his mind.

As the room spun and the lights flashed, T'Challa saw the skeletal face, the shadowed limbs of Baron Macabre. He saw another face with malevolent eyes, a wide, toothy grin that emanated evil. A green face that bubbled. Flesh composed of fungi and blossoming spores, small fountains that popped and oozed small bulbs of green slime.

"T'Challa! How does it feel to be in the presence of a true king?" Baron Macabre said. "Enjoy this feeling because it will not last long."

The Black Panther fell to his knees and clawed at the sides of his mask, as Baron Macabre's voice burned the inside of his skull.

"That's right, T'Challa. Bow, pledge allegiance to the king of the underworld. The pain you feel… King Cadaver can make it all go away." Baron Macabre laughed.

The mirrors reflecting the misshapen faces and the light blinded T'Challa, pushing him to the edge of madness. Collapsing images, his father lifting a black boy into a ball of white light, G'Sere's eyes evoking polished obsidian, M'Jumbak reaching for his hand.

T'Challa waved his arm to find his balance. Four steps and he stumbled to his knees for the second time.

"The pain must be horrendous." King Cadaver stared at the Black Panther and smiled. Equine, yellow teeth spread a wedge of gold into the green, the patina, leafy boils that flowered and burst across his cheeks, chin and forehead. "You can make the pain go away right now, T'Challa. Swear your allegiance to Killmonger. Surrender Wakanda to her rightful ruler. Set your people free."

The Panther King screamed as the voice scraped between his temples. He screamed despite himself, despite his training and his conditioning. Every time the voices spoke, the Panther King felt something tearing his mind, ripping through his nervous system. He gouged at his mask and raised his head to blinding light that turned the mirrors and the marble floor into the walls of a life-sized oven, a crematorium.

"Aren't you tired of being king? So much responsibility. So many lives depend on you, and none of them appreciate you. None of them appreciate your sacrifices. Wouldn't it be easier to let all of it go right now? Aren't you tired of protecting Monica? You have failed. Your Tribunal Council will sentence her to death. The blood will be on your hands. Even you are bound by the laws of your ancestors. Heavy lies the crown."

Monica! T'Challa screamed in his mind. He refused to say her name aloud. He saw her smiling image floating just beyond his reach. Her eyes and her smile radiant with stage lights. She sang to T'Challa and reached for him. Her fingers stretched less than an inch before his own. He struggled to grab her hand.

When the last dance is through, and there's no one left that loves you.
Baby, you'll think about me. Monica sang in T'Challa's mind. She
threw her head back and laughed. Then, she stared down her nose at
T'Challa. Her eyes wide and bright with avarice and condescension.
You'll think about me, T'Challa.

"No, please, don't leave me," T'Challa said. He cried and reached
for the open air. He saw Monica running from him. She turned
back and looked over her shoulders with disapproving eyes before
she disappeared into the all-encompassing light.

"Yes, T'Challa, think of Monica." The voices raked the Panther
King's mind. "What would you give to be with her right now?
To hold her? The price is so simple. You have so little to lose, so
much to gain." The voices of Baron Macabre, King Cadaver, and
Erik Killmonger coalesced into one horrid utterance that smashed
T'Challa's forehead like a hammer on anvil.

"No," T'Challa roared. "You will not take Monica. You will
not take Wakanda. She is mine." Even with the chaos assaulting
his mind, the Panther King grabbed Baron Macabre. T'Challa
swung the Baron like a cyclone before using the Baron's body to
smash the mirrors.

Broken shards fell to the ground, revealing the darkness of
grinding machinery, a latticework of intertwined cables and pipes.
Under the wreckage lay Baron Macabre, unconscious and sprawled
on his back, his arms extended, and one foot folded under the
other leg at the calf muscle. T'Challa could not help noticing how
the position made the Baron look like a dancer, ready to spin on
the tip of his toe.

Revulsion, disappointment as bitter as hemlock, furrowed the
Panther King's brow. How many of his people had been corrupted,
ensnared by Killmonger's poisoned whispers? *What is your endgame,
N'Jadaka?* T'Challa thought with a clenched fist.

"We only want what's best for Wakanda." The barbed-wire voices
clawed T'Challa's mind again. King Cadaver's face was reflected in
the remaining mirrors. Yellow eyes filled with childlike buoyancy
and brilliance. Yellow teeth, smiling wide as the dawn, cracking

across some dark fertile horizon. The fleshy boils, a steaming swamp covered with mold and dead film. "The medicine that we need the most often tastes the worst."

Now the contemptuous voices mocked T'Challa. That was Killmonger. All superego. T'Challa stared into the fragments of mirrors that swung in broken shards.

"The mirrors do magnify my power," King Cadaver said in chorus. "But even without them I will crush your brain. You will follow me just like the farmer you love so dearly, on your hands and knees."

The voices cut the insides of T'Challa's skull. He grunted and blinked as the words blurred. He gritted his teeth, grabbed King Cadaver's neck, and slammed the Death Regiment member through another mirror.

It's in your mind. The pain is not real, T'Challa thought. He glanced at Baron Macabre lying on the floor, the broken mask, and the broken Wakandan. The Panther King grabbed the green, squirming mess that covered King Cadaver's face.

King Cadaver cackled as T'Challa's hand sank into green ooze and fungus that wrapped around his fingers. A crowd of voices laughed in King Cadaver's voice. The loudest belonged to N'Jadaka, belonged to a dark, basement nightclub in Harlem. The laughter filled T'Challa with a rage beyond comprehension. He used King Cadaver like a shield, a club, swinging Killmonger's monster around and around until he broke every mirror that he saw standing.

Panting, the Black Panther stood on the mess of broken glass; a bloody lump of flesh heaved in the Panther King's grip. He dropped the unconscious King Cadaver, taking heavy breaths as his anger quelled and sank back to the latent depths from which it arose. The shattered mirrors now revealed a shocking discovery. He found himself in a secret room filled with computers and lab equipment. T'Challa opened a door and stepped into a vast cavern of darkness and twinkling lights. *A secret underground network.* What the Panther King saw next assured him of his utter failure, his disconnection with the lives in his charge.

As far as he could see were conveyors, huge stretches of monorails, platforms. He looked up at the underbelly of Central Wakanda. And he realized. N'Jadaka was using all of Wakanda against the Panther King—the people, the animals, the land, the air, the resources, the heart and soul of his beloved nation were all bound in league against him.

His mind reeling through bouts of horror and confusion, T'Challa wondered what wellspring of life, what secret arcane mysteries, what elusive uncharted regions of Wakanda had N'Jadaka accessed? He stood in the vast darkness, amid the streaking beacons and the humming machinery, an alien standing for the first time before uncharted terrain that sprawled farther than he had ever imagined.

CHAPTER ELEVEN

THE PROBLEM WITH DRAGONS

AFTER EXPLORING the underground network, T'Challa returned to the spot where he had left Baron Macabre and King Cadaver. The Panther King made a mental note to have W'Kabi and the Taifa Ngao shut down the series of underground passages after thorough inspection. The pair had been incapacitated but were still breathing. Their souls had not crossed into Death's Domain. Not yet. But, amidst the broken mirrors, he found only two marks scorched into the floor where the Baron and King Cadaver had sprawled only minutes before. Black ooze bubbled and popped where the pair had lain. The sight disgusted T'Challa, but he made himself look. He bent to one knee and produced a slender vial nestled in his sleeve. T'Challa pulled a small stick from the container and dipped the tool into the burned goo.

"One more clue, N'Jadaka; one step closer to the source of your power. Once I find it, I will destroy it, and I will end you." T'Challa considered the farm boy, Kantu, who had lost his father to the Death Regiment. T'Challa had been about that age when T'Chaka was assassinated.

The Kimoyo beads fastened around T'Challa's wrist buzzed and flashed neon green, black, and yellow.

The combination of colors signaled a message from Taku. T'Challa returned to the weapons depot. Staring into the vast expanse, he raised the Kimoyo beads toward his mouth.

"This is T'Challa. Come in, Taku," the Black Panther said. He spoke in measured tones, drew all his strength to hide the utter shock, the dismay that came with being violated.

"Your Majesty, when are you returning to the royal palace? I have gathered a highly sensitive piece of intelligence I do not wish to share with anyone except you."

"We are all learning today, my friend. I have information of my own that will prove useful in our pursuit of Killmonger."

With a mental command, T'Challa cut the transmission on the Kimoyo beads. He stared at Killmonger's handiwork.

"You think you can turn Wakanda against me," he said aloud. "This is my country. I love Wakanda and she will never fall to you. By the power of Bast, Wakanda forever."

T'Challa returned to the path that had led him to this terrible discovery. He climbed the chasm, leaping from wall to wall through the pitch dark until he found himself back in the City of the Dead. He had emerged not too far from M'Jumbak's farm. The thought of the kind farmer being forced into such horrid bondage after death pained T'Challa. He would ask the shamans of Mount Kanda to find a way to put the farmer and the other poor undead souls to rest. For now, he searched the Necropolis for M'Jumbak, to capture him and return him. He slipped through the shadows, making his way around the old tombstones as he called M'Jumbak's name. He searched to no avail until sunrise vanquished the darkness, expelled the primal hunter pacing his heart.

The sun hung over the Golden City, a burnished disk illuminating the sky. Ethereal morning eased the Black Panther's troubled heart, filled him with new hope as he returned to the royal palace. Racing across the beaming rooftops, T'Challa imagined the fantastic fields of Djalia, the royal seat of Bast herself. His father had brought all that splendor to life right here in Wakanda. As he moved through the city, a dark shadow, he noticed a gleaming white building, newly constructed, that he didn't recognize. So much progress had sprung up in the dark time after his father's death. He could see the evidence of long held dreams.

Metallic beauty shining all around reminded T'Challa of the precious gift that had powered Wakanda's unparalleled success. The Golden City also exemplified his responsibility, and the terrible fate that N'Jadaka posed to this treasured world—everything his father had died trying to build and enhance.

Monica. Her name, her face flew from the darkness in his subconscious as he re-entered the palace, freezing his feet to a marble floor set aglow with long swaths of sunlight filtered through tall stained-glass windows. He thought about the knife that had killed Zatama. Monica's fingerprints. *I must re-examine the blade right away.*

An automatic door across from T'Challa split open with a barely audible hiss, even with his enhanced hearing. Taku strode into the parlor with a brisk stride and furrowed brow. Known for his poise and reserve, Taku entered wearing a grim expression.

"My King, I have gathered critical intel from the prisoner who calls himself Venomm." Taku took a deep breath. "He has revealed vital information concerning Erik Killmonger's base of operations. I've come to find Horatio is one of Killmonger's most trusted allies."

"You two are on a first-name basis, now?" T'Challa asked. The question was simple enough; still the Panther King kept his voice even, kept his suspicion from showing. Taku was an astute councilor. His eye for decoding the body's language was unmatched. But T'Challa had been trained to mask his emotions since he was a child.

"The relaxed tone of our discussions helped to win his trust," Taku answered. "But there is something else, My King. Venomm is a tortured soul. He has been crippled by social anxiety. Tormented since his youth, he has suffered unimaginable cruelty. Killmonger is one of the few people in the world that has ever shown him any kindness. If someone else had gotten to him first, showed him a better way, showed him that he was beautiful despite his injuries,

177

Venomm might be a different person today. Would you like to go down to his confinement chambers and question him yourself, My King?" Taku held out his arm and gestured toward the door.

"That won't be necessary. I have gathered some critical intelligence of my own. Come, we can strategize and trade intel along the way." T'Challa headed for the door. He did not stop or look back. He knew that Taku would follow him.

The pair walked and talked. Taku explained what he had learned from Venomm. He told T'Challa about Killmonger's base, a secret village that used a cloaking system to hide itself from the world. A system that bore a strong resemblance to the devices that had kept foreign powers from penetrating Wakanda for decades.

"But Killmonger's setup is… different," Taku added. "Venomm claims that it's powered by magic, not science."

"Magic? I don't think so." T'Challa almost laughed, despite his doleful mood. MIT graduate, esteemed professor; the last word that T'Challa associated with N'Jadaka was magic. The staunch empiricist had been even more hard-nosed than T'Challa about many of the traditions and practices that the man had dismissed as arcane spook-doctrine.

"I have seen Killmonger's so-called magic up close and personal," T'Challa said. "His tactics are all smoke and mirrors, relying on the power of vibranium to control his followers. He wants people to believe that he is some kind of shaman or demigod to secure their loyalty."

"Your strongest critics and detractors say the same thing about you, My King." Taku lowered his voice and his eyes. "Please forgive my rash speech."

"If you cannot express your true mind to me, I am not fit to rule. That would substantiate the rumors about the panther demon, as some of the rebels have taken to calling me. They say I'm the spoiled, rich brat who abandoned his people to become the lap dog of the superhumans in the West." T'Challa wrapped his arm around Taku's shoulder and squeezed the communications specialist's shoulder playfully.

"Now, let me tell you what I have learned," T'Challa said.

The Panther King recounted the events from the night before. By the time T'Challa finished, the idea of N'Jadaka employing magic or some arcane art did not seem so strange.

T'Challa did not accompany Taku to Venomm's confinement chamber. Instead, the Panther King led Taku to the quarters where Monica Lynne had been confined under house arrest. An opulent, luxurious prison, but a prison, nonetheless. The soldiers W'Kabi had stationed in front of the chambers parted. Taku remained outside with the soldiers, while T'Challa went inside to comfort Monica.

His visit would be short, however. There was too much to do. Still, he could not stay away. He had to see her. If he could, he would imprison himself just so he could be with her. But he needed to find Zatama's true killer before it was too late. Rules were rules, and even though he was king, T'Challa could only delay the Tribunal Council's judgment for so long.

Again, he found Monica singing. This time she was pecking away at a keyboard that someone had mercifully brought her. This is Taku's work, T'Challa thought, with a slight smile raising one corner of his mouth. Monica was so engaged in her music that again she failed to notice T'Challa's entrance. If she did know, she did not give a clue. T'Challa thought of the poise, the reserve required of a queen. The solid, unshakable reserve of his stepmother, Ramonda. And he thought to himself, not for the first time, that he had chosen well. He had chosen his queen well indeed.

"Climb mighty woman, even as the world, this cruel world snaps at your heels," she sang. *"Fly, fly oh mighty woman, even as the sun threatens to burn your wings."* Her voice was soft and rich, yet powerful and furious all at once.

When she finished her song, she stared at the keyboard. She sighed and dropped her head, and at that moment it looked as if she had given up all hope.

"Beautiful as always," T'Challa said. He clapped his hands, softly and briefly.

Monica looked up with a start, whirled around with a speed that surprised T'Challa. In one moment, she was turned, poised on her elbows, her foot pointed, ready to kick the intruder. For one second her brow furrowed in confusion. Then her demeanor relaxed when she saw that it was T'Challa standing before her.

"I'm sorry, Monica. I did not mean to frighten you," T'Challa said. Now he felt like an intruder.

"So, now you come to check on me?" Bitterness replaced the sweet tenor that had filled the room only moments before. "The king has finally taken time out of his busy schedule to see about me. Glad to know where I fit in on your list of priorities."

Monica's anger cut through T'Challa, lodged itself inside his heart. He could not blame her for her anger. In fact, he wondered why it had taken her so long to vent her frustrations toward him.

"I am sorry, Monica, but you are correct. There is much to do. Right now, clearing your name and freeing you is my number one priority. *You* are my number one priority."

T'Challa reached for Monica, but she pulled away from him.

"You have every right to be cross with me," T'Challa responded to Monica's cold gesture. "But you must understand, I am very close to finding Zatama's true killer. You must also understand that I am the king, and my country is tearing itself apart. Bringing peace to Wakanda is also my responsibility."

"I know. I know," Monica answered, the sarcasm dripping from her voice like snake venom. "How can I compete with an entire country?"

"This is your country, too, Monica." T'Challa reached for her again, and this time she did not pull away. "These are your people. One day soon, you will rule them by my side. One day you will be their queen."

She raised an eyebrow, the hurt in her eyes softening. "But first, I must be free."

Monica allowed T'Challa to wrap his arms around her, but she would not look at him. Instead, she focused her attention on a life-sized statue of the Panther God, Bast. She sighed and rested her head against T'Challa's chest. He felt the weariness in her bones, and it took all his strength, all the training he had received as a young prince to keep himself from breaking down and crying all over her.

With great reluctance, T'Challa left Monica with a deep, passionate kiss and a promise to uncover the treachery that had split his house and imprisoned the woman he loved. After leaving Monica, the Panther King had Taku summon all of the military personnel and all the Dora Milaje.

In the gardens behind the royal palace, T'Challa stood before scores of warriors. Shield of Wakanda, Dora Milaje. Mounted on red-eyed metal horses, with manes and tails that surged with vibranium-powered electricity. The warriors stood still, staring up at their king from all around the gardens. Every gaze penetrated T'Challa. He allowed every eye to enter his spirit: he felt the weight of his entire kingdom, everything T'Chaka sacrificed, everything Bast had given them. The Panther King pictured N'Jadaka smiling, raising a shot glass, wishing T'Challa a safe return to Wakanda. A deadly silence hung above the columns of soldiers and palace security. Their faces blank and expressionless, their eyes filled with the rage of war. The same rage that T'Challa found himself fighting to control. The Panther's rage. The rage of all Wakanda. The rage of Bast herself. T'Challa clenched his jaw.

Rage will not destroy you, unless you destroy yourself, Monica sang in T'Challa's head. Her voice came to him with a host of memories. He promised himself that he would free his love. He had found evidence, and now he needed a trap to bring the killer into the open. But the trap would have to wait—even though T'Challa knew that he was running out of time.

On T'Challa's left, Adebisi stared at the gathered mass, bottled fury shining in her eyes. On his right, W'Kabi turned to him and nodded. T'Challa wondered if W'Kabi was nodding at the assurance of bloodshed that would soon take place on Wakandan soil.

Wakandans fighting Wakandans, T'Challa thought with a terrible sense of grief. He would try his best to neutralize N'Jadaka as quickly as possible. That would be the key to reducing the casualties. The wounds T'Challa incurred during his fight with the crocodile and Baron Macabre's zombies throbbed in dull, achy concert.

T'Challa stepped to the edge of the raised patio that hung over the palace gardens to address his soldiers. As he spoke, he thought about his own father delivering a similar speech the morning he was murdered by Klaw.

"I have allowed a great sickness to spread through our land," T'Challa said. He called out to his people with the spirit of his father, the spirit of every Panther King that had come before, emboldened by the spirit of Bast and the Heart-Shaped Herb flowing through their veins. "Today, we will extract the deadly poison that has stricken our nation and reduced us to the barbarity of civil war. I will not mislead you. The exile who calls himself Erik Killmonger poses the greatest threat this country has ever faced. My father's murderer, Ulysses S. Klaw, was nothing. Killmonger has managed to infiltrate every corner of our beloved country."

T'Challa looked over the mass of soldiers. He stepped so close to the edge of the balcony, the black toes of his boots in the air, that he could no longer see the marble filled with precious stones glittering under his feet. Couldn't see anything but the soldiers. They stretched through every corner of the gardens, their numbers spilling over into the grassland that led to the river where Monica had found a half-dead T'Challa floating only days before.

"I was gone. I left Wakanda, the seat of my throne, but I never turned my back on any of you. Wakanda is my life, and I will always be the first to sacrifice myself in her defense." T'Challa felt something burning, filling him with heat. He thought about Monica and all she had done for him. She had saved his life, and he had failed her.

Like I failed my father, like I failed Wakanda…

"I left you because I was sick. I left you because I needed time to heal. Had I stayed I would have destroyed myself and ruined everything that our predecessors built." T'Challa bent down on one knee and raised his fist above his head. "Know that your king is here. I am here, and I pledge my life to the preservation of my country, my people. I believe in the Wakandan way of life, and I will not have our world destroyed. Come. Fight with me. Help me defend our traditions, our culture. Help me defend the heart of the Panther God. Help me defend Wakanda."

All around T'Challa, the hordes bent their knees and raised their fists. He stood and stared as his people, his soldiers, cheered and roared. The Black Panther crossed his arms, raised the ancient symbol of his country for all to see—mortal and spectral eyes were invited to bear witness.

"*Wakanda forever!*" T'Challa shouted. Then he roared, with all the power of his lungs. The soldiers returned the ancient greeting, and with their arms crossed they all yelled in mighty, thundering unison.

"*Wakanda forever! Wakanda forever!*"

T'CHALLA LEAPT from crag to stony outcrop on the balls of his feet, his gloved palms and anti-metal claws. Leaping down the steep drop, he allowed the scents to guide him down the mountain, the warm wind filling his nose with the cat tails strewn along the stony hillside. T'Challa smelled other things from the valley below, which looked empty to the naked eye. He could barely discern the ripples of energy that covered the belly of the valley. The air at the bottom of the valley twinkled only slightly. A casual observer would have blamed the sun and the specks of vibranium dust rising from the soil on the mountainside. But T'Challa caught an assortment of scents that betrayed the image of the empty field that he saw beneath him. He smelled human sweat, fire, and machinery.

At the bottom of the steep hillside the valley shimmered. The displaced light soaked the grass, the sparse trees, and the low-level buildings. Here the smells of a thriving settlement were strongest.

"This cloaking device…" T'Challa raised his hands, framing the picturesque valley for the Wakandan soldiers gathering behind him. "This is Wakandan technology." The vibranium in his mask amplified his voice, blasting the sound through the Kimoyo system so all the Panther King's subjects could hear.

"Erik Killmonger wants to turn Wakanda against itself," T'Challa said, then roared with the fury of the slain screaming through his memories. He saw them all at once, watching him. He would not fail. "But they do not understand. The gifts of Bast were meant to protect and uplift our people. Woe to the sowers of discord, woe to those who would misuse the gifts that Bast has so generously given."

T'Challa turned and faced the soldiers gathered around him. W'Kabi, Taku, and Adebisi stood at the head of the mass. W'Kabi stared at him as if searching for the Panther King's heart. W'Kabi's nose flared with the same disdain that twisted his face the night of Zatama's murder. He wore polished vibranium that covered his forehead, his temples, and his throat. The metal gleamed and purple streaks of light danced across his arms. His spear bore the records of battles that stretched back to the first challenges faced by Bashenga. The blade at the top of the spear was much wider than the average spearhead, black and shiny, cut into a shape that evoked a panther's head and the curve of a sickle.

"W'Kabi, I will disrupt the cloaking shields," T'Challa said. "I am picking up the vibrations from the field covering this area. I don't know why we did not detect it before. Still, I can disrupt the shields. Hopefully the feedback will destroy the sources—or at least cripple them long enough for our soldiers to cross over. But if the cloaks resume or remained undamaged, stand down. Do not proceed." The Black Panther turned to Taku. "Looks like the intel you gathered from Venomm was true indeed. Good job." T'Challa squeezed Taku's shoulders.

"Horatio spoke to me in confidence, and I betrayed his trust." Taku lowered his eyes and shook his head.

"This could still be a trap, My King," said W'Kabi. "You, yourself, should certainly understand the dangers of trusting foreigners."

"I understand the dangers of narrow minds and antiquated thinking, W'Kabi," T'Challa said. He patted W'Kabi's arm. "Watch, old friend."

"May Bast be pleased," Adebisi said, lowering her voice, she stared at the valley below. "The Death Regiments will answer for their effrontery to the Panther God." Adebisi turned to T'Challa. "Killmonger will answer for hurting my king."

T'Challa walked into the valley, walked until the light sang and bubbled. Invisible to the human eye—and scientific observation, apparently—the waves rose from the grass and spoke to T'Challa, spoke to him through the Heart-Shaped Herb that coursed through his veins. He heard the condescending laughter that could never be mistaken—not through a thousand celestial planes or Djalia itself.

"What took you so long?" Killmonger's voice buzzed through the pulsing light. "You were beginning to worry me, but here you are, just in time." Killmonger spoke with joy. His voice was playful, mischievous even.

T'Challa raised his arm, pressed his open palm into the wall of light that glittered like a polished window. A wall of light that bordered a glittering mosaic of shorn grass and crooked, pruned trees, and small houses arrayed in vibrant rows of colored stucco. W'Kabi raised his Kimoyo beads to his mouth and whispered a gruff command. Throughout the mountain pass, the Wakandan soldiers readied themselves, gripping their weapons. Some whispered small prayers and affirmations. Many of the soldiers carried pictures of their loved ones packed in wallets, framed in lockets, and these soldiers gripped the pictures and kissed the faces frozen in timeless poses.

T'Challa had one of these pictures tucked inside his sleeve. Not a selfie, but a picture taken with his cell phone, a picture of Monica laughing with her hand over her heart. Her hand pressed against her chest as if the laughter might actually pop out of her. He kept the picture tucked in his sleeve. He never looked at it. He never would, unless his time was short and he knew that would be the last image that he would see. All that he had sacrificed during his life, he would give himself that much if it came down to it. He had to.

T'Challa's suit began to absorb the energy emanating from the wall of light. The vibranium implants in the palms of his gloves went to work siphoning massive amounts of energy. The suit T'Challa wore, the hybrid of metal mesh and braided thread, every inch fashioned from some form of vibranium, analyzed the vibrating waves and presented the information to him through readouts flashing across the lenses that covered his eyes.

The vibrations from the field were generated by a material that was not quite vibranium, but a highly developed approximation of Wakanda's sacred mineral. So much of it made sense now. N'Jadaka's enhanced weapons. His own enhanced strength. He must have used this synthetic metal to synthesize his own version of the Heart-Shaped Herb.

The energy soaked into T'Challa's gloves, as the wall began to glitch. On and off. Off and on. T'Challa heard the soldiers behind him gasp as the energy drew and gathered around him, surging, an electrical storm centered around his person that made him think of Ororo. All those years ago, he had watched her summon the most severe thunderstorm he had ever seen.

Megahertz of vibratory energy were being drawn into the gloves of T'Challa's suit. The energy was not a bother. However, the cells in T'Challa's suit also detected a significant amount of psionic energy being transmitted. The computers in the suit tried to trace the psionic energy and came up with nothing. T'Challa hated mysteries, and this one scared him more than any other he had ever encountered. He wondered with horror, raising his eyebrows inside his mask. *What is the true source of N'Jadaka's power?*

"T'Challa, T'Challa, you never cease to amaze," Killmonger said. His voice a series of pulses and warbled sequences, vibrations coursing through the surging energy and psionic waves coursing through T'Challa's uniform. "Welcome to my humble abode. I know it's not what you're used to, but we do our best here."

The glitching wall of light revealed a small township, made up of wide dirt roads and old, weathered flats. The light surged around T'Challa, and for a moment the outside world seemed far away.

He could have been back in Harlem or even walking along the starry shores of Djalia. It would not have mattered. He heard the screaming and jeering of war all around him, but the sounds were distant and muffled. The wall of light disappeared completely into a scant trail of ash that stretched across the dirt roads and sparse patches of grass. T'Challa stood with his feet planted, rubbing his hands and wrists, where the remaining currents of energy sparked and picked at his bones.

He watched as his soldiers stormed the small village. The dirt roads and spartan dwellings reminded the Panther King of the ruined neighborhoods and the burial grounds where he first encountered Baron Macabre. This place had the same deathly smell, but the scent was stronger here, even stronger than the stench T'Challa found in the graveyard. The odor of death, of Killmonger.

With the Taifa Ngao and the Dora Milaje running through the settlement, the buildings opened their doors, and soldiers marked with the skulls and the scars of Killmonger's Death Regiments ran into the streets to meet them in a flourish of metal, pulsing rays, screaming, and splattered flesh. He saw a line of Death Regiment soldiers further down the road, led by Malice, Baron Macabre, and another he did not recognize. A man with a bald head and a bare chest wore a green cape that rose from his shoulders and dropped behind his calf muscles. He brandished two handguns that he fired into the oncoming crowd of royal soldiers.

The hunter pacing inside T'Challa's heart took over. Instead of running into the village, he leapt into the trees branching over the settlement, and from there to the rooftops. Building to building, thatched roof to thatched roof, he leapt in silence, using the faded shadows of mid-morning as best as he could. Keeping himself as low to the rooftops as possible. In his mind he saw N'Jadaka. That haunting smile mocking T'Challa, stringing him along with a trail of corpses and half-dead superhumans—Killmonger's Death Regiments.

T'Challa crept across a roof covered with straw and over a layer of solid metal. T'Challa judged the material to be steel from the silver gleam and the grainy texture that scratched softly as he shifted his weight across the thinly disguised surface.

Just enough disguise to fool anyone who might come by, T'Challa thought. He shook his head at the idea of another clue or door that opened upon the mind of N'Jadaka, the psychotic genius who called himself Erik Killmonger.

Voices rose from the ground below. Two familiar voices that T'Challa would have recognized anywhere. He did not need to peek over the edge of the rooftop to know that it was Tayete and Kazibe talking beneath T'Challa's hidden position. Along with the voices, T'Challa caught a savory waft of spiced lamb and white fish that made his stomach grumble. For a moment he thought that he had compromised his position, but T'Challa dismissed the fleeting sensation as soon as it crept into his mind.

The scent reminded him of the dishes that he had been eating all week. T'Challa sniffed the air. In fact, the scent was exactly the same. As if Tayete and Kazibe were eating food cooked in the royal palace. Maybe someone who cooked for the royal family had prepared this meal as well. Maybe someone was smuggling food out of the royal palace to feed N'Jadaka's soldiers—just as N'Jadaka had found his way into the abandoned mines and turned Wakanda's weapons against itself.

He's taking my country bit by bit, T'Challa thought, the rage climbing from his stomach. Tayete laughed out loud, the sound incensing the Panther King even more. *Traitor by traitor...*

T'Challa craned his neck so he could see the two traitors. The two fools, as they had been called around the royal palace during T'Challa's youth, before he took the throne. Before his father died in his arms and changed everything. He did not need to see them to know they were below him relaxing in the shade, resting their backs against the cool stucco. T'Challa did not need to see them to know they were stuffing their faces with food too heavy for breakfast. He smelled them and their meal quite clearly. He heard them stuffing their mouths, but he wanted to see. He wanted that reminder.

Tayete and Kazibe had begun their service in the Wakandan army under King T'Chaka. The two fools had mourned the terrible death of the Great Isolationist, and they had fought bravely beside T'Challa to expel Klaw from Wakanda. When he returned to kill T'Chaka's son and pillage Wakanda for its precious vibranium, Tayete and Kazibe had been heroes—celebrated throughout the royal palace and all Wakanda. Yes, T'Challa needed the reminder. Many people, many parts of the nation that he loved, were against him now. The thought ignited the rage he had fought so hard to suppress. T'Challa took a deep breath, and somehow, he controlled his anger. But he made himself look, so he would never forget.

These were the men who killed G'Sere, T'Challa thought. *The two fools.* The irony tasted bitter and forced him to picture Tayete and Kazibe torturing G'Sere. He saw the pair in his mind as clearly as he saw them in the shade below, stuffing their faces with spiced meat and couscous. He saw them taunting G'Sere as they stabbed him. Laughing as the old griot's blood ran through the bars of his suspended cage and puddled in the grass.

"Wait, Tayete. I heard something," Kazibe said. He looked around, eyes darting, face greasy. "Did you hear that?"

"Hear what?" Tayete laughed and stuffed a piece of braised lamb into his mouth. With the juice running down his hand, he smacked his lips and licked his fingers. "You haven't been right since that night in the graveyard. The panther demon has you spooked." Tayete tore off a piece of injera bread and swiped a thick gob of sauce from a plate resting between his legs.

"You are a grown man, Kazibe. A soldier—a member of Killmonger's Death Regiments. We are the most feared men in all of Wakanda, yet you tremble at the sight of your own shadow!"

"I guess I should be more like you," Kazibe said, resentment brewing in his throat.

"That's right. Look and take notes. Every time I fought the panther demon, I sent him running back to his precious Golden City with his tail tucked between his legs."

"Is that so?" Kazibe asked.

"That is so!" Tayete answered.

"Is that why you cry in your sleep? *No, stop. Please don't!*" Kazibe laughed, a low-pitched, anxious chuckle. An uncomfortable silence spread between the two fools. "At night you call his name from your dreams."

"Who are you calling?" T'Challa leapt from the roof and kicked Tayete in the chest. The vibranium embedded in the Black Panther's boot released a shockwave that knocked both the fools into the side of a blue cottage.

Kazibe fell on top of Tayete, and the pair stumbled over each other as they stood. The two fools pressed their backs against the wall. Tayete fumbled with the holster under his armpit until he produced a .50-caliber handgun, which he pointed at the Black Panther. He gripped the pistol with two trembling hands. Nostrils flared, sweat shone on his forehead.

"I am not afraid of you, panther demon," Tayete said.

"What are you doing, Tayete? You know that won't work on him." Kazibe pulled at his partner's free arm.

"I will warn you, once," T'Challa said. His voice low and grim, he remembered their derisive laughter, G'Sere howling in agony. "Pull that trigger, both of you die."

"You're lucky, panther demon." Tayete's eyes and voice grew wide and desperate. "Killmonger wants you for himself."

"Tayete, remember what you said?" Kazibe patted his partner's shoulder. "There he is. Now, you can tear him apart like you promised." Kazibe's voice dropped, and he leaned toward Tayete's ear. "You have a gun pointed directly at him, and you're still trembling."

"What did you say to me in your nightmare?" T'Challa stepped toward the two fools and the gun.

"I—I—we need to find Killmonger," Tayete said. He backed away, pointing the gun with one hand, pulling Kazibe with the other.

The pair backed away clumsily before Tayete ran and left Kazibe stuck between fear and his job as a soldier. When T'Challa started toward Kazibe, the fool stumbled backwards and ran after his partner down a narrow path of brown and black stones bordered by rows of painted stucco. The strip of stones that served as a back alley between the arrayed dwellings and commercial spaces opened up to a wide area of packed earth and scattered patches of grass. By the time T'Challa stepped into the circle, he found Captain Adebisi putting Tayete and Kazibe into headlocks under each of her arms.

Rows of soldiers adorned with the decorative skulls of Killmonger's Death Regiments emerged from between the stucco buildings. The soldiers wore grim faces, void of expression. They brandished spears and knives with black blades, pulsating dark, deadly energy stored inside the forged metal.

The sight of the Wakandan weapons and the vibranium blades—whether stolen from the Great Mound or synthesized in one of Killmonger's laboratories—stoked the Black Panther's anger. It took a good deal of strength to swallow the fury rising from his chest.

"My people, children of Bast, I will give you one chance to drop your weapons and return to the welcoming arms of your king. If we fight here today, it will be Wakandan fighting Wakandan, Wakandan killing Wakandan. That is not what I want for our country. Return to me now. Take up arms with the descendant of our beloved Bashenga, the chosen avatar of our Panther God. Help me rid our country of this pestilent discord."

The soldiers said nothing, gripping their weapons even tighter. The Death Regiments formed a circle around T'Challa. A door opened on a brown bungalow. The bare-chested bald man with the green cape stepped onto the porch. The green cape was bordered with gold embroidery, and a heavy cord of gold rope fastened beneath his throat. T'Challa recognized the glyphs sewn into the cape's fabric and the story that the ancient characters told—the story of K'Liluna, the Betrayer.

"You are in no position to offer anyone anything, T'Challa," the bald man said. He smiled with bright, evil eyes and a wide, hungry smile. "Do not underestimate the danger that surrounds you. Your power in Wakanda is nominal at best. I have an offer for you, panther demon. Surrender your crown to Killmonger. Your death will be quick. Your family will be safe."

The bald man smiled, raising his open palms high above his head. He evoked an old memory of G'Sere raising his arms, offering his praise song to Bast and the ancestors watching from Djalia. The stucco houses sank into the earth, wall by wall, until a circle of shiny laser cannons surrounded Panther King. The cannons gleamed, the sunlight streaking across the shiny, deadly metal.

"Killmonger should have told you. These cannons will not suffice. This entire base is surrounded. That goes for the underground tunnels as well." T'Challa crouched, his claws growing into sharp, black knives extending from his fingertips.

From all around the perimeter of Killmonger's base, royal soldiers appeared. Ten times more than the thousand loyals who had followed T'Challa into the town. The reserves on the hilltops fell like an endless shadow.

"Listen well, panther demon," the bald man said. He reached inside his cloak and produced a gray rifle capped with a nest of twelve rotating gun barrels. The barrels revolved with a series of clicks and lights surging through the rifle stock. "My name is Lord Karnaj. You've already met the Baron and King Cadaver. We are Wakanda's new aristocracy. Killmonger is the new ruler."

"Why doesn't Killmonger speak for himself?" T'Challa asked, but the answer did not matter. The Panther King had come to destroy this place, and nothing would stop him.

"Wakanda's rightful ruler appreciates your concern," Karnaj said. "He admires your tenacity. Even with your world crumbling, you chase your own destruction." His rifle hummed, and the nest of gun barrels glowed with fury and caged power.

"Don't worry. I'll be all right," T'Challa said with confidence, as he started toward Lord Karnaj. "Ask yourself why your new ruler would sacrifice you."

The cannons turned with a loud grinding noise, each mounted weapon yawning and surging. They blasted T'Challa. He flexed his arms as the vibranium in his panther suit absorbed the sonic blasts until a ball of red flame, a growing burning heart, hurled streams of red fire spiraling through the wind. Seconds later, T'Challa's suit released a shockwave that incinerated the cannons and sent Lord Karnaj leaping from the exploding porch.

Green and gold cape billowing in his trail, Lord Karnaj managed to roll on his shoulder and land with one knee planted firmly into the ground. The gun barrel on his rifle spun and hummed, with the synthesized vibranium unleashing a deadly charge. Karnaj pointed the weapon and screamed, but he did not aim at T'Challa. Instead, he turned his weapon onto W'Kabi, who had leaped from a neighboring bungalow. He twirled his double-edged spear so quickly that the spinning blades evoked a single sheet of polished metal. The glyphs carved into the staff glowed until the air all around W'Kabi was marked with glowing, red characters. The fire from the twirling spear blocked most of the shots from the sonic-powered rifle.

Behind W'Kabi, the Taifa Ngao and Dora Milaje flooded the decoy village. Two royal soldiers supporting W'Kabi's rear did not move quick enough to dodge the sonic blasts. The first was obliterated quickly, his body vaporized before he could even scream. The second fell, hands spread before him, face bright with agony, legs melting from the knees down.

"Do not doubt the strength of our weapons," Lord Karnaj said, calling out in triumph over the din. "Killmonger has given us power beyond reckoning. He has turned us into gods, and you will call me Lord." Karnaj screamed and fired his rifle at the royal soldiers rushing into the open mall behind W'Kabi.

The sight of the wounded soldier dressed W'Kabi with a grim sneer and eyes void of mercy, features consumed in the gray haze of war. His mind filled with memories of the young soldier crawling at his side. He refused to look down; refused to focus on anything but the memories of his beloved compatriots. Raising his spear over his head, W'Kabi yelled while the silver-black blade spat purple vibranium discharge.

In a flourish of green and gold, Lord Karnaj dove across the open mall, gripping his rifle to his chest, as he dodged the red flames and blades cutting at his head, his pliant limbs obscured in the folds of his cape. As he fled, W'Kabi stepped on Lord Karnaj's cape, pinning the flowing material to the ground. The fiery tip of W'Kabi's spear flickered with purple light emitted from pure vibranium conversion. Karnaj aimed his rifle at W'Kabi's midsection. The barrels spun, and red light surged inside the weapon.

Soldiers marked with the neon skulls of Killmonger's Death Regiments poured from the metal shelters revealed by the collapsing stucco houses. *Kill, Kill, Killmonger!* They called his name as they stormed into the melee. The Death Regiments kept advancing over and over, a rolling river of screaming faces and howling gun blasts. The sheer number of N'Jadaka's followers disturbed T'Challa. As he watched them pour from the center of the base, row after row, his heart sank. Once again, he felt like a failure. If someone would have asked at that moment, he would have given up the crown with no protest—none at all.

Even so, a part of T'Challa watched all this with a scientist's detached sentiment. He watched the swarming soldiers. The fighting, the killing and the gushing blood, pooling on the ground. He watched W'Kabi and the Death Regiment officer who called himself Lord Karnaj point their weapons at each other. He watched with amused fascination as Baron Macabre crept from the confusion of the fray, from behind a corner of ultramarine stucco. The Baron smiled, gray and black rot stretched to reveal a set of teeth, tombstone gray. The Baron reached out as W'Kabi focused his attention on the felled enemy lying in front of him.

W'Kabi, W'Kabi, W'Kabi, T'Challa thought. *How many times have I told you? Watch your surroundings.* T'Challa darted forward, leaping past the ruined blaster cannons and grabbing the Baron's arm just as the crooked claws raised ominously behind W'Kabi's head. The sudden disturbance startled W'Kabi and Lord Karnaj, who aimed his rifle toward the greater threat.

T'Challa moved quickly, but the Baron managed to grab W'Kabi's shoulder with his free hand. He heard flesh searing inside the Baron's palm. Smelled burned hair and skin. The sight of W'Kabi grimacing from the pain brought the memories of T'Challa's first encounter with the Baron and his zombified goons to the forefront of T'Challa's memory; the image of M'Jumbak smiling in the sun. The thought stoked the rage burning T'Challa's belly.

T'Challa did not remember the crashing blows he delivered to the Baron's face, chest, and stomach. Before he realized anything had happened, the Baron was lain at his feet, a mess of blood pouring from his face. T'Challa could feel the vibranium along his knuckles and elbow reverberating from the shock of the blows. With war boiling all around, spears and bullets flying, T'Challa heard W'Kabi calling him, but when T'Challa looked up he did not see W'Kabi. Instead, he saw Lord Karnaj aiming a rifle. Lord Karnaj wore a mischievous smile that reminded T'Challa of N'Jadaka.

All this death and destruction. How did you do it, N'Jadaka? T'Challa wondered to himself as he swung the Baron in a complete circle and hurled the unconscious body into Lord Karnaj, sending the pair of Death Regiment officers flying backwards to crash into a smoldering heap that had been a deadly laser cannon only minutes before.

T'Challa watched Lord Karnaj help the Baron to his feet as the pair scurried away, disappearing into the melee. Wakandan against Wakandan, kin against kin, spilling each other's blood. The spectacle saddened T'Challa, but rage burned inside him, a rage that would not allow rest until N'Jadaka was an ancestor.

"That was Baron Macabre," T'Challa continued. "The one in the green cape calls himself Lord Karnaj. It was the Baron who led Killmonger's pillaging of the abandoned mines where Ulysses Klaw died." It was hard for T'Challa to say the name of his father's murderer. Speaking that name brought back old feelings. Old rage that T'Challa thought he had overcome with the help of Monica. *Monica.* In his mind he saw her face and heard her voice. The thought of returning to her lifted T'Challa's spirit, gave him something to fight for besides revenge.

"T'Challa, I know I've been difficult," W'Kabi said. "But you left Wakanda alone when we needed you most. You turned your back on us and aligned yourself with the same powers that have been trying to conquer us for centuries."

"The Avengers are allies, W'Kabi: so are the Fantastic Four. They have proven their loyalty and their friendship a thousand times over." The Panther King turned to his Shield. "Is that why you were so upset about Monica?"

"My King... I—," W'Kabi lowered his head. "I should have never doubted you, but I thought you had abandoned us. We have seen so many leaders in other countries turn their backs on their people. Even offering their own lands to the foreign powers willing to pay the most. When I heard of your travels with the Avengers, that's what I assumed. When you returned with an outworlder on your arm, expecting us to accept her, even revere her, I... I didn't know what to think."

The crashing noises of war and bloodshed surrounded the pair. T'Challa's Kimoyo beads buzzed around his wrist and glowed like a chain fashioned from star fire. Smoke rose high and thick: even through the layers of his vibranium suit, the stench of gunpowder and blood irritated his nose.

"What do you think now?" T'Challa asked.

"I think you are full of surprises. I think you are still My King. I think you are the same young man who I trained, filled with the potential to change the world. In fact, you may be better now than you ever were."

W'Kabi extended his hand in a gesture of friendship and respect that surprised T'Challa. The gesture encouraged him and renewed his sense of confidence as Wakanda's rightful king; as the son that his father and mother had raised and taught and sacrificed so much for so that he would be prepared to lead Wakanda into the future and defend the nation during times of danger and unrest.

"I've waited a long time to hear that conviction in your voice, W'Kabi," T'Challa said. He gripped W'Kabi's hand in his own. For a moment the gesture of friendship, the significance of it all took T'Challa's mind from the battlefield.

o———————o

T'CHALLA'S MIND took him back to the previous night. Back to the chambers where Monica waited for Wakanda's Tribunal Council to pass their judgment and decide her fate. Incense and perfume replaced the scents of gunpowder and char. Monica's voice replaced the sounds of war. Her face replaced W'Kabi's stern features—her brown eyes deep as the Great Mound's interior. Her round cheeks, her black hair as real in his mind as the battle raging around him.

The chambers were dark, barely lit by torches that surrounded a thick black rug covered with pillows. The pillows were so soft underneath T'Challa's head, with Monica's soft skin pressed against his own, he almost forgot that the lavishly adorned apartment was a confinement unit.

"I'm trying, T'Challa," Monica said. "But it's hard. I feel like I'm coming between you and your people. That's the worst part of all this." She waved her arms, demonstrating *all this* included the furnished apartment.

"The world has gone mad," T'Challa said. "This is not the Wakanda that I knew as a child or even as a young man. I wanted to show you the country I fell in love with." T'Challa stroked Monica's cheek. "Killmonger has incited so much fear, so much violence and mistrust. My people have internalized much of this unrest. Their world is in peril. They don't know who to trust. It's not just us. They don't trust each other."

"This is more than mistrust, T." Monica rested her chin on his chest, stared into his eyes. "When it was all about mistrusting the foreigner, I could handle that. I knew I would grow on them sooner or later, but I'm not just the foreigner anymore. I'm the outworlder accused of murder. Not only that, I'm accused of cutting a councilor's throat in the royal palace. They have my fingerprints. They have my face on camera. Even if you prove my innocence, in the eyes of some, I will always be guilty no matter what."

Doors on the far side of the room opened and Tanzika entered, bearing a silver tray filled with spiced fish and vegetables. T'Challa smelled braised meat, grilled cabbage, the collards prepared for Monica. Tanzika nodded to T'Challa, bending her knee in reverence.

"Do you need anything else, My King?" she asked. Her eyes low, her voice deferential, she spoke as if T'Challa was the only person in the room.

"No, that will be fine, Tanzika." T'Challa watched her place the tray on the floor, nod again, and turn to the doors that opened for her as soon as she approached them. He returned his attention to Monica, but he remembered the subversive tone Tanzika shared with Zatama the night of his murder.

"I have found Zatama's murderer, and I have the evidence to prove it," T'Challa said just as the doors slid shut behind Tanzika.

"Why didn't you wait until she was gone to tell me that? You're not helping, T. In fact, you're making things worse. Your people believe you're protecting me because I'm your woman. Be careful. Someone could use this against you. Especially with all the turmoil your friend is causing." Monica spoke with mildly irritated sarcasm that reminded T'Challa of Shuri. Then she paused and stared, eyes wide with knowing before mouthing the words.

"You wanted her to hear. Didn'you?"

Later that night, T'Challa stood over Monica and watched her sleep. He blew her a kiss before he crept out of the room. W'Kabi's guards stiffened when they saw T'Challa. He nodded at the soldiers but kept his stride brisk, quickening his pace until he stood once again in the gardens behind the palace. His panther suit materialized around his body, and he leapt into the trees with the waxing moon shining through the night.

The Black Panther found a thick limb in the treetops that branched over the trail that led to the river, poised between a green canopy of leaves and the worn grass below. Both loomed quietly, bathing him in silvery moonlight. Sleuth that the Panther King was, he waited, hoping for his bogie to arrive sooner rather than later. He wondered if he had arrived too late but dismissed the thought. No, the prey he was hunting needed time to prepare. The

security around the royal palace had been set on high alert, and nothing had come through his Kimoyo beads. T'Challa used the neural sensors in his panther suit to link into the computer system and dial the palace security system back to normal alert, then to standby.

After a few minutes, T'Challa heard rustling in the bushes below. He caught the scent of a person who had followed him out to the riverbank, recognizing it instantly. The Panther King did not know whether to be enraged or amused. Both emotions fought for space in his head. T'Challa leapt from his place on the tree branch. He timed his jump perfectly. As his pursuer stepped into the clearing beneath the tree, T'Challa planted the balls of his feet between the hunter's shoulder blades. The Black Panther landed on the ground and crouched as the man who had followed him fell hard, smashing his chest and face into the dirt and grass.

"W'Kabi, what are you doing here?" T'Challa asked. By the time he finished his sentence, he was already on top of him. The Panther King wrapped his hand around W'Kabi's throat and held W'Kabi to the ground. "Following your mad king?" T'Challa kept his voice low even as he growled in W'Kabi's face.

"I had to. You have been acting entirely strangely lately. Your woman is accused of murder." W'Kabi started to raise his voice but lowered his tone when T'Challa raised a black gloved finger and set the finger to his black mask.

"You are not the same man whom I fought with when we avenged your father. You have betrayed your country and taken up league with foreigners. You have brought a murderer into the royal palace built by your ancestors…"

"Shush," T'Challa said. Even through W'Kabi's grumbling, he heard the footsteps sliding through the grass. He considered W'Kabi for one more moment. "You want justice for Zatama's murder? Follow me, but not too close. You make too much noise."

With those words, T'Challa left his old friend, the most reliable and formidable of all Wakanda's soldiers, lying on his back. The Black Panther returned to the trees, leaping as fast as the strength in his legs would allow. He jumped and flipped and darted from branch to branch. The darkness gifting him with stealth, the Panther King landed in a clearing. This time he allowed the suit to absorb all the sound from his landing. He did not want to take any chances.

He watched the figure standing by the river. Even without the moonlight he would have recognized this person by scent alone. This was a woman who always smelled like spice and the sweat that came with working in kitchens. Still, to be sure, he took note of the moonlight shining on her bun, the long, slender muscles in her arms, her long neck a sign of regality in her bloodline. The woman carried a satchel on her arm. When she reached into it, T'Challa reacted. He knew the woman was about to throw something away, and he planned to stop her before she did.

He sprinted toward her in total silence, even the sound of rushing wind absorbed by his panther suit. When he grabbed the woman, she opened her mouth to scream or shriek, but no sound came out. Through the neural sensors connected to his nervous system, linking his brain to the vibranium-powered tech in his panther suit, T'Challa sent a message to cease the absorption of sound in the surrounding space. The noise of the world returned, rushing back with intense clarity.

The Black Panther heard the river flowing past, the light breeze and vegetation rustling all around. He heard W'Kabi running through the dense foliage that separated the palace gardens from the River of Grace and Wisdom. He heard the air rushing from the woman petrified in his grasp. He heard her heart thump with the fear.

"These are dangerous times, Tanzika," T'Challa said. The growling in his voice hinted at the rage that swam in his belly. "A woman of the royal house should not be out alone at this time of night."

"My—My King, you, you don't understand. Please, let me explain," Tanzika said.

"I have already heard everything I needed to hear." Regret and sadness, the swirling emotions of failure, replaced the rage in T'Challa's voice. "And I have seen almost everything I need to see." T'Challa grabbed the bag hanging from the woman's arm.

"No, Your Majesty, you don't understand." Tanzika made a feeble effort to grab the bag back.

"Figuring out how you got Monica's fingerprints on the murder weapon was easy." T'Challa spoke with a calm, matter-of-fact tone. He allowed the pragmatist in him, the researcher sharing empirical data, to speak. "The carving knives that Monica used to eat. You removed the steak knife blade and replaced it with a dagger. Now, getting Monica's face on camera killing Zatama: it took me a little longer to figure that one out, but not too much longer." T'Challa allowed his mask to dematerialize, so Tanzika could see his face and look into the eyes of her king.

T'Challa expected the sight to humble Tanzika. Instead, he saw fury in her eyes, and he wondered if her anger had been triggered by the rage pent-up in his heart—the rage he struggled to suppress even at this moment.

"You think you know so much." Now Tanzika spat her words, as disgust and contempt filled her voice.

"On the contrary. I understand that I know very little, especially with the developments of recent weeks." He tugged at the bag that she seemed to cling on to for dear life. He did not pull hard though. Instead, he stared into Tanzika's eyes, allowing the rage in his heart to seep into his face.

By the time she released the bag, W'Kabi had made his way from the dense underbrush. He ran to the Panther King. The old soldier, the Shield of Wakanda, looked confused.

"Tanzika, what's going on?" W'Kabi said. His voice was filled with uncertainty.

"Let's see," T'Challa said. He released Tanzika's arms and rifled through her bag. She tried to jump into the river, but W'Kabi grabbed her before she could escape.

"Actually, it is a fortunate accident that you followed me tonight, W'Kabi. I would call it a blessing," T'Challa said. For the first time that night, he smiled. "As the Americans say, Bast is good all the time."

T'Challa began to empty Tanzika's bag. First, he pulled out a wig, then a set of clothes that matched the dress that Monica had worn the night that Zatama was murdered. Then he pulled out a mask and held it up to the moonlight. Even with its slack, drooping expression, the truth was evident. The mask had been made to mimic Monica's face.

"This doesn't change anything," Tanzika hissed. "Killmonger will be the king of Wakanda, and I will be his queen."

"That's what he told you?" T'Challa laughed.

"Tanzika," W'Kabi said, shaking his head. Disappointment and pain filled his voice.

"Laugh if you want to." Tanzika continued her tirade. "You brought an outworlder to our country. You made us serve her. You would dare to make *her* queen. Your father must be ashamed." Tanzika spat in T'Challa's face.

T'Challa did not call his mask to shield him. Instead, he allowed himself to feel the saliva spraying his cheeks and his eyes. It was as if Wakanda itself had just spit in his face. However, T'Challa did not question his place in Wakanda, his place on the throne, but he did think of Monica. He thought about everything she had done for him, all that she had experienced. She had given him his life back, even before they fell in love. It was Monica's support that reassured him and girded his spirit. T'Challa knew what he had to do about Killmonger, about Monica's place in Wakanda, about everything.

The Panther King turned to W'Kabi, but Wakanda's Shield stared at the ground—his shame a sharp contrast against Tanzika's self-righteous hatred.

"T'CHALLA, LOOK out!" Adebisi screamed at the Panther King.

The captain's voice returned T'Challa to the present. The sounds of the river and the jungle creatures were replaced by the sounds of war. The bright, blinding light of battle replaced peaceful darkness. Adebisi pulled his arm as a spear flew so close, it grazed the Black

Panther's cheek, the metal in the blade sparking the vibranium that covered his face.

T'Challa watched the spear break through the blue stucco behind him. When he looked up, he saw Malice. The smell of Killmonger, the stench of death hung heavy in the air, and he wondered why he had never caught N'Jadaka's scent on Tanzika.

Another mystery I will soon uncover, he thought.

But for now, T'Challa would deal with the work at hand. He watched as Lord Karnaj and Baron Macabre emerged from the smoke and confusion of the battle, taking their places at Malice's side. There they stood, three of Killmonger's Death Regiment officers.

"Did you think you would rout us so easily, panther demon?" Lord Karnaj laughed hard, the barrels on his rifle spinning, glowing with dark red light.

"You take the one with the bald head. I'll handle the woman and the skeleton," Adebisi growled, twirling her own spear with one hand.

"No, you won't," W'Kabi said. "You'll save one for me."

"All three of you are fellow Wakandans," T'Challa said, calling out to Malice, Karnaj, and Macabre. "I feel generous today, so I will offer you one final opportunity to lay your weapons at your feet and turn yourselves over to Wakanda's royal court."

"Your court lost its authority a long time ago," Malice said. "This is for Killmonger."

"*Kill, kill, Killmonger!*" She raised her palm and caught her flying spear as it returned to its owner. She shouted, "Death to the panther demon!" before hurling the weapon at T'Challa. Her comrades followed her lead and fired their weapons. Karnaj shot his rifle and ran for cover. Macabre extended his open palms, black flames swirling from his fingers toward T'Challa with the fury of a thousand howling souls clawing their way from Death's Domain.

T'Challa leapt ahead, flipping forward to kick Malice in the chest. Adebisi went low, diving to the ground to block Macabre's flames with her double-edged blades.

The stucco behind T'Challa and his comrades exploded. Everything afterwards was a blur. T'Challa's instincts took over; before he knew it, he was trading blows with Malice. The woman was quick and agile. She dodged T'Challa's flying kick, landing a blow of her own and planting her knee in his stomach.

Malice reminded him of Monica. It wasn't just her natural beauty or the flawless brown skin. It was her fire, her conviction. It was Malice's staunch adherence to her beliefs and the code that she fought for. Her resemblance to Monica made it difficult to fight her, but not impossible. Still, instead of punching her, T'Challa subdued Malice, locking her arms behind her back. He covered her mouth, allowing the knockout gas emitted from the palm of his glove to do its work. Malice slumped, her entire body relaxing in the Black Panther's grasp.

T'Challa looked to his side and saw the Baron lying on the ground, Adebisi's blade pressed beneath the Baron's chin while W'Kabi pushed his spearhead against the Baron's heart. T'Challa also noticed the burn marks on W'Kabi's arms, where the Baron had laid his fiery grip. Another reminder of the depth and mystery of N'Jadaka's power source. A part of T'Challa had to acknowledge Killmonger's resourcefulness.

T'Challa surveyed the former farm village, laid to waste and ruin, destroyed by the onset of civil war. The colorful stucco houses smoldered. Soldiers on both sides of the conflict lay strewn about the battleground. Most were dead. A few moaned and tossed on the ground, or limped through the ruins, suffering from multiple injuries. Some wore the insignia of the panther clan; others wore the skulls and neon war paint of the Death Regiments. All wore the stamps of their mother country. All were Wakandan. This fact saddened T'Challa, filling him with regret, even as the surviving, victorious Taifa Ngao rallied and cheered, fists in the air.

"Wakanda forever!" they cried, voices ragged from combat.

Zatama had hoped for another way to solve the conflict with

Killmonger, but T'Challa saw the truth.

There would be much more suffering before this unhappy business concluded. The sound of surging energy turned T'Challa's head. Lord Karnaj stood over a young soldier, one of T'Challa's own. The boy held up his hands and cried for mercy as Karnaj unloaded his rifle into the boy's chest. Taku tackled the Death Regiment officer. Too late to stop the killing, Taku did what he could and ripped the blaster from Karnaj's grip. Soft-spoken man of peace, communications specialist with the heart of a poet, Taku screamed and cursed. His eyes mirrored the rage of civil war—its fruit scattered about the sacked village.

"You murdered an unarmed child begging for mercy," Taku screamed. "How could you be so cruel?" With blow after blow, he battered Karnaj's face. The Death Regiment officer laughed and spat blood at Taku, incensing the communications officer further. Taku swung until the laughter stopped, reduced to blood-soaked gurgles, but he kept punching, even when the battered flesh turned into broken bone. Eyes glassy with rage, something held in Taku's heart his entire life was finally expelled.

T'Challa understood rage. He understood Taku's need to release, so he watched. W'Kabi stepped forward to restrain Taku, T'Challa raised his hand in protest.

"Aren't you going to do something?" W'Kabi asked, in shock. Like Zatama, Taku had been a peacemaker all his years. "He is going mad."

"This is what you wanted, isn't it?" T'Challa said. "To see the dragon in Taku? In me?" T'Challa could not hide his irritation. "This is the end result, old friend. This is what happens when we give in to the dragon—give in to rage."

"You call yourself 'Lord,'" Taku panted, every syllable accentuated by the sound of fists plowing into flesh, shattering the bones in Karnaj's face. "Your leader knows your title is meaningless. If you were a true lord, he wouldn't have left you here to murder children, wouldn't have left you here to die."

"Please, stop. Mercy!" Karnaj pleaded, his voice reduced to a ragged whimper.

"Lord Karnaj wants mercy?" Taku asked, mocking him. He smashed Karnaj's bloody face into the ground. "Look at the boy you just killed. A recent recruit, barely out of childhood. This was his first battle. You will receive the same mercy you offered that boy."

Taku raised his fist, but Adebisi grabbed his wrist. Tugging at the Dora Milaje's grip, face twisted with rage all too familiar, Taku looked the way T'Challa felt.

"Enough," the Black Panther said, in a low voice, hoping to calm Taku.

"Did you see what he did to that child?" Taku's voice rose. His eyes widened. Spittle flew from his mouth.

"His death will not bring you peace. Trust me. Look at W'Kabi." T'Challa leaned close to Taku, so that their noses almost touched. "Look at me. You know my pain better than almost anyone. Is this what you want? Once you kill someone up close and personal like this, the memory never leaves you. You can never go back."

"He's right." W'Kabi stepped forward. "Don't end up like me." Wakanda's Shield patted Taku's shoulder. "On this day I witnessed another side of you, but I regret seeing it, seeing you like this."

Taku ignored W'Kabi's words and pulled until Adebisi released his wrist. He lifted the deceased boy lying next to the sniveling Lord Karnaj. Turning his back on his King and Wakanda's Shield, Taku cradled the limp body in his arms, as if he had birthed him himself.

"I want both of you to look at me and pay heed," Taku said. "This is the product of your war with Killmonger. How many of Wakanda's children must die before Killmonger is neutralized, and all this foolishness is put to rest?"

Taku walked back toward the ravaged village. T'Challa wondered where the communications specialist was taking the young Taifa Ngao. To bury him, perhaps? T'Challa decided that he did not want to know, but he would learn his name. *So many new names to fill the pages of his secret book.* The incalculable cost of his choices weighed heavily on him. Taku's words had pierced his vibranium armor and sunk deeply into T'Challa's heart. He stood beside W'Kabi and watched Taku carry the dead child until the pair disappeared.

"All this and still no Killmonger," W'Kabi said. He spoke in a faraway voice, full of disbelief.

N'Jadaka, where are you? T'Challa thought. With the aid of the Taifa Ngao and the Dora Milaje, he had won a key victory against Killmonger's Death Regiments, but at what cost? He considered Tanzika's treachery and Taku's violent outburst. War was poisoning them all. Who else would turn against him? Who else would lose their minds to the savagery of war? The weight of the dead soldiers lying around the bloody ruins hung heavily over his head.

That's the problem with dragons. They destroy everything—even after they've been slain.

CHAPTER TWELVE

BLOOD ON THE ALTAR

HIGH WITHIN a mountain range that borders the northern region of Wakanda, the Land of Chilling Mist was a strange place. The climate was markedly different from that of the Golden City or the fertile fields of Alkama. It was a mythical place where aircraft were said to fail or disappear in the mists. T'Challa could count the times that he had been there on one hand, and those times, like this one, had been on foot.

T'Chaka had hated the cold. Even though he had walked every inch of Wakanda with a young T'Challa in tow, T'Chaka had only taken his son to the Land of Chilling Mist once or twice. T'Challa could not quite remember. The pink skies and the snowcapped mountains in the distance looked familiar, but the purpose of his journey filled him with an ominous sense of déjà vu. Like something bad had happened there long ago. Something that T'Challa had done his best to wipe from his memory.

The Panther King stood before a long rope bridge stretched over a vast canyon, steam and mist obscuring the true depth of the wide chasm. The wind blew and howled, rocking the bridge from side to side. Behind T'Challa stood Tayete and Kazibe. Both of the two fools looked fearful. Behind Tayete and Kazibe, Adebisi stood with her arms crossed over her chest, and Taku held a small stun pistol aimed at the traitors. Unaffected by the icy wind rushing over the canyon, the Dora Milaje captain had refused to wear a coat or even a light jacket over her armor.

Monica had come as well. T'Challa had tried to stop her but she ignored him. She would not go into the Land of Chilling Mist, but she had been adamant about escorting him to its borders. After spending several days under house arrest, another week confined to the safety of the Golden City, she needed to get out and see as much of the world as possible, despite the dangers. She needed to feel free.

Most of the Death Regiments had been captured, but a few had fled into the Land of Chilling Mist. According to the two fools, that was where N'Jadaka ran an underground operation called Resurrection Altar.

"Tayete, it's time to test the validity of your information." T'Challa stared at the rope bridge that stretched across the canyon toward the towering icy mountains and the sky gray in the distance. With warm air pressing his back, T'Challa marveled at the stunning, scenic view. The mountain rose above the surrounding plains, its peak looming over the Wakandan grasslands. As beautiful as it was, the Land of Chilling Mist was said to be the home of evil spirits and strange creatures. Few ventured there, and those who did refused to return. When he turned back to Tayete and Kazibe, T'Challa found the pair with wide eyes and fearful expressions. Tayete was trembling, and T'Challa knew that it was not because of the cold.

"I know you're afraid, Tayete," T'Challa tilted his head and raised his eyebrows. "At this point it doesn't matter what's across that bridge. It doesn't matter what you believe Killmonger will do to you for leading me to him. Right now, you should fear my wrath more than anything else."

"I'm not afraid of anything, panther demon," Tayete said.

Adebisi punched him in the mouth. "Show some respect, traitor."

Tayete licked the blood from his lip and stuck out his scrawny chest when he spoke, but the fear in his voice was evident. "It's just… You haven't seen what we've seen. I must warn you. There are things on the other side of that bridge that you must take into… *consideration*."

"The only thing I need to consider, Tayete, is the punishment you will receive for your treachery," T'Challa said. Allowing his rage to seep into his throat, he pointed. "Your actions today will affect my decision, and ultimately save your life or condemn you."

T'Challa gave Tayete and Kazibe a hard glare before he turned to Monica. She stood with Taku beside the Quinjet that had brought the group out to the cliffside. She wore a black bubble goose coat that reminded T'Challa of their time in Harlem. He fought against the regret he felt for bringing her to Wakanda. If he had known what she was going to encounter, he would have left her in the United States despite the love that he felt, even at that very moment. He walked over to Monica and slipped his arms around her waist. In turn, she pressed herself against T'Challa and wrapped her arms around his neck.

"I'm not going to ask if you really have to do this," Monica said. She stroked the back of his neck in that way that always drove him crazy. "I know you have your duties, T, but what about us? What if you don't come back? What am I supposed to do then?"

"What's the name of that singing group you always used to talk about?" T'Challa asked before answering his own question. "The Isley Brothers. What do they say in that song, 'Voyage to Atlantis?'" He tightened his grip around her waist, lowered his voice and did his best to croon the words and mimic Ronald Isley.

"You better come back to me," she said and smiled, "pounding her fist against his chest playfully. "There's only one singer in this group."

"Will you sing to me before I go?" T'Challa asked.

Monica stood on her tiptoes and raised her lips to his ear. "When you get back. I want you to have something to look forward to." She nuzzled her nose against his neck. Then, abruptly, she pulled back and stared at T'Challa with one curiously raised eyebrow. "But I don't understand. Why do you have to go alone? Why can't you take W'Kabi or Adebisi with you?"

"W'Kabi is Taifa Ngao, the Shield of Wakanda. It is his sworn duty to protect Wakanda from all threats, both foreign and domestic, as they say in the West. With much of N'Jadaka's Death Regiments confined in the Golden City and the rest on the run, W'Kabi has his hands full. Adebisi leads the Sacred Eighteen, who hold my life in the truth of their hands and their training. They are protecting my heart. Adebisi says you have more training to finish." T'Challa wrapped his arms around Monica's shoulders, allowing her to rest her cheek against his chest. He stared over her head at the steam rising from the canyon, and the rope bridge whose end disappeared in the billowing mist in the distance. "This conflict ultimately rests between N'Jadaka and me. I have to deal with this threat alone."

Monica huffed in protest. "For the record, I never liked him."

"You never said anything."

She shrugged. "If you like 'em, we love 'em. But I never trusted him. I saw through his BS the moment you introduced us." She looked up at T'Challa with a frustrated smirk and weariness in her eyes. "But I could never have imagined this."

That makes two of us, T'Challa thought. *She's a better judge of character than me.* Instead of speaking, he kissed her. Slowly and deeply. He tasted as much of her as he could, took in her scent, hoping that this moment would carry him through the difficult journey ahead. T'Challa sighed and stroked her head once more before he let her go and turned to Adebisi.

The Panther King nodded, a signal for Taku and Adebisi to remove the fetters that bound the wrists of Tayete and Kazibe. The two fools looked at each other, their faces long and bright with confusion.

"Why are they freeing us, Tayete?" Kazibe asked. He spoke in a low voice, almost a whisper.

"It is obvious, Kazibe. He wants to… He wants to…." Tayete frowned as if his next words had lodged themselves deep in his throat.

"I am not Killmonger," T'Challa answered the question himself. "I do not rule through tyranny and oppression. My rule comes from the divine decree of Bast, the most beloved. Just as she has taught me the virtues of compassion and forgiveness, it is my job to teach those qualities to my people. What better way to teach these principles than to embody them?"

After removing the manacles that bound their wrists, Adebisi handed each of the men spears adorned with steel blades. She eyed the former rebels suspiciously.

"My king has instructed me to arm the two of you. I do not agree with this decision, but His Majesty's wisdom is far greater than my own. But let me warn you. If either of you attempts any treachery against him, you will face the wrath of an entire country, and I will be there to kill you myself."

"No need for threats, Adebisi," T'Challa said. Even though he spoke to the Dora Milaje captain, the Panther King kept his focus on the rebel soldiers who would soon escort him across the bridge and into the greatest challenge of his life.

"Why trust them?" Monica scowled at the two traitors.

"I don't. They understand the precarious nature of their situation. Besides, if I detect the slightest instance of treachery from either one of these two, I will release the anger that I am doing my best to control. Then they will answer for G'Sere, M'Jumbak, and the rest of the lives that have been destroyed because of Killmonger's lies."

With those words, T'Challa hugged Monica one more time before turning to Tayete and Kazibe. The Panther King did not speak again. The time for talking was concluded. Instead, he pointed at the rope bridge and stared at the two fools. Tayete and Kazibe heeded the gesture and made their way toward the rope bridge. The pair stepped onto the bridge nervously. Just then, a strong wind blew across the canyon and rocked the rope bridge from side to side like a cradle. Tayete turned his head back, his eyes wide, pleading, begging T'Challa to turn around before it was too late.

It's already too late, T'Challa thought as he stepped onto the bridge. *It was too late for me the moment I saw my father's corpse, the moment I heard the name Ulysses Klaw.* The mist from the canyon felt warm, and T'Challa felt the contrast with the cold wind blowing from the other side of the chasm. He walked slowly. Not that he was afraid of falling. In fact, falling off the bridge might be easier compared to the battle that he would face when he crossed it.

He knew that Monica was watching him cross over into the mist. He wanted to turn around and see her face one last time, but he would not allow himself to do so. He needed to focus. He knew there was a high probability that he would not return. That's why he had asked her to sing for him. He had wanted her voice, her song, fresh in his memory. In case her voice was the last thing he heard. It would have been a most proper send-off to the realm of the ancestors. But she had refused. Now he had to settle for memory. And he would. He would cling to that last night in Harlem, when she had stood on the stage in that crowded basement lounge and sang like T'Challa was the only person in the room. He would take that memory to the grave with him. But N'Jadaka had been there that night as well. T'Challa hated to share that memory, but it was all he had.

As if cued by T'Challa's reverie, steam and heavy mist rose from the canyon, so thick he had trouble seeing through it—even with his enhanced vision and the infrared sensors in the lenses of his armor. More wind blew in from the frozen landscape on the other side of the canyon. The bridge blew back and forth, and T'Challa watched with great amusement as Tayete and Kazibe grabbed the ropes for dear life. The mist rising from the canyon made the wooden slats of the bridge slick and slippery, and even T'Challa had to mind his footing. He could only imagine the difficulty that Tayete and Kazibe were having.

Watching the pair inch their way across the bridge, T'Challa could not help remembering G'Sere dying in his arms and the burning villages that Killmonger had sacked shortly after the Black Panther's return from the United States.

It would serve them right if they fell, T'Challa thought. He watched them stumble and inch forward nervously, knowing he would not let them fall, knowing he would save the pair. He needed them to lead him to N'Jadaka.

Half an hour passed before T'Challa and his hostage guides made it to the other side of the bridge. T'Challa stepped off the bridge onto the packed snow with feelings of impending dread and angst fighting for space in his head. He surveyed the endless miles of snow and the black, snowcapped mountains that formed a huge wall of rock and ice that blotted out everything behind them and made him feel as if he were imprisoned. As quickly as Monica was freed, he found himself trapped.

Tayete and Kazibe huddled together in a shivering mass of fur-and-hideskin coats. Sinking, legs up to their calves in the snow, they used the spears that Taku had given them as walking sticks to keep their balance and to help them navigate the icy terrain. Suddenly, Tayete stopped in the middle of his icy march. He quit walking so quickly that Kazibe almost tumbled over him into the snow. Had it not been for the spear that Taku had provided earlier, Kazibe would have disappeared into the white cold.

"Aren't you cold, *p-p-p*-panther demon?" Tayete asked. His teeth chattered as he spoke, and he patted himself furiously. He wrapped his arms around himself as if to stop himself from breaking into pieces. "Don't you have some kind of gadget in that costume that can keep us warm?"

"Keep moving," T'Challa answered. "The quicker you lead me to Killmonger, the quicker I can get you out of the cold."

T'Challa spoke with a gruff tone even though he wanted to laugh. Still, he had to be careful. This was not a time when he wanted either of the traitors to feel at ease or comfortable. They were not forgiven.

The panther armor did have instruments that could control his temperature. However, T'Challa had disabled the climate controls. This place, however well isolated, was part of Wakanda. If there were people living out here, they were his people as well. He had chosen to walk among them, so it was only fitting that he chose to see how they lived. The thermometer gauge inside the suit measured the outer temperature worsening rapidly. T'Challa looked up at the round, yellow sun burning its way through the hazy pink mist that covered the sky.

What powers are in control here? What kind of force keeps this place cold in the middle of a sweltering jungle and blazing savannah? T'Challa wondered as he continued his trek into the frozen wasteland. He was confident that the source of this power would reveal to him the root of Killmonger's strength as well. T'Challa wondered if he really wanted to find out what had created Killmonger and the Death Regiments.

The wind kicked up around T'Challa and his weary companions, tossing snow to and fro, all around. That's when he heard the voices. Faint and distant, riding the wind. The voices were coming from miles away, and Tayete and Kazibe could not hear them. Even with his enhanced hearing T'Challa struggled, but he heard them all the same, dancing in the wind like so many tumbling leaves. Two voices stood out from the others. Despite the distance and the snow between them, T'Challa identified them the moment he heard them. The Panther King remembered the so-called King Cadaver's throaty, saliva-drenched gurgles. He had intimate knowledge of Cadaver's voice. In fact, the knowledge was too close for his liking. He remembered the telepath's words shredding through his head like razors. Scraping the inside of his skull. Digging and clawing through the Panther King's brain.

Still, it was N'Jadaka's voice that caused T'Challa the most discomfort. Too many memories. Too many mixed emotions bouncing around in the fractured darkness of his mind and heart. T'Challa could have recognized that voice in his sleep, and he could have picked that voice from a din of thousands. It was the arrogance, the condescension that he recognized. But mostly he was familiar with the anger that always managed to seep into N'Jadaka's voice. Sometimes it was buried beneath platitudes and well-spoken arguments. Other times it had been out in the open, blaring uncontrollably. But it was always there. The anger was near the surface, but T'Challa had misunderstood its source.

This seemed like it was one of the times that N'Jadaka's anger was buried deeply. So deeply that the people around him could not detect it at all. But even through the snow and ice, and howling winds that separated them, T'Challa heard the controlled anger and listened with great care.

"I used to be so afraid of this place. All those stories." King Cadaver's voice traveled with the wind. "When you first brought me here, it was my first time seeing snow. I had only lived in my village." His teeth chattering, he sloshed through the snow behind his massive leader. "It feels like a lifetime ago."

"You were a different person then," Killmonger said. That rage that T'Challa had been acquainted with moved stealthily beneath a veneer of fraternal compassion. "Back then you were merely a man. You were lost, searching for purpose. Now look at you. You are a king among men. When this is all over, you will rule Wakanda by my side. A portion of this great land will be yours to command."

"Yes, you are a king now," N'Jadaka continued. "You have power beyond reckoning. Unfathomable power. Your enemies will kneel before you and beg you to spare their minds. You have been given the power to invade the thoughts of anyone you choose. Even the great Black Panther himself barely escaped your plundering of his mind. How is a mystery I must solve. One day soon."

The voices in the wind angered T'Challa, but he smiled in the darkness under his mask. "You will learn more than you bargained for, much sooner than you think, old friend," T'Challa muttered.

"What was that? Did you say something?" Tayete stopped and turned back, yelling through the wind at the Panther King.

"Keep moving," T'Challa said.

"Please, Tayete, let's just go," Kazibe pleaded, teeth chattering. "We've done enough to upset him already."

The wind blew without reprieve, forcing Tayete to ball himself inside the heavy bundle of furs and coats that protected him from the cold. Kazibe pulled at Tayete's arm, urging his friend to resume their march. T'Challa took a deep, calming breath and focused his thoughts on the chattering voices propelled by the freezing blast.

"The Black Panther is resourceful, commander." The frozen breeze hissed as it brought King Cadaver's voice to the Black Panther's ear. Struggling to match Killmonger's long strides in the snow, Cadaver's voice, weighted with exhaustion, worked its way in and out of his lungs. "Aren't you concerned about the news from the base? He has sacked the training grounds and captured the remaining Death Regiments. Everyone except for me."

The sounds of footsteps crushing through the snow ceased, replaced by a rageful whisper, a swift rush. Killmonger's hand closed around Cadaver's throat.

"I could never be concerned with the actions of a spoiled, insolent child. T'Challa is doing exactly what I want him to do. Never question my actions or decisions again, Cadaver. Remember, I'm the one who gave you your powers. I made you, and I can just as easily destroy you." The snowstorm gave N'Jadaka's voice a hissing effect that clawed T'Challa's ears.

That's it, my friend, he thought with a rueful smile. *Let the rage consume you.* The thought of Killmonger losing control at the mere mention of the Black Panther's victory filled him with satisfaction. N'Jadaka's arrogance would be his undoing, and it would help to make T'Challa's job that much easier.

T'Challa continued to listen in on the party marching ahead. He listened as the sound of steam, of hot air meeting the frigid wind, grew all around. He heard the rhythmic undulations of warm air, the crush of snow surrendering to the footsteps crossing over stone. The timbre, the echo of each boot told T'Challa that the stone was hewn and polished. T'Challa also heard another set of footfalls rising to meet the party. The Panther King listened to the swishing sound of silken robes rustling across the smooth stone floor—and the slithering voice that followed.

"Erik Killmonger, welcome back. I trust that you had a safe journey. I see that you have brought the good King with you. Where are the rest of your Death Regiments?"

"Lord Sombre," N'Jadaka said. The rage in his voice disguised by a false veneer of deference. "King Cadaver has been marveling at the wondrous landscape we've created. I would be remiss if I did not remind the good King that the land claimed by the line of Bashenga belongs to me now. I have chosen to share the land with the people of Wakanda. All of Wakanda's people will share the fruits of her bounty, not merely a chosen few." N'Jadaka paused and sighed. "As far as my Death Regiments go, let's just say that they've been delayed."

A FEW more hours passed, taking T'Challa and his guides into the late afternoon, when the trio encountered a great flowing river populated by huge chunks of broken ice floating dangerously downstream. They stood at the edge of the water, watching the frozen blocks float past. T'Challa could feel the cold air coming off the river, and he knew that his guides must have been freezing. He wanted to turn around, and a big part of him could not help thinking of a warm beach. He imagined Monica stretched before him in a two-piece bathing suit, sunlight dripping off her brown skin. The thought warmed T'Challa and emboldened him. Monica alone was more than enough reason to make it back to the Golden City and the royal palace.

"There's no bridge here, panther demon. We must turn back, now," Tayete said, his eyelids lowered. He waved a hand as if dismissing the entire outing and T'Challa.

"Will you shut up?" Kazibe demanded. "You've gotten us into enough trouble with your smart-alecky mouth and your ridiculous antics."

T'Challa shook his head and smiled to himself, careful not to show too much mirth at the banter between the two fools. He took a deep breath, spread his arms.

"Move back," T'Challa said. He knelt by the edge of the flowing water and planted his arms deep into the ice until he was covered up to his elbows in the frozen material. He planted his feet, tensed his arms. Grunting, T'Challa pulled until he broke a huge chunk of ice from the edge of the flowing stream.

Tayete and Kazibe stumbled backwards until they both fell on their backsides in the cold snow. With expressions of awe stretching their faces, they watched T'Challa pick up a chunk of ice three times his size and set it down, creating a makeshift bridge crossing over the freezing water.

"Now we can cross," T'Challa said. He pointed to the chunk of ice and stared at Tayete and Kazibe. "Move," the Panther King demanded.

With hesitance, Tayete and Kazibe made their way to the frozen hunk. Kazibe crossed first. With fear in his eyes and puffs of warm breath steaming the air, he ran and stumbled across the hunk of ice until he fell onto the other side of the stream. Tayete stood trembling before the frozen block. He raised one boot to step onto the bridge, but T'Challa grabbed his arm, giving it a not-so-gentle squeeze.

"One more thing, Tayete," T'Challa said.

"What's that, panther demon?" Tayete stammered.

"I am the chosen avatar of the Panther God, the descendant of Bashenga, the true King of Wakanda." He grabbed two fistfuls of Tayete's coat and pulled the frightened soldier so close that their noses almost touched. "If you call me panther demon one more time, I will leave your remains to freeze out here in the snow and the ice. No one will ever hear from you again. Do you understand?"

"Yes," Tayete said, his eyes wide. He trembled so hard in T'Challa's grasp that the Panther King could not tell whether it was cold or fear that made Tayete tremble uncontrollably.

"Yes, what?" T'Challa growled.

"Yes, Your Majesty," Tayete conceded.

"Good. Now go." T'Challa pushed Tayete toward the frozen hunk that bridged the icy stream.

Tayete's feet were heavier than his companion's; as soon as Tayete stepped onto the makeshift bridge, the ice began to crack.

"Careful, Tayete," T'Challa said. He did not attempt to hide the amusement in his voice. "If you fall into the river, that's it. You will freeze almost instantly. There will be nothing that anyone can do to save you—not even me."

Tayete tripped as the ice cracked beneath his feet. He screamed and stumbled forward in a frantic flailing run as the ice crumbled beneath his feet. As soon as he dove onto the snowy bank on the other side of the bridge, the ice shattered completely and fell into a mess of frozen chunks that were carried downstream. Tayete turned over on his elbows and watched the broken chunks fall into the water as the current swept them away. He jumped up, dusting the snow off his hide coat. He laughed and pointed a derisive finger at the Black Panther.

"Ha! Your ice bridge is gone panther... *king...* what are you going to do now?" Tayete asked.

No sooner than the words had escaped Tayete's mouth, than T'Challa crouched and leapt into the air, jumping across the freezing water in one easy stride. He landed right in front of Tayete and Kazibe in a crouching stance, sending flakes of snow spraying through the air, knocking Tayete back into the arms of Kazibe. This time, Kazibe caught Tayete and kept his partner from falling on his backside. T'Challa stood, stretching his shadow across the pristine, white snow. He looked at the pink mist that obscured the sky and watched the sun lean towards its eventual destination behind the mountain ranges stretching in the distance.

"Do you see, Tayete, Kazibe?" T'Challa pointed at the orange orb burning through the misty sky. "The sun will be setting before long. When nighttime approaches, the temperatures here will drop. Then even breathing will kill you, as the air inside of your lungs will turn to ice. Now, where is Killmonger, and what is the quickest way to get to him?"

Tayete's eyes widened with fear, but there was something in his face as well. Insolence. T'Challa did not know whether he should admire or curse the wayward soldier's stalwart nature. Then, without warning, Kazibe stepped in front of his partner, almost knocking Tayete to the icy ground where he had almost fallen.

"There in the mountains, Your Majesty," Kazibe said, pointing **220** toward the upthrust of black rocks reaching toward the pink sky.

"There is a place called Resurrection Altar; that is where Killmonger has gone."

Tayete gave Kazibe a look of disapproval, but Kazibe ignored his friend and kept explaining to T'Challa the directions that would take them to Killmonger's lair.

"The altar is buried deep inside the mountain," Kazibe said, pointing the way toward the black escarpment. "The entrance is hidden, but we can show you the way in."

"Why do you call it Resurrection Altar?" T'Challa asked.

"The altar is a place of immeasurable power," Kazibe said. "Killmonger has harnessed the dark secrets of this place, and he uses it to bestow super-human talents on the Death Regiment officers who pledge their loyalty to him."

Tayete grabbed Kazibe's arm, but he snatched away, breaking the grip.

"Why haven't the two of you received any of these special enhancements?" T'Challa asked.

"There are side effects for those exposed to the chambers in the altar," Kazibe said. "The side effects are unpredictable, so Killmonger does not force anyone to step into the altar who does not want to go."

"That is enough, Kazibe," Tayete said. This time he stepped between Kazibe and T'Challa.

"I have told you, Tayete," T'Challa said. "In your present situation, Killmonger's wrath should be the least of your worries."

From there, the party of three continued. They tramped through the snow and ice, the sun moving across the sky toward the tips of the snowcapped mountains. After around three more hours of walking, the party came to a metal door in the base of the mountain. T'Challa folded his arms and watched Kazibe type a code into the security lock on the side of the door. After a series of button mashes, beeps and buzzing lights, the door opened with a swish of fallen snow displaced from the top of the door.

From the dark opening, T'Challa caught the scents of flesh and sweat, fire and molten rock. There was another scent that T'Challa found even more disturbing—vibranium. A molten stream of the precious metal seemed to be flowing somewhere underneath the mountain. Remaining silent, T'Challa pointed at the dark entrance. For a moment, Tayete and Kazibe elbowed each other until Kazibe took the first brave steps into the dark opening.

Inside the mountain, T'Challa found himself inside a long corridor with metal walls and strips of neon lights that gleamed and pulsed along the floor and the ceiling. He assumed that the lights were meant to guide visitors through the hall. He also found the remnants of a stench that could only be Killmonger's work, of blood and death and burning warfare, that was much more pungent inside the corridor.

They are leading me in the right direction, T'Challa thought to himself with no small amount of surprise. Either the pair were actually attempting to make up for the death and destruction they had caused, or they were leading T'Challa into a trap.

Doesn't matter, T'Challa thought. *Either way, the business between N'Jadaka and I will be settled tonight.*

After a series of sharp corners and steep staircases that took T'Challa and his guides deeper into the mountain, T'Challa found himself in a huge dark room, where the air was thick and heavy with scents of perspiration, singed hair, and molten vibranium. He crouched in the dark and hid behind a huge stone banister, forcing Tayete and Kazibe to hide behind him. The Panther King did not want to be discovered until the time that he chose. Hidden in shadows, with the scents of vile experimentation wafting from the floor below, T'Challa peeked his head over the stone balcony and stared down at the floor below, at the open sanctuary that Tayete and Kazibe called Resurrection Altar.

T'Challa watched as strange scents and even stranger voices rose from the ceremonial chamber. Scanning the dark room half covered in shadows, half covered in flickering firelight, he noticed an uneasy mixture of modern architecture and traditional Wakandan decor. The room was sealed inside sets of large metal doors centered on each of the chamber's four walls. An assortment of decorative shields and ancient runes covered the walls between.

A set of concentric circles had been painted on the floor. The rings, designed like ripples, stretched from the altar in the middle of the floor to the edges where the floor and the walls connected. On the altar a solitary figure rested, bound to an ornately carved block of vibranium meteor rock covered in unrecognizable runes. The figure was restrained by sets of ceremonial chains covered with jewels that glimmered in the failing light. Even though the figure was chained to the table, he did not look perturbed by his situation. In fact, the figure looked at total ease and peace. Even from the heights and the shadows of the balcony, T'Challa could see the green fuzz and the boils animating the figure's skin.

Cadaver, T'Challa thought. Even the memory of Killmonger's so-called king made his head hurt. How were the faux king's telepathic powers created and magnified in this place? The possibilities worried him, but he would deal with that when the time presented itself. For now, the Panther King focused his attention on the tall, thin figure dressed in long purple robes whom N'Jadaka had called Sombre, the creaky voice, the horrifying golden death mask fused to the mystic's face.

And yes, down below with his back turned to the shadows and the heights that hid the Black Panther, there stood N'Jadaka with his fists set against his hips. He stared at the altar and the chained King Cadaver. He seemed to be lost in concentration, totally enraptured by the moment.

T'Challa poised himself. He wanted to leap over the balcony right then and toss N'Jadaka into the crater in the center of the floor. Suddenly, T'Challa saw himself plummeting down Warrior Falls; he remembered the glee on N'Jadaka's face and that laugh, that condescending, self-righteous laugh. T'Challa gripped the balcony and narrowed his gaze on the best-friend-turned-worst enemy standing below.

"The first time you brought him here, he was scared out of his mind. Do you remember the way he screamed?" Sombre asked Killmonger. The elaborately robed man had more than a little mirth in his voice. He seemed to enjoy the spectacle of King Cadaver chained to the altar. Even more so, Sombre seemed to enjoy the suffering of the Death Regiment warlord in this unholy ritual.

"He was merely a man then, and not even a particularly strong one, but look at him now. He is a god ready to hold dominion over all he sees," N'Jadaka said, his voice triumphant and gleeful, echoing throughout the dark chamber. "He understood the necessity of sacrifice. He relinquished his flesh only to be born again as a god, right here on this slab in Resurrection Altar."

His boots crunched on the gravel as he strode through the cavern, Lord Sombre at his side.

"Most fear the physical transformation induced by the ancient mineral and the mists we have harnessed from deep within the earth, but that's what separates the Death Regiments from the average soldiers. Not only are they willing to kill, willing to die, but they are willing to live with pain, with disfigurement. Vanity flees in the face of infinite power!" he cried. "They are willing to endure a lifetime of pain, if necessary. This is the caliber of soldiers I need. The misfits who have nothing left to live for, nothing left to lose. The rejected and scorned. The world has turned its back on them, but I have chosen them. Together we will bring Wakanda to its knees. Together we will kill that spoiled brat who calls himself king, and we will establish a new Wakanda. No more isolation. No more coveting a treasure that could free the whole world. We will build the world anew. A Wakanda that will rule the entire Earth."

T'Challa could stand no more. He heard N'Jadaka's bombastic speech and the anguished screams of all the dead and the undead. He remembered the flames and the ruined villages. He remembered the beasts that N'Jadaka had sacrificed. *No more! Not one more life will be sacrificed in service to your maniacal dream,* T'Challa thought.

"N'Jadaka!" T'Challa shouted, as he jumped atop the balustrade and stared down at him and his minions. T'Challa stood there in darkness, allowing the lenses in his mask to adjust, glowing bright yellow. He growled and balled his fists, the hatred creeping from his belly.

Staring at N'Jadaka, the Panther King saw the death that had consumed Wakanda. In that madman were visions of burning villages and the strewn, bloody casualties of war.

"Perhaps you care to discuss your plans for Wakanda face to face, up close and personal?" T'Challa said. He roared and leapt from the balustrade, soaring through the dark, a deadly black missile, claws bared, ready for blood and death. For a moment, T'Challa lost himself in the rage that he had fought so hard to control ever since he returned to Wakanda and found his home splintered by civil war. The rage T'Challa had felt ever since he killed the man who murdered his father. The rage he felt ever since he held his dead father and cried over the body, forever still.

"Or has your affinity for intrigue and manipulation finally corrupted the last dregs of humanity and dignity that you had left?" T'Challa shouted as he sank his claws into N'Jadaka's bare arms.

Coming from the darkness into the light, T'Challa stared at the face of his nemesis. The Panther King expected to see pain. Instead, T'Challa found the same insolent smile. The same evil, the same nefarious mischief that had always filled N'Jadaka's eyes. A wide smile, bright and pristine, a smile that had wooed countless beautiful women and conned countless unsuspecting marks, across his face from ear to ear. N'Jadaka fell backwards, allowing T'Challa to land on top and straddle the exile's wide, muscular chest. T'Challa wrapped his arms around N'Jadaka's wide neck and sank the sharp, bloodthirsty black claws into his sinewy flesh.

Still, there was no fear in Killmonger's countenance, only mirth.

"I have waited many moons for this day," T'Challa said, growling as he squeezed N'Jadaka's throat.

Somewhere in the back of T'Challa's mind, flashbacks of Harlem rushed through his subconscious. Fragmented images of N'Jadaka feeding the homeless in the soup kitchen where the pair had worked alongside Monica. N'Jadaka reading, laughing, raising a glass in honor of the king whom he had been blessed by Bast to encounter so far from home.

"Lies, they were all lies," T'Challa said, bitterness consuming him, dashing the fond, haunting memories with the flames of rage and revenge.

"No one has spread more lies and deception than you, ukatana," N'Jadaka said. T'Challa hated the Zulu word for kitten. Now there was more than mirth in Killmonger's voice. Laughter followed his words. Deep, hearty, and rich. Laughter that lifted his chest and rolled from the sides of his mouth in waves that echoed throughout the dark altar room. "But your lies, your deceit, your hindrance of Wakanda will end today. Here in the fire that surges deep beneath our precious homeland."

With a sudden display of strength that T'Challa had not expected, a display of strength that shadowed even the infuriated warrior that had hurled T'Challa from the top of Warrior Falls, N'Jadaka flipped T'Challa over, the pair locking their fingers in a deadly power struggle for life and death.

"I was wondering what kept you so long, ukatana? For a moment I worried that Tayete and Kazibe had failed to guide you here as instructed. Good help being so hard to find nowadays." N'Jadaka laughed.

T'Challa felt the moment of shock and betrayal blast through his chest, even as N'Jadaka kneed the Panther King's stomach, punched him in the gut and raised him above his head in a deadly moment of déjà vu that mimicked their previous battle, that mimicked the only moment in T'Challa's life when he had known true defeat.

"You see, ukatana. I am Wakanda's true destiny, and you are nothing more than a mere distraction. A brief bump in the road on Wakanda's way to the success and the glory that it truly deserves."

T'Challa struggled to free himself from Killmonger's grip, but the more he struggled, the tighter the hands around his throat squeezed until the world around him spun in a cracked mess of smoke, darkness, and spinning broken Wakandan runes.

"Don't worry about Monica, either. I will take wonderful care of her," N'Jadaka said. With a glorious grunt of strength and unrestrained fury, the exile threw the Panther King into the crater in the center of the floor—which led to the fiery depths that ran underneath Wakanda like a series of flaming blood vessels.

Monica's name coming out of N'Jadaka's mouth struck something deep inside T'Challa, something that burned even hotter than the fiery river and the flaming steam rising beneath him. With Monica's face in his mind, and her beautiful voice singing in his heart, T'Challa grabbed onto a jagged piece of hot stone jutting from the wall of the crater. Though the heat from the stone intensified, his panther suit maintained control as he held onto the searing rock. He used it as a handhold and a brace to pivot and launch himself back up from the burning depths.

T'Challa somersaulted through the air to land on top of the suspended altar, his feet parted over the restrained King Cadaver.

He looked up and saw Tayete and Kazibe staring down from the balcony above. Even through the dark and the distance, T'Challa saw the fear in their eyes. He saw Tayete tremble. He heard Kazibe's gasp and Tayete's fearful outburst.

"I told you, Kazibe," Tayete whispered. "T'Challa is not human. He is a demon sent here from Death's Domain to torment the world of the living."

The thought made T'Challa chuckle, and in that moment, he promised himself that Tayete and Kazibe would not have to wait for Death's Domain to experience eternal fire. They would pay for their crimes with blood right here in the living world. He would see to that duty himself.

The Panther King crouched on the stone slab and stared at N'Jadaka, and for the first time T'Challa saw something that resembled surprise and frustration—maybe even fear.

"What's wrong, N'Jadaka?" T'Challa asked. "I thought you were waiting to face me again, to kill me and make me pay for all the pain that you have suffered through your life. Well, here is your chance. Come, old friend. Teach me the lesson that you have been waiting to show me."

When the hand grabbed him from behind, the Panther King

wondered how someone, how anyone had managed to sneak up on him. He had not heard or even smelled him coming.

Remember, T'Challa, your enhanced sensors are only products of your mind. King Cadaver's voice scratched though T'Challa's skull like a brush covered with rusty nails. *And if it occurs or takes place inside your mind, it can be manipulated by King Cadaver.*

The unseen flames that leapt from the hand burned through the vibranium-laced armor all the way into T'Challa's bones. As the Panther King fell to his knees, he noticed three things.

One, when he looked down, he saw that King Cadaver was smiling up at him. Two, the burning hands that clutched and incapacitated him with the sensation of flame searing through his flesh belonged to Lord Sombre. Three, the look of bewilderment had been washed away from N'Jadaka's eyes and replaced with a look of absolute confidence. The look of certain victory. After that, everything went black. The last thing T'Challa heard before he was submerged in the brutal walls of unconsciousness was the maniacal laughter of N'Jadaka and the monsters who called him commander and master.

WHEN T'CHALLA awoke, the intense heat that had rendered him unconscious had been replaced by searing cold biting through his black armor, digging into his flesh. The hot stone and chains where T'Challa had collapsed had been replaced by the frosty, shifting grain of snow clinging to his limbs, his chest, his face.

Another move, and T'Challa heard the growling of wild animals. For a moment, he wondered if N'Jadaka had sent Preyy back to finish the job and get revenge for the pain the leopard had endured on top of Warrior Falls. Then T'Challa realized that the growling was coming from a canine. Not just any canines—a pack of wolves. He raised his head to find himself surrounded by at least two dozen hungry gray wolves. T'Challa could not tell how many there were exactly. The pack moved as one living animal that seemed to be connected, and he could not see beyond the mounds of gray mangy fur and the cold black night that encased and swallowed them all.

Before T'Challa could react, the wolves dove on him from all directions. Still groggy from the burning, telepathic assault of King Cadaver and Lord Sombre, T'Challa's muscle memory, his enhanced reflexes augmented by the Heart-Shaped Herb flowing through his veins, let him leap to his feet and grab a spear stuck in the ground beside him. It was the same spear that Taku had given Tayete. For protection. He thanked Bast for the divine providence and N'Jadaka's characteristic arrogance. T'Challa also asked the Panther God to forgive him for the lives of the creatures that he was about to slay.

One wolf leaped toward T'Challa, biting at the Panther King's throat, and caught the sharp end of the spear straight through its mouth. T'Challa pushed the spear until the head burrowed through the wolf's throat and lodged deep inside the creature's belly. T'Challa shut one eye as the wolf's blood splattered and gushed onto the black armor. He did not try to pull the spear free from the wolf's mouth. Instead, he swung the spear, using the wolf's dead body like a baton. A cruel club, he smacked the other wolves as they jumped toward him. Snarling, their coal-red eyes ignited the frozen night as they sped around him like wheeling stars and comets.

T'Challa fought until the rage rose from his heart, transforming him from cornered prey fighting for its life to a malicious predator, killing for the hunger and thirst of blood and violence, killing for the sake of violence and malice. T'Challa fought and fought until the snow was covered in blood and the few remaining wolves went yelping into the night, running for their lives.

T'Challa fell to his knees in the snow, panting, struggling to catch the precious breath that turned to ice as soon as it hit the open air. One name crossed T'Challa's mind. *Monica.* He remembered N'Jadaka laughing and promising to take care of the Harlem songbird. The thought lit something within him that all the snow in the Land of Chilling Mist, in all the frozen wastelands of the world could not freeze. With Monica's face in his mind and her song in his heart, giving him strength, T'Challa pulled himself to his feet once more and started toward the cold mountains that sheltered N'Jadaka, the Death Regiments, and the blasphemous place the Wakandan exile had named Resurrection Altar.

IF T'CHALLA had not gone in search of N'Jadaka, if he had gone with Monica, Taku, and Adebisi back to the warmer climate of his beloved homeland, he would have seen Karota working the fields beside her son Kantu. He would have seen the little boy bravely assuming the responsibilities of his unfortunate dead but undead father, M'Jumbak.

T'Challa would have heard Karota crying for her son to stop one of the bulls from escaping the fence that had fallen into disrepair after M'Jumbak's disappearance. He would have seen Taku and Adebisi aiding the young Kantu in cornering the beast and bringing it back to join the other farm animals. He would have seen Monica pat Kantu's shoulder and Karota screaming for Monica to get away from her child, to get her outworlder hands off Karota's last living relative, Karota's last reason to keep living herself.

"Go away, outworlder! Ever since you have come here, nothing but bad luck has befallen my family. My husband is dead! Our fields are almost barren, my farm is in ruins, and it's all your fault!" Karota yelled.

"I was only trying to help," Monica said with humility and compassion. She reached toward Kantu, who had sustained a long gash on his arm trying to corral the bull.

"Go away with your outworlder trickery! We don't want your medicine. We don't want you here. If my son is hurt, I will take him to Mendinao myself. Kantu is all I have left. I have already lost my husband. You are just like all the rest of the outworlders. All you do is take and take until there is nothing left."

"I'm sorry, Karota," Monica offered in halting Wakandan. "Believe me, I know what it's like to lose people you love. To witness suffering and to feel helpless. I know what it's like to feel pain without any hope of balm or healing. That's why I'm here. I only want to help. That's all. Right now, I don't know if I'm good at anything. The one thing I could do better than anything else has been... taken from me. Please let me help you. Maybe we can get through our pain and our troubles together."

Karota resisted for a moment, but it was not long before she gave herself over to Monica's loving embrace. Monica wrapped her arms around Karota as the Wakandan woman broke down into tears. She held Karota there, stroking the widow's hair, singing softly the first lines of "O-o-h Child" into her ear. Slowly, sweetly, the same way she had sung to T'Challa back in Harlem when he had been on the edge of destruction.

CHAPTER THIRTEEN

A SOMBRE SACRIFICE

MUSCLES EXHAUSTED, frozen blood coating his black armor, T'Challa tramped across the frozen ice and snow of the Land of Chilling Mist. He still felt the burning of Sombre's hands streaking through his bones, but he ignored the pain and focused on Wakanda's invader from within—N'Jadaka. Even now he heard his enemy laugh and when he looked at the pink mist swirling across the orange dawn, he saw N'Jadaka's mocking face. Laughing as T'Challa tumbled down Warrior Falls. Laughing as the pungent flames and smoke of Resurrection Altar threatened to consume the Panther King. Laughing as villages burned and Wakanda died in a storm of war and blood.

T'Challa crested a hill and found an encampment nestled at the bottom of the icy ridge. A ring of tents. Small campfires struggling to stay lit, reaching as far as they could with their smoke and flames into the frigid cold. A half dozen men wrapped in furs and hides warmed themselves against the fires and with the bottles they passed between them. The smell of liquor and cooked meat brushed T'Challa's nostrils. He saw one more thing that aroused his curiosity and his anger. More wolves. Like the ones that had attacked him, when he had awakened and found himself left for dead in the snow.

T'Challa did not wait. He did not ask questions. He already knew the answers. These men belonged to N'Jadaka. These men had helped to carry his unconscious body. Had dumped the Panther King in the snow. These wolves were kin to the ones that had attacked them. T'Challa would spare the beasts if he could. They were not responsible for the death and destruction that had beset his country. But N'Jadaka's Death Regiments would not be granted such mercies.

T'Challa leapt from the top of the hill and landed in the middle of the camp in a flourish of black-clad muscles and lightning-quick movement. Before the soldiers could react, one had been kicked in the mouth—the jawbone cracking around T'Challa's foot gave him an inhumane sense of satisfaction that he would have admonished himself for on any other day. But this was a different time. The climate of war had triggered something deep inside T'Challa—the rage that he had fought to control since the day his father died. Since the day that T'Challa had killed his first man and felt the satisfaction of revenge.

If you could only see me now, father. What would you feel? Pride or revulsion?

"How did he escape?" A tall, lean man raised an automatic weapon, his accent marking him as a citizen of the northern mountain ranges near Wakanda's shared border with the Republic of Mohannda. Wakandan military issue, the rifle hummed a deathly song of war and bloodshed. Scars covered the man's face in a latticework of swollen, glazed scar tissue. "We left two dozen wolves behind to finish him. Killmonger will not be pleased." Anxiety and worry seeped into the man's speech.

"I do not know, but don't worry. He will not make it to Killmonger, nor even Lord Sombre," another man said. This soldier was even taller than the first and much wider. He swung a weapon that looked like a cross between a flail and a cat-o-nine-tails, huge, spiked balls that buzzed with deadly electricity connected by a chain that had been dampened by a rope and plastic casing.

"I don't know how you made it past our wolves or how you survived the frozen night without shelter, but you will die here, panther demon!" called out the taller man. He had one good eye and another eye, white and sightless, that bulged from the socket as if it were about to fall from his head. He smiled when he spoke. Thick spittle fell from his mouth and froze in a thick beard that grew down to the collar of his hide coat.

"I will give you one chance to live. Where is Killmonger? Where has he taken the rest of his Death Regiments?" T'Challa crouched and bared his claws. He heard growling and hissing enter his own voice. This did not surprise him. He remembered the words of Mendinao. In his anger, his feral side had begun to take over. T'Challa was tired of suppressing his animal nature. Maybe it was time for him to let the panther loose. Where had practicing self-control gotten him so far? His kingdom had been torn apart. The people he loved the most had been murdered and imprisoned. Maybe it was time for him to embrace the fire and use it to his advantage. Anger and murder seemed to be working very well for N'Jadaka.

"Killmonger is gone and so are the Death Regiments, but you needn't worry. You will die long before you meet them, panther demon."

First, the man with the automatic rifle fired. T'Challa knew the mineral used in N'Jadaka's weapons was not vibranium, but some sort of alloy synthesized from the sacred metal and some other substance. *Maybe plutonium,* T'Challa thought. He could tell by the thrumming. The reverb was not quite as strong as the undulations and the warbling created by the sound-absorbing metal that was Wakanda's most precious resource.

He knows how to synthesize vibranium. The thought sent a chill through T'Challa, one much stronger than the cold from the frozen ice that currently surrounded him.

The bearded man twirled the electrified balls over his head; with the glee of a raging madman, he swung the surging weapon at

T'Challa. Caught in the middle of his reverie, T'Challa managed to avoid the deadly blow, with the surging spiked balls screeching a hair's length in front of his face.

"We will deliver your carcass to Lord Sombre, an offering to the gods that protect our land with ice and cold mist." The bearded soldier laughed as he swung the spheres and watched T'Challa leap out of the way, a second before the weapon crashed into the frozen earth.

"Kill, Kill, Killmonger!" the scar-faced man screamed. He followed his partner's assault with a volley of gunfire that nipped at T'Challa's heels.

The Black Panther spun through the air. With his left hand he raked his anti-metal claws through the weapon's chain, sending the spiked balls flying in all directions. With his right hand, he punched the man's throat before spinning again and planting his heel in his temple.

"Is death and destruction the only thing that Killmonger teaches his followers?" T'Challa said regretfully. He charged the man with the scarred face, knocking the gun from his hand and pinning him to the ground. He wrapped one hand around the man's throat and raised his other hand, claws bared, ready to end the man's miserable life and stain the snow with blood.

"I am feeling generous this cold morning, and I am tired of the killing that has overrun my country. I will give you one more chance to save yourself. All you have to do is answer this one question. Why does Killmonger only subject some of his followers to the smoke and flames of Resurrection Altar? If he wants to conquer Wakanda, why doesn't he create an army of superhumans with augmented abilities?"

Instead of answering the question, the scar-faced man spat a glob of blood and mucus into T'Challa's masked face. The red saliva froze instantly, spattering a frozen red crust across T'Challa's mask. T'Challa imagined himself sinking his claws into the man's throat, slashing the man's windpipe. Underneath his mask, a nascent smile curled the edges of his mouth. He felt the primal fury, the rage, creeping through the muscles in his neck and his stomach.

Then he saw Monica's face, heard her voice. He wondered what she would have done if she had been standing there. If she was able to see him in his present state of near-madness. Suddenly, T'Challa felt ashamed of himself. He did not feel like a king at all. Once more he felt like a failure, but this time he promised himself that he would not fail. He would not give into the rage. He was not N'Jadaka—and he never would be.

"Do it, panther demon. Do it." The scar-faced man laughed. "Either way, you are a dead man. Killmonger will destroy you, and he will display your corpse in the Golden City for everyone to see."

T'Challa retracted his claws, balled his fist, and put an end to the man's senseless yammering. Not a permanent end. The man would wake up, sooner or later, in the snow. His end would be none of T'Challa's business, but that of Bast. The blood would not be on T'Challa's hands, nor would it be on his conscience.

T'Challa left the remains of the camp and continued his trek across the snow toward Resurrection Altar, his mind full of what he had seen. Killmonger's Death Regiments had been full of Wakandans, many from the outer villages, who clearly felt isolated and left out of the Wakandan dream. A northerner, from the nomadic mountain tribes, who sounded part Wakandan and part Mohanndan, might have a markedly different point of view about the nation's isolationist policies. These thoughts weighed heavily on his mind as he charged onward.

At first, he let the wind guide him. He listened to the sounds of Sombre's swishing robes marching through the snow, miles ahead. He wondered if Sombre knew that someone was following. He wondered where Sombre was going, and he hoped that Sombre would lead him back to Killmonger. He decided this war would end this day. One way or the other.

T'Challa noticed tracks in the snow. Tracks larger than any human could have made—larger than M'Baku's footprints, even larger than the Hulk's. The tracks were signals: signs of danger yet to come, danger T'Challa knew he must face to free Wakanda from N'Jadaka's savagery. It was a danger T'Challa welcomed.

Marching through the snow, he thought of M'Baku and the Clan of the White Gorilla in the distant Jabari-Lands, who worshiped the ivory-furred beasts and challenged Wakanda constantly over the boundaries in the north.

MEANWHILE, FAR beyond Resurrection Altar, where the Land of Chilling Mist surrendered its cold to steaming humidity and sweltering jungle, another remote section of Wakanda teemed with dense vegetation and beasts that had not contacted the outerworld in countless millennia. In this place, called Serpent Valley, N'Jadaka had set up another base of operations. A place where he indulged in training exercises of a more nefarious, arcane nature.

Through dense jungle, Killmonger marched with Tayete and Kazibe following close behind. Tall grass brushed against their legs. Long vines dropped from the treetops and swung in front of their faces. They approached a hill covered with patches of grass, bordering a stone path that wrapped around the hill that led the trio to the base of operations.

Killmonger walked with confidence, with the stride of a man who was sure of his destiny, and even more sure of the road and the means that would lead him to victory. Tayete and Kazibe walked with shaky footsteps and wide eyes that betrayed their trepidation and uncertainty.

"Are you certain that the path has been cleared of serpents, commander? I mean, what if one of your soldiers were attacked or poisoned. We are far from the village where we left the medical supplies, or even the healing powers of Resurrection Altar," Tayete said. "It's not like I'm afraid of anything. If I met a serpent, I could slay the beast straight away, no problem. I'm merely thinking of some of the other soldiers who aren't as skilled at combat as I am."

Kazibe rolled his eyes. "I don't know if it's wise to bring our column through these hills," he said, quietly. "They are uncharted for one thing, and—." He stuttered. "What if someone gets bitten? They could die out here without any antidote."

"Don't worry, Kazibe," Killmonger said. "We are hunting a different kind of serpent, and the good Lord Sombre has already scouted these hills. He found a den of beasts that will prove themselves very useful to our cause when we sack the Golden City and take control of Wakanda's precious royal palace," Killmonger boasted. He walked with his chin held high, sweeping his way carelessly through the vines that hung along the path before them.

"I hope the Black Panther did not survive. What if he comes after us?" Kazibe asked, his voice quaking with fear.

"T'Challa is dead!" Killmonger cried, a vein rippling across his temple. "But even if he survived the wolfpack and the traps that we left behind in the ice with Sombre, he will get more of the same if he comes here. I will use his head as a standard to announce our presence when we invade Birnin Zana." Killmonger stopped in his tracks and rubbed his chin thoughtfully. "Which reminds me…"

In a sudden flash of terrible agility, Killmonger produced a whip covered with black spikes that crackled with pulsating energy. He brought the whip down on Kazibe with a mighty force, smacking the helpless soldier across the face and chest.

Kazibe screamed in pain and fell to the ground, his clothes ripped open from his throat to his waist. Blood ran down his face and chest. He raised his hands and begged Killmonger for mercy.

"Please, commander," Kazibe cried. "I'm sorry, please—please don't kill me."

"It was you who led T'Challa to Resurrection Altar. Instead of proving your worth, instead of showing that pampered brat what a member of the Death Regiments would do to him. Instead of fighting with honor, you cowered before him. You have shamed me. You have shamed the Death Regiments. You have shamed yourself."

With every word Killmonger brought down the sizzling whip, burying the spiked leather inside Kazibe's flesh. The helpless soldier screamed and howled until his voice went hoarse from the pain. All he could do was writhe in the suffering, constricting his muscles with each terrible blow.

238

"You wanted us to lead the panther demon to you, commander. Please stop! You are going to kill him," Tayete pleaded, pointing an assault rifle at Killmonger's back, his hands trembling. "Kazibe is like my brother. I am loyal to you, but I will not allow you to take his life." He growled and clenched his teeth. "Please, don't make me shoot you, commander."

"Shoot *me*?" Killmonger spun in a blinding flash of fury and wrapped his whip around Tayete's throat. The rifle fired one solitary shot before Killmonger knocked the weapon from Tayete's hands. "I said, 'kill him in the mountains.' The two of you combined could not stand a chance against T'Challa, and you have the nerve to challenge me? I should kill both of you right now."

"Wait, wait, commander, please forgive us. We had to lead him to you. That was the only way." Tayete raised his hands in acquiescence, as if he were praying to Bast herself. "Please have mercy. Can't we talk about this? We will do anything you command."

Killmonger smiled at the sight of the sniveling soldiers. He stood over them with his fists resting against his hips, the spiked whip sizzling at his side. Preyy appeared behind him, growling. The giant black-and-gold feline stood ready to finish the deadly job Killmonger had started.

"Easy, girl," Killmonger said. He rubbed the leopard's ear and stared at the bleeding pair as if he had just completed a masterpiece. "These two might serve us yet." Killmonger stepped forward and placed his boot on Tayete's chest, pinning the soldier to the ground. "I admire your loyalty to your friend, and your courage—foolish as you are. Even more, I admire your willingness to die for him. Follow me. I have an opportunity for you, a chance to prove you are not a coward who deserves a coward's death."

N'Jadaka turned his massive back on Tayete and Kazibe and continued the trek up the stony hillside. Preyy snarled at the pair to emphasize her master's dissatisfaction and joined Killmonger, following at the exile's heels.

"Tayete, you were willing to die for me," Kazibe whispered. He coughed and spat blood into the dust and the grass.

"That's what friends are for, right?" Tayete said, exhausted. His lips smiled weakly, but his eyes were hard, staring at Killmonger's back.

DEEP IN the snow and ice of the Land of Chilling Mist, T'Challa made his way up another hill. Here the tracks were larger, fresher than those he had encountered miles back. The sounds of Sombre's robes swishing and blowing in the freezing wind were much louder. He expected to find Sombre and the beast that had accompanied Killmonger's henchmen at the top of the hill.

There were other sounds too. Sombre's voice rose with the wind, sharpened with ancient incantations uttered with the thrall of a dervish consumed in feverish prayer. Alongside Sombre's arcane chanting were the sounds of animals snarling and growling. The combination gave T'Challa reason to pause, but he continued his march. Whatever was on the other side of this hill, whatever had made these tracks in the snow, T'Challa would face it—come what may.

The sky glowed with orange and yellow hues as the sun made its way toward another set and lit the pink mist ablaze. The scene had a sense of wonder that would have charmed T'Challa beyond words, had not the circumstances been so dire. Even at this moment he could not help but to recognize the beauty of the idyllic landscape. With ice cracking in the joints of his panther suit, and the freezing winds slowing his pace to an exhausting crawl, he finally crested the hill. What he found drove the words from his breath.

In the valley below, Lord Sombre held court. His hands were raised to the wind, making a series of arcane gestures and symbols that T'Challa had only seen in the dances of the oldest griots who had danced for his father. T'Chaka had been more accepting of the ancient ways of conjuration than T'Challa had ever been or ever would be, considering the empiricism and science that he leaned on for understanding.

A clan of giant white gorillas surrounded Sombre. Their eyes, yellow stars burning with primal ferocity, stared at Sombre attentively. Their ravenous jaws, filled with unnaturally sharp teeth, dripped with eager attentiveness as they watched every movement of the robed figure with his raised hands and enthralling incantations.

T'Challa wondered what M'Baku would have thought if he had seen these terrible creatures.

These could not be the gods the Jabari Clan have worshiped over the centuries, T'Challa thought. The Black Panther himself, the avatar of Bast, had only seen the Panther God through the powerful visions brought on by his ingestion of the sacred Heart-Shaped Herb and in dreams. The sight below made him glad that he had never seen Bast in real life, and he wondered how a sight this terrible might test the faith of the most pious worshiper.

"Lords of the snow and ice! You have drawn near, sensing my presence. I have brought you a sacrifice to appease your appetites and to win your favor." Sombre pointed at the top of the hill, pointed at T'Challa. "Look, my lords. Up on the hill I have brought you a king. What better sacrifice to present as tribute to living gods? There is your feast and your sacrifice. Now, great gods of ice and snow, feast on your offering. This offering of panther flesh!"

T'Challa stood frozen by the weight of the responsibility of what lay ahead of him. He could not turn back, and yet to move forward meant a terrible deed he would always regret. Before he decided his next move, the decision was made for him.

A giant white gorilla charged up the hill. The sight was the stuff of legends, the old stories Griot G'Sere told T'Challa in his youth. A reverse avalanche of white fury and indiscriminate rage. Yellow eyes glared at him, saliva dripped from its fearsome fangs and fell steaming into the snow.

The Panther King stared at the enraged beast and saw the empty glare, the pointless anger, the same unconscious frenzy he had seen in the rhinoceros he fought in the Fields of Alkama and the crocodile that he wrestled in the River of Grace and Wisdom.

This beast is under Killmonger's control, T'Challa thought. Before another could enter his mind, the beast swung its mighty arm with a lightning-quick speed uncharacteristic of its massive size. Before he could dodge the blow, the beast's fist smashed into T'Challa's chest and face, knocking him off the hill and into a huge block of ice jutting from the ground. The beast pounded its chest and screamed into the night, a victorious cry that chilled T'Challa to the bone.

He lay half-covered in broken ice. The world swam in a dizzying carousel of fractured images and memories. He recalled the time when he sat with his father and a group of Wakanda's most famous griots led by the man himself, G'Sere. T'Challa had only been a boy then, around seven years old. He had just begun his education in the customs and practices of Wakandan royalty.

He remembered the warmth of the fire and the warmth of his father's loving embrace. They had come to the borders of the Land of Chilling Mist for the first, and what he thought would be the last, time. T'Challa remembered how G'Sere had danced around the flames and told the ancient stories of the white gorilla. A godly creature who ruled with brute strength, it was one of Bast's unsuccessful competitors. Griot G'Sere had sung of the mythic creature's power. He had promised them that, one day, the white gorilla would return in all its glory to assume its place next to Bast as her faithful companion and ally.

Now, T'Challa watched the beast of stories standing over him, screaming in primal rage. The mythic creature made flesh, brought into the real world. This was where myths turned to ashes and legends became real-life monsters, agents of tyranny.

The gorilla roared once more as it brought both its massive fists down into the ice in a desperate effort to crush the offering that would not stop moving or fighting. Even in his dazed and injured state, T'Challa summoned enough speed to avoid the fatal blow. More chunks of ice went hurling through the air. After evading the assault, he leapt and punched the white gorilla in the face.

T'Challa's blow managed to daze the white gorilla, but only for a moment. When the behemoth grabbed him, the Black Panther thought of the overpowering strength of Ben Grimm or the Hulk. The beast lifted him into the air like a fetish or a shiny black trophy. The creature screamed in triumph and T'Challa felt the beast attempting to pull him apart, attempting to rip his legs from his torso. Luckily, the vibranium in his Panther armor absorbed the sound waves from the roaring white gorilla. The harnessed vibratory energy strengthened the armor and kept it intact, kept T'Challa's body from being ripped into pieces.

T'Challa took the moment of stalemate and used it to his advantage. He channeled the harnessed energy through the claws extending from his black-gloved hands, digging them into the gorilla's eyes as deeply as he could, with all the strength he could muster. The claws punctured the soft flesh of the white gorilla's eyeballs, and the harnessed vibratory energy exploded in the white gorilla's face.

The creature flung T'Challa into the snow like a rag doll as it screamed and covered its eyes with its hand. Blood rushed from the creature's face, gushed between its fingers, turning its fur a pale, sickly pink.

"You miserable, wretched man!" Sombre screamed. "It is just as Killmonger said. You are a true demon. You have spilled the blood of a god. May your soul suffer eternal damnation!"

"What do you and Killmonger know of Wakanda's gods? How dare you speak of souls, abomination?" T'Challa asked as he stood to his feet, panting. "You have desecrated this land and perverted its inhabitants. You have defamed and soured all we hold sacred. I promise you, Sombre, just like Killmonger, you will pay for Wakanda's blood with your own."

"On the contrary, panther demon. It's you who shall pay," Sombre said, his long, bony fingers gesticulating, strange signals conjuring a great white light that consumed his hands and spread across his arms. "Oh, Sacred Great One, you do not need eyes. I will see for you. Kill your offering. Feast on the panther demon's flesh. He is standing right in front of you. Kill him now!"

Sombre laughed and leapt from the hilltop, disappearing in the snow and wind that blew in his wake.

With a scream that shook the ground and opened the sky with primal rage and hunger, the creature brought down both of its fists. T'Challa avoided the blow, but the impact broke the ice that composed the ledge where the pair stood, sending them both flatlining into an avalanche of broken ice. Huge chunks, sharp and deadly, threatened to crush them both and bury them underneath an icy grave.

No time to think. T'Challa's muscles and instincts took control. Before he knew it, he had buried his claws into the icy hillside, clinging, sinking deeper until he came to a screeching stop, his body dangling above the icy depths below. Exhausted, panting against the hillside, T'Challa stared down. The white gorilla had not been so lucky. The mythic creature lay sprawled below, half covered in ice, impaled on a huge icicle jutting from the ground, its bloody tip protruding through the white gorilla's chest.

After making the long, arduous climb down the icy drop, T'Challa knelt beside the dying white gorilla. The creature moaned and coughed, choking on its own blood until its life expired in a pool that turned the white ice into red slush. T'Challa stared at the beast and cried. He had killed one of the mythic creatures from his childhood. He had killed a god. He wondered what M'Baku and the order of the white gorilla would think of him now.

"This god from my childhood was controlled by Sombre and N'Jadaka." Another soul the exile would answer for, the first god in his book of names. The shame filled him. *So much death that could have been prevented.*

"How many more?" the Panther King asked himself aloud. "How many more of Wakanda's children will die before this scourge of war ends?"

WHILE THE Black Panther lamented, a crowd of Wakandans gathered around a gleaming white building newly erected in the middle of the Golden City. The building was Wakanda's newest medical facility. A new kind of hospital that combined ancient healing practices with the scientific advancements of modern medicine that flourished under the late King T'Chaka and his son. The sight of the building would have warmed T'Challa's heart and renewed his faith in his ability to lead his people.

Monica led Karota and Kantu into the medical facility. Through a flourish of doctors, nurses and other medical professionals. Past the front gate where a receptionist gave Monica a stern nod that betrayed mistrust intermingled with forced nicety. The trio—Monica, Karota, and Kantu—walked down a series of pristinely lit hallways until they encountered a door adorned with a sign that read: Dr. Daktari Mganga, PhD, MPH.

Inside the room, Monica and her companions found Mganga sitting atop a large cherry oak desk. The room was decorated with a mixture of traditional Wakandan decor that included ceremonial masks and kente design wallpaper borders. Upon the visitors' entrance, Mganga looked up from an open book spread across her lap. Her eyes twinkled with new discoveries and her smile welcomed the visitors.

"Ah, Monica, so glad to see you this morning. And you've brought visitors," Mganga said. She wagged her finger at Karota. "I remember you, Karota, you too, little Kantu. I haven't seen you since—" Suddenly a dark realization covered her face, clouding her eyes. "—since your last visit to the royal palace. I am so sorry for your loss, Karota. How have you been holding up since M'Jumbak's disappearance?"

"We've been managing the best we can," Karota said. The stiffness in her demeanor seemed to relax in the presence of Mganga, her fellow Wakandan.

"Tell her about your headaches," Monica said. She patted Karota on the back. Over the course of the day, Monica had managed to pierce Karota's rough exterior and her distrust for outworlders. In Monica's mind they had become something like friends—or at least cordial associates.

Karota glanced at Monica, then focused her attention on Mganga. "Ever since M'Jumbak disappeared in the burial grounds,

I've had these migraines. Some days I can fight through the pain, but other days all I can do is lie in bed. Thank Bast I have my little Kantu to take up the slack around the farm. I don't know what I would do without my little man." She wrapped her arm around Kantu. The boy blushed and stared at his feet. "But this burden is not for a child. Something must change."

Monica tousled Kantu's baby locs, sprouting an inch from his scalp.

"It's hard, but my mama needs me. I just do my best to make up for papa's absence. That's what he would want." Kantu returned his mother's embrace and stared at Mganga with eyes bright and shiny with sadness. "Isn't that what the king did, when his father died?"

Mganga leaned toward the young man and smiled. "That is certainly correct, young man. But he had a lot of help, and we shall help you. I see you've been studying your Wakandan history."

She rose to her feet and shared the same smile with Karota. "Most likely your migraines are stress induced. I will need to run some tests to be sure. However, we have been working on a new form of treatment for stress-related illnesses. As in we, I mean Ms. Lynne and I."

Monica smiled. This time it was her turn to blush.

"Ms. Lynne? Are you talking about Monica?" Karota looked confused.

"No need for alarm, Karota. Here in Wakanda, our vibranium resources have enabled us to develop treatments rooted in sound. These advancements allow us to employ the songs and histories of our griots to help heal all kinds of illnesses, a kind of intensive music therapy. Luckily for us, Ms. Lynne is an extraordinary singer. Using her voice and certain frequencies, we can treat your headaches. But more importantly, we can reduce the stress that causes them."

Karota laughed and scoffed, waving a dismissive hand toward Monica. "So, you are going to let the outworlder sing to me to get rid of my headaches? I traveled all the way from Alkama Fields for this foolishness? Find yourself another guinea pig, Mganga. Come on, Kantu." Karota grabbed Kantu's wrist and dragged her son out of the doctor's office.

"Karota, wait!" Monica called, but it was too late. Monica stared at the open door. Her spirit sank, and helplessness draped itself around her shoulders.

"It's all right, Ms. Lynne. She'll come around, especially when the Wakandan Interior arrives to help with the farm. When she and her son get relief from their tireless labor, she may feel differently. Karota is a fine person, but she has always been stubborn. It is her strength and her weakness. The fact that she came here with you says a lot. She cares for you more than you know. I can tell. But she's always had trouble expressing her feelings, except when she's angry."

"I don't know, Mganga. This has been the story of my life ever since I came to Wakanda. I'm trying to fit in. Trying to get the people to love and trust me. Even after everything I've been through. But nothing seems to work, and I know respect must be earned and that can be hard. I love T'Challa, and I want to be here with him. I feel like he needs me, but I just don't know. Maybe I should just pack my things and go back to New York."

"No, dear one. I know it is difficult but give it time. Wakanda needs you, even if its people don't realize it. Even if you're not yet sure how. They—and you—will know soon. I will assist you, personally. We have much to do."

BACK IN the royal palace, W'Kabi slumped into the loft apartment he shared with his wife, Chandra, and their two children. Exhaustion weighed heavily on his neck and shoulders. He unbuckled the gun belt from his waist and took off the bandolier that was filled with heavy rifle shells. He set his weapons on a table in the foyer that led to sitting chambers, where he assumed his wife would be—watching television like she did every day. He took a few sniffs, hoping to smell something like dinner cooking. Nothing, which was not a surprise. Irritation mixed with the empty hunger in his gut.

"Chandra," he called as he walked through the house. The boys had gone to their room. Even though he loved his wife, he had always hated her name. It sounded too much like the name of an outworlder. She might as well have called herself Shanequa and joined a singing group with the outworlder Monica, in W'Kabi's opinion.

Inside the sitting room, W'Kabi found his wife. She was sitting in the half dark underneath a reading lamp, an open book spread inside her hands. The title on the book's cover read *Half of a Yellow Sun*. W'Kabi shook his head.

"Where are my children?" he bellowed. "Why haven't you prepared my dinner?"

"Your dinner is in the kitchen, cold as usual. I prepared it hours ago. Your children ate hours ago. Now they are sleeping. Please don't wake them." She spoke with the frustration of disturbed concentration, only looking up from her book to stare at W'Kabi a moment before returning her attention to the open pages.

"You know my responsibilities. I am the Shield of Wakanda. I am sorry I couldn't make it home earlier. We are in the midst of civil war. Our prisons are overrun with half of Killmonger's traitorous Death Regiments, while the other half runs amok throughout Wakanda. What do you want me to do, run home and kiss my wife while the country falls apart? You sound like that outworlder woman." W'Kabi raised his voice.

"I want a husband who knows I am alive and that his children are alive, too. What I want is a life. I sit in this house every day. Cooking your food. Cleaning your dirty clothes. Tripping over your weapons. This is getting old, W'Kabi. This was not our dream when I married you. You treat me like a prisoner, and I'm tired of it. I'm telling you, if things don't change…"

"Chandra, you are a free woman with the empire at your feet. You could do or be whatever you choose. No one forces you to remain in this house, unhappy. Don't blame me because you gave up on the dream you dreamed for yourself. If things won't change until you do," W'Kabi yelled.

She flinched, his words hitting their mark, but she continued reading, as if she had not heard him speak. Frustrated, he snatched the book from Chandra's hands and ripped it in half. "You're not the only one who's tired."

"You—you've become a monster," she said, quiet and low, "no better than the rebels fighting in the streets. You claim to protect us from traitors, but it is *you* who have betrayed our family. You abandoned us, long ago. This war is just your latest excuse."

Chandra picked up the torn halves of her book, walked into her room and slammed the door. W'Kabi looked to see his two boys peeking from their bedroom, their little faces sad and confused.

W'Kabi started toward them, but fearing their father's wrath, the children ran back into their room. Alone with nothing but his anger and frustration, W'Kabi sat in the dark and sulked.

CHAPTER FOURTEEN

SPIRITS OF THE JUNGLE

FROM SNOWCAPPED mountains to burning jungle marshes, T'Challa tracked Lord Sombre into the oppressive humidity and the scorching heat of the one place in Wakanda he had never been— Serpent Valley. His father had been there only once when T'Challa was a child. T'Chaka had left the royal palace at Birnin Zana with a company of five hundred men, but only two of them had returned: T'Chaka and W'Kabi. The latter had sustained massive injuries in his efforts to protect his king.

T'Challa remembered his father speaking furtively of a place infested with evil spirits and creatures that only existed in the ancient mythologies sang by the griots. T'Chaka had decreed Serpent Valley off-limits. No Wakandan would be permitted to make the journey to the primeval jungle land. T'Chaka's word had been law. No one questioned his orders. No one dared to ask about the terrible fate that had befallen the soldiers lost to the mythic valley.

After tracking Sombre all day and night through freezing wind and snow, T'Challa had finally crossed a sudden, abrupt change of landscape to a dense jungle, so hot that it triggered the cooling system in his panther suit. Bright colorful plants rivaled the curated gardens in the courtyards behind the royal palace.

T'Challa leapt through the treetops in pursuit of Sombre. There was something different about this place. A sense of psionic energy pervaded the air. T'Challa heard murmuring voices drifting from the lush treetops, the twisting vines and wind. The animals calling each other through the wilderness penetrated his mind in a way that he found invasive, reminding him of King Cadaver's mental attacks.

Every sound in the jungle seeped into the Panther King's brain, into his blood and his very core. Normally, his panther suit would flex slightly as it absorbed the cacophony of vibratory energy; however, the material remained unaltered, as if T'Challa was surrounded by complete silence. Despite the mysterious chorus of voices that fell like cosmic rain from the trees, the audio spectrum displayed in his lenses showed zero movement—or at least no sound or vibrations that the suit could register.

Puzzled, he shook his head, but the incomprehensible voices grew louder. Shadows flitted around him, forms that flickered just out of view. He spun and swiped at them, but they dissipated, fading into the camouflage of green. He had tracked Sombre for almost a week, hoping that the purple-robed Death Regiment member would lead him to N'Jadaka, but now T'Challa found himself in the middle of a cathedral-like forest with lush undergrowth. The voices increased with the chattering of insects and creatures unseen. His patience was growing thin.

Sombre is weaving his sinister magic, he thought angrily. Though the Panther King did not trust magic and believed only in the power of Bast, he was a man of science. He was sure that Sombre was behind the mysterious chatter. Sombre had not shown any sign that he knew he was being followed, yet he must have known.

Irritated, T'Challa could not stand the whispering voices and shadows any longer. He chose to attack right there. He would beat Sombre until he drove the invading voices from his head. Then he would make Sombre take him to N'Jadaka. T'Challa had decided he would end the madness of this civil war once and for all. He would kill Sombre, N'Jadaka, and anyone else who dared to intervene in his royal duties as the sovereign protector of Wakanda.

T'Challa crept through the trees, getting as close as he could without being seen by Sombre. He leapt from the branches, a flying black spear, straight and true, composed of lean stretched muscle and black luminescent vibranium.

The Black Panther pounced on Sombre, kicking the violet-swathed villain in the back of his golden-masked head. Sombre hit the ground. T'Challa watched as the fiend struggled to stand. Somehow, the Death Regiment officer's robes managed to stay clean. The mud fell from his garments, leaving not the slightest trace of scum nor any evidence of his fall.

Sombre stood almost motionless and stared at T'Challa, his robe billowing in the breeze. The golden mask fused to Sombre's face curled itself into an unlikely smile.

"You didn't know you were being followed?" T'Challa asked. He crouched and allowed the black claws on his gloved hand to extend another inch. "You thought the white gorilla would kill me for certain, didn't you?"

Sombre did not answer. Instead, he raised his hands above his head, moving his fingers with the same gesticulations that he employed in the presence of the massive white gorilla. The god that T'Challa had left for dead in the snow. The thought of the beast's sacrifice, the machinations of N'Jadaka, the manipulation performed through Sombre, and the rest of the Death Regiment enraged T'Challa.

"But you had to leave me, didn't you?" T'Challa asked. "If you had stayed, the white gorilla would have turned on you after you finished me." T'Challa screamed, barely able to control himself, barely able to keep from strangling Sombre right there in the jungle.

The rage proved too formidable an adversary. T'Challa reached out and wrapped his hands around Sombre's throat. He felt the burning in his hands as soon as he tightened his grip. The pain permeated his panther suit and sank deep into his flesh, deep into his bones. He was transported back to the memory of the burial grounds, to Baron Macabre and the zombified minions of the Death Regiments.

T'Challa tried to release his grip, but his arms were constricted, and his hands were glued to Sombre's neck by some unseen force, some intangible substance that had wrapped itself around his hands and refused to release them. He fell backwards with Sombre landing on top of his chest. Before T'Challa realized what was happening, Sombre wrapped his taloned fingers around his neck and squeezed.

The Black Panther did not think it possible, but the burning he felt coursing through his hands, through his arms, through his neck, made the sensations he felt in the graveyard battling the Baron seem warm and gentle—like one of Monica's sweet caresses. Monica. T'Challa wondered what would happen to her if he died here in the Valley of the Serpents. His authority as king had been her only saving grace, the only thing that had protected her from his mistrusting brethren. The ones like W'Kabi who despised outworlders and didn't mind showing their disapproval and their antipathy.

Fire and darkness consumed T'Challa. Darkness and fire. He felt himself drowning in a black, burning sea. He smelled his flesh burning, the blood boiling in his veins. He gritted his teeth as the darkness washed over him. If it was the will of Bast for him to die there in the Valley of the Serpents, he would not die alone. With the dregs of his evaporating strength, he squeezed Sombre's neck. The weight of flesh and bone collapsing, cracking in his grasp gave him some solace. He smiled, even though the burning tears welled in his eyes, knowing that Sombre would never bring harm to any more of Wakanda's creatures. Knowing that he had avenged the white gorilla would have to be solace enough. It would be the peace that he would take with him into the darkness of the darkness of Death's Domain, and it would have to do.

Are you giving up so easily, Panther King? The voice inside T'Challa's mind spoke as clearly as if someone had been standing next to him, watching him succumb to the powers of Sombre. *I heard that you might be the greatest of Bast's avatars. I must say, Panther King, I am somewhat disappointed.*

The voice inside T'Challa's head startled him. It was not his own voice, and it did not sound like any other voice that he had heard before. The voice did not belong to T'Chaka or G'Sere, W'Kabi or Taku, Mendinao or even his beautiful Monica. It was a derisive voice, playful and mocking. At the sound of it, T'Challa bucked and kicked and sent Sombre flying across the grassy jungle floor until the nefarious priest slammed into a tree in a billowing explosion of purple robes and flailing limbs.

T'Challa tried to stand but ended up falling to his knees. The pain was too great. He could still feel the searing heat coursing throughout his body, clouding his mind like an incessant fever. T'Challa held his brow with one hand and shook his head. When he looked up, Sombre was floating over him, purple robes fluttering in the wind. Sombre raised his hands once again and some unseen hand had grabbed his throat to lift the Panther King into the air.

"Killing the white gorilla should have been tantamount to killing your own Panther God with your bare hands. It should have been an epiphany for you, a sign of your ineptitude and your worthlessness, your inability to lead Wakanda." Sombre worked his fingers in an array of archaic gestures. The invisible grip on T'Challa's throat began to squeeze, cutting off his air supply.

"You should have crawled back to your precious Golden City, to your outworlder. At least you could have confided in her in your disgrace. Now you will die here in the marsh and the jungle land, and no one will ever know what happened to you. No one except Killmonger, that is."

Again, the golden mask welded to Sombre's face bent itself into a smile that projected evil and malcontent, satisfaction in the act of murder that Sombre was about to commit. The eyes of the mask glowed like two pieces of molten magma, two distant red stars. T'Challa could not help himself. With the life force draining from his limbs, he began to lose himself in those glowing eyes. The more he stared, the more the eyes began to look like distant planets. Distant worlds that would take him to the realm of his ancestors. Distant worlds that would take him to Djalia. No more war. No more pain and uncertainty.

No more anything.

You are a selfish one, Panther King. Bast must be truly ashamed to call you her avatar, to have entrusted the wellness of so many people in your care.

Again, the sound of the voice shook T'Challa from his dying reverie, sent a bolt through him that shocked him back to reality: back to the waking world. A bolt that strengthened him and shamed him all at once.

This time when T'Challa awoke, he spun and brought his heel down like an ax blade on the back of Sombre's neck. The bones cracking under T'Challa's foot made a sickening sound. The time for talking was done. Without any utterance of pain or victory, T'Challa grabbed Sombre's wrist. Gritting his teeth, enduring the burning spreading through his body, he flipped Sombre over his shoulder and sent the sorcerer hurtling into a pool of mud and marsh. The surface looked solid but revealed itself as a swampy quagmire once Sombre hit its surface. T'Challa stood over Sombre and watched as he struggled to free himself from the swamp that trapped his arms, disabling Sombre from working his archaic, cryptic magic.

T'Challa watched as the quagmire sucked Sombre down, covering his arms, his waist. Submerging Sombre until the thick mire covered the purple-robed priest to his chest and armpits.

"You brought this upon yourself, Sombre," T'Challa said. "You came here to warn Killmonger. To tell him that the wolves and the cold had not killed me. That you left me as an offering for the white gorilla, but you still could not be sure of my demise. Now look at you. It would be a fitting end for you, would it not. Covered in muck. Seeping into the same destruction that you had hoped would drown my kingdom."

T'Challa waited for a reply, for some cryptic retort, some signal of defiance, or some eternal pledge to the power and might of Erik Killmonger. But Sombre remained silent. Instead, he stared at T'Challa, that golden mask still stretched into its hideous smile. The eyes inside the mask were lit with nefarious delight. A madman's glee. In T'Challa's mind, he pictured Killmonger laughing at him. Mocking him. Deriding the rage that T'Challa had failed to control.

You are a great disappointment, Panther King. The disembodied voice intruded on T'Challa's thoughts once more.

"The penalty for treason against the crown, against the line of Bashenga, is death," T'Challa said. Talking to the world. Declaring his intention to anyone who was listening. Sentient or not. Tangible or immaterial.

But you promised to usher in a new Wakanda. A new age of enlightenment. If you allow this helpless man to die, what makes you any different from this Killmonger, with whom you are obsessed?

"N'Jadaka," T'Challa muttered to himself. He knelt as close to the quagmire as he dared and extended his arm. "Take my arm, Sombre. You will return with me to the Golden City and answer for your crimes, but you will live."

Sombre did not move. He did not make any effort to reach for T'Challa. Instead, Sombre smiled and stared until the quagmire covered him to the chin. Then, that evil golden smile. Another moment passed and all that was left were those red eyes glowing with all the evil in the world. Staring at T'Challa until they disappeared in the quagmire, never to resurface again.

T'Challa watched Sombre sink to his muddy death with neither satisfaction nor regret. Only a cold, desensitized awareness. The kind of iron resolve that accompanied the horrors and the reality of war.

"Are you satisfied, Panther King? Does this man's death, this man you call Sombre, bring you any peace?"

T'Challa looked up through the sweltering heat and mist. Now the voice that had been inside his head rang through the jungle with a striking clarity. In the treetops above, a man sat perched on a huge, twisting branch that stretched over T'Challa's head. The man wore a yellow vest and green beads that gleamed over his bare chest. He also wore a yellow wrap around his pelvis, clamped and held in place by a shiny green belt. The man's brown skin shone like polished copper. His head was shaved bald, but his thick dark eyebrows framed wide dark eyes that rose with his brilliant smile. The man sat in the tree and stared at T'Challa with all the mischief of a gleeful child at play in the sweltering jungle.

"Who are you?" T'Challa asked. "Are you with Killmonger's Death Regiments?" T'Challa's voice went cold, and he bore black claws that hungered to end this civil war.

"Killmonger? Death Regiments?" The mysterious man managed to stretch his smile even more. "Do you want to kill these men too? Tell me. After you have done your killing, will you take your corpses and leave Serpent's Valley forever?"

"Answer me, damn you," T'Challa yelled and leapt toward the high branch, a blinding blur of black muscles and razor-sharp claws.

Just as T'Challa was about to wrap his clawed hands around the man's throat, he disappeared in a flourish of laughter and smoke.

"Are you looking for me?" a voice called to T'Challa, a voice filled with mirth.

T'Challa turned to find the strange bald man perched on another branch directly behind the Panther King. Neither the branch nor the tree had been there a moment before. T'Challa spun around to discover more trees, as if their trunks had sprung up in mere seconds. Leafy branches stretched across the sky overhead, blotting out the sun.

"Where did you get such powers?" T'Challa asked. "You don't have the signs of physical deformities, the mutations of those subjected to the inner chambers of Resurrection Altar."

"Resurrection Altar?" The bald man laughed again. "Is that what you call that place? It seems that you and your friends are more concerned with killing than rebirth, Panther King."

"Who are you, little man? I don't want to hurt you, but I will if I must. I am looking for someone who came through these jungles ahead of me. A man who calls himself Erik Killmonger. He would have had an entire retinue trailing him."

"You can't find him on your own, Panther King?" The bald man disappeared. This time he reappeared right in front of T'Challa. "Can't you smell him? The ones you are looking for? They have brought the stench of death to this place. It's a smell we work desperately to steer clear of, and we haven't had those kinds of visitors since another Panther King, who dressed just like you, came here many years ago. We sent him on his way. Now, you need to find this Erik Killmonger and take him with you."

T'Challa ignored the old man and raised his nose to the wind. At first, he could smell only the earthy, wet scent of the flora around him. The forest was three-dimensional. At T'Challa's feet, the air was damp, hot and still. He climbed over the thick, powerful buttress roots of the trees, past wide trunks that stretched and climbed hundreds of feet in the air. Darkness crowded around him as the dense sea of leaves rustled overhead. And there, in the wind, he caught it—the unmistakable stench of death that N'Jadaka carried on him. T'Challa wondered why he hadn't tried that before. Immediately, he took to the treetops, leaping from branch to branch. Swinging on the vines, he glided through the lush trees.

He was the Black Panther, ghost of the forest, silently stalking the hothouse jungle and blending with the night. As he stealthily slid through the darkness, he noticed the death scent grew stronger. He was going in the right direction. But there were other scents as well. The heavy perfume of overripe winged fruit and strange blossoms, mixed with monstrous scents that reminded him of the white gorillas. But these scents were different. T'Challa looked to his side and was astonished to see that the bald man was right beside him, swinging through the trees, as effortless as a spirit.

"What are you?" T'Challa asked, his voice filled with confusion and more than a slight bit of wonder.

"I am called Mokadi, Panther King."

"And what is this place? Why do they call it Serpent Valley?"

"Serpent Valley? Do we breed serpents or attract them, Panther King?"

"Why do you answer my questions with questions?"

"That is all I have," the strange man said, his yellow wrap billowing as he floated by, vines twisting beneath his feet. "You are the one who thinks he has all the answers. I can't help but wonder: how is that working out for you, Black Panther?"

T'Challa growled and shook his head as he lithely bounced off a giant leaf. The leaf reminded him of the Heart-Shaped Herb that flowed through his veins and heightened his senses, even at this very moment. The scent of N'Jadaka had grown strong. T'Challa was close. His muscles tensed with the anticipation of battle.

"Do you know there is another land that lies beyond the ice and the snow, one that protects the secrets of this place?" T'Challa asked.

"Oh?" The man tilted his head, curiously. "I have never had any reason to leave. This is my home. Everything I need is right here. The forest protects itself."

This made T'Challa think about the Golden City, the lush lands of Wakanda and the bounty that he had known ever since he was a child. *If Wakanda is so great, why do you keep leaving? What are you searching for?*

"Exactly," Mokadi said. "You took the thought right out of my mouth." Mokadi laughed and leapt ahead of T'Challa. "The beautiful, wondrous sunsets. The gold buildings in your mind with all their splendor. Why do you keep leaving them behind, Panther King? What are you looking for? What are you running from?"

T'Challa did not answer. Instead, he looked to the hills and the valley. He stood on a vast cliffside and stared at the valley below. Here, the sun burst through the trees, dipped into its afternoon march, and the sky filled with hues of orange and purple and flaming red, setting a stark backdrop against the green treetops.

Down in the valley, T'Challa noticed a river where the indigo waters were filled with great beasts milling about. *Prehistoric beasts.* Beasts that should have been extinct millions of years ago. And yet they lived. The behemoth descendants of the brachiosaurus, the giant creatures craned their long necks, tromping around the river in large patches of sludge. T'Challa noticed men working near the banks of the river, manning machines. Huge cranes that dumped gallons and gallons of dark black sludge into the river. The great creatures, an astonishing sight, were covered with nets—and they looked angry.

Regret filled the Panther King as he thought of the black rhinoceros, the flying crocodile, the white gorillas that had been deployed against him. Beasts driven mad by a rage not their own. This was the work of N'Jadaka. The scent of death was strong here. Even if T'Challa had seen none of this atrocious scene, he would have smelled N'Jadaka. The air was full of his bitterness, the stench of unrelenting avarice and pain. The Panther King's friend-turned-nemesis was close. T'Challa balled his fists, anger rising from his stomach, seeping into the back of his mouth like acrid bile.

"You talk of beauty and splendor, Panther King, but behold. This is the work of man. This is the work of the men you have followed here. Would you destroy my home in order to build your own?" Mokadi asked.

T'Challa did not answer. Instead, he took a cue from Mokadi and posed a question of his own. "Why didn't you speak to them the way that you have spoken to me, the way that you spoke to my father?"

"Only virtuous hearts can hear us in this place." Mokadi turned to T'Challa. This time the bald head man did not smile. His face was sorrow. This time he spoke with pain, something akin to anger. "Why speak to those who refuse to listen?"

DOWN IN the valley, Killmonger watched over the men carrying out his orders. Flanked by Tayete and Kazibe, the Wakandan exile looked upon his handiwork with pride and approval.

"What's wrong, Tayete, no jokes to tell? Relax, we are here to master these creatures. These beasts are going to be instrumental in our conquest of the Golden City. In fact, if you please me, perhaps I will allow you to train with the special militia who will ride these great beasts, and then you may trample Wakanda into the ground. We will shatter the throne," he said, eyes shining with malice and glee. "Reduce the royal palace to rubble and stone! How does that sound?"

Killmonger bellowed and smacked Tayete in the back. The force of the blow knocked the scrawny soldier into the brown sludge that had been used to fill the river, immobilizing the dinosaurs who were now being captured and herded underneath nets. Killmonger watched Tayete struggle, without success, to free himself. He found the scene entirely amusing and reared his great head back, his laughter echoing through Serpent Valley.

"Come now, Tayete. I thought you were light on your feet. There is far too much work for an afternoon swim." His body shook with laughter, enjoying Tayete's panic as the oil sucked at his arms.

"Um, Commander Killmonger, sir," Kazibe said, venturing beside Killmonger, eyes filled with fear.

"What is it, Kazibe?" Killmonger could barely stop laughing to speak. "Are you feeling like a bath yourself? You want to join your partner?"

"No, no sir. It's just... I'm worried that Tayete might drown. It doesn't look like he can get out."

"Nonsense," Killmonger said and knelt beside the riverbank. "Tayete can't wait to ride these great beasts! He's just a little overzealous, that's all. You know your friend better than me. He's always full of sly jokes, like the little trick he pulled, leading T'Challa to the Land of the Chilling Mist. Hope you've learned your lesson!" he called out to Tayete.

Tayete's eyes bulged, but he did not answer. Kazibe gulped and stared at a bird struggling in the sludge, flailing like his friend. Tayete reached for the struggling animal, but Killmonger grabbed Tayete's collar and snatched him from the river before he could rescue it.

"What are you doing? Time is of the essence. If we stop to save every helpless creature, we will miss an opportunity." Killmonger turned his back on the little bird drowning in the muck and pointed at the huge dinosaurs straining against the netting. "After we capture a few more of these rare specimens, we will leave this cursed valley that time forgot and return to Birnin Zana with an epic surprise."

Tayete smiled uneasily, averting his eyes from the defenseless creature, its cries unheeded as Killmonger set the fool on the dry shore. Dripping in the oily, sticky substance, Tayete brushed himself off, then noticed something standing atop the hill. He focused for a moment before he gasped.

"Commander Killmonger. Up there on the hill, do you see? It's the panther demon!"

"You're not supposed to call him that, Tayete," Kazibe whispered.

"What? That can't be," Killmonger roared, the red beaded necklace tight around his throat. "The Black Panther is dead, or else we would have received word from Lord Sombre." Killmonger sneered and cupped his hand over his eyes, staring at the mountain's crest. Nothing stood in the distance now but an empty crown of trees.

"If he lives, it speaks to his endurance. Despite his pampered lifestyle, he'd prove a worthy adversary after all. But either way, it doesn't matter, even if our little panther demon has managed to survive and follow us here. Let's make sure that he doesn't get out. The Golden City will be much easier pickings without their mascot to rally them."

Killmonger held out his hand, waiting for Tayete to pass him a small remote control. He took it and pressed a red button, laughing as he marched briskly, with Tayete and Kazibe trudging behind him, along the trail that led out of the valley.

T'Challa watched as an enormous glass cage rose from the brown sludge in the river. Inside, a huge dinosaur thrashed its great tail against the walls of the cage. T'Challa recognized the beast from the textbooks he'd read as a child and the science fiction movies he had grown to love during his stay in the United States. *Tyrannosaurus rex, king of the tyrant lizards.* A siren rang out: as if on cue, the panels of the glass cage sank back into the river. When the T-rex realized it was free, it reared its head back and roared.

Serpent Valley shook, the sound echoing over the river and across the mountainside. A burst of wings took to the air as the birds fled from the frightening sound.

"Wow! That's a big fella," Mokadi said, stroking his green necklace thoughtfully. "What will you do, Panther King?"

"Mokadi, right now I need solutions, not questions," T'Challa said, his shoulders set with grim determination.

THE TYRANNOSAURUS rex chased T'Challa through the jungle. It swiped its claws, forcing him to jump over the swatting talons. The beast's fist slammed into an outcrop of rock that jutted from the hillside, sending a shower of rubble spraying in all directions. The ground shook all around them. Killmonger's remaining Death Regiments fled in terror, scrambling for safety. T'Challa wondered where Mokadi had disappeared to, as he dodged the enormous animal's attacks.

He bounced and flipped through the jungle until he came to a cliffside. With the beast chasing him, he had no choice but to dive off the cliff. Luckily for the Panther King, the Heart-Shaped Herb enhanced his kinesthetic senses and perception, making his leap of faith onto a tall palm tree less of a gamble. T'Challa grabbed the tree and held on as his weight pulled it to the ground, allowing his panther suit to absorb the vibrations around him.

T'Challa channeled the stored energy into a boulder that had landed next to him. He placed the huge rock on the treetop and let the makeshift catapult snap upright, hurling the sonic-charged boulder into the dinosaur's face. The homemade missile exploded and sent the beast staggering back, falling to the ground.

T'Challa stood over the unconscious beast and checked its wounds. They were bad but not serious. The beast would be out for a while, but he thought it would live. T'Challa thanked Bast.

"Nice work, Panther King," Mokadi said.

T'Challa found Mokadi standing behind him. The bald man held a bird, cradled like a newborn baby. Mokadi wiped the bird's head, its wings and breast, removing the sticky goo from the bird's feathers with each gentle stroke. Then Mokadi released the bird into the air.

Watching it fly away, T'Challa remembered the name. Mokadi. It was a word that he had learned long ago from Griot G'Sere. It was a word that his father had hated, almost as much as magic. Now, T'Challa understood why.

Mokadi was an ancient word that meant "spirit".

At Resurrection Altar, the Black Panther saw the dangers of

interfering with the world of the spirits, mixing magic with science. How vibranium's properties might be used to amplify mystical properties to a devastating and dangerous effect. Like science, the mysteries of magic could be weaponized. T'Challa did not understand the meaning of the words and incantations Lord Sombre had used to wreak such havoc on the Land of the Chilling Mist and Mokadi's beloved Serpent Valley. But he knew he had to stop the fiends spawned from the profane altar.

Until we meet again, Panther King, may the love of Bast protect you and keep you safe.

When T'Challa turned around, Mokadi, Spirit of the Jungle, had disappeared.

BACK IN the Golden City, in the courtyards behind the royal palace in a place called Tranquility Temple, W'Kabi sat with his two sons. The trio stared out at the beautiful, manicured gardens that filled the marble courtyards. W'Kabi sat with one child under each arm. The sun, near the horizon, bathed the entire garden in a shower of honey and gold.

"T'Challa has gone again, but this time he left me in charge. There are great things I must attend to. That's why I haven't been around as much as I would like." W'Kabi sighed, looking down at one boy and then the other. "I'm afraid my absence has taken a toll on the bond between your mother and I, but no matter what happens, please remember that I love you more than anything in the world. I would give my life for you if necessary."

W'Kabi dropped his head, his voice full of shame.

"I'm sorry, boys. This is no excuse, but I have been a warrior all my life. I have defended Wakanda against some of the Earth's most powerful fighters. But right now, I am so afraid. I don't know what to do. Someone like your Uncle Taku is much more suitable for this kind of thing. I can't believe I'm saying this, but right now, I wish I were more like him. Maybe then I could keep from losing my wife, keep from losing you."

They sat in silence, listening to the chittering of insects, the whisk of tiny wings. After a moment, his eldest boy rubbed his grizzled cheek. "Don't be afraid, Father," he said. "Bast will protect us." His little brother lay his head on W'Kabi's shoulder.

The Shield of Wakanda held his sons and wept.

Taku stood off in the distance with Monica Lynne. The pair watched W'Kabi and his sons rise from the marble steps, walking back toward their apartment. Taku's face was grim, but Monica had a sadness in her eyes and sense of foreboding about her entire demeanor.

"W'Kabi seems really upset, Taku," Monica said. "This war is taking its toll on everyone, even our strong ones."

"I don't think it's the war, Ms. Lynne," Taku said. "W'Kabi loves to fight, and he's good at it, but when he goes home, he enters a different kind of war. He is not so suited for that kind of battle."

"All this time, I had W'Kabi pegged as a muscle-bound xenophobe, but since T'Challa has been gone, he's actually been rather sweet. At least sweet for W'Kabi."

Taku laughed. "There is definitely more to our Shield of Wakanda than meets the eye." They watched W'Kabi and his children walk away until the trio disappeared as the sun set. "Everything is just so confusing now."

Taku turned to Monica.

"When we raided Killmonger's base, I saw a boy, barely out of his teens, murdered right in front of me. I haven't been the same since. All my life I had a good handle on the world around me, you know. I thought I knew how things went. But now..."

"I know what you mean, Taku. When T'Challa invited me to come here, I thought I was going back to the motherland, reconnecting with my roots, but now I feel more lost than ever. And if something happened to T'Challa, I don't know what I would do."

"Everyone is on edge. The prisoner Horatio keeps asking me for word about his snakes. When we raided the village, W'Kabi had the snake pits burned. This news will upset Horatio, but I must tell him the truth. I don't know any other way."

"The one who calls himself Venomm, with two *Ms*? I heard he's a survivor: strange but strong."

Taku cracked a smile.

"That's the one. You're right. He is strong but misguided." He peered at her. "I see why the king admires you so much. Good day, Ms. Lynne."

"Monica," she said. "Call me Monica."

They parted ways. Monica returned to the gardens, and Taku went back into the royal palace. He took a series of corridors and elevators until he arrived at the holding cells beneath the royal palace where the captured Death Regiments were being held. He found Venomm waiting at the front of the cell, his face pressed to the plexiglass, looking out into the dark corridor expectantly.

"I am here, Horatio," Taku said evenly. "I must tell you something I have held back from fear of hurting you. General W'Kabi set fire to the pits where you trained your snakes. If it's any consolation, it appeared that most of the snakes had escaped by then. There were a few left at the bottom, and I don't think any of them made it out. I am sorry. I tried to stop him, but these are desperate times. Compassion is a rarity that few can afford."

"Damn," Venomm cursed and flinched. When he looked out at Taku from the darkness, his eyes were brimming with tears. "That's all right. I guess you did all that you could do. Thanks for telling me."

"No need to thank me, Horatio," Taku said sadly. "I'm just doing my job."

"Outside of Erik, you're the only person I've ever known who wasn't disgusted by my face. You treat me like a human being."

"You are a human being, Horatio, and you deserve respect. I know how it is to be different, to be scorned and ridiculed."

Venomm looked Taku over. "Listen, Taku, before long I'm gonna bust out of here. And I suggest you stand aside and let me do what I gotta do. I mean, I like you and all, but don't get it confused. I'll kill you if I have to."

CHAPTER FIFTEEN

HEART OF POISON

WALKING THROUGH Serpent Valley, T'Challa reflected on how much he had gained from personally experiencing the true terrain of Wakanda. Making his way back to the Land of Chilling Mist, T'Challa came to a vast forest filled with thick bramble and thorny briar. He made his way through the briar until he reached a small stream—clear as polished crystal, untouched by N'Jadaka's treachery. He knelt by the river and allowed his panther suit to dematerialize around his face and arms. He dipped his hands in the water, splashing himself with the cool liquid. T'Challa winced at the burned tissue that covered his arms, amazed at how Sombre's touch had scarred him through his panther suit without damaging the vibranium-enriched fabric. The painful reality sparked T'Challa's sense of scientific curiosity and wonder. He promised himself that he would discuss these phenomena with Mendinao back in the Golden City.

T'Challa paused as he heard movement deep in the briar behind him. The sounds were subtle and faint. Something was attempting to be stealthy. Or *somethings*. Nevertheless, the Black Panther heard them with his enhanced senses.

The sound of inhalation and held breath. A heartbeat's increased rapidity. A slight shift of grass underfoot. Grass brushing flesh. A taut string pulled and held, vibrating ever so slightly. Then, much louder, the sound of the taut string's release. T'Challa realized the sound slicing through the air was a missile before he saw it.

T'Challa dodged the arrow, which exploded as it struck the water. He smelled the ammonium nitrate, then dove deep underwater as he realized the arrows were dipped in explosives. Now below the water's surface, he observed a group of men inspecting the bank, searching for his remains.

"It was definitely the panther demon, Salamander," one bare-chested man said as he squatted by the stream. "I'm sure of it. Killmonger was correct, this panther demon indeed has many lives."

"Killmonger is always right." Salamander's voice rolled like thunder. "He has proven himself time and time again. Ever since he came to our village with news of his revolution and what it would mean for us to overthrow the so-called Panther King."

The bare-chested man waded further into the stream. Armed with a long machete in one hand and a Wakandan-issued handgun in the other, he searched through the seemingly placid water.

"There is no way he could have survived that explosion. Your aim is always true, Salamander, but where is the body?"

T'Challa leapt from underneath the water and wrapped his hand around the man's throat. T'Challa sank his fingers into the muscular flesh of the man's neck. Raised the man into the air.

"Are you looking for something? Seek and you will find. Ask and you will receive." T'Challa laughed as he punched the man in the face and hurled him into the briar.

T'Challa stood face to face with the one called Salamander. T'Challa noticed the waxy greenish skin and lurid lavender boils, oozing pus and blood, that covered the man's athletic body, the military grade recursive bow, and the case of explosive arrows slung across his shoulder. *Was Salamander another unholy sacrifice on Resurrection Altar?*

"You are hard to kill, but you will die today, King of Wakanda. Enjoy that title while you can. Soon, you will be king no more." In one lightning-quick movement, Salamander loosed an arrow and nocked another before the first could finish its deadly flight.

T'Challa jumped over the arrow, and when the missile exploded behind him, the momentum propelled him forward, transforming him into a speeding rocket, a black warhead composed of honed muscle and the power of caged fury. Another Death Regiment soldier dove from the dense foliage to protect Salamander. When T'Challa crashed into the man, he heard breaking bones. He watched as the bare-chested man flew past Salamander, slammed into a tree, and fell unconscious.

"No more men to hide behind. There's insufficient distance for your arrows to be effective unless you're willing to explode with them. What now, Salamander?"

"My name is Salamander K'Ruel," the man said, laughing. "Don't worry. I have a few more surprises. The Death Regiments are very resourceful, thanks to Killmonger and the sacred flames of Resurrection Altar."

Disgusted by N'Jadaka's profane experiments that mutated its victims into grotesque distortions of themselves, T'Challa charged. Engaged in combat, Salamander exhibited an unexpected amount of strength. He wrapped his arms around T'Challa and held the Panther King in a locked embrace.

T'Challa watched as the mauve boils on Salamander's face burst open. He shuddered as hundreds of metal quills sprung from Salamander's sores, penetrating the Black Panther's armor. *Vibranium!* T'Challa thought as the needles sank into his flesh. His muscles grew numb as he collapsed by the stream.

"You're not the only one with gifts," Salamander K'Ruel mumbled as the world went black.

T'CHALLA WOKE to excruciating pain. Thousands of tiny pinpricks covered his arms and his chest; each puncture burned as if lit by a tiny match. T'Challa tried to move but found his arms and legs bound to a pair of tree trunks, flanking his sides.

"I am sorry, panther demon, but I must leave you now. Don't worry—I have brought plenty of company to escort you into Death's Domain." Salamander raised his hand and presented a tiny green lizard. "Funny thing about salamanders. They are not venomous, but their skin is poisonous. Lucky for me, I'm immune to poison. What about you? You will find out soon enough." Salamander set the lizard on the ground and chuckled as the tiny beast crawled up the sole of T'Challa's boot.

A screeching sound, bestial and primeval, unlike anything T'Challa had ever heard, pierced the sky and made the King of Wakanda shudder.

"Ah, that's another friend coming for you. He will be here before long. With that I bid you farewell. He might confuse me for the tasty morsel I left for its dinner. Remember, T'Challa: this is for the best. You are sacrificing your life for a new era, a new Wakanda. Let that thought comfort you."

T'Challa watched Salamander walk away until the hideously disfigured man disappeared into the thorny forest. T'Challa sighed with relief and relaxed his muscles. Staring at Salamander's boils disgusted the Panther King and reminded him of the poison that N'Jadaka had brought to his homeland. He watched the lizard creep across his leg, leaving a trail of poison slime, until the beast crawled up his chest and came to rest on top of T'Challa's head.

He wondered if the poison from the salamander's skin would soak through his panther suit but found he did not care.

Either Bast will see me through or call me home. Either way, I have done all that I can do for my people. For Monica.

The piercing screech penetrated the sky once more, and T'Challa looked up to see a huge flying creature with its outstretched wings blacking out the sun. Another beast he had read about in his science books when he was a child—a pterodactyl. The creature swooped down from the sky and grabbed T'Challa. The salamander leapt from T'Challa's head for safety as the flying reptile wrapped its claws around him, breaking his fetters, and snatching the Panther King into the air.

○━━━━━━○

TAKU, ADEBISI, and Monica Lynne walked through the fields of Alkama. Monica had not seen Karota and Kantu since the episode at the hospital, but with all the rumors of war, with all the death and destruction, Monica wanted to check on her. She remembered the brightness of M'Jumbak's smile and knew how it felt to have a loved one disappear under perilous conditions. She wanted to comfort this family, but she also needed comforting herself.

"Do not beat yourself up, Ms. Lynne," Taku said. "Karota is used to working with griots and medicine men, but the kind of song therapy that you are suggesting is new to her. Give her time. She'll come around."

"I hope so. Back in the US I sang pretty much my entire life. For money and adoration mostly, when I think about it, but the prospect of using my voice to heal people… Well, that's an idea that I need to get used to myself."

"You possess more power than you realize, Ms. Lynne," Adebisi added. "Once you learn to harness and control your abilities, you will wield a force more powerful than you can imagine."

The trio found Kantu playing on the porch outside of the farmhouse where M'Jumbak had waved to T'Challa and Monica, brilliant love shining in his eyes. When the boy saw Monica, his face lit up with glee. He jumped up and ran to her, wrapping his arms around her waist.

"Monica!" the boy yelled, pressing his face against her stomach. "We've missed you so much. Wait until mama sees you." Kantu ran into the house pulling Monica by the finger, calling for his mother. "Mama! Look who came to visit us."

"I didn't think you would dare show your face around here again, outworlder." Karota emerged from her kitchen with the scents of stewed meat wafting around her.

"But mama, you said that you missed Ms. Monica," Kantu said, his eyes bright with confusion.

"Silence, child. Go set three more places at the table." Karota frowned. "You're here: you might as well sit down and eat. Maybe some real food can force some of that outworlder poison out of your system. My old friend, a professor at the university, visited the United States, and was sick for three weeks after eating what Americans call food."

Taku stared at Adebisi and shrugged his shoulders as Karota returned through the door that led to her kitchen. Monica smiled, shook her head, and followed Karota into the kitchen with Taku and Adebisi in tow. *The women of Wakanda will shade you, if nothing else.*

"Can I help you with something?" Monica asked. She grabbed a spoon from the kitchen counter and stirred a big smoking pot that smelled like stewing beef simmering on the stove top.

"Out of the way," Karota said. "You outworlders always want to take over."

"Monica only wants to help," Adebisi said. "You don't have to be so cross."

"Adebisi, Taku, can y'all check on our young friend? I got this," Monica winked before turning to Karota. "You're right. It's hard being an outworlder. That's why I'm here. I want you to teach me a better way, and I know what it's like to miss the one you love. Maybe we can help each other. With hard times like these, no one should be alone."

BACK AT the royal palace, W'Kabi sat in his living room with Chandra. The two sat on opposite sides of the room. Neither one spoke to the other. W'Kabi wanted to reach out, but he did not know what to say. He did not know what to do. This was no villain he could head-butt or kick or punch. This was his wife, but she did not want to be married any longer. W'Kabi did not know about these modern ways of living. A husband and wife were supposed to stay together no matter what—that was what W'Kabi and Chandra

272

had dreamed of when they had been married, fifteen years ago—but this was a new day.

o———o

IN THE sacked village where T'Challa's troops had fought and captured the majority of Killmonger's Death Regiments, N'Jadaka stood with King Cadaver, staring at the charred remains—burned under W'Kabi's orders.

"They burned our home to the ground," King Cadaver said in anger. "Savages. The House of Bashenga will pay."

N'Jadaka was silent. Wordless, he raised his face to the bright sky and laughed, knowing that T'Challa was dead. Knowing that the Golden City and the throne would soon be his. Anticipation rippled through his muscled body, twisting through the laughter curled in his throat.

o———o

BACK IN Serpent Valley, the pterodactyl flew through the sky, clutching its prey. T'Challa struggled in its grasp and asked Bast for forgiveness before he punched the beast, forcing it to drop him. The creature squawked and dove, swooping toward the ground to retrieve its plummeting captive. It grabbed T'Challa, but this time he rolled and flipped onto the pterodactyl's ridged back, guiding it through the sky like a winged stallion. The flying reptile fought for a bitter moment but soon surrendered.

The pterodactyl soared until T'Challa saw Salamander walking through the jungle, making his way back to the Land of Chilling Mist and Resurrection Altar. T'Challa called Salamander's name. The Black Panther thought he saw the Death Regiment officer marvel for a brief second at the sight of Wakanda's true king riding the prehistoric beast, before loosing one of his exploding arrows.

T'Challa leapt from the beast and the pterodactyl rolled, dodging the exploding arrow. Salamander nocked another before the plummeting Black Panther kicked him in the face and knocked him out cold.

T'Challa dragged Salamander through Serpent Valley, through the Land of Chilling Mist, back to the Golden City and the royal palace. A trek that took another week. T'Challa checked in using his Kimoyo beads but refused assistance, deciding instead to walk and reacquaint himself with the Wakandan landscape, a form of penance and pilgrimage. He had bound his enemy with strong vines, and every time Salamander woke up, T'Challa used the nerve gas stored in his gloves to render Salamander unconscious.

Exhausted, T'Challa passed out on the marble steps that led to the rear of the royal palace. When he woke up, Monica was cradling him in her arms and calling for Mendinao.

He looked at her beautiful face and smiled. "You have saved me once again, my love. We have to stop meeting like this." He laughed, wanting to touch her face but too weak to raise his arms. "My sunbird hero."

Monica smiled as she stared at him with great love and intention, finding the hurt parts inside of him, singing them whole again.

CHAPTER SIXTEEN

ANOTHER NAME FOR REVOLUTION

AFTER A week in bed healing from the wounds he endured while trekking through the Land of Chilling Mist and Serpent Valley, T'Challa rose feeling refreshed, craving fresh air and sunlight. Bedridden, he had realized that Monica had seen little if any of Wakandan's thriving beauty. That in mind, he took his sunbird to his favorite place in the countryside. He had loved the scenic beauty of Lake Nyanza since his first family vacation when he was five years old, the same year his father taught him to swim.

Monica welcomed the chance to spend quality time with T'Challa away from the stress, even for a little while. Even with the need for open security links through T'Challa's Kimoyo. The opportunity to learn more about Wakanda and T'Challa's childhood intrigued Monica, and she read as much as she could find on the outdoor getaway before they left the palace. T'Challa was as open and genuine as always; before long, Monica forgot that anyone was listening.

Now the lovers raced under the water of Lake Nyanza, each pulled by a giant sea turtle. These creatures were born on distant shores. Having escaped the hunts of bestial and human predators alike, the sea turtles had found peace here in these placid waters. They seemed to enjoy the underwater romp even more than the humans who rode their backs.

Monica was the first to leap from her turtle, spinning through the water. She smiled, and T'Challa could see the joy in her eyes even inside the dark, churning lake. The pair raced for the surface. They came here to spend some quality time away from the concerns of war. Monica was a much better swimmer than T'Challa, and she broke the surface first. T'Challa surfaced soon after. The two laughed and splashed water on each other—then T'Challa swam towards her and took her in his arms. The two kissed, long and passionate, turning in the warm water as the afternoon sun burned overhead.

They swam toward the shore and found a nice round rock on the beach where they held each other, admiring the wondrous view. T'Challa knew that he needed some alone time with Monica, but he hadn't known how much. Four months ago, stepping off the plane with his sunbird, he was beset with news of civil war. After that, G'Sere was killed and everything went downhill, but now, at least for today, everything was good. He had left all his problems back in the Golden City. Focusing on Monica, he lost himself in the totality of her. Her eyes, her skin glistening with the drops of lake water. Her smile, as bright as the open sky reflecting in the lake's surface. Most of all, her voice. It had been her voice, her singing, that brought him from the edges of madness. It was no wonder that Mendinao had discovered a way to help Monica heal people with her voice. It didn't surprise T'Challa at all.

"I'm glad you're back home. I don't just mean here with me, even though my heart is your home. I'm your Monikanda." She laughed and placed her hand over T'Challa's. "Your presence brightens everything around you. I understand why your absence hurt your people so much. You mean more to them than you know."

"I am Bast's avatar. When they see me, they see the spirit of Wakanda, the spirit of the Panther God."

"It's not just that, T'Challa. It's you. I saw the same light when we met in New York. This glow around you: everybody sees it no matter where you go." She leaned back and shook her head in the sun. "Even now, you're the brightest thing out here."

T'Challa stared at the sea turtles floating happily. A part of him was afraid to face Monica. Emotion brimmed in his eyes, and he felt ashamed for her to see.

"All those days trekking through the snow in the Land of Chilling Mist, the ancient jungle in Serpent Valley, I realized that my vision of Wakanda was… limited. This is the Wakanda my father wanted, but what if my father was wrong? What if I'm wrong? Maybe Wakanda has its own vision."

"You know you and Taku are a lot alike. Both of you are heavy thinkers, and both of you also put the needs and wants of others before yourself. That's all well and good, but you must understand, T'Challa, your people need *you*. They need you to lead them. You are not your father, and you will never be. You are *yourself*, and that's more than enough."

They sat together and watched the sun drop in the sky, a brilliant sunset dancing across the surface of the lake.

"When I think about you, sometimes I feel selfish because I need you, T."

"I need you too. Before we met, I knew exactly what I wanted out of life, but now things have… changed. I want more. I want you to be my queen, and lead with me."

"Queen Monica has a nice ring to it," Monica chuckled and wiggled her ring finger, as T'Challa embraced her. "Sounds like my next single."

"Do not forget about us little people who supported you from the beginning, Queen Monica. Especially your number one fan."

They shared a kiss and held each other. They lay in the sand as the sun set over the lake and the sea turtles played joyfully.

TAKU ENTERED a cage he had visited quite a bit over the past few months, even more so since T'Challa's raid on Killmonger's village. Inside the cell, Venomm stretched out on a twin-sized cot, his hands behind his head, staring at the ceiling. He lay there, perhaps dreaming of the snake he missed, or maybe about escape. Ever since Taku had brought him news of the burning of Killmonger's village, Venomm had become increasingly cagey, talking more and more about escape as the weeks passed.

"You are silent today, Horatio, even more so than usual," Taku said. He sat back in a folding chair and stared at the Death Regiment prisoner. "I remember we discussed your love for poetry. I would have hoped that you would have taken this time to write down your thoughts on paper."

"Poetry?" Venomm threw his head back and laughed. "Heck, that was a long time ago, Taku. I haven't written any poetry since my accident. All that stuff's just mumbo jumbo anyway. None of it means anything in the real world. Nope. The only thing that matters in real world is strength. I thought you would have learned that by now. With all the crap you've been through. Where was your poetry when you watched that child die?"

Taku paused. His mouth hung open as if he were searching the words to fill it. Before he could answer Venomm, W'Kabi appeared at the door to the cell. He spoke a low, gravelly command into the Kimoyo beads clamped around his wrist and stood grim-faced as the sliding doors to the prison cell opened. He stood over Venomm and pointed his finger.

"This charade that Taku has played with you has lasted long enough. Your so-called revolution is doomed. You will tell me where Killmonger is now, or you will die here by my hands." Taku sputtered, but the general continued, waving him away dismissively.

"I don't care what Taku has told you. First, I want to know how Killmonger smuggled an outworlder into our country. I want to know how Killmonger got his hands on Wakandan weapons undetected, and most of all, I want to know how Killmonger was able to raid our vibranium storehouses right under our noses."

"Ask your questions, Wasabi. It's not like my boy Taku here can stop you anyways." Venomm smirked. "But you might not like the answers."

"W'Kabi, this is not necessary, and it's totally against protocol. Wait until King T'Challa hears of this."

"Go ahead and tell him, Taku. The king is just as tired of this charade as I am, especially after killing Sombre and dragging Salamander halfway across Wakanda." W'Kabi smiled at Venomm. "Who do you think gave the order to burn your village? I declared it publicly, but the king gave the order."

Seething rage shot through the veins in Venomm's face, a dark poison.

"Killmonger played your king from the start," Venomm said, vitriol slurring his words. "Mr. Physics-Know-Everything ain't so smart after all. It all began when a Wakandan exile showed up at the Avenger's mansion and introduced himself as N'Jadaka. That war orphan played your boy like a fiddle! He laid out a sob story about being exiled and kidnapped, so sweet, he had ol' Ta'Charlie eating out the palm of his hand."

Venomm slapped his scaly palms against his chest. "Next thing you know, the two of them are best friends. They worked together feeding the poor, mentoring troubled teens back in New York City. Real follow-the-leader type stuff. I guess King Ta'Charlie ain't never had a friend. He was so grateful to meet a fellow Wakandan, he even fixed it so Killmonger could become a full citizen, 'with all the rights thereof reinstated' and everythin'. Ol' Ta'Charlie knew that Killmonger's parents had been killed by Klaw, right in front of him, but he didn't know that Killmonger worked for Klaw as a mercenary. Kind of slick, ain't it."

"What does this bedtime story have to do with what I asked you?" W'Kabi said coldly.

"*Everything*," Venomm said, scratching a dry patch of scales on his peeling arms. "See, Killmonger hated the ruling class of Wakanda. 'Cuz he blamed them for his parents' death and his own messed-up childhood. Working in the mines with the other orphan children, then sold off to Krazy Klaw? What kind of childhood was that? Killmonger was a regular Oliver Twist, 'cept he grew twisted for real," Venomm said, tapping his thick skull.

"He promised himself that he would do anything to avenge his family and free Wakanda from the rule of the *weak line of kings,* who went from hiding within their borders to bowing and scraping in front of the world superpowers, begging for a seat at the colonizer's table. Anyway, when Ta'Charlie sent his private jet to bring Killmonger home, I snuck into an underbelly galley. Killmonger already had everything figured out. Whatn't nothing to it but to do it. With all the trouble Ta'Charlie ran into when we touched down in Wakanda, I was able to sneak off the jet no problem.

"And *ssseee, here'sss* the thing," Venomm said, hissing like his beloved pet snakes. "Killmonger had been going back and forth between the States and Wakanda the whole time. This plan of his has been over a decade in the making. There's no way he can fail now. So, see, it don't matter what you do, Wasabi. Your Golden City's about to fall real soon and Killmonger will be the new ruler of Wakanda. Mark my words."

W'Kabi pulled out his gun. Taku screamed and jumped in front of Venomm, but the snake charmer grabbed the communication specialist from the back, pulled Taku's gun from his holster, and lodged his own service pistol under his chin.

"I told you I was busting outta here," Venomm said. "And I told you to stay out of my way."

"Horatio, this will not help. Not in the long run. You must confront your demons if you ever plan on defeating them."

"Shut up, Taku. Right now, all I'm thinking about is busting out of this cage and nothing's gonna stop me." He stared at W'Kabi. "Put your gun down, Wasabi, or your Wakandan brother is going to die. Just imagine: an outworlder killing your comrade, and the blood will be on your hands."

W'Kabi did not put his gun down. Instead, he gritted his teeth and stared through Taku. He stared through Venomm even, as if they weren't there. W'Kabi's eyes had gone dark and empty, pitiless. He extended his arm. Aim as true as ever, he pointed the barrel of the pistol at the space between Venomm's bushy eyebrows.

"I am not Taku. I understand the products of war. Blood and killing are natural products of the conflicts between men."

"You—you wouldn't dare," Venomm stammered. The story wasn't ending the way he planned it. This time, when he spoke, his voice shook in nervous expectation. "What would King Ta'Charlie say? Huh? Blood all over the royal floor?"

"You do not know Wakanda at all, outworlder. The penalty for attacking the line of Bashenga is death. You have been spared because we thought you possessed information that our king would deem useful. Your value does not extend beyond that."

Moving quicker than he would have imagined, Venomm ducked behind Taku and pushed the communications officer into W'Kabi. Caught between the choice of setting his aim or catching his friend, W'Kabi chose the latter. Venomm dropped to one knee and fired Taku's pistol until he had emptied the clip. With one eye closed, he managed to shoot between Taku's flailing limbs. Fifteen bullets. Three of them found their marks deep inside W'Kabi's flesh. The rest of the bullets ripped straight through tendons and lodged in the gray wall of the prison cell.

Taku fell on top of W'Kabi. For a moment, there was so much blood, so much confusion, it was impossible to tell who exactly had been injured by the gunfire. But Taku pulled himself to his knees, and W'Kabi moaned, sprawled with his arms stretched out beside him. Not one bullet had touched Taku. Venomm's latent military skills were still intact. Taku's brown tunic was covered in blood that was not his own. He stared at Venomm with more sadness in his eyes than anger.

Venomm waved his pistol in Taku's face.

"I told you not to get in my way," Venomm hissed. "There's at least four more bullets in this clip, but you and I both know it only takes one."

"Horatio, please, this decision will only hasten your own destruction," Taku said. He spoke calmly, as if none of this had ever happened, as if he and Venomm were still in the dark conversing like civilized men.

"I'm sorry, Taku, but he burned my snakes. Your valiant king had no mercy on them. My babies come before everything, even my own life. They're the only creatures that never judged me."

Venomm pressed the gun barrel to Taku's forehead. His arm trembled. Somewhere deep within the pale disfigured face, a lifetime of sadness and regret shaped the tormented countenance. Venomm raised the pistol and struck the side of Taku's head. Again and again, he swung the butt of the gun until he was sure that he had rendered Taku unconscious. Unconscious and banged up, but not dead. He owed Taku at least that.

Venomm left the communications officer and the security chief covered in blood and shadows and ran through the black hallways. Pistol held tightly, Wakandan blood dripping through his clenched fist.

LATER THAT evening, W'Kabi lay in a hospital bed. The dimmed light softened his features, reducing the grizzled soldier to the young man once filled with hope and an unwavering sense of justice. T'Challa and Monica stood by his bedside. She held T'Challa's waist tightly and pressed a cheek wet with pity and sadness against his chest.

On the other side of the bed, Taku stood with Mendinao. Taku held W'Kabi's hand and shook his head with the confusion and bitter hopelessness that often accompanied the tragedy of war. Mendinao stood at the head of the bed. The old physician's face impassive and stern, he studied the digital display that showed W'Kabi's vital signs: his heart rate, oxygen levels, and the electrical charges that raced throughout his nervous system and powered his brain.

"Has Chandra been notified?" T'Challa asked. He raised his head and stared at his communications officer.

"Yes, My King, she is on her way. She said she had to find someone to watch her children," Taku answered.

"I could have done that," Monica said, worried.

"She should have been here hours ago," Mendinao grumbled.

"So, this was going on while we were out at the lake?" Monica asked, her voice hoarse from sorrow.

"This is not our fault, Monica." T'Challa used his finger to lift her chin until her eyes met his own. "This is the work of N'Jadaka's minion." He turned his attention to Taku. "Venomm injured two of Wakanda's top military personnel and managed to escape the royal palace?" Anger and doubt crept at the edges of T'Challa's voice. He pondered the possibilities of the incident, what Venomm's escape revealed about the lapses in Wakandan security. "Could someone have assisted him?"

Taku and Venomm have cemented a formidable bond over the past months. One might even say they have developed a friendship. T'Challa shook the thought from his mind. Taku had proven his loyalty to Wakanda to the line of Bashenga time and time again. *At this point no one is beyond suspicion,* the Panther King thought regretfully.

"I do not know, My King. I admit that my pity for Horatio— for Venomm—compromised my objectivity, but I think I know where he is. If it would please Your Majesty, I would like to be the one who recaptures him."

"No, Taku, that will not be necessary. Nor is Venomm your responsibility now. You have injuries of your own that need attention."

"Speaking of injuries," Mendinao said. "I believe it is time for Ms. Lynne to put that voice of hers to use." He looked at her and smiled. "I trust your gift and believe that you can help heal W'Kabi. In fact, the song treatments that we have developed might be his only hope."

VENOMM STOOD in the burned ruins of N'Jadaka's village and covered his eyes as the sun rose, casting its stark cruel light over the charred remains of Killmonger's training ground. He walked through the scorched remains of stucco houses that had once glittered with so much beauty, until he stood before the snake pit where he had trained with his pets. His snakes. The only creatures who had ever truly understood him. The only creatures that he had ever called friends.

Ta'Charlie, hurt over one fake friend, Venomm thought. *I've lost a legion of real ones.*

"What about Killmonger? What about Taku?" he mumbled to himself. His lip trembled and the confusion of it all filled his eyes with bright, shiny tears.

"They call themselves civilized," Venomm growled, "but they betrayed me like all the rest. And Ta'Charlie had the nerve to call himself a hero."

Venomm stared into the pits, at the remains of the charred snakes that he had trained and fostered—even slept with—down in their hole. The sight was heartbreaking. Black bodies curled into long black ribbons. The open mouths stretched upward. The eyes burned from their sockets.

Venomm leapt down and sat in the middle of the pit. He pulled his hair by the roots and cried out to the morning sun burning away the night's mist.

"You're going to pay for this, Ta'Charlie. I promise. I'm going to watch your loved ones burn. Then we'll see how you like it." Spit flew from his mouth, and he raked his fingers against the flaky skin of his burned scalp.

As if on cue, at the sound of his grieving voice—as if the creatures had been hiding, waiting on their master to return—snakes began to crawl from dark holes set into the ground and the sides of the pit. Nests of snakes crawled from the darkness, slithering through the charred remains of ash and soot. The snakes called to him, hissed, wrapped themselves around Venomm's legs, slid up his arms, rubbed their cold scaly faces against his, as if to comfort him.

"My babies!" Venomm cried. He grabbed an armful of snakes and laughed as he rolled around in the ash and the dirt, streaks of tear-stained smoke across his relieved face.

T'CHALLA LANDED his Royal Talon Fighter miles away from the remains of Killmonger's village, near a spindly stream that stretched near the outposts of the Death Regiments training camp. The late afternoon sun shone, blazing behind an escarpment and a seesaw row of trees that spiked the distant horizon. T'Challa walked slowly along the riverbank. He was in no hurry to meet up with Venomm.

He watched the sun set behind the mountain and the light play along the water and lost himself in the tranquility. He walked along the beach until he noticed someone crouched in the sand, running their fingers through the water as it trickled along the riverbank. A few more yards, more lengthening shadow, and T'Challa saw that it was M'Jumbak's son, Kantu, sitting in the dirt.

Staring dreamily at the water, contemplating some unknown misfortune, the fatherless boy reminded T'Challa of himself.

"Kantu, why are you here alone by the river? Your mother is probably worrying herself sick. You should return home before it gets late." T'Challa stared at the darkening sky, the sunset mimicked the darkness that grew inside him. "These are not safe times for children to wander alone." T'Challa lowered his head. The statement reminded him of his failure as protector of Wakanda.

"My King," the boy said. He stood and faced T'Challa. Pain and confusion, a child's sense of utter loss and hopelessness, shaped the boy's eyes.

"This man that they call Killmonger. They say he is the reason that my father has disappeared. They say he wants to destroy Wakanda. He wants to kill you and take your throne." Kantu's voice trembled, and tears rolled down his round cheeks. "I wish I could kill him myself. I would make him pay for what he did to my father."

T'Challa thought of his own father. Indeed, he shared a great deal with this child. Memories of his youth and his little sister Shuri's innocent childhood, cut short by the machinations of war, bombarded the Panther King. Shuri was only a couple of years older than Kantu. One lived in a palace, the other on a farm, but they shared the same pain. He grabbed Kantu's shoulders and walked the boy toward his Talon Fighter, waiting on the darkening riverbank.

"Losing your father hurts," T'Challa said, bending to kneel before Kantu. "But that anger in your chest, your fists, has the power to destroy you. For far too long, I have allowed rage and the need for revenge to consume me. But that time must end. I've lost too much, and if I allow the rage to conquer me, I could lose everything, including my soul. Kantu, nothing is worth that.

"Killmonger will pay for his crimes, for what he did to your father, I promise. But vengeance is not your responsibility. Your king will shoulder that burden. It is your responsibility to take care of your home, your mother, and to grow to be the young man your father taught you to be."

T'Challa escorted a silent Kantu back to the farm where the boy lived, to beautiful Alkama Fields. The Panther King nodded graciously to the imploring streams of *thank yous* and *praise Basts* that Karota hurled about as she hugged her son and showered his face with kisses and tears. Watching Karota reminded T'Challa of what his mother must have felt when he left to face Klaw to avenge T'Chaka's death, or what Monica must have felt when he left her to journey into the Land of Chilling Mist.

After T'Challa watched Karota cry over her son and drag the embarrassed boy back into the fatherless house, he flew his Talon Fighter back to the stream near Killmonger's village. This time nothing deterred his return to the sacked village. The sun already set, had covered the golden savannah with a dark shield, most comforting to the Black Panther, most conducive to the hunt and combat he loved the most.

He walked through the dark and bore witness to the destruction left behind by his own men. When W'Kabi had burned the village, T'Challa did not protest. Now looking at the products of that destruction, the results of a rebellion that he had failed to quash, T'Challa could not help the overpowering feeling of sadness and inadequacy building inside him.

That's when he heard Venomm's heavy breathing, the accelerated heartbeat that marked the serpentine poise of the disfigured Death Regiment lackey. T'Challa crouched and stalked his way over to the hole that had once been a snake pit. Inside the man-made crater he found Venomm. Arms akimbo, balled fists resting against his hips, Venomm raised his head and smiled. A hideous grin of gray, deformed flesh and long, crooked teeth.

"Ta'Charlie, I figured you'd show up here sooner or later," Venomm said. "You're a smart enough fella, I reckon. You knew I'd come here to see about my babies. Heck, it took you so long I started to worry. Thought maybe something had happened to you." The twang in Venomm's voice teemed with derision and chained anger.

"I knew you would come here. So did Taku," T'Challa said. "It would have been better for you if you had run back to Killmonger, but it would not have mattered. I would have tracked you down regardless. Either way, you will answer for the blood that you spilled in my royal palace."

The Black Panther leapt down into the snake pit and stood face to disfigured face with Venomm. The stench inside the snake pit, the smell of burned flesh and waste, permeated T'Challa's nose.

"You got some nerve coming after me after what you did to my babies. Who's going to pay for their blood?"

T'Challa heard the snakes hiss and slither before they emerged from their hiding places in the loose dirt under his feet and the sides of the pit. A king cobra stuck its head out of the ground and wrapped itself around his ankles before he could escape. He grabbed the snake's head and choked its neck until the scaly body went limp around his black boots. Two more snakes shot through the dirt wall behind him and coiled around his arms. Another fell from the top of the pit and wrapped around his neck.

The snakes squeezed T'Challa and dropped him to one knee with their strength. *Enhanced in Resurrection Altar*, he thought.

The walls of the pit collapsed, and before the Panther King could react, a host of snakes fell on top of him. Squeezing him, they pressed their fangs against the metallic fabric with all their might. T'Challa tried to stand but collapsed under the weight of the slithering mass.

"Horatio!" Taku called. His voice boomed from the top of the snake pit. "You will call off your snakes and release my king. This is the only warning I will give you. You have already spilled blood in the royal palace of Wakanda. If you surrender, your children will be spared. If you murder our king, you and all your children will die. Including the pretty magenta-and-black rock python that we still hold back in the glassed ciborium underneath the Golden City. Jolene's a beauty: we might just keep her," Taku said, noting the discoloration in Venomm's already sun-averse face.

"You wouldn't dare, Taku. I thought we were friends. That's why I let you live when I shot Wasabi."

"Horatio, my heart has gone out to you over these past months but make no mistake: I am a servant of Wakanda, of the line of Bashenga, the great Panther God Bast. I will not allow you to murder the sacred avatar."

A host of masked soldiers surrounded the snake pit. They wore black, fireproof suits and were armed with flamethrowers aimed into the pit. Aimed at Venomm and at the cluster of snakes that were crushing T'Challa.

"I won't forget this!" Venomm raised his arms, and made a low-frequency, guttural sound, a signal that called all his snakes back to their master. The serpents released the Black Panther, and he fell to the ground. Taku leapt into the pit to join his king.

"Revolution is here, Taku," Venomm said, retreating. The snakes coiled themselves together, a giant braid, bearing Venomm upon their writhing backs. "And there's nothing that anyone can do. Especially you, Ta'Charlie. Erik Killmonger will be the new ruler of Wakanda. You might as well get your people out of here. Save as many as you can," said Venomm, riding the serpents like a dragon into the darkness.

CHAPTER SEVENTEEN

WAKANDA FALLS

MONTHS AFTER returning to Wakanda with the love of his life and finding his kingdom embroiled amid civil strife, T'Challa woke up to the sounds of war raging outside the royal palace. Killmonger's rebellion had finally arrived in the Golden City. Sirens blared. T'Challa's Kimoyo beads flashed around his wrist.

He tried to wake Monica. At first, he shook her shoulders gently, but that didn't work. She yawned in her sleep and turned over, pulling the black sheets over her shoulder.

"Leave me alone, T," Monica mumbled and smiled.

A rocket whistled outside the bedroom window, followed by an explosion that rocked the royal palace like an earthquake. Monica fell on the floor. T'Challa rushed to her side. Still half asleep, she looked confused. A second or two passed before recognition flashed across her eyes. The next moment, terror raised her eyebrows and opened her mouth into the shape of a small, dark *O*.

"Get dressed as quickly as you can," T'Challa said. "We must leave this place."

Palace guards shouted outside. He heard the Dora Milaje barking beyond the door.

Monica ran to a black chifforobe next to the bed and grabbed a pair of jeans and a gray tank top. She slipped on the clothes almost as quickly as T'Challa materialized his panther suit. The Panther King was impressed. The training with the Dora Milaje and Shuri had changed Monica from the woman who once needed a separate car for her suitcases. He wondered if she could see the difference.

She threw on a pair of black sneakers and ran toward the window. Automatic gunfire rattled outside. Across the Golden City, a dinosaur stepped between a pair of gold and glass-plated skyscrapers.

"T'Challa, what's happening?" Tears filled her eyes, slid down her cheeks. "Did I just see a freaking dinosaur?" Terror blazed across her face. "What the—?"

Instead of answering her questions, he raised his Kimoyo beads to his mouth. Any other time he would have called W'Kabi, but the Shield of the Nation still lay in a hospital bed, suffering from gunshot wounds in his chest and stomach that brought him to the threshold of Death's Domain.

"Come in, Taku. Are you there?" T'Challa said, half expecting the static scramble of radio silence.

"I'm here, Your Majesty. Are you and Ms. Lynne alright?" Taku spoke slowly. His tone was measured and calm. In the background, a cacophony of yelling and gunfire contrasted his composure.

T'Challa was surprised in a good way. He hoped that Taku would prove to be a good substitute for the chief of security.

"I need a group of Taifa Ngao to escort Monica to the research hospital." More than a cutting-edge research facility, the structure also served as a shelter.

T'Challa stared at Monica. One part of his mind said, *I should have never brought you here.* Another part admitted the truth. *But I need you. I can hardly stand being away from you for a full day, much less indefinitely. Honestly, all this time, what would I have done without you?*

290

"All the Shields have been deployed, sir."

"And the Dora Milaje?"

"I am heading toward you now, Your Majesty." Adebisi's throaty voice buzzed into the Kimoyo transmission.

"Who else is guarding the palace?"

"All the Shields and most of the Dora Milaje are outside, doing their best to keep the Death Regiments out of the royal palace."

"You need someone to watch Monica?" Shuri chimed in through the Kimoyo.

"Shuri," T'Challa said more forcefully than he had intended. He had no idea how she managed to tap into the secure line. She was a constant wonder with her ingenuity. "Stay in your room. Someone is coming to escort you to the research hospital as soon as possible."

"I'm not in my room, brother," Shuri said. There was a knock at the door. "Surprise!" she said. "I'm going with you."

"No, dear princess. I know you have been training, but this is neither the time nor your battle, young warrior-in-training. I need you safe, far away from what comes next, but please protect Ms. Lynne," he said, winking at Monica before the young princess could protest.

Monica's eyes were worried, but she put on a brave face.

"I would love that, thank you," she said.

Okoye and Nakia bowed their heads as they entered the room. Adebisi and two more of the Adored Ones stood, waiting.

"May Nakia and I help guard Ms. Monica, Your Majesty?" Okoye asked. Nakia looked frightened, but she stood with her back straight, her eyes darting from the Panther King to Monica.

"Of course," T'Challa said and signaled Adebisi to go. He held Monica one last time, kissing Shuri atop her forehead.

"You're doing the most, T'Challa!" Shuri cried but squeezed her brother's hand.

He kissed Monica for a long time. It felt like forever, but finally he pulled away, allowing her to leave with Shuri and the others. As another explosion shook the palace walls, Shuri, the Dora Milaje, and Monica all headed to the medical facility to wait in the bomb shelters underneath the hospital with Mendinao and Dr. Mganga until the encroaching threat had been vanquished. T'Challa would return for them himself.

Monica's tears were a reminder of the night she had been framed for Zatama's murder. She had endured so much suffering since she had arrived in Wakanda. It had not been his plan, that night she sang at Minton's. T'Challa promised himself that he would make everything up to her as soon as all of this was over, as soon as he defeated N'Jadaka for good.

T'Challa ran to the roof of the royal palace and saw giant, prehistoric monsters—brachiosauruses and tyrannosaurus rexes—stomping through the Golden City, smashing buildings, destroying the work paid for with his father's blood. He looked at the streets below and saw hundreds of soldiers marked with the neon skulls of the Death Regiments running through the streets. Screaming. Setting the city to flame. Shooting innocent citizens. Screaming the name of T'Challa's nemesis, Erik Killmonger.

Kill, Kill, Killmonger!

So many more than T'Challa had known, he pondered the reserve's origins and cursed himself for underestimating N'Jadaka's resources, again.

Frozen in disbelief, what the Panther King saw defied all logic. He saw his beloved city crumbling before his eyes. He remembered N'Jadaka smiling, laughing, toasting to the good Panther King's health back in Harlem. The memories stirred an anger in him that he could no longer control. He had to finish this war today. Nothing else mattered.

"You will pay with your blood today, N'Jadaka." T'Challa raised his black claws to the morning sun and the destruction boiling all around. "I promise. You will not leave Wakanda alive."

A blue-black brachiosaurus stumbled into the Black Panther's line of sight. It was a magnificent creature, beautiful in all its terror. A huge foot, raised high, came pounding down from the sky, bashing the royal palace's roof into rubble, forcing T'Challa to dive from the roof to save his life.

He heard the brachiosaurus roar, unconscious wrath directed at no one in particular. He remembered that these beasts were not acting under their own volition. They were captives, forced from their home in Serpent Valley to be battering rams in someone else's war.

A hailstorm of gunfire rattled from above, bullets trailing the Black Panther, shattering the golden glass that encased the royal palace.

"*Kill, Kill, Killmonger!* Wakanda's rightful ruler!" someone yelled.

A giant gray tail swung through the air, sliced the wind beneath T'Challa. He used the great limb as a springboard, reversing his trajectory and sending him back into the sky, propelling him toward the Death Regiment soldier firing his rifle from an open carriage on the dinosaur's back—another brachiosaurus—screaming at the top of his lungs like the madman that he was.

T'Challa jumped into the carriage atop the beast and kicked the assault rifle out of the man's hand. The man's face was painted neon to look like a skull. The fronts of hollowed-out skulls cupped around his shoulders. He wore a belt and a necklace that hung to his navel, both decorated with bones. The man pulled a knife and screamed Killmonger's name again. The black blade glowed with a shifting purple light that pulsed in time with the man's screaming.

Vibranium, T'Challa thought. Anger burned his eyes and rang inside his head as the carriage shifted with the movements of the lumbering dinosaur. The skull-faced man, off-balance, stumbled toward T'Challa and swung the knife. T'Challa shook his head as he ducked the swinging blade. In one motion, he grabbed the belt decorated with human bones and tossed the man from the carriage.

Another Death Regiment soldier cowered in the corner of the carriage. His painted face fearful and trembling, his arm shaking, he pointed a handgun at T'Challa. The Panther King crouched and bore his claws. He felt the feral panther side that guided his spirit rise inside him. The Heart-Shaped Herb surged inside his veins and charged him with unfathomed, inexhaustible power. With the points of his panther claws thirsting for blood, he leaped toward the man. Instead of firing the handgun, the lackey dropped the pistol and leapt from the carriage.

T'Challa watched the screaming man plummet to the ground. His broken limbs arranged in impossible positions. His neck twisted. His face half-smashed against a gleaming street paved with gold and multicolored lights.

There were screaming voices all around. Crashing metal and stone. Prehistoric monsters roared and yowled. Gunfire. Missile fire. The Golden City collapsing to the ground. T'Challa heard Monica screaming. When he looked up, he found the brachiosaurus that he rode was stumbling toward the research hospital.

T'Challa was furious.

Monica and Shuri stood in front of the building, surrounded by crowds of confusion and upheaval. She kneeled in the midst of chaos, cradling an unresponsive Mendinao.

They hadn't made it inside.

The sight of the old physician lying in Monica's desperate embrace took T'Challa all the way back to the beginning of the rebellion. He saw himself cradling G'Sere as the griot died in his arms. There was too much loss.

"Return home, old one. Tell your brethren we are not your enemies," T'Challa whispered to the creature. Cutting the ropes, he somersaulted from the carriage as it crashed to the ground, then he slid down the side of the brachiosaurus, vaulting himself into the air with cat-like grace. He landed beside Monica just in time to move her and Mendinao from the path of the stumbling dinosaur.

"Shuri, are you alright?" T'Challa shouted, directing the princess. "What happened to Adebisi and the others?" Fire was in his voice.

"Something worse came up," she said, horrified.

A bloodcurdling roar filled the air. *The T-rex!* T'Challa thought.

He grabbed her face with both hands and, for a moment, the chaos of war disappeared from her eyes.

"Shuri, I will not fail you," T'Challa said as Adebisi made her way back to the princess's side.

"Your Majesty," she said, shaking her head at the Panther King. "I know. Take them, now."

"I'm fine," Monica said. Dirt and soot covered her face. Her shirt torn to rags. A long cut bled along the length of her bicep.

"No, you're hurt." T'Challa reached for the cut but she avoided his touch. "Inside they will help you."

"I'm good, T'Challa. It's just a scratch. I appreciate the effort." Somehow a smile etched itself across Monica's face. "You've been saving me since we met, but Mendinao's hurt. We'll get him to a safe place."

There is no safe place, T'Challa thought. *No place in the world...* He looked around, incredulous, surrounded by dinosaurs destroying the city he had worked most of his life to build and protect. His father's legacy, the foundation of his own.

Someone grabbed T'Challa's shoulder. With reflexes quicker than his conscious mind, he turned and raised his claws, ready to draw blood. He found Taku by his side.

"My King," Taku said. T'Challa stared at his communications specialist and friend; in that moment, the violence and determination in his eyes made him look a lot like W'Kabi. "We are concentrating our forces in two key areas—the royal palace and the research hospital. These seem to be the two focal points of Killmonger's attack."

Seem to be? T'Challa started to ask but restrained himself. Instead, he squeezed Taku's shoulder in confidence and admiration and thanked him for his service. The communications officer was already faced with the difficult task of filling W'Kabi's combat boots. T'Challa had to admit: Taku was not doing a bad job.

"I want you to help get Monica and Mendinao to safety," T'Challa said. "See that Mendinao gets medical attention from Dr. Mganga right away."

"Yes, Your Majesty," Taku said. "One more thing..."

T'Challa raised an eyebrow, the inquisitive facial expression shaping the eyes of his black mask. Above the horizon, he spied a fleet of Talon Fighters blacking out the sky. The aircraft formation was a deadly bird of prey that swooped through the city, streaking across the skyline. Below them, the sound of thunderous trumpeting as a herd of giant mech elephants ran at full charge, their golden tusks glistening in the sun.

"The Force Majeure—the citizens' militia—have mobilized themselves throughout the city," Taku said. A hopeful smile stretched crooked across his face. "The people are leaving their homes and taking up arms against Killmonger's forces. Wakanda will not fall."

NEAR THE outskirts of the city, a small boy armed with nothing more than a dagger and a heart filled with the spirit of revenge, ran through a battalion of marching dinosaurs and armed rebels. The boy ran as fast as he could. He did not wipe the tears from his eyes. The memories of his father drove him, triggered the adrenaline rushing through his slim body. The boy carried the final memories of his home and his mother, who was hard and cross, but she loved hard. The dinosaurs had marched through his village and destroyed his home. His mother had been reduced to madness and incessant screaming. The boy's name was Kantu. Running toward the Golden City, he had one name on his mind.

Erik Killmonger.

T'CHALLA STOOD watching as a horde of N'Jadaka's Death Regiment soldiers charged toward him. He laughed to himself and ran to meet the charge. His black claws, thirsty for more blood, extended another inch from his fingertips. A hundred soldiers would not be enough to stop the Black Panther. A thousand soldiers would not be enough. He sliced his way through the Death Regiments with ease. The more he fought, the stronger he felt. The rage that had been pent up inside of him for the past year, for the past ten years since his father's assassination, was rising and burning more than ever.

T'Challa, the Orphan King, did not try to suppress the burning wrath. He did not ask for forgiveness. He realized this is what he had wanted all along. An excuse to destroy. An excuse to spill blood and sink his claws into pliant flesh.

Fighting his way through the hordes of the Death Regiments, the Panther King found Tayete and Kazibe. Fleeing a pair of stampeding mech elephants that flung Death Regiment soldiers left and right, the two fools had been cornered by a swarm of the Force Majeure, as fierce as anything imagined by the Spirit of the Jungle. The host of Wakandan civilians were armed with shovels and hammers, kitchen knives and flagpoles. Tayete and Kazibe received the brunt of these homemade weapons, as well as an ample share of punches and kicks. One old man even gnawed at Tayete's calf muscle, an indignity that earned him a swift kick in the chin. The pair saw T'Challa brawling his way toward them. Full of fear, their hearts sank into their bellies.

"Oh no, Kazibe, the panther demon is coming this way. Of all the misfortunes imaginable!" Tayete covered his face as an old woman smacked the back of his head with a black skillet.

"What are you telling me for?" Kazibe cried, panic across his face. "You're the one who keeps calling him *panther demon...*" he whispered, looking around anxiously. "What if he hears you with his great panther ears?" Kazibe backed away and bumped into something.

"*Aiyeee!*" a young woman cried, swinging a belt covered in cowrie shells. "No Death Regiments here!" she shouted and lassoed it around his neck. Kazibe flapped his arms, trying to fight off the woman. He was certain that the belt had once been a musical instrument.

These were peaceful people. Killmonger had forced them to take up arms wherever they stood, wherever they may find them.

T'Challa stopped to observe the beatdown. Huffing and puffing, Tayete and Kazibe had fallen a long way since that bright morning he'd found them torturing G'Sere. He smiled at the absurdity of the punishment being meted to the pair of treacherous fools. If they were lucky and Bast had forgiven them, perhaps they would live long enough to learn from their disastrous choices.

Perhaps I will, too, T'Challa thought.

The Black Panther joined his people, swinging his elbow into the painted face of a Death Regiment officer twirling a spear charged with an electric blade. Another stolen Wakandan-issued weapon. He had to give it to N'Jadaka for waging a war with your enemies' own weapons.

"Ukatana," a voice called from above. It bellowed over the writhing crowd, drowning out the din of war and chaos.

T'Challa looked up and saw N'Jadaka. The exile who called himself Killmonger stood on top of a giant statue dedicated to Bast, set atop the royal palace.

"I see you are still alive! That makes me happy. Now I get the chance to kill you myself."

The exile faced the Panther King, two orphans fighting for wildly different visions.

T'Challa growled and flexed his hands, claws extended. He imagined himself wrapping his hands around Killmonger's throat, pressing his claws into Killmonger's flesh and watching the blood flow, red and incessant.

"But this is no place for our final battle. Fighting amongst all this disorder. Come to Warrior Falls. There we will fight as men to the death. Until I rip your head off your shoulders with my bare hands." Killmonger reared his head and laughed heartily.

INSIDE WAKANDA'S new research hospital, W'Kabi lay in his bed, barely conscious. His two boys stood by his side, their eyes filled with fearful tears. Chandra stood by the window, watching the city being destroyed around them. W'Kabi wanted to go to her, hold her in his arms, but all he could do was raise his head from the pillow.

He studied the hospital room with suspicion—the pristine yellow walls, the tubes running in and out of his arms, the humming machines buzzing around, the lights and gauges pulsing—lit brilliant with the security chief's lifeforce. He did not trust the machines monitoring his vital signs. He did not trust hospitals. For W'Kabi, hospitals were places where weak men went to die. Strong men died in battle. The idea of the civil war raging outside of his hospital room without him hurt even more than the bullet wounds ripping through his chest and stomach.

"The king was here earlier, you know, before you got here." W'Kabi knew that the sarcasm in his voice did not help matters but he could not help himself. "He had his outworlder woman with him. He tried to speak to me of love." W'Kabi's speech broke into a coughing fit.

"You probably should have listened, W'Kabi," Chandra said. "You probably could have learned something."

"Learned something? What does he know about my pain?" W'Kabi asked bitterly. "He has a woman who loves him, who can barely go one minute without being in his presence."

Chandra winced. The state of their union had never been so starkly stated. A study in contradiction.

"From what I've heard, the feeling is mutual." Chandra stood beside the bed. Lying in it, her brave and once-beloved husband seemed frail and small. "From what I heard, the king nearly sacrificed his entire kingdom for the love of his woman."

A series of explosions shook the hospital room. Cement from the ceiling fell all around. W'Kabi gritted his teeth; using all his strength, he managed to sit upright in his bed. Chandra went to the window. Whatever she saw made her scream and tumble backwards.

The thought of his family in danger filled the Taifa Ngao with a strange power, renewed strength that replaced his pain and dread. *This must be what the Heart-Shaped Herb feels like,* he thought. With the sudden surge of adrenaline filling his veins, W'Kabi dove from the bed and grabbed his wife, just as the head of a huge brachiosaurus crashed through the wall. The floor beneath their feet buckled. W'Kabi knew that the building was crumbling before their eyes and would soon collapse. He grabbed his wailing children and screamed for his wife to join him quickly.

"Follow me now, Chandra!" W'Kabi yelled, yanking the IV from his arm. "No time for anything. Let's go."

Just as W'Kabi made it out of the room with his wife and children, a huge claw broke through the wall and smashed the bed where W'Kabi had lain half unconscious, half medicated out of his mind. W'Kabi thanked Bast for placing him on the first floor of the research hospital. They did not have far to go. Soldiers and doctors, nurses and patients stricken with all kinds of infirmities ran to and fro. They all made their way toward the exit, a giant wave of deathly frightened people.

W'Kabi limped along, his family huddled around him, through the intensive care and ER units. Through the sections of the research hospital designated for families and patients awaiting admittance. When the glass doors of the hospital's exit came into view, W'Kabi felt relief brighten his spirit. Then another roar—louder than any he had heard in his life before—bellowed through the hospital entrance. A huge gray foot blocked the door. The building shook; pieces of cement, broken tile, and torn wires crashed all around him.

W'Kabi took a deep breath, summoned his strength, and ran for the exit doors. He managed to get his family to an open space surrounded by ambulances and covered by a stone canopy. Chandra shrieked, and W'Kabi looked up. Guided by the direction of her horrified gaze, he saw an avalanche of broken rock falling from the canopy overhead. Instinctively, before W'Kabi fully realized what was happening, he shoved Chandra and his two children out of harm's way, allowing himself to take the brunt of the collapsing stone.

Buried up to his shoulders in a pile of broken rock and debris, W'Kabi moaned. The world around him was obscured in a haze of destruction, mounds of rubble, gunfire, and screaming voices. Over the din, he heard Chandra crying and felt his wife press her wet cheek against his forehead. It had been so long since he felt her touch. So long since she seemed to feel anything but frustration and resentment. Even with his extensive injuries, with the world slipping in and out of consciousness, W'Kabi felt his heart flutter.

300   *Hope.*

W'Kabi reached for Chandra, his battered, stoic soldier's heart racing with the excitement of a schoolboy's first kiss. He turned his head to his wife and smiled. He was grateful to Bast that he had lived long enough to see her smile back. W'Kabi wrapped his free arm around her shoulders and held her with all his fading strength.

"Chandra," he groaned weakly. "I speak to you now as your husband, not as Wakanda's Shield. Are you alright, dear one? Where are our children?"

"I am well, W'Kabi. The children are fine. Rest your eyes and listen. We are all right here."

W'Kabi heard his sons crying. He wanted to take his family in his arms and comfort them, but he could not move beneath the large pile of stones that buried him.

"Chandra..." He clutched the back of his wife's blouse. "All this time, you were right. I've been so busy protecting my king, protecting my country, I forgot about what was most important. You. Our children. You are my Wakanda. I would gladly give my life for you. It would be currency well spent."

"Oh, my dabbar dutse," Chandra cried.

He laughed, a pained sound. "Heh, mountain beast? You haven't called me that in a long while, dear."

She smiled despite her fears. "I haven't forgotten how you earned that name." She covered his laughter with gentle kisses. It had been too long since they laughed together.

A tear rolled from W'Kabi's eye. Such grace to find this hope again when the entire world was cast into darkness.

KILLMONGER'S DINOSAUR-MOUNTED forces had destroyed Wakanda's research hospital, reduced the state-of-the-art medical facility to a mound of rubble, a glorified quarry. Meanwhile, more dinosaurs and Death Regiment fighters had stormed the royal palace and razed most of T'Challa's gilded home to the ground.

In the confusion of the pulverized palace, all the prisoners in the underground holding cells escaped. Malice, Baron Macabre,

Lord Karnaj, Salamander K'Ruel—all the Death Regiment officers captured in N'Jadaka Village. The escapees ran in every direction, slithering away like Venomm's pet snakes. Except these minions fled without form or logic to their flight.

Broken stones from the wrecked palace, crushed statues, and monuments dedicated to the Panther God rained all around. A pile of rubble buried Salamander; he lay screaming for help as Malice and Lord Karnaj hurried past him. Neither stopped to lend their fallen comrade a helping hand.

With rage, a king's wrath taking control, T'Challa went after the Death Regiment officers. He punched through Baron Macabre's mouth, sending decayed gray teeth flying. He slammed Lord Karnaj on his back so hard that the Black Panther heard bones break. T'Challa watched Karnaj convulse on the ground, foaming at the mouth. Malice stared into T'Challa's eyes for hardly a sliver of a second. Recognizing the unbridled fury standing before her, she did what any mortal would have done in the face of a primal force of nature. She ran. She ran as fast as she could, and she didn't look back. If they were smart—and fast—they would all run.

T'Challa heard someone shriek. To his surprise, he saw Monica leaping from behind a pile of broken rock and warped metal. She had picked up an energy spear abandoned by a felled combatant. The black vibranium glowed and surged with sonic energy, drawn from Monica's voice.

Malice raised her arm quickly, but the move was far too slow, insufficient. The charged blade pierced Malice's right shoulder. The stored sonic energy exploded. The blast blew both women in opposite directions.

T'Challa was surprised. *She was always talking about blowing up back in Harlem,* he thought. He hoped for the chance to tease Monica if they survived the day; if he survived his appointment with N'Jadaka at Warrior Falls.

Taku ran from the smoke and the chaos and kneeled beside Monica. Malice lay stunned, unmoving. He helped Monica stand

and brush the dirt from her clothes and hair. Then someone called his name from behind. It was a shrill, fragmented voice. Derisive.

"Taku," King Cadaver called. He smiled as he walked toward the communications chief. Cadaver's voice echoed through Taku's head.

Killmonger's file claims you are an expert in various mediums of communication and psychology. Have you ever communicated in this manner, Taku? Have you ever had someone dig through your mind? How do you like it?

Taku grabbed the sides of his head and fell to his knees. A single string of blood ran from his nose and dripped around the corner of his mouth. He screamed as if he were dying, as if his brains were frying inside of his skull.

Growling, gritting her teeth, Monica balled her fists and made toward King Cadaver. She had grown tired of war, tired of watching the people that she cared for being attacked and assaulted. Before she could take a second step, a snake sprang up from behind and wrapped itself around King Cadaver's throat. King Cadaver reached for the snake, but the end of a bullwhip wrapped around his wrist.

Venomm appeared at Taku's side. Two of his pet snakes leapt from his shoulders and sank their fangs into Cadaver's green, fungus-covered face. This time it was Cadaver who dropped to his knees. More snakes crawled from the smoke and the piles of broken stones. They coiled around Cadaver, biting him all over his body. He fell to his knees, then to the ground in a slithering green mass of coiling scales, flailing limbs, and desperate screaming.

"I'm sorry, Caviar, but I ain't sorry. Taku is my friend, and good friends are hard to come by."

T'Challa left King Cadaver breaking under the weight of the snakes, convulsing with snake venom speeding through his veins. The Panther King could not look at Monica. He could not turn around, even when she called his name. All he could do was hope that Taku and Adebisi would have the sense and the strength to restrain her and keep her from following. With the image of his woman soaring through the air, screaming for blood and vengeance like one of his Dora Milaje, screaming like a warrior born, T'Challa walked faster. Then he jogged. Before long he broke into a full sprint.

There can be no delay. You are my destiny, N'Jadaka. I see that now.

T'Challa ran until he arrived at the foot of Warrior Falls. He climbed up the steep drop with as much agility, as much dexterity as always. Since his childhood, Warrior Falls had always been a special place. His father had first taught him about mastering his emotions here. Particularly the emotion of rage, which T'Challa felt growing and pulsing throughout his entire body, as sure and tangible as the blood that coursed through his veins.

T'Challa had gone through the sacred rights of coronation here. He had suffered his first defeat at the hands of his most formidable adversary here. How fitting it would be for everything to end here. He promised himself, if his life ended today on top of Warrior Falls, he would do his best to take N'Jadaka with him to Death's Domain.

Isn't that what friends are for? he asked himself with bitter irony.

The rocks beneath his hands were slick with the spray of the waterfall, round and polished from years of erosion. Sweet blossoms in the air, the great thunderous rushing of the waterfall drowning out all other noise around him. The great hissing of flowing water emboldened the Panther King and reminded him of his Panther God watching over him, guiding the sacred avatar, strengthening him. He realized that he was more than prepared to meet his powerful adversary. The Black Panther realized that he had prepared for this moment his entire life.

AT THE top of Warrior Falls, he found N'Jadaka standing beside the rushing river, looking down at the Golden City the Wakandan exile had just destroyed. His chin held high and strong, N'Jadaka looked over the land below as if he already ruled it, as if he had already defeated the Black Panther and become Wakanda's newest ruler.

The sight brought out every last bit of rage that the Panther had been holding inside. He could not contain the wrath burning in his heart. Before the Panther King could stop himself, he was leaping through the air, lunging toward his greatest foe, his black claws extended and thirsting desperately for N'Jadaka's blood.

"T'Challa! Coming in hot!" N'Jadaka said. "It's nearly sundown. But no worries, I will not make you wait to die. I know you miss your father, poor ukatana. Trust me, I understand your pain. But don't worry—you'll join him very soon. You will greet your father long before I greet mine!"

Looking out over the waterfall, the emerald expanse and the golden wreckage sprawling below, Killmonger had spoken with an air of confidence and assured victory. For a moment, T'Challa thought the arrogance had the better of N'Jadaka, but just before T'Challa could sink his anti-metal claws into the back of N'Jadaka's head, Erik Killmonger turned with lightning speed, slashing with the spiked whip that surged and cracked the air with thousands of deadly volts.

T'Challa twisted his body enough to avoid the deadly blow. Instead, he landed a blow of his own, planting his fist squarely on Killmonger's jaw. The blow forced N'Jadaka to stumble backwards, sending a mouthful of blood into the cool Wakandan wind that blew with intense force at the elevated heights of Warrior Falls.

"You dare speak of my father," T'Challa growled as he threw another punch, one that slid past N'Jadaka's face as the Wakandan exile spun just beyond his reach.

N'Jadaka swung the spiked whip again. This time, the charged spikes caught T'Challa along his rib cage, sending a shock through his midsection.

"Your father was weak—just like you, ukatana. He hid in the comfort of his kingdom while the world superpowers conquered and plundered the lands surrounding your precious Wakanda. Even your mother knew he was weak. That's why she left."

"You are unworthy to speak my mother's name," T'Challa said as he blurred across the wet rocks to slash Killmonger's chest.

The man stumbled back, that arrogant smile still on his face.

"Oh, you're sensitive now. Poor kitten. Don't get mad, blame your dad. He's the one who allowed Ulysses Klaw to enter these lands. Just like you brought me. Because of your spineless father, my parents were burned alive. They died horribly. They didn't deserve that, but T'Chaka did. And *so... do... you!*"

Killmonger roared like the beasts that he had conquered and brought under his control. He released a series of vicious attacks that pushed T'Challa back until the Panther King's heels teetered on the edge of the cliffside.

Instead of pressing forward to regain his balance, T'Challa fell backwards off the cliffside. Just as he did at Resurrection Altar, he caught hold of a jutting rock and used the protrusion to pivot and swing himself back up to the cliffside. Killmonger was waiting, but it did not matter. This time, flying through the mist, T'Challa caught the crackling whip inside his clenched fist as he crashed into him. He tackled N'Jadaka where the pounding waters were swallowed by granite rock, pummeling the exile with haymakers, blow after blow. T'Challa punched him repeatedly, one for every Wakandan brick torn down, one for every Wakandan home burned and pillaged, until N'Jadaka's face was a red river running on its own.

"All those people you murdered, beginning with Griot G'Sere. All those villages your minions burned. The animals you captured and sacrificed for your god. Where is she now? The lives of the confused, the misled souls who sacrificed themselves for your cause. For the grass you trod upon, your every step is a violation. All of them will be avenged today," T'Challa said, his rage replaced with resignation and clarity.

Anger had consumed him in waves and fits, the stages of grief and powerlessness urging him forward, battle after battle. Now, facing the object of his ire, T'Challa realized that rage was a dangerous elixir that could consume one's whole self. He did not wish to become a prisoner to the past, to the trauma that so clearly ruled his former friend. The Panther King watched the fallen man who had once been an innocent casualty of another war with a mixture of genuine pity and disappointment.

Killmonger raised his head, weak, and wobbled like an old drunk. He spat more blood and teeth, stared at his red-stained hands and the Panther King through one swollen eye. But instead of Erik Killmonger, the Black Panther saw N'Jadaka again.

A TINY hand emerges from the darkness. The boy climbs out of the pit, barefoot, soil-stained clothes ragged. He cups his hand, shields his eyes from the sun. In the light, the red dust on his hands and feet make it appear as if he is bleeding. The boy no longer fears death. He has seen the old specter, its appetite fiery and deep. The boy's parents were fed into death's fire, the red lolling tongue, just as the boy was fed to the fiery temple of the strange man the others called Klaw.

The boy has spent hours working inside the pit. The boy has worked so long in the mines, night is where he wakes, and daylight is where he sleeps. He no longer dreams of a rescue. The people of Wakanda have forgotten him. Deep in the mines, there is no sound, only thoughts. The boy has become very good at feigning silence. Inside, his thoughts are loud, violent, blood-red howling things. Now above ground, daylight breaks his skin into patches of want. He proudly holds up the fruit of his labor: a silvery-purple chunk of vibranium, the iridescent mineral shimmering in the afternoon light.

Children like the boy were not seen at school. The boy and the other children-who-are-no-longer children are largely unnoticed in a nation that prided itself on its lush tropical forests, and hills, and mounds of the extraterrestrial mineral. One day the boy will learn to master the mineral. One day the boy will escape, and when he returns, he will seek his revenge.

"IF THIS is how it must end," Killmonger's face was swollen, his words distorted but the meaning clear, "then let it be so, ukatana. Kill me now. My name will be remembered throughout Wakanda. Let the people know that I tried my best to liberate them from a lineage of tyranny, from traditions that no longer serve the people they claim to revere."

With a heavy sense of duty, T'Challa wrapped his hands around Killmonger's throat and squeezed until the words no longer spilled out. The Black Panther poured the rage that had nearly consumed his heart into his hands. He listened to N'Jadaka choke and gurgle. The blood, a waterfall in its own right, ran down the exile's chin.

"N'Jadaka, Erik Killmonger, whoever you once were," T'Challa said. "Make your peace with Bast. Here, at Warrior Falls, you and your rebellion die today."

Instead of dying, Killmonger smiled at T'Challa. A secret gleamed in his eyes. Eyes that gleamed with as much anger and cruelty as they had ever possessed. Killmonger grabbed T'Challa's arms and pulled the Black Panther's hands from his neck, even as the anti-metal claws broke N'Jadaka's skin and drew more blood. Squeezing T'Challa's wrists, N'Jadaka stood, all six-foot-six of him, overpowering the Panther King in a display of unadulterated, unapologetic strength.

N'Jadaka held T'Challa's wrists and headbutted the Panther King. Rivulets of blood trickled down Killmonger's face. Blow after blow, the exile bashed his head against T'Challa's until the Black Panther's legs went limp, until blood ran down the Black Panther's forehead, pooling inside his mask, rendering him blind and powerless.

N'Jadaka grabbed T'Challa's throat and one of his legs, hoisting the Panther King into the air above his head. T'Challa's body hung limp: with the sky turning twilight pink, streaks of gold and orange above his head, the blood running across his face, the crashing waterfall filling his ears, he thought of his father. Of his mentor G'Sere, M'Jumbak, his country, all the people and the animals that died. He thought not of failure, but of his commitment as king. Of his little sister Shuri, who relied on him, who he could not let down again, and he thought of Monica. Her face. Her song. Remembered the taste of her lips, the warmth of her skin.

Find harmony in chaos, he heard in the wind. The words of G'Sere.

"I'm gonna break your back on my knee, ukatana."

A high voice came screaming from the rocks behind Killmonger. For a moment, T'Challa imagined it was Monica, that his love had followed him, and was now trying to save his life as he had once saved hers.

"No," T'Challa whispered and shook his head. But then he recognized the voice and his mind filled with alarm. It was not Monica. The voice belonged to the child Kantu. T'Challa heard the same rage he had seen in the boy days before when they spoke by the river near N'Jadaka's village.

The boy landed on Killmonger's back and stabbed the leader of the Death Regiments with the black vibranium dagger. Killmonger spun around swinging, but Kantu held on.

Killmonger yelled, more from irritation than pain. The boy was an annoying tsetse fly, buzzing in his ear. He flung T'Challa's limp body to the side, grabbed Kantu's throat and lifted the boy into the air with one hand. He drew back his fist, ready to end a grieving child's life with one cruel blow.

"I know you," Killmonger said and laughed. "I have seen you. My Death Regiments turned your father into a zombie. Then we killed him when he outlived his usefulness. Your vengeance is well earned, but unfortunately for you, it looks like I will be killing a pair of orphans today. Two for one at the bargain counter," Killmonger said.

"Spare him!"

Struggling, T'Challa strained to pull himself to his feet. He could hear the crash of the waterfall, the clash of weapons fighting below, the creak of buildings collapsing in on themselves. Dinosaurs screaming in anger and pain, the cries of his people fighting for Wakanda. His ears were filled with the din of war but then, in the clamor, T'Challa could hear harmony in the chaos—

Monica weaving a healing song.

Concentrating on the sound of her healing voice, T'Challa felt the power of the Heart-Shaped Herb growing, reaching through his veins.

"You talk way too much, N'Jadaka. You always did." T'Challa caught Killmonger's arm and turned the exile around, forcing him to release the boy.

Killmonger dropped Kantu, swinging his elbow to bash the side of the Black Panther's head. This time T'Challa relied on speed, an advantage N'Jadaka could not match. He ducked the flying elbow and grabbed Killmonger by his throat, digging into the giving flesh.

Anti-metal claws extended. With one swipe, the Black Panther shredded N'Jadaka's throat. With a look of mortal shock, N'Jadaka staggered near the waterfall's cascading edge, his hands rushing to stave off the mortal wound.

"Nothing to say," T'Challa said. "That's a first."

Then the Black Panther heard footsteps, running hard and fast. He turned, surprised, to see little Kantu shove N'Jadaka, pushing the exile over the cliff into the waterfall. Shocked, Killmonger and the Black Panther locked eyes, both staring in disbelief, before N'Jadaka fell, no words escaping his mouth, only silence, as he plummeted through the air, down into the crashing white rapids, five hundred feet to his death.

Neither T'Challa nor little Kantu spoke. Still stunned by the boy's actions, the Black Panther knew that they would never forget the look on their enemy's face.

Finally, Kantu rushed to T'Challa's side and wept. The Panther King hugged the boy with a sense of regret. The child was too young to bear such burdens, but he would carry this pain for the rest of his life. For a long while they stood still, the sound of the powerful falls thundering behind them.

No one spoke, neither boy nor man. Each desperate soul went to rebuild their shattered worlds anew, fatherless boy and fatherless king.

Just before they descended Warrior Falls, T'Challa pressed his Kimoyo beads. "Killmonger is dead."

One by one, the shouts rang up from the valley and drifted into the Wakandan sky.

EPILOGUE

PRAY FOR MADAME SLAY

WRECKAGE LAY all around as far as T'Challa could see. An entire city razed to the ground. Decades of work overseen by his father. A culture that stretched back two thousand years. T'Challa surveyed the destruction with a mix of emotions fighting in his belly. A conflict just as intense as his personal battle with Killmonger only days before. Entire buildings demolished. Whole neighborhoods and patches of masonry and roadway torn from the earth. The carcasses of huge prehistoric beasts, as dead as their lost prehistoric brethren, littered the streets. The streets filled with the dead and the injured. Death Regiments, the Shield of Wakanda, the Force Majeure. All Wakandan, all tragic casualties in a civil war that should never have been.

T'Challa crouched on a stone panther head that had broken off a statue mounted over the entrance to his throne room. Now the statue, and the royal palace itself, lay in mounds of broken stone, cracked metal, and shattered jewels. The scene filled T'Challa with a dismal sense of the past—but a hopeful view for the future. He stared at the ruins and promised himself that he would rebuild his father's beloved creation. With his own hands, brick by gold brick, if necessary.

In fact, we will build a new Golden City greater than anything the world has ever seen, T'Challa thought, resolve and determination swelling his chest, raising his chin to the smoky heavens.

A blend of strumming guitar and song drifted over the wind. T'Challa closed his eyes and allowed Monica's voice to lift him up. He imagined himself flying above Wakanda. Soaring through the clouds propelled by love and music. A part of him wondered how Monica could find the spirit to sing in the aftermath of such destruction.

Monica was not far away. She sat on the steps of the razed research hospital with her ankles crossed. A guitar in her lap, the magic of twilight beaming on her skin. She closed her eyes and rocked from side to side as she strummed. A crowd had gathered. Shuri, Okoye, Nakia, and Adebisi hummed and clapped in time as Dr. Mganga sat beside Monica, playing her kalimba. Mendinao stood behind the quintet, singing his own fine tenor underneath Monica's saucy contralto.

Monica sang of the land. She sang of healing. She sang of a new day in Wakanda. A new day for the entire Earth. T'Challa wanted to join her side, but now wasn't the time. The cleanup had already begun. There was much to do. Much to prepare and restore. He allowed himself the pleasure of Monica's song for a few more minutes before he left to join Taku. In W'Kabi's absence, the communications officer had taken over the responsibility of overseeing the prisoners.

Taku led a line of chained rebels that started with the two fools, Tayete and Kazibe, and ended with Malice, Baron Macabre, and the other Death Regiment officers.

"We saved Wakanda, too!" Tayete cried. "Long live the Panther King!"

Kazibe smirked and shook his head, trudging behind his friend.

Venomm walked beside Taku. The former Death Regiment allegiant was not shackled. T'Challa stood before Venomm and placed his hands on both of his scaly shoulders.

"You saved Taku's life," T'Challa said. "For that I am eternally grateful. I hope that you will remain among us. An outworlder living here will be a first, apart from Ms. Lynne, but in light of your service, I think we can make good use of your talents here."

"I gotta admit, Ta'Charlie—" Venomm said.

Taku elbowed Venomm in the ribs and shook his head.

"My apologies. Old habits die hard, Your Majesty." Venomm bowed respectfully. He looked up with a smile and newfound hope shining in his eyes. "When Taku asked me if I wanted to stay, I thought he'd gone plumb crazy, but honestly, I think me and Jolene are gonna like it here."

"Don't forget, we have more snakes than you can count," Taku said. He patted Venomm on the back and laughed.

W'KABI'S APARTMENT sat in ruins and rubble, but he didn't care. He had both of his children sitting beside him. One of his arms was lost, crushed to jelly underneath the broken rock. It had been replaced with a prosthetic arm made of vibranium alloy. The arm moved with W'Kabi's thoughts, and it felt like it was part of him, like it was organic in some strange way. He did not understand this technology at all, and the functionality of the arm felt strange and unnerving.

"My captain of security," Chandra said. She stood behind W'Kabi, wrapped her arms around his shoulders and kissed his cheek.

"No, you are my security," W'Kabi said. He leaned back, enjoying his wife's embrace. "And you too," W'Kabi said and tickled each of his sons with his flesh hand.

OUT IN the wild lands near Wakanda's southern border, two tribesmen crept through the dense jungle. Armed with rifles and vibranium-tipped spears, the pair followed the trail of a spotted leopard they had tracked for almost ten miles. Sweat covered their foreheads, their bare chests and arms. They moved as carefully and as silently as they could. They heard the leopard snarling, and one of the men pointed at a dense patch of elephant grass. The leopard poked its head through the tall shrubs and growled at the two hunters. One man raised his rifle and fired. The other launched his spear at the spot where the leopard disappeared.

The hunters both craned their necks to see through the dense bush. One man cupped his hands over his eyes. The other pointed toward the elephant grass and pushed his partner forward to investigate. In single file, weapons raised, eyes wide and fearful, the hunters crept toward the bushes.

Inside the high grasses, hidden in the brush, they found the leopard laying on its side; its belly inflating and deflating furiously with its expiring breaths. The first hunter, using his rifle to balance himself, knelt beside the beast to examine its wounds.

"Wait," the second hunter said. "I don't see any blood. There should be blood."

The grass around the hunters rustled and shifted. Snarls and growls filled the surrounding brush as more leopards padded their way through the elephant grass and encircled the hunters. The hunters huddled together, back to back. Their faces long and bright with terror. One of them raised his rifle only to have it caught by a huge hand that poked its way through the bush. The huge ebony hand was dressed in a set of iron rings clamped around the wrist and extending up a muscular forearm. Silent as the padding leopards, a tall, bald-headed man appeared behind the hunters.

Armed with a machete as long as the hunter's rifle, the bald-headed man frowned with hatred and disgust, furrowing his brow and twisting his mouth into an angry snarl of its own. The hunters cowered in the silent man's presence. One of the men took a step backwards, only to be frozen by the sound of snarling—at once both feline and human.

The hunter turned around to a sight so frightful he fell on his backside and dropped the rifle he had clutched as if it could somehow save his life. The other hunter dropped to his knees and begged for mercy in tearful supplication.

The leopard that had led the hunters into the elephant grass stood on its hind legs. Huge knots bubbled under the leopard's skin, rising and falling, shifting as the muscles underneath the cat's pelt rearranged itself. The cat's fur fell to the ground, revealing dark brown skin, lustrous with slime and mucus. The cat reared its head. Snarling. Screaming. Its wet nose retracted to a dark brown button. The fangs in the corners of its mouth retracted with the sound of cracking bones, black gums becoming the raw pink color of human flesh. The chest heaved up and down as the breast bones surrendered to supple brown mammaries. The creature—half leopard, half beautiful brown woman—shook her head until a flowing crop of black locs dropped and bounced around her shoulders.

The leopard-turned-woman squatted before the cowering hunters. Poised with the instinctive movements of the feline spirit pacing inside her, she leaned towards the hunters and smiled.

"What's the matter, boys? It's no fun when the Preyy takes the gun, is it?"

The leopards sitting around the bush clearing leapt forward, digging their teeth and claws into the hunters. Having their fill of flesh, terrible screams rang out through the sweltering savannah.

A DAY later, accompanied by W'Kabi, T'Challa entered the dense flora skirting Wakanda's southern boundary. The pair had come to this location to investigate reports of poachers hunting the protected animals of this region. But there were other reports as well. Hunters spotted entering the region were going into the jungle, but they were not returning.

W'Kabi walked through brush, hacking his way through the tall grass with a long, black blade that jutted from the end of his mechanical arm. T'Challa searched through the trees, leaping from branch to branch, scanning the area with his eyes, his advanced hearing and enhanced sense of smell.

W'Kabi spoke into the Kimoyo beads built into his metallic

wrist. "Nothing out of the ordinary here on the ground, My King. What about you? Can you see any signs of the missing poachers?"

"None at all, W'Kabi," T'Challa said. "We will keep looking until we find something. Is that all right with you?" T'Challa spoke, a slight edge of sarcasm raising the notes of his voice.

"The corpses were found here, My King, mangled almost beyond recognition," W'Kabi said. "The creatures who have been mauling the poachers should be around here somewhere. We should have brought some meat that we could have used to lure them."

"I don't believe that will be necessary, W'Kabi. Our flesh should prove sufficient as bait. Remember, the bodies ravaged in these jungles have been all human," T'Challa said, a morbid sense of irony and humor coloring his words.

W'Kabi and T'Challa entered the clearing at the same time— W'Kabi on the ground, T'Challa in the trees. The scene they found did not disturb T'Challa as much as it would have months ago, before the civil war and the rebellion that almost took his life.

The bodies were tied to trees. They had been mutilated beyond recognition, mangled into lumps of bloody flesh and broken bones. A pack of hyenas picked and pulled at the remains. When the pack noticed W'Kabi on the ground and T'Challa perched in the tree, the feral canines pulled together to protect their carrion meals. They growled at T'Challa and W'Kabi, baring their fangs to frighten away the potential threats.

W'Kabi pointed his metal arm at the pack and watched as the blade transformed into a metal fist, then broke down into a series of whirring metal parts that rearranged themselves into a firearm gleaming at the end of his wrist. W'Kabi fired a single warning shot over the hyena's heads and watched the pack yelp and scatter in every direction into the dense bush.

T'Challa leapt from the tree branch to stand beside his security chief. The blaster on the mechanical arm sent a thin ribbon of gray smoke into the air.

"What do you think could have done this?" W'Kabi asked.

"Something possessing extreme power," the Black Panther said. He studied the broken bones and noticed there seemed to be a pattern in the way they were arranged.

Again, the huge brown hand, the arm swollen with chiseled muscles, reached through the brush. This time, the arm grabbed W'Kabi's throat.

With blinding, soundless speed and accurate deadliness, the brown man with the bald head lifted W'Kabi and slammed the security guard into the tree, knocking him unconscious.

The bald man wore the same impassive grim expression. With his chest protruding and his fists balled at his sides, the man stared at T'Challa. After fighting N'Jadaka and the Death Regiments for the past months, T'Challa had grown accustomed to loud, boisterous adversaries. He found this man's silence unnerving.

"I have many questions to ask of you, silent one," T'Challa said. "I hope you are prepared to give me the answers I need. You will save yourself a world of pain."

The Black Panther dodged the bald-headed man's fist and kicked him in the face and chest. The mute warrior stumbled back a couple of steps, but beyond that T'Challa's blows did not seem to hurt the silent giant. Not at all.

T'Challa bounced on his feet and circled the bald man. The Panther King could not believe what he was seeing. The impossibility of the man's strength was even more disquieting than his lack of words. The brute seemed even stronger than Killmonger.

T'Challa heard the leopard snarl and move through the grass before it stepped into the clearing. He had only seen one cat that huge in his life, and it had belonged to N'Jadaka.

"Preyy?" T'Challa wondered aloud.

The leopard roared at T'Challa. A flurry of memories and images drawn from the past year accosted his mind. He crouched, extended his panther claws. He wondered if N'Jadaka would leap through the bushes behind the leopard that had nearly given its life to defend the exile on top of Warrior Falls.

Confusion spang T'Challa's world from its tethers and gave the silent bald man the distraction necessary to flank him. By the time he saw the giant stone crashing toward his face, the impact had already sent the Panther King falling into a bottomless pool of black unconsciousness.

T'CHALLA AWOKE with a start. In his dream he had been falling endlessly. Tumbling through absolute darkness without shape or perceptible depth. His head felt as if someone were punching his temples from the inside of his skull. The world spun in continuous circles. His head hung like a rag doll, and when he tried to lift it, shockwaves of pain stabbed him between his eyes.

When his vision refocused and the pain in his head subsided to a dull ache pounding between his ears, the Panther King found himself surrounded by leopards. The leap of golden spotted cats lay around the room in lazy bunches. They purred and licked themselves and yawned like the Panther King was the most boring thing they had ever seen. A woman sat in a stone chair, a throne surrounded by the spotted leopards. Her feet were propped on one cat's spotted back. Another huge cat stretched across her thighs. She rubbed another feline, gently brushing its head and stroking the underside of its ear with her fingernails.

The woman looked familiar to T'Challa. He had seen her face somewhere before, but he could not place it, and trying to remember made his head throb.

"Greetings, T'Challa," the woman said. Her smile sly and knowing, she raised her high cheekbones and exposed a pair of deep dimples.

T'Challa stared at the woman. He blinked, not knowing if he should try to speak, wondering if the attempted communication would make his head hurt.

"Of course, you don't recognize me, ukatana," she said. "Let me fill you in; we used to share a mutual friend. Until you killed him."

318   *N'Jadaka*, T'Challa thought. That's when the realization bashed

T'Challa's brain, just like the stone that the silent fighter had used out in the jungle. It was the thought of N'Jadaka that triggered the memory, and the woman's smile cemented T'Challa's recollection.

A year ago. T'Challa's last night in New York. The woman had been in the club that night when he had sat with N'Jadaka. It was the same woman who had smiled and flirted with T'Challa from across the room, the one wearing the leopard scarf around her neck. T'Challa had sent her a drink right before he had received the message about Regent N'Baza. That's when T'Challa realized. N'Jadaka had played him the entire time, from the moment the Panther King had met the Wakandan exile.

And there was little doubt that N'Baza's death was not due to natural causes.

There had been a time that T'Challa would have gotten so angry he would have ripped the chains from his shackled wrists and choked or killed everyone in the room. But the past months had taught T'Challa a great deal about rage. T'Challa had learned to never give in to the rage. Not ever. It was the constant control of human emotion that separated good from evil, the just from the unjust, heroes from villains, sentient intellectuals from raving madmen.

"I see you. You finally see me," the woman laughed. "I might as well tell you my name, see as how we're old friends and all." The woman stood before T'Challa. All muscles and brown skin; under different circumstances, T'Challa might have mistaken this ebony woman for one of Bast's avatars or even a god of some sort in her own right.

"In this form, I am known as Madame Slay, but you are probably more familiar with my other form."

Standing before T'Challa, the woman's lustrous brown skin began to swell and deflate, as the muscles underneath shifted and arrayed. Bulging in some places, shrinking in others, Madame Slay howled and screamed. Screamed and howled as she fell forward to her hands and knees. Black-and-gold fur sprouted in small ridges then grew until it covered her back, her arms, her face, her entire body. The shiny black locs that curled around her face fell to the floor. Her nose and mouth stretched into a split-lipped snout. Fangs stretched and creaked from the corners of her mouth. The woman-turned-leopard padded toward T'Challa, her muscles flexing and jumping underneath her spotted fur.

T'Challa had seen many things in his life, but for the first time found himself horrified beyond comprehension. Madame Slay was right: he did recognize this form much more intimately than the former. He watched the giant leopard, the faithful pet that had fought valiantly at N'Jadaka's side.

It was Preyy, T'Challa thought. *It was Preyy all along.*

T'Challa struggled to free himself from the manacles and chains that bound his wrists and ankles. He watched in terrible dismay as the leopards, who only moments before moved so lazily around the room, rose to their feet and padded behind their leader until they formed a circle around T'Challa, surrounding him on all sides.

Chained to the wall next to T'Challa, W'Kabi pulled at his restraints as well. W'Kabi's arm reacted on its own, the metal segments of his firearm folding in on itself until it took the form of a circular saw. W'Kabi used the spinning blade to free himself from the binding chains.

T'Challa heard the saw blade spinning, the sparks thrown from the saw's blade drawing only half of his attention. He watched Preyy rear back on her hind legs. With adrenaline and the Heart-Shaped Herb strengthening him, he pulled with everything he had inside until one of the chains broke, allowing the Panther King to dodge one of Preyy's vicious claws.

One of the smaller leopards leapt at T'Challa. He greeted the lunging beast with a right hook that sent the creature flying across the room. Another jumped at him, aiming for the side of him that was still chained to the wall. In a flash, W'Kabi's prosthetic hand transformed from a blade back into an energy blaster. He shot the spotted cat down with the metal gun barrel that sat smoking at his wrist.

T'Challa managed to free his other arm as two more leopards attacked him. The Panther King grabbed the forepaws of one of the leopards and swung the beast like a bat into the other, knocking both unconscious.

T'Challa and W'Kabi stood back-to-back as the rest of the leopards in the room padded around them in a snarling circle of bared fangs and swinging claws.

"Feels like old times, my friend," T'Challa said.

"There's no one else who I would rather fight beside," W'Kabi answered.

The two nodded at each other and began to fight their way through the leopards towards a light that soon revealed itself to be a cave entrance. T'Challa punched and kneed, elbowed and kicked, and headbutted the attacking leopards. W'Kabi blasted the advancing cats with his mechanical arm. As the Panther King and his security chief approached the cave entrance, the dwindling number of leopards fought with increased desperation.

Behind them, in the dark, Madame Slay returned to her human form. Before them, a dark presence occupied the cave entrance. The silent one blocked the way. The silver rings that stretched from his wrists to his elbows glimmered, as did his eyes. He did not smile. He did not move. He stood in the cave's entrance; a door just as formidable as the stone that surrounded him.

"I'll take care of big boy," W'Kabi said. He smiled. "We got a score to settle." The mechanisms in his arm whirled and popped as the blaster at the end of his arm broke down. The metal parts rearranged themselves into the shape of a hand. "You stole on me back in the jungle. Let's see how you fare now that I can see you coming."

T'Challa turned toward Madame Slay who smiled at the Panther King and retreated further into the cave. T'Challa pursued her, but he did not hurry. He knew that she would not try to escape. She had brought him here to exact revenge. If anything, she was leading him into a trap. But the cave was dark, and darkness was his friend. *Nighttime was the right time for panthers*, T'Challa thought. He smiled as Monica's voice sang in his head, crooning the lyrics to an old Simon and Garfunkel song she had introduced to the Panther King not long after they had started dating.

"There is no use hiding, Madame Slay," T'Challa called into the darkness. "I know you brought me here to kill me, but the killing must stop. Too many have died already." T'Challa heard Madame Slay's heartbeat quickening. He heard her bones pop and the strained grunting sound that accompanied her transformation. T'Challa assumed that turning was painful. "I know what it's like to lose a loved one. I know you are in pain. However, if you continue this gambit, you will only cause yourself more suffering."

The echo in the cave amplified T'Challa's voice. He listened as Preyy padded further into the depths. He heard her tail sliding across the rock. T'Challa's eyes had adjusted well to the absolute blackness. Still, there were so many twists and turns, crags and crannies in the cave that T'Challa still could not see. He made a mental note to add thermal vision to the lenses in his mask.

Turning one last corner, T'Challa faced a rock wall. Chunks of uneven stones, packed dirt, and the roots of what looked to be baobab trees hung from the ceiling. T'Challa looked around, but he did not see Preyy. He stopped and crouched. His arms stretched at his sides. He sensed the shadows moving behind him, but by the time he turned it was too late. Madame Slay was standing behind him. T'Challa found himself confused and alarmed. He had heard her assume her leopard form, had listened to the tell-tale sounds of her transformation carefully. Without mistake, he had heard the footfalls of a cat, the swishing sound of fur against rock.

But the woman standing behind him and the vibranium blade piercing his panther suit assured him that he had been mistaken. But how?

"Silly black kitten," Madame Slay said, as if she had read T'Challa's thoughts. "You men are all alike." She pushed the blade deeper into T'Challa's side, twisting and turning the dagger as she exerted more force. "You see something once, and you think you know it for true. But things change, ukatana. Yes, things change very quickly."

The shockwave from the energy dagger sent thousands of vibrational charges throughout T'Challa's intestines and broke the Black Panther down to his knees. He fell to the floor and turned onto his back. He winced from the pain and stared up at Madame Slay, his own blood dripping from the black blade.

"Erik and I shared many things," she said. "We served the one true goddess, K'Liluna, and Erik was to be her avatar—ruling not just your kingdom but the world. It is through her power and mine that Erik was able to control the minds of your creatures and synthesize your precious Heart-Shaped Herb. It was I who helped Erik camouflage his scent; that's why it was so difficult for you to follow his trail. We had a *vision* for Wakanda. And it lives yet. It would be a shame to let all that planning go to waste, don't you think?"

Madame Slay lunged at the Panther King, transforming quickly. By the time she landed on top of him, she had turned into Preyy again. Pinning T'Challa's shoulder to the ground, she opened her mouth, fangs poised to sink into the Black Panther's throat.

T'Challa clenched his teeth and rammed his forehead into Preyy's snout, releasing a blast of vibratory energy. The blow stunned the were-leopard long enough for T'Challa to grab the vibranium dagger that Madame Slay dropped when she transformed. T'Challa plunged the blade into the shapeshifter's chest. The huge cat stumbled and released a heart-stopping, long sawing roar that echoed through the room, ricocheting off the cavern walls. With her waning strength, she tried to use her powerful jaws and fangs to rip out his throat, but the Black Panther sent the feline flying through the air. Preyy's body smashed into the stone wall at the end of the cave and collapsed to the floor.

Writhing on the ground, Preyy reverted to her Madame Slay form, the dagger jutting from her wound. For a few moments the wounded creature seemed to be caught between shiftings. She morphed back and forth from woman to cat, from cat to woman.

Clutching his side, T'Challa leaned against the cave wall. He caught his breath and stared at what remained of Preyy and Madame Slay as W'Kabi rushed around the corner to find his King.

"Your Majesty, you are injured! I am sorry—I could not get here sooner," W'Kabi said, blood trickling down his chin. "But I see you handled it." He stared with astonishment at Madame Slay's half-transformation.

"It's over now," T'Challa said. He looked down at the gash in his side. "The wound looks bad, but a session with Mendinao should heal me right up."

"Maybe we can get Monica to sing to you," W'Kabi said with a smile.

"My outworlder has finally grown on you," T'Challa said. He laughed for a second then winced in pain.

Madame Slay lay on the ground, holding her lone black-and-gold leopard limb that had not transformed. Her beautiful fur matted, she panted in pain, her mouth opening and closing in shock. The Black Panther could hear her fading lifeforce coursing through her veins, the pain in every drop of blood, each grain of bone. Hatred rippled out of her throat, in a ragged, blazing line of obscenities. "You killed him!" she cried. "Our one true king! You killed him!"

T'Challa bent to one knee and touched her trembling paw, but she recoiled as if she had been burned.

"Don't make us take your life as well, Slay. You and I both know Killmonger was not worth it."

"Yes, there has been too much suffering," W'Kabi added. "Too many Wakandan lives have been lost."

T'Challa nodded.

"This rebellion has taught us a great deal, Your Majesty. You're not the only one who has learned to control his rage," W'Kabi added.

T'Challa grabbed Madame Slay and threw the incapacitated shapeshifter over his shoulder.

"What happened to the silent one?" he asked.

"Big boy's taking a nap," W'Kabi said. He raised his metal arm in triumph. "You know what? The more I use this thing, the more I like it."

The trio left the back of the cave. They found Madame Slay's bald-headed companion sleeping silently near the entrance—just as W'Kabi had said. Face swollen and bruised, the brute lay on his stomach, wrists and ankles hog-tied with slim manacles. Wakandan technology, the restraints would have squeezed around the silent man's wrists and ankles had he resisted them. The more resistance, the stronger the tightening, until the restraints crushed the limbs held inside of them.

T'Challa decided that the four of them would walk back to the royal palace. Every one of them needed time to think. W'Kabi grumbled, but no more than T'Challa expected from the grizzly curmudgeon.

Madame Slay cursed the Panther King until W'Kabi pointed his blaster at the shapeshifter's face. Finally, she raised her head to the burning afternoon and called out to Erik Killmonger, as if he were floating in the sky above them.

"Don't worry, my love, the soul always returns, in one form or another. Greatness never dies."

"And there is none greater than Bast," the Black Panther responded. "None greater than her kingdom." T'Challa crossed his arms and joined W'Kabi in calling out the ancient affirmation born from the line of Bashenga.

"Wakanda forever!"

ACKNOWLEDGMENTS

WRITING FOR *Black Panther* is a dream come true!

There are so many people who helped and blessed me along the way, and some who don't even know they did. Thank you for the kind words, the generosity of time and spirit, and the willingness to share your insights with me. Thank you for your support and good will in these interesting times. Thank you to Stan Lee & Jack Kirby for creating this legendary character and world; thanks to Dan McGregor, Rich Buckler, and Billy Graham for writing and illustrating the first *Black Panther* comics, making *Panther's Rage* a self-contained, multi-issue story arc and a thrilling graphic novel. Thanks to Christopher Priest for creating the Dora Milaje and Reginald Hudlin for introducing Shuri! Thanks to all the contributors to the world that is Wakanda: the writers and artists who keep the Black Panther alive. Thanks also to the fans of Black Panther around the world! Your love and enthusiasm inspire new adventures every day!

I would like to thank my family:
My firstborn, Jackie B. & Jada
My dear parents, Jacqueline Thomas & Eddie Thomas
Mailane & Jerry Plunkett
Darrell & Carolyn Jerry

My younger sibs, Terrence Thomas, Brian Thomas,
Ebony Thomas, Xavian Thomas
My nephew, Akira Wolfgang

Many thanks to:
My editor, George Sandison, Michael Beale, Kevin Eddy, Andy
Hawes and the Titan Books team
Brian Overton, Sarah Singer, and Jeff Youngquist at Marvel
Jesse J. Holland, editor of *Black Panther: Tales of Wakanda*
Tananarive Due, Linda D. Addison, and Chet Weise,
who believed in me
Gordon Van Gelder and *The Magazine of
Fantasy & Science Fiction*
My agents Kristopher O'Higgins and Marie Dutton Brown, who
started this with her faith in the *Dark Matter* anthologies

With much love and gratitude to:
Daniel and Isaiah Coates
Andrea Hairston, Pan Morigan, James Cameron Emory
Reynaldo Anderson, Clairesa Clay, Danielle L. Littlefield

Finally, all my love to:
Danian Darrell Jerry

ABOUT THE AUTHOR

SHEREE RENÉE THOMAS is an award-winning writer, poet, editor, and a 2022 Hugo Award and Ember Award Finalist. Her work is inspired by myth and folklore, natural science, music, and the culture of the Mississippi Delta. She is the author of the short fiction collection, *Nine Bar Blues: Stories from an Ancient Future,* a Finalist for the 2021 Locus Award, Ignyte Award, and World Fantasy Award for Year's Best Collection. She is the winner of the 2022 Dal Coger Memorial Hall of Fame Award and is #339 in the Walter Day Science Fiction Hall of Fame Trading Cards. She is also the author of two hybrid/multigenre collections, *Sleeping Under the Tree of Life* and *Shotgun Lullabies: Stories & Poems.* She edited the two-time World Fantasy Award-winning *Dark Matter* anthologies, co-edited *Trouble the Waters: Tales from the Deep Blue* with Pan Morigan and Troy L. Wiggins, and *Africa Risen: A New Era of Speculative Fiction* with Oghenechovwe Donald Ekpeki and Zelda Knight.

Sheree Renée Thomas is the editor of *The Magazine of Fantasy & Science Fiction,* founded in 1949 and is the associate editor of *Obsidian,* founded in 1975. Widely anthologized, Thomas' work appears in *The Big Book of Modern Fantasy* (1945–2010), edited by Ann & Jeff VanderMeer, *Year's Best African Speculative Fiction.* edited by Oghenechovwe Donald Ekpeki, *Year's Best Dark Fantasy & Horror,* vol. 2, edited by Paula Guran, and Marvel's *Black*

Panther: Tales of Wakanda, edited by Jesse J. Holland. Her essays have appeared in *The New York Times* and other publications. She is a collaborator with Janelle Monáe on the artist's fiction collection, *The Memory Librarian: And Other Stories of Dirty Computer.* A former New Yorker, she lives in her hometown of Memphis, Tennessee, near a mighty river and a pyramid. Follow her @blackpotmojo on Twitter, @shereereneethomas on Instagram and Facebook, or visit www.shereereneethomas.com.